TOF

Lt. Colonel Brenna Duggan was torn between the overwhelming evidence that Staff Sergeant Andrew Lang was high and deep into perverse sex when he died and a growing list of new facts that cast the shameful death in a shocking new light.

Brenna was torn between loyalty to the Air Force and sympathy with spunky, passionately loyal Janeen Lang, who was carrying the dead airman's baby and would move heaven and earth to prove his innocence.

Brenna was torn between her mounting suspicion of mocking and macho Dave Sanderson and what happened to her when she surrendered to the blaze he ignited with his touch.

Somehow Brenna would have to fly on torn wings above the swirling clouds of doubt and deception to pursue the truth no matter how cruel it turned out to be. . . .

LINE OF DUTY

What happens when you cross it?

LINE OF DUTY

DUTY

Merline Lovelace

AN ONYX BOOK

ONYX
Published by the Penguin Group
Penguin Books USA Inc., 375 Hudson Street,
New York, New York 10014, U.S.A.
Penguin Books Ltd, 27 Wrights Lane,
London W8 5TZ, England
Penguin Books Australia Ltd, Ringwood,
Victoria, Australia
Penguin Books Canada Ltd, 10 Alcorn Avenue,
Toronto, Ontario, Canada M4V 3B2
Penguin Books (N.Z.) Ltd, 182–190 Wairau Road,
Auckland 10, New Zealand

Penguin Books Ltd, Registered Offices:
Harmondsworth, Middlesex, England

First published by Onyx, an imprint of Dutton Signet,
a division of Penguin Books USA Inc.

First Printing, November, 1996
10 9 8 7 6 5 4 3 2 1

 REGISTERED TRADEMARK—MARCA REGISTRADA

Printed in the United States of America

PUBLISHER'S NOTE
This is a work of fiction. Names, characters, places, and incidents either are
the product of the author's imagination or are used fictitiously, and any
resemblance to actual persons, living or dead, events, or locales is entirely
coincidental.

BOOKS ARE AVAILABLE AT QUANTITY DISCOUNTS WHEN USED TO PROMOTE PROD-
UCTS OR SERVICES. FOR INFORMATION PLEASE WRITE TO PREMIUM MARKETING DIVI-
SION, PENGUIN BOOKS USA INC., 375 HUDSON STREET, NEW YORK, NEW YORK 10014.

This book is dedicated
to the men and women
of the 552d Air Control Wing,
who fly high and fly proud.

With special thanks to:

Captain Kim Boone, USAF, for her expert technical assistance, outstanding professionalism, and great sense of humor

The personnel of the Office of Public Affairs, 552d Air Control Wing, for giving me the extraordinary privilege of seeing the 552d in action

Mr. Larry Ringler, U.S. Customs National Aviation Center, for the guided tour of CNAC and terrific insights into its vital mission

Mr. Vince Bonds, U.S. Customs Service Office of Public Affairs, for keeping me straight on roles and missions

Colonel Bob Sander, USAF (ret.), and his family for showing me the sights of Seiling, Oklahoma, and for the best hamburgers this side of the Pecos

Lt. Colonel Laura Jones, Captain Linda Tutko, and Sgt. Katherine Huffmaster, USAF, for their impromptu sessions in front of the camera

and most especially,

Mr. Harry Plagman, formerly with the U.S. Customs Service, for a sunny afternoon of golf and the fascinating conversation about his profession that inspired this book!

Chapter One

The call came at 0357 hours.

Later, much later, Brenna would feel a warped sense of pride that she could pinpoint the precise moment her life began to spin out of control. But right then, squinting at the blurred numbers on the clock radio through heavy lids, she felt only a vague irritation that it wasn't even four o'clock in the morning. Why didn't her hot line ever ring *before* midnight?

"Lieutenant Colonel Duggan," she croaked, her throat thick with the cotton of sleep.

"This is Sergeant Adkins at the Tinker Command Post. Sorry to wake you, ma'am."

"This better be good, Adkins," she mumbled, running her tongue over dry lips while she fumbled for the switch to the bedside lamp. "I just got down a few hours ago."

"I know. Must've been a rough flight in this weather."

Brenna tugged at the sheets tangled around her

hips and struggled upright. "I've had better. We had to circle for almost an hour before the front moved off."

"Glad it was you up there and not me." The controller paused. "You ready?"

Sergeant Adkins was good at his job, Brenna acknowledged grudgingly. Damn good. He always gave the folks he jerked so unceremoniously from their sleep time to work the sludge out of their brain cells before he laid the latest disaster on them. Cradling the phone on her hunched shoulder, she reached for the pad and pen on the nightstand.

"I'm ready. What've we got?"

She braced herself for his answer. In the ten months she'd been the commander of the 552d Training Squadron, her middle-of-the-night calls had run the gamut from aircraft crashes to an hysterical nine-year-old pleading for help in finding his lost dog. After her long, turbulent flight, Brenna muttered a silent prayer that all she had to contend with tonight was another stray pet.

"We've received notification of a death of an active-duty member assigned to your squadron," Sergeant Adkins told her.

"Oh, no." Her pen skittered across the pad. "Who?"

"Staff Sergeant Andrew Lang. One of your air surveillance techs."

Lang. Andrew Lang. Brenna's still sluggish mind tried to fit a face to the name. With more than seventy instructors and two hundred plus students assigned to her squadron, half of whom were gone at any one time, it took a moment for the image of a lanky, fair-haired man to surface. A man with smiling blue eyes, she remembered, who carried himself with the self-confidence of a natural athlete.

"What happened?" she asked the controller, her voice still raspy from sleep.

Adkins hesitated. "I've got the Casualty Affairs rep on the other line. I'd better let him brief you."

While the duty controller made the connection, Brenna shed the last of her grogginess. With the precision that characterized her, she began to tick off in her mind what she knew about Sergeant Lang. Although relatively new to the squadron, Lang had seemed to fit in well and had excelled as an instructor. In the check rides Brenna had flown to observe him and the other instructors assigned to her squadron, she'd been impressed by the sergeant's patience with his students. If she wasn't mistaken, Lang was on temporary duty in Panama right now, working an extended training mission.

Brenna sat up straight in the bed, her brows snapping together as another bit of information clicked into place. Lang was from a small Oklahoma town, not too far from their home base here at Tinker. So was his wife.

Oh, Lord!

Tentacles of dread began to curl in Brenna's stomach as she thought of the duty she'd have to perform in the next few hours.

"Colonel Duggan?"

"Yes."

"This is Brian Hollywell, from Casualty Affairs."

"What do you know about this so far, Mr. Hollywell?"

"Only that Sergeant Lang was found a couple of hours ago in the back room of a bar in Panama. Naked."

"What?"

"He, uh, had a rope knotted around his neck. The apparent cause of death was self-strangulation."

Brenna gripped the phone. "Self-strangulation? You mean he hung himself?" That cheerful young sergeant with the lopsided grin? She couldn't believe it, couldn't accept the horrific image that sprang into her mind.

"Well . . . Not exactly."

Hollywell's hesitation jerked Brenna from her tumultuous thoughts. She'd worked with the grizzled civilian once or twice in the past. Those brief encounters had taught her that little fazed a man who'd been in the Casualty Affairs business for over ten years. The fact that he was not groping for words set off a warning alarm in her mind.

"Then what, exactly?" she asked.

"We won't know for sure until the autopsy's completed," he replied slowly. "But initial indications are that the death may have been accidental. It seems Sergeant Lang was, ah, engaging in some kinky sexual activity involving ropes."

Brenna felt her jaw sag. She wasn't ready for this. Not at four a.m., after a flight from hell. Not with a member of her squadron, a man with a young wife who'd have to be told the gruesome details.

"The Panamanian police took their time calling in the U.S. military authorities," Hollywell continued. "There's some confusion over times and a question about who, if anyone, was with him at the time of his death. The investigation's still ongoing."

"Any idea when I'll have more definitive information?"

"I doubt they'll finish the investigation for a few days. The Army Medical Examiner should have an autopsy report in sooner, though." He paused, his voice taking on a note of sympathy. "Makes it tough, doesn't it? Breaking it to the next of kin, I mean."

Brenna raked a hand through her tumbled, shoulder-length hair. "Tough isn't the word I'd use."

Resuming his brusque professionalism, Hollywell read the scant details provided in the initial casualty report. Brenna listened carefully, but learned little more. The Air Force wouldn't make any assumptions about Lang's death until the full investigation was completed and the autopsy done. Still, she wished fervently she could tell the woman she'd have to face in the next hour more than the bare fact that her husband had been found naked, in a bar in Panama, with a rope knotted around his neck.

"I assume his wife is listed as next of kin on his Emergency Notification Form?"

"Right. Janeen Lang." Hollywell rattled off an on-base address.

"I got it, Colonel," the listening command post controller interjected.

Brenna's throat closed. Janeen Lang. She remembered her now. A shy, brown-eyed young woman with honey-colored hair and a full, rounded figure. They'd met at a couple of squadron functions, including the annual family picnic only a few weeks ago.

With a muttered curse, Brenna threw off the sheet and swung her legs over the side of the bed.

"What, ma'am?" Adkins asked.

"Nothing. Have you notified the duty chaplain?"

"He's on his way in. He'll meet you here at the Command Post."

"Okay. I'll be there in half an hour. And Adkins?"

"Yes, ma'am?"

"Call the hospital and alert the Medical Officer of the Day. I want a physician with me on the notification." Her fingers tightened on the phone. "Mrs. Lang is pregnant. Very pregnant."

Spurred by a driving sense of urgency, Brenna hurried into the bathroom. She washed quickly and applied only a swipe of lipstick to relieve the pallor induced by lack of sleep. Ruthlessly, she tugged a brush through her thick fall of sable-colored hair, then pinned it up in its usual twist at the back of her head. With the deftness of many years' practice, she pulled on a starched, light blue uniform blouse and tucked it into the waistband of her skirt. But her fingers fumbled with the shiny, nickel-plated belt buckle for several seconds before she could get it to catch.

God, she hated the thought of what was to come. But she couldn't avoid it, even if she wanted to. This was part of her job. The hardest part. As she slipped on her black leather pumps, a dozen clichés from the countless leadership courses she'd taken over the years ran through her mind.

With authority comes responsibility.

A commander's duty extends not just to his or her personnel, but to their families as well.

The Air Force takes care of its own.

None of the time-honored truisms seemed to help tonight. Her mouth tight, Brenna reached for the tailored jacket with the silver oak leaves designating her rank on the epaulets. Shrugging the uniform coat on, she shot a quick glance at the mirror to make sure her nickel-plated aircrew wings and Weapons Director badge were properly aligned above the three colorful rows of ribbons. Satisfied, she stuffed her flight cap with its thin cord of silver braid along one edge into her purse and headed for the door. She was ready, as ready as anyone could be.

The steaming August night wrapped around her the moment she backed her convertible out of the garage. Instantly, the Miata's windshield fogged to an opaque whiteness. Swiping her forearm across the window only made the condensation streak. Her jaw tightening, Brenna turned the air-conditioning up full blast and drummed her fingers on the leather-wrapped wheel while she waited for the window to clear.

Normally, she would have lowered the top and enjoyed the sting of hot wind in her face as she drove to the base. Nudging the speed limit with the little cherry-red Miata was one of the few lapses in discipline Brenna allowed herself. But she wasn't in the mood to indulge herself tonight. Not with what she had to do.

By the time she pulled onto the empty streets, the dread in her stomach had solidified into a hard, aching lump. She gripped the steering wheel and headed for the interstate that would take her to Tinker's back gate. Pavement still slick from the rain a few hours before hissed under her car's tires as the dark countryside rolled by unseen. The few miles from her small, lakeside condo on the south side of Oklahoma City to the sprawling Air Force base seemed to stretch interminably. Brenna used the time to rehearse the words that would inform a young woman her husband had just died.

There were no words, she knew from past experience. She'd done this duty once before, as part of a notification team that informed heartbroken parents of their son's death in a vehicle accident. The memory of that long, painful night haunted her now.

The first few hours would be the worst. Nothing Brenna could say would ease Mrs. Lang's shock. Or temper the disbelief, the denial, the surge of blinding rage that this could happen. Nothing Brenna could say would lessen her pain.

After a while, when word got out, friends and family would gather to give the widow what comfort they could.

After a while, she might take some comfort from their presence.

But in these first few hours, in these terrifying first few hours, Janeen Lang would have with her only the members of the Initial Notification Team ... the duty chaplain, the MOD, and the squadron commander.

The circumstances of Sergeant Lang's death, as sketchy as they were, made the notification even more difficult. Brenna searched her mind for some way to soften the stark, ugly facts. There'd have to be an autopsy, she reminded herself grimly. The exact cause of death hadn't yet been determined. She couldn't, wouldn't hazard any opinions at this point. Somehow, the uncertainty made her task even worse.

Calling on the rigid control that was as much a part of her personality as a result of her years of training, Brenna swallowed the knot in her throat and steeled herself for the hours ahead.

Janeen Lang grunted as the baby's kick brought her out of a fitful doze. Sighing, she curled her legs to shift some of her belly's weight onto her thighs and relieve the pressure on her back.

She hated sleeping on her side. Of all the discomforts she'd experienced in her advancing pregnancy, the only one that really bothered her was not being able to sleep on her stomach. She didn't mind the swollen ankles and the fingers so full of fluid she couldn't wear her wedding ring. Or the pressure on her bladder that sent her to the bathroom constantly for relief. She didn't even mind the cramps that tugged at her lower body. The pulling sensation was normal, the doctor had assured her, something called Braxton Hicks syndrome. Her uterus was stretching and retracting in preparation for the baby's passage. Janeen was sure that if she could just roll over and assume the sprawled position she normally slept in, arms outflung, face buried in the pillow, she'd stretch enough to ease the passage for both her and the baby.

She smiled into the darkness while her fingers traced light circles on her taut stomach to quiet the rambunctious child within. Andy always teased her about the way she slept. Bed-hog, he called her. Mattress rustler. He'd threatened several times to buy another bed, just so he could get some sleep before or after a mission.

Janeen's smile widened as a slow, delicious heat spread across her chest. He wouldn't buy another bed. Not hardly. Not even if she pushed him clear off the edge. Andy might complain and tease in that exaggerated Okie drawl he used when he had a mind to, but he surely wouldn't buy another bed. He enjoyed tusslin' with her for sleeping space on this one too much.

The heat climbed up Janeen's neck, then speared downward into her belly. Her vaginal muscles clenched in a spasm that had nothing to do with Braxton Hicks. That was another thing about being pregnant that surprised her. Here she was, all swollen up like a sow and just about as ugly, yet the slightest hint of how she got that way was enough to make her wet her undies with sudden craving. Thank goodness her ballooning belly hadn't inhibited Andy. For a small-town boy, he was sure developing some interesting tricks for dealin' with a woman's needs. She arched her back a little, enjoying the way the cotton sleep shirt rasped across tender, enlarged nipples.

The sound of the doorbell made her heart leap and the heat between her legs intensify to a hot, rushing wave. He was home! Two days early. Andy was home.

She wiggled to the edge of the bed and pushed herself up, a grin of anticipation curving her lips. Andy always rang the bell and waited patiently for her to let him in. He knew she was nervous about living alone, and him gone so much on training missions. Even here on base, with neighbors on either side, she didn't feel comfortable alone. This was her first time away from home, away from the security of a small town where everyone knew everyone else. Away from her large, boisterous family. She still wasn't used to locked doors and nightly reports of murders and shootings on the local news.

Over her objections, Andy had taught her to use the snub-nosed .38 he kept under the bed. And he'd promised never to come in unannounced from a late mission. He surely didn't want to get himself shot by his own wife, he'd told her with the crooked grin that had made her tumble into love with him the first time she'd seen it, back when her brother Bobby brought home the gangly, scrape-kneed kid whose parents had bought the old Matthews place.

Tugging her sleep shirt down over her stomach, Janeen speared a hand through her tangled hair. She should've taken time to wash it, she thought as she moved through the darkened living room toward the front door. It felt as dry and brittle as the straw they baled up for the cattle her daddy ran. Probably looked about as appealing, too. She'd threatened to cut the heavy, blond mass, just to get it off her neck during the awful summer months, but Andy had a fit whenever she mentioned lopping it off. 'Course, he hadn't been around much lately to listen to her complain about it. He'd been gone so much, learning this instructin' business and pulling his share of temporary duty. But he was home now, she reminded herself with a leap of anticipation.

Flipping on the porch light, Janeen raised up on tiptoe to peer through the peephole. Even with her blood thrumming fast and hot in her veins and her welcome smile ready in place, she took time for that quick look.

Instead of the expanse of green Nomex flight suit she expected to see, her eye caught a glitter of silver against a dark blue background and an array of colorful ribbons. Her smile fading, she adjusted her vision. Gradually, she made out a woman's shape, distorted by the curved lens of the peephole.

Janeen's sensual haze faded, to be replaced by confusion and the first stirrings of unease. Swollen, pudgy fingers fumbled with the chain of the door guard. It took her three tries to get it off and open the door. By then, her unease had deepened to a gut-wrenching fear. She might be young and not very experienced as a military wife, but she knew that officers in fancy uniforms didn't show up at your front door in the middle of the night unless something bad had happened.

"Mrs. Lang?"

She gripped the edge of the door with one hand. "Yes."

"I'm Colonel Duggan, from the 552d Training Squadron. I'm your husband's commander. We've met at a couple of squadron parties."

Fear sliced at Janeen's throat. "I . . . know who you are."

The tall, dark-haired woman took a step forward. Janeen heard the click of a heel on the concrete stoop and glanced down. She's wearing high heels, the young woman thought numbly. Shiny,

21

black high heels. I'm in a rumpled cotton sleep shirt and she's in heels.

Weeks later, when she could think of that night without crying, Janeen would remember that wayward thought and cringe in shame that something so meaningless would snag her attention. But at this moment, she clung to it desperately, wanting to focus on anything other than what she feared was to come.

"Mrs. Lang?"

She raised her head and met Colonel Duggan's eyes. They gleamed in the porch light, a misty, gray-blue color, filled with a look that made Janeen's hand clench on the door.

"May we come in?"

For the first time, she noticed the shadowy figures behind the commander. Instinctively, her hand moved to the swell of her stomach.

Colonel Duggan took another step toward her. "I'm afraid we have some bad news."

Janeen gave a small, frightened whimper.

It was worse, so much worse, than Brenna had feared. Sergeant Lang's wife stared at them, her brown eyes dark pools of fear in a white face. Her terrified little moan hung on the night air.

"Please, may we come in?"

"It's Andy, isn't it? He's hurt."

Brenna hesitated, not wanting to say what she had to say out here, on the front stoop.

"Is he hurt bad? Tell me."

"We should go inside," the chaplain interjected softly.

"Tell me!"

Brenna bit her lip, then answered the urgent plea in the frantic brown eyes. "He's dead, Mrs. Lang."

"Oh, my God!"

The young woman started to crumple. Leaping forward, Brenna caught her around her thickened middle. The doctor rushed up the steps and wrapped his arm around her other side.

"Let's get her into the house."

The sobs began then. Low, ragged, rasping cries that tore at Brenna's heart. Stumbling, searching for a way through the unfamiliar house, she led the small group to the living room. Her own throat ached as the woman she held spasmed with each racking sob.

She wanted desperately to tighten her arms and offer the weeping woman some support, if only for those few, endless moments, but Janeen wrenched free of her hold. Sinking onto the couch, she hunched her shoulders and wrapped both arms around her distended stomach. Rocking back and forth, lost in her own private haze of pain, she moaned her grief.

The chaplain eased down beside her, murmuring low, soft words Mrs. Lang gave no sign of hearing.

Brenna stared at the two figures on the brown plaid couch. She knew this scene would stay with her for the rest of her life. A T-shirt-clad woman, her legs bare, her tangled blond hair falling forward as she rocked forward and back, forward and back. A gray-haired man in a blue uniform, the silver cross on his breast pocket proclaiming his calling.

Never had Brenna felt so helpless. She was used to taking charge, to bringing order and rational thought to any and every situation. But there was nothing rational about this situation. There was nothing neat and orderly about watching a young wife racked with pain.

She caught a slight movement as the doctor moved toward the couch. The concern etched on his face made her stomach clench. He hunkered down beside the weeping woman, his black bag in one hand.

"Mrs. Lang, I checked your medical records before we came."

She gave no sign that she heard him, didn't cease her rocking, her sobbing.

"You visited the OB clinic a week ago, reporting mild cramps. I'd like to give you a sedative."

After a long, tense moment, her head lifted. The stark pain on the tear-ravaged face hit Brenna like a blow.

"No," she whispered.

"Just to help you through the next few hours. To ease the strain on you and the baby."

She shook her head, her arms tightening around her stomach. "No. Please. Not yet. Not now. Not until I know what happened." Her swimming, red-rimmed gaze shifted to the woman standing beside her. "I need to know."

Brenna drew in a deep breath, then nodded to

the chaplain. He stood up, making room for her on the couch.

This was her duty, she told herself as she sat down. Her responsibility. No one else could tell Janeen Lang how her husband died.

She took the chaplain's place on the sofa and reached across the nubby fabric for the young woman's hand.

Chapter Two

"Hello, Duggan."

Brenna glanced up from the checklist she held in one hand. The sight of Buck Henry's stocky figure and handsome face generated a tired smile of welcome.

"Well, well. If it isn't the world's greatest Intelligence Officer," she mocked gently. "When did you get back from D.C.?"

"An hour ago."

"How did your meetings go?"

Grimacing, Buck strolled into her office. "Two days spent locked in a room with the folks from the DOD budget office is my idea of un-fun."

"Bad, huh?"

"Worse than bad." He settled his solid frame in one of the chairs facing her desk. "You try explaining our counternarcotics mission to some pointy-headed auditors who think that everything on God's green earth can be reduced to dollars and cents. Hell, I don't even fully understand all the military and civilian law enforcement requirements for counterdrug operations, and I'm up to my ass in it. All I know is that we need more collection points, more analysts, more ..."

"I've got the picture, Buck."

He gave a rueful laugh. "Sorry. Guess I'm still wound up. I can't believe that some people really think we should watch our pennies in this drug business. They don't seem to understand we're in a war here, a real war, with the baddest guys we've been up against in a long time."

Brenna nodded absently. She'd been seeing Buck on and off for the past six months and had often heard him voice his frustrations about the limited intelligence assets dedicated to halting the flow of illegal drugs. Usually, she agreed with him. Sometimes, she deliberately agitated him with the reminder that counterdrugs was not, after all, the military's primary mission. Today she couldn't work up the emotion or the energy to pursue the issue either way.

At her halfhearted nod, he cocked his head and studied her face. "You okay?"

"I'm fine."

"You don't look fine. You look about as whipped as I've ever seen you."

"Thanks," Brenna responded dryly, tucking an errant strand of hair back into the thick twist.

"Which isn't to say you don't look gorgeous, of course. Just not up to your usual, General MacArthur-ish, knife-edged precision."

"I've had a bad couple of days, too."

He nodded sympathetically. "I heard about Sergeant Lang. How did the notification go?"

"Rough. Worse than rough," Brenna admitted, paraphrasing his words. "His wife took it hard. I was with her most of yesterday, until her family arrived. We were worried we'd have to hospitalize her at one point."

"Anything I can do to help?"

Brenna sent him a grateful smile. Not for the first time, she wondered why she couldn't respond to this thoughtful, considerate man in the way he wanted her to. Under that lighthearted, teasing exterior, Lt. Col. Buck Henry was as dedicated to the Air Force and to his career as she was. They thought alike on most issues . . . except football, of course. Despite her Irish Catholic roots, Brenna's years at the Air Force Academy made her take the long-standing feud between the Academy and Notre Dame personally. To his credit, Sean Patrick "Buck" Henry only reminded her a few times a month that his alma mater had stomped the cadets into the ground the last four times they'd met.

With a small shake of her head, Brenna declined his offer of help. "I think I've got everything working that needs to be working. I was just reviewing the checklist when you barged in. Isn't that just like the military? We even have a checklist for death."

"Death is a complicated business," he replied, his voice even.

Brenna slanted him a quick look. Although he'd

lost his wife to cancer nearly five years ago, she knew his wounds were still raw. She also knew how much he hated to talk about it.

"Yes, it is," she agreed, her tone brisk. "And you need to haul your carcass out of here, so I can get on with it. Not all of us have the same light schedules you staff toads do. Some of us have to work for a living."

The long-standing rivalry between operations and staff brought a grin to his face. "Right. And if you work hard enough, maybe someday you'll get picked for a cushy staff job, too."

"Hah," she snorted. "Not if I have anything to say about it."

"Want to have dinner tonight?" he asked casually, moving to the door.

"Thanks, but I'd better pass." She gestured to the papers on her desk. "I've only got two working days to complete the Line of Duty Determination. I'm struggling with it now."

"Call me if you change your mind." He sketched her a salute. "Later, Duggan."

When her office door closed behind Buck's familiar figure, Brenna leaned back in her chair. Her pen tapped idly against the papers scattered on her desk while she tried to recapture her previous concentration. After a few moments, she gave up and swiveled her chair to stare out the window behind her.

The crepe myrtle that shaded her window drooped pathetically, its fuchsia blossoms shriveling in the brutal, hundred-degree Oklahoma heat.

She felt about as lively as that poor tree, Brenna thought with an uncharacteristic tiredness.

Normally she thrived on her work. Her long days and erratic flight schedules never bothered her. A true professional, she took a deep satisfaction at being part of the military institution and a fierce, personal pride in her position as a commander.

Brenna knew how lucky she was to command the 552d Training Squadron. In a pilot-oriented Air Force, choice command billets for officers without wings were few and far between. Her squadron was the only one of its kind in the Air Force, providing academic and simulator training for crew members who flew aboard the Airborne Warning And Control Systems, called AWACS for short. Every officer who flew in the back end of the AWACS had his or her eye on Brenna's job. It was common knowledge that bagging this billet meant you were being groomed for future promotions.

At this particular moment, however, Brenna felt the full weight of her command on her shoulders. The hours she'd spent with Janeen Lang had wrung her emotions and sapped her usual energy. And the task ahead of her would be almost as draining. Swinging her chair back around, she shuffled through the papers on her desk and picked up a single-sheeted form.

AF Form 438. Line of Duty Determination. The LOD, in unofficial Air Force parlance.

All she had to do was mark an X in one of the

innocuous boxes on the bottom of the form, then sign her name. With that simple act, she'd officially determine whether Sergeant Lang's death occurred in the line of duty or because of his own misconduct. Whether he was responsible for what happened, or a victim of unfortunate circumstances. Whether his wife would be entitled to extended benefits while she decided what to do with the rest of her life, or not. So much hinged on that simple X.

The intercom's shrill buzz interrupted her intense concentration on the form. Setting it aside, she picked up the receiver.

"Yes?"

"Mr. Richards is here to see you, ma'am," her military clerk announced.

Brenna had been waiting for his arrival. Special Agent Richards would have the formal report of investigation she needed to complete the LOD.

"Send him in, Pete."

She flipped off the intercom and rose, smoothing her tailored, dark blue skirt over her hips in an unconscious carry-over from her long-ago academy days. Wrinkled skirts were about as acceptable in a female cadet as long hair. It had taken her years after graduation to grow her hair out to the shoulder length she preferred.

Brenna held out her hand to the thin, unsmiling man who entered her office. Although he wore a conservative gray suit and a maroon tie, Richards was her peer and a commander in his own right. Agents assigned to the Office of Special Investigations didn't advertise their military rank, however. Not when they might have to investigate anyone from an airman to a general. The OSI preferred to keep their anonymity and their distance from other officers.

"Afternoon, Colonel."

"Good afternoon, Mr. Richards." Brenna waved him to one of the chairs placed at a small, round table in the corner of her office. "I appreciate your coming over. I'm impressed that your folks finished the official investigation so quickly."

Richards gave a small shrug as he set his briefcase on the table. "When someone with Sergeant Lang's security clearance dies under suspicious circumstances, we move fast."

Brenna waited quietly while the agent pulled out a sheaf of notes.

"As you're aware," he began after a moment, "Staff Sergeant Andrew Lang's unclothed body was found in a back room of the Purple Parrot, a bar in downtown Panama City, at approximately oh-one-hundred on August seventeenth. A rope was knotted around his neck."

The stark, ugly facts didn't sound any better to Brenna in the light of day than they had when she'd first heard them at four o'clock in the morning.

"The other end of the rope was looped over the door and tied to the knob on the other side. Apparently Sergeant Lang leaned into the rope, causing self-strangulation. The official cause of death has been listed as asphyxiation. We've concluded that it was an accidental death. There was no note, nor any other evidence to indicate Sergeant Lang intended to kill himself."

Brenna felt a rush of guilty relief. Aside from the official complications a suicide involved, she was glad that Sergeant Lang hadn't intentionally left his wife ravaged with doubt as well as grief. It was bad enough that he'd left her the way he had.

As if reading her mind, Richards continued in a dry, unemotional voice. "The evidence indicates that Sergeant Lang was engaging in sexual self-stimulation, either alone or with another partner. None of the bar girls at the Purple Parrot will admit to being in his company at the time of his death, however."

Self-stimulation. Brenna assumed that was the official OSI term for jerking off.

"Use of a rope or other form of constriction around the neck to cut off the air supply is a standard technique in autoeroticism."

"Autoeroticism." Her lips curled in distaste as they formed the words.

"It's a form of sexual stimulation. It reportedly heightens the orgasm at the moment of ejaculation."

"I know what it is, Mr. Richards. I'm just having a hard time believing that Sergeant Lang . . . that any responsible adult would do anything so stupid."

The agent gave a small shrug. "This particular sexual technique has been around for a long time. The Chinese have practiced autoeroticism for thousands of years. One of the Chou dynasty sex manuals describes various methods for knotting a silk scarf around the neck, and just where to place the knots for maximum effectiveness."

Brenna stared at him, trying to connect a bar in Panama with an ancient Chinese dynasty. She failed, utterly.

"Death occurs more frequently than you'd believe," he added. "The victims lean into the rope and unintentionally cut off the oxygen flow to the brain. They pass out, then slowly strangle."

Brenna's flesh prickled. She considered herself relatively sophisticated. After all, she'd been married for several years before she and her husband's separate careers had caused them to drift apart. Nor had she been completely celibate since her divorce, although her natural fastidiousness precluded casual encounters. Still, she couldn't imagine anyone, much less the smiling, easygoing Sergeant Lang, participating in such dangerous sexual practices.

"Actually," Richards said, "we think there are probably a lot more deaths attributable to auto-eroticism than ever get reported. Family members often try to cover it up by clothing the body and hiding evidence before calling the police. Understandable, of course, but it makes our business more difficult."

The contrast between Richards's calm, flat voice and the sinister subject under discussion was beginning to get on Brenna's nerves. Unable to sit still any longer, she stood and began to pace the small office.

"I'm having trouble absorbing this. I can't believe Sergeant Lang would do something so ... so bizarre."

"We've had three similar deaths in the Air Force this year alone."

"Not in my squadron," she snapped.

"That's less than the national average," Richards continued evenly, "but still cause for concern."

Brenna whirled to face him. "What do you guys do, keep score?"

"As a matter of fact, we do. It's our business."

At his level response, Brenna reined in her distaste. "I'm sorry. You're right. It *is* your business, and now I guess it's mine as well. So you think Sergeant Lang was indulging in this particular ... sport at the time he died?"

"We do. The position of the body and the presence of semen indicate that he ejaculated before death occurred."

For a quick, resentful moment, Brenna wondered if this man ever showed any emotion. The few times she'd dealt with Richards on other matters, he'd come across the same way. Cool, efficient, bloodless. She knew he had to stick to the facts in the case, but his dispassionate account of Sergeant Lang's last moments grated on her. How would he like it if someone discussed his ejaculation, his semen, in that precise, dry manner?

"Of course, the use of drugs increases the risks

associated with autoeroticism, as much as it increases the pleasure. Lang probably checked out on a real, sustained high."

"Drugs?" Brenna stopped in midstride and turned to face him. "Are you saying Lang was on something?"

"The preliminary lab analysis indicates the presence of crack cocaine in his system. We're waiting on the autopsy report for confirmation."

"I don't believe it," Brenna said flatly.

Her mind whirled. None of what she'd heard in the last few moments fit her mental picture of Andrew Lang. Although she didn't know him as well as other members of her squadron, he just didn't seem the type to use crack or practice kinky sex in a shabby bar in Panama. Not the tall, gangly man with the easy smile and gentle, if thoroughly competent way with his students.

"The Army medical examiner who processed the body noted fresh tracks on Sergeant Lang's arm."

She bit her lip, unable to refute that bald statement.

Richards frowned slightly at his notes. "That surprised me, actually. Most crack users snort it or cook the stuff up and smoke it. Very few mainline. It's too risky these days, given the AIDS threat." He shook his head. "But it's fast. Damn fast, which I supposed is what Sergeant Lang wanted."

"I suppose."

Rising, Richards drew an envelope out of his

briefcase and placed it on the table. "This file contains datafax copies of the pictures taken at the scene and the official OSI report."

Brenna stared down at the manila envelope. Distaste, quickly controlled, shivered down her spine.

"The file also contains copies of the witness statements, not that they add anything. The three men who were with Lang that night left him around ten o'clock to return to the base. Still, they were the last to see him alive, and you'll need their statements for the Line of Duty Determination." He consulted his notebook. "Technical Sergeant Martinez. Staff Sergeant Dobbs. And a Mr. Dave Sanderson from . . ."

"The U.S. Customs Service," Brenna supplied.

At her clipped reply, Richards looked up sharply. "You know him?"

"I've had to deal with Sanderson personally on a couple of occasions."

Richards's eyes narrowed. "Something I should know about?"

Brenna shook her head. Her opinion about this particular civilian Customs agent, one of several who flew aboard AWACS on designated counter-drug missions, was just that, a personal opinion.

"We've disagreed once or twice on procedures," she replied. "I understand the witnesses will be arriving back at Tinker tonight. I'll read through their statements before I interview them tomorrow."

A faint frown creased the OSI commander's

forehead. "You don't really need to interview them. Our agents in Panama were very thorough. There's nothing more those three men can tell you about what happened."

"Maybe not. But maybe they can help me understand why it happened."

"You don't need that for the LOD."

Brenna's eyes hardened, and she leaned forward, planting both palms on the table. "I may not need the details for the LOD, but as the commander I need to understand a few things. Like why a man assigned to my unit was shooting dope while participating in a highly sensitive mission. Why he knotted a rope around his neck, then played with himself, either alone or in the presence of some bar girl, and managed to kill himself in the process. If I get the answers to those questions, then maybe, just maybe, I'll understand why a man like that left behind a pregnant wife who thinks he's a combination of John Wayne and Saint Francis. Or use to think that, anyway."

Richards stared at her for moment, as if processing her answer, then picked up his briefcase. "We should get the autopsy report this afternoon. I'll send a copy over as soon as it comes in."

You do that, Brenna thought.

Her mouth tightened as she watched him leave. She knew damn well that her belligerence toward the OSI commander was a transference of her own anger and frustration over what had happened. But recognizing the source of her anger and being able to control it were two different matters.

She stood beside the table long after the echo of Richards's footsteps on the tile floor outside her office had faded. From the administrative area, she heard the clatter of a keyboard and the low hum of conversation as the clerks went about their business. Someone laughed in the outer hallway, making Brenna's brows draw together. Laughter seemed so inappropriate, given what had just been discussed in her office. Given what she still had to read.

With the tip of one finger, she slid the folder a few inches across the polished surface of the table. Why in the world was she so reluctant to open the damn thing? She'd seen bodies before. And parts of bodies, for that matter. As a young lieutenant, she'd been detailed to an aircraft accident response team. The experience of picking up the pieces after a KC–135 tanker crash wasn't one she'd soon forget.

But this seemed worse somehow. This wasn't an accident where the world exploded in a bright flash of flame. This was slow strangulation with dark, sexual overtones. She felt like a voyeur about to peer through a murky glass at something that should be private. Secret.

Reminding herself that there was nothing private about death, Brenna sat down and opened the folder.

The OSI report was bad enough. The autopsy report, when it arrived later that afternoon, was worse. Not even the long, convoluted medical terms could soften the stark details.

Brenna forced herself to read through it, looking for answers that weren't there. When a knock sounded on her door and her chief administrative specialist poked his head inside the office, she looked up in mingled irritation and relief.

"It's after six, Colonel. You need anything before we shut down?"

"No thanks, Pete. I'm just going through the report the OSI sent over. It'll keep me busy for a while."

"Kinda weird about Sergeant Lang, isn't it?"

"What do you mean?"

"That rope stuff, and him doing dope like that."

Brenna stiffened. "Did you read this report before you gave it to me?"

Her sharp tone took the clerk aback. "No, ma'am. I wouldn't read something marked 'Sensitive, Commander's Eyes Only.' "

"Then how do you know . . . ?" Comprehension dawned. "I take it the rumor mill is already working."

"The crews talk to each other," the airman admitted, shrugging. "You know how word gets around."

Brenna rubbed a tired hand across her forehead. "Yes, I know. Go on, go home. I'll lock the safe when I leave."

While the outer office slipped into a half quiet, Brenna glanced at the clock on her wall, wishing it was too late to call Janeen Lang. If only the OSI hadn't been so damned efficient, she might have delayed this visit until tomorrow. If only the rumors weren't already circulating, she could have waited until she felt more prepared to face the young widow again.

For a few moments she toyed with the idea of shirking her responsibilities and taking Buck up on his offer of dinner. Lighthearted companionship and hot, spicy food were what she needed right now. Enchiladas maybe, or a big, greasy pizza. Her mouth watered at the thought, and she realized suddenly she'd forgotten to eat lunch.

She knew the Air Force too well to delay, however. During times of crisis, people converged on the scene to volunteer aid and assistance. Neighbors came with food. The squadron spouses network would offer emotional support. She suspected that friends and neighbors had already called on Janeen Lang, had already offered to help her dazed parents. Brenna couldn't take the chance that someone might inadvertently let something slip. Mrs. Lang deserved to hear the official report from her husband's commander, not a neighbor. The pizza would have to wait.

Brenna felt a stab of guilt as she reached for the phone. Here she was, regretting a lost dinner when another woman had just lost her husband. When she heard the report, Mrs. Lang would no doubt lose the last of her illusions as well.

Gnawing on her lower lip, Brenna dialed Sergeant Lang's home phone number. A half hour later, she faced the young widow across a white-washed kitchen table.

"No." Stubbornly, Janeen shook her head. "Not Andy. Not my Andy."

She didn't believe it. She refused to believe it. Her mouth tight, she glared at the woman seated across from her, a cup of coffee cradled in both hands.

"Mrs. Lang, I know it's hard to accept, but—"

"There are no 'buts,' Colonel Duggan," Janeen interrupted fiercely. "My Andy wouldn't do any of those . . . those things you say he did. And he doesn't take drugs."

She heard the rising note of hysteria in her voice and pressed her fingers against her lips. As if to shut out the ugly words that still hung on the air, she closed dry lids over eyes that felt as though they'd been scraped with sandpaper. She'd cried all the tears clear out of her body, she thought bitterly. She didn't have any more left in her.

"I didn't come to argue with you, Mrs. Lang, or try to convince you. I just didn't want you to hear the facts from anyone else."

Janeen's eyes flew open. "You mean these disgustin' lies are being spread about? Have you been talkin' about Andy with other folks?"

"I haven't gossiped about your husband, if that's what you mean," the colonel replied quietly. "But you know we have to conduct an investigation in cases like these, where death is due to other than natural causes. Reports are . . ."

Janeen's tenuous control over her emotions disintegrated. She slapped both palms down on the pine table. "Don't call him a case," she hissed. "Don't call Andy a case. He's not a case. And he's not remains."

Her fingers curled into the woven place mats on the tabletop. The green-and-white-checked fabric bunched as her anger gave way to waves of grief.

"That's what the man this afternoon called him," she moaned. "Remains. He said Andy's remains will be shipped home within the next couple of days. Oh, God."

Her head dropped as dry sobs tore at her raw, aching throat.

The colonel shoved aside her coffee mug and reached out to cover the clenched hands with her own.

"Don't touch me," Janeen gasped, snatching her fists back. "People been touchin' me all day. People I don't even know. Huggin' me and telling me they're there if I need them. I don't need them. I need Andy."

The panic in her own voice frightened Janeen. She couldn't lose control again. She couldn't. She had to think of the baby. Stuffing a knuckle into her mouth, she bit down hard.

While she struggled for control, the kitchen door opened and her mother peered into the dim, shadowy room, lit only by the dying rays of the afternoon sun.

"Janey, honey, are you okay?"

No! she wanted to scream. No, I'm not okay! I'll never be okay again. But she cut off the agonized cry before it ripped out of her throat. She wouldn't scream out her anger and pain like some wounded animal. Her momma and daddy were hurting, too, and Janeen didn't want to add to their burdens.

Lowering her hand from her face, she swiveled her bulk around in the ladder-back chair.

"I'm . . . I'm just talking to the colonel, Momma. 'Bout Air Force . . . I mean, there's some . . ."

Brenna's heart wrenched at the young woman's struggle to contain her emotions. Smoothly, she came to her aid. "I know this is difficult for your daughter, Mrs. Wilson. I won't keep her much longer. Unfortunately, even in distressing moments such as these, we have business that has to be conducted."

The gray-haired woman stood at the kitchen door, clearly reluctant to intrude but concerned. Her clouded brown eyes skittered from Brenna to Janeen, and back.

"I thought those people who came this afternoon took care of Air Force business," she said in the same soft, rolling drawl that characterized her daughter's speech. "They talked to Janeen about the funeral and gave her all that money."

The six-thousand-dollar death gratuity check probably seemed like a lot of money to Janeen's mother, Brenna realized, but that emergency fund had to sustain the widow through frozen bank accounts and adjudication of Sergeant Lang's insurance benefits. She'd need that much and more to help her through the coming weeks.

"I'm afraid it'll take a while to settle everything

that has to be handled. I won't keep Janeen much longer."

Still concerned but realizing she'd been dismissed, the older woman nodded and closed the kitchen door.

"Thank you."

Janeen's voice had lost its touch of hysteria, Brenna noted with relief.

"I wouldn't want momma to hear . . . what you've been telling me."

Sergeant Lang's in-laws were bound to hear the sordid details sometime, Brenna thought. But not from her. Lord, not from her.

"She and Daddy love Andy like a son," the younger woman continued in a slow, ragged voice. "They just about raised him."

"You and your husband grew up together?"

"Andy's folks bought the farm next to ours when he was no bigger than a lick of spit, as daddy used to say."

With relief, Brenna saw the hard, hurt glitter in the red-rimmed brown eyes ease a fraction.

"Andy spent more time at our place than at home, playing and scrapping with my brothers. He was an only child, you know."

"No, I didn't know."

Janeen nodded, the stark lines of her face softening as she thought about happier days. For the first time Brenna caught a glimpse of the beauty that lay beneath her drawn cheeks and lank, lifeless hair. She kept still, not wanting to disturb the widow's fragile moment of peace.

"Andy never much noticed me when we were growing up. I was too young, I guess, and too scrawny. But I noticed him all right. The first time I set eyes on him, there in the lane leading to our house, I went all silly and giggly. I must've been five or six years old."

"How old was he?"

" 'Bout eight, I suppose." Janeen's lips curled in a small smile. "I thought he was so nice. Then he put a bullfrog down my back, and I hopped and screeched all the way home."

Brenna held her breath as Janeen's smile deepened. The young woman stared across the kitchen, seeing something other than the bland, government-standard cream-colored walls and outdated appliances. Probably a farm road of red Oklahoma clay, hard-baked by the summer sun, and a gangly, laughing boy. For a moment, Brenna could almost see him, too.

Janeen's gaze fluttered back to the woman opposite her. The sunshine and laughter faded away. Reality settled around them like a cold fog.

"That's why I know Andy didn't do any of those things you told me were in that report, Colonel Duggan," the younger woman said, her words fierce. "I know him. I've known him since I was in first grade, and I've loved him just about as long. He's the only man I've ever been with. And I'm the only one he's . . ."

Her voice caught. Swallowing, she forced herself to continue.

"I'm the only one he's ever laid with. I know

it. He wouldn't have sex with a bar girl. He wouldn't put drugs in his body and ... and masturbate like that. Not Andy. Not my Andy."

Brenna bit her lip. Although she'd never suggest it to this distraught woman, people stationed far away from home sometimes did things they'd never dream of doing around their families. She'd taken a whole course on situational ethics at the Academy, one structured around Lieutenant Calley and the men who participated in the My Lai massacre during the Vietnam War. Many of those men had been loving husbands. Caring fathers.

No, Brenna had done her duty. She'd told Mrs. Lang the circumstances of her husband's death. If the widow chose not to believe her, that was her right. Her refuge.

She stood and waited patiently while the other woman planted both hands on the table and pushed herself to her feet.

"I'm sorry, Mrs. Lang, more sorry than I can express. I wish I'd known your husband better. It sounds as though you had a rare and wonderful relationship."

Janeen nodded, attempting a smile. "We did."

With a jolt, Brenna realized that the young widow had just spoken of her husband in the past tense for the first time.

The other woman seemed to recognize that fact at the same moment. Her skin paled to a stark white. A pain so raw leapt into the wide brown eyes that Brenna could only mumble a farewell and turn away.

Chapter Three

The look in Janeen Lang's eyes haunted Brenna during the interviews she conducted the following day. Over and over, she tried to find something in the other crew members' accounts to explain why Andrew Lang would put that pain in his wife's eyes. Why he would compromise his career and his life for a few moments of sordid pleasure in the back room of a bar.

"Are you sure there's nothing more you can add, Sergeant Dobbs?"

Sweat glistened on the black staff sergeant's forehead. "No, ma'am. I've gone over that night a hundred times in my mind, and I don't know why Andy decided to stay at the bar. He wasn't the kind to hang out in those kind of places."

"What kind of places did he usually hang out in?"

Dobbs frowned, then shook his head. "Guess I really don't know. I've only flown with him a couple of times. Last time was to Saudi, and we never left the base."

Swallowing her disappointment, Brenna dismissed him. After two interviews, she knew no more than when she'd started. Neither of the men she'd talked to so far could offer more than the basic facts detailed in the OSI report. Lang and Dobbs had eaten dinner at a downtown restaurant, not far from the Purple Parrot. On their way back to the base, they'd spotted two other crew members, Martinez and Sanderson, going into the bar. The four men had downed a couple beers. About ten, they'd decided to leave. Lang alone had insisted on staying.

With only one more individual to interview, Brenna was close to concluding that she would never understand why Lang had stayed—any more than Janeen Lang would.

One more interview. Then she had to finalize the Line of Duty Determination. Frowning, Brenna shot a look at the clock on the wall. She might have known Sanderson would be late.

He arrived some ten minutes later. Tall and deeply tanned, he sported an undisciplined mane of sun-streaked brown hair and an attitude that immediately set Brenna's teeth on edge.

"You wanted to see me, Colonel?"

She glanced pointedly at the clock. "I wanted to see you at ten-thirty, Mr. Sanderson."

Hazel eyes more green than brown traveled over her face. Brenna thought she detected a subtle hardening in the harsh planes of his cheeks, but it was more of an impression on her part than an expression on his.

"I'm here now," he drawled, strolling into her office.

Without waiting for an invitation, he settled his long frame into one of the chairs in front of her desk. Leaning casually back, he crossed one leg over his knee, folded his hands across his stomach, and waited for her to proceed.

Deliberately, Brenna took her time. Her previous encounters with Sanderson had been brief and mutually terse. She didn't know much more about the man than the little that everyone else in the squadron knew. That little didn't particularly impress her.

A former Air Force officer whose casual approach to regulations had reportedly ended his military career prematurely, Sanderson spent the last six years in a succession of different jobs. Some of the wilder rumors around the squadron had tagged him as a free-lance "consultant" for unspecified agencies operating in Central America. He'd started flying as a civilian Customs Agent aboard the AWACS about six months ago, after requalifying on its surveillance systems in minimum time.

Raking him with a hard glance, Brenna tried to reconcile the man's reputation to his appearance. Although he needed a haircut and his scuffed boots looked like they'd taken him through the last two wars, he possessed a lean, muscled body that hinted at some degree of inner discipline. Well-washed jeans hugged his thighs and a faded, blue cotton shirt, its sleeves rolled up in concession to the muggy Oklahoma heat, stretched taut across his shoulders.

They were shoulders that any woman with half a hormone left in her body would notice, Brenna admitted. Too bad the man's personality was so much less attractive than the rest of him.

"As you're aware, Mr. Sanderson," she began, her voice cool and clipped, "I'm required to ascertain the facts surrounding Sergeant Lang's death in order to complete a Line of Duty Determination. You were one of the last people to see him alive. I'd like you to tell me what happened that night."

He measured her from behind a screen of sun-bleached lashes. "I've already told the OSI."

"I have the OSI report, Mr. Sanderson. What I want now is your personal account."

"I can't tell you any more than what's in the report."

"Try."

His eyes narrowed fractionally at the unmistakable command. "Martinez and I met Lang and Dobbs in the street outside the Purple Parrot. We had a few beers together. Around ten, we left him at the bar and headed back to Howard."

"You just left him there? In a part of town that no one with any sense wanders around in alone?"

Like all AWACS crew members, Brenna had pulled her share of temporary duty stints in Panama. Despite its lush climate and profusion of exotic flowers, the capital city wasn't exactly a paradise. There were some pretty rough districts just a few blocks from the wide sweep of the bay. What's more, a groundswell of resentment had built up since the U.S. had intervened to take Noriega out of power. Most crew members made it a point not to travel through the city streets alone.

Sanderson shrugged off her concern. "He's a big . . ." He stopped, correcting himself. "He *was* a big boy. He knew the risks when he decided to stay."

The callous response flicked at something raw inside Brenna. "Why did Lang stay after you and the others left?" she asked coldly. "Was he intoxicated?"

"Not that I could see."

"So what kept him there?"

He surveyed her across the wide expanse of her desk. "You ever been to the Purple Parrot, Colonel?"

"No."

"I didn't think so," he murmured.

"I gather that you're implying Sergeant Lang stayed because of the bar girls."

"It sure as hell wasn't because of the decor."

Brenna's jaw tightened. "Just answer my question, Sanderson."

She sensed rather than saw him stiffen. He didn't alter his comfortable sprawl, but she caught the subtle tensing of his jaw and the ripple of his shoulders under the blue cotton shirt. Good. She hoped she annoyed him. He certainly annoyed her.

"I don't know why he stayed at the bar," he

replied after a moment. "He *said* he was going to have another drink, then head back to base."

"Did Lang show any evidence of having used drugs while you were with him?"

"No."

"Have you ever known Sergeant Lang to use drugs before?"

His hazel eyes glinted. "Now how do you suppose I'm going to answer that? You know as well as I do that anyone with knowledge of substance abuse is supposed to report it."

"And do you always do what you're supposed to, Mr. Sanderson?" Despite herself, Brenna couldn't keep the acid out of her voice.

"When it suits me."

The simple arrogance of his answer lit small, angry fires all along her nerves.

"Answer my question, Sanderson."

"You'll have to repeat it. I want to make sure I get it right. For the record."

At the gleam of mockery in his eyes, Brenna decided it was time to set one shaggy-haired civilian straight. Rising, she walked around her desk and leaned one hip against the front edge.

"This isn't a judicial hearing. You're not under oath, giving testimony that can later be held against you. Nor are you facing any kind of administrative action. *Yet.*"

That got his attention. He tilted his head to study her, his gaze sharpening.

Without raising her voice, Brenna sliced into him. "I suggest you listen, and listen good. You may think because you're a civilian you can get away with the line of bull you've been handing me. Think again. If I don't get some straight answers out of you in the next five minutes, you can kiss your flight pay good-bye."

Uncoiling his long legs, Sanderson pushed himself out of the chair and turned to face her. Without the desk between them, he towered over Brenna's own five-feet-seven. His powerful shoulders blocked out the rest of her office, narrowing her field of vision to a broad chest molded by faded blue cotton and a weathered face that was a study in hard lines and uncompromising angles.

"What the hell are you talking about?"

"You were scheduled to fly the day after Sergeant Lang died."

"So were twenty other people."

"Twenty other people weren't at the Purple Parrot, consuming alcohol less than twelve hours before a mission."

The look he gave her might have raised the hackles on the back of anyone else's neck, but all it produced in Brenna was a fierce stab of satisfaction. She had him by the short hairs, and he knew it.

"I checked the flight schedules, Sanderson. By staying until ten o'clock at the Purple Parrot, you violated crew rest. So unless you want me to haul you in front of a flying review board, I suggest you sit down, wipe that sneer off your face, and answer my questions."

Silence spun out between them, heavy and tense.

"I don't repeat myself," she warned softly. "Ever."

Pinpoints of green fire flared in his eyes.

Brenna let them burn.

Expelling a long, harsh breath, he muttered something she didn't ask him to repeat and sat down. Breathing a little hard herself, she turned and walked back to her chair. By the time she was seated and facing him, Brenna had herself under rigid control.

He had to search back through their exchange for the question she'd thrown at him before their confrontation.

"No," he ground out after a few moments, "I've never known Lang to use drugs before."

By the time Duggan dismissed him from her office, Dave Sanderson's jaw had locked tight. Heat singed his cheeks as he strode through the squadron's corridors. Ignoring the casual greetings from other crew members, he shoved open the door with a hard palm and stalked across the huge parking lot behind the 552d headquarters complex. His mud-spattered Ford truck sat in a haze of shimmering heat, squatting on the asphalt like some sorry-eyed, molting brown hen.

He wove through the parked cars toward it, his body taut with anger. The whole damn lot had been full when he arrived for his appointment this morning, still groggy from the long flight home last night. Circling the lot several times in the hundred-degree heat hadn't improved his mood at all. Nor had Duggan's snippy reference to his tardiness when he entered her office. His reluctant willingness to cooperate with the authority she represented had taken a direct hit the moment she looked up and speared him with those frosty blue eyes.

Dave climbed into the truck, slamming the door so hard the glass rattled in the half-opened window. Christ, he couldn't remember the last time he let someone get to him like that. He'd learned long ago to tune out and turn off officers with minds as starched as their uniforms. Officers who lived and died by the goddamn book.

Lived by it? He snorted in derision. Hell, Lieutenant Colonel Brenna Duggan probably slept with the Manual for Courts Martial tucked between her slender white thighs.

He cursed as a vivid image leapt instantly into his mind. Clenching his fists on the steering wheel, he shook his head in disgust. Why didn't he admit it? It wasn't the colonel's attitude that had sent his temperature soaring, but the colonel herself.

He'd only seen her a few times up close and personal in the months he'd been flying with the 552d Air Control Wing. But those few times had made his hands itch to bury themselves in her thick, silky-looking mane and do some serious damage to its disciplined coil. Just a glimpse of her long, lithe body strolling down the corridor was enough to generate a late-night fantasy, one that centered on tugging down the front zipper on her flight suit, inch by tantalizing inch.

Despite his fascination with the woman, or perhaps because of it, Dave had made it a point to steer clear of her as much as possible. Those long legs of hers might kick a few of his more basic male instincts into overdrive, but he had no intention of letting himself get involved with an uptight, acid-edged, do-it-by-the-book commander. An Academy grad, for God's sake.

Even if she hadn't been a commander, Brenna Duggan wasn't the kind of woman he should be fantasizing about. She was too smart, too wrapped up in her career, too intense. He'd journeyed to hell once with a woman like her. He wouldn't, couldn't, do it again.

Not that Lieutenant Colonel Duggan wanted to journey anywhere with him, Dave admitted with a wry grimace. Not after he'd done his best to rub her with almost as much friction as she'd rubbed him.

She didn't rub easy, he thought ruefully. That dewy soft skin covered a core of solid steel. He'd met a few tougher officers in his time, but not many. He was surprised there wasn't any blood on his shirt from the strip she'd torn off his hide.

What the hell, he thought, raking a hand through his hair. Given the circumstances, it was probably just as well they'd struck sparks off each other from the moment he'd walked into her office. He sure didn't need the kind of complications a woman like her would bring into his life. Not with all that was coming down. Not with one man already dead.

Twisting the key in the ignition, Dave shoved the gearshift into drive and headed for the west gate. He'd better get his mind off Brenna Duggan's legs or he'd wind up just like Lang. Thank God it was a long, hot drive to the airport on the northside of town where his contacts waited. He was going to need every mile to get himself under control.

The men he had to do business with demanded every ounce of his concentration.

"Kill him, Spider! Kill him!"

"Ice him down!"

A chorus of raucous shouts and colorful epithets rose from the men and women clustered around the pool table. The climactic, final contest began in the crud tournament—a convoluted, energetic team sport invented by Canadian fighter pilots some years ago and now played with demonic enthusiasm by uniformed men and women all over the world.

The attacking Red Team player maneuvered for position at the far end of the felt-covered table, his body bent at an impossible angle. He lifted one leg to the broad edge for balance. The crowd around him quieted momentarily. The referee warned a few anxious teammates back, out of the three-foot clear zone.

The young Weapons Director with the call sign

"Spider" peered down the length of green felt at his target. His left hand caressed the cue ball, rolling it lightly back and forth on the table, warming it up, arming it for the kill. Then, with a flick of his wrist, he sent the ball spinning. It careened off one side, whirled across the table to the other, then shot back to the center.

The Blue Team defender leaped to avoid the attack, but Spider's aim was deadly. The snap of wooden balls colliding rang through the noise in the crowded lounge. The Red Team erupted into whoops of victory. Spider went under as his teammates expressed their appreciation for his skill by pummeling him into the table.

Brenna cheered the victory along with the rest of her troops. When the grinning, red-faced Spider glanced over to her table, she gave him a thumbs-up. His grin widened, then was lost as a throng of jubilant well-wishers surrounded him.

"Your squadron just might get the trophy back," the major beside her commented.

"Might, hell," she responded with a grin. "It's in the bag."

The noise in the bar subsided to its normal, deafening level. On Friday nights the casual lounge at the Tinker Officers' Club was AWACS country. Only about a third of the wing's personnel were home at any one time, but those who were partied, and partied hard.

No one seemed to care that the place reeked of stale smoke, old popcorn, and the tang of bodies baked by the Oklahoma heat. No one noticed the less than inspiring decor, with its old-fashioned brown leather bar stools and dark-paneled walls. No one paid any attention to the fact that the jukebox shoved up against one wall played nothing but Garth Brooks and George Strait. In any case, the music could barely be heard over the shouted conversations and loud laughter.

Taking a sip of beer from the dew-streaked glass in her hand, Brenna surveyed the room and tried to capture the feeling of camaraderie she usually felt at these Friday night gatherings. Her gaze swept the crowd, passing over men and women clad in green flight suits or camouflage fatigues, incongruously labeled "battle dress uniforms" by some anonymous Pentagon staff puke long ago. There was nothing "dress" about BDU's, with their baggy pants tucked into heavy black boots and their oversized shirts worn outside the pants.

Here and there amid the mass of green and black and brown, occasional splashes of light blue and white denoted wing staff officers and their Navy counterparts. Other nations were represented as well. Arms lifted and hands moved in parallel, swooping gestures as a small group of Canadians and Turks and Americans described their maneuvers in the universal language of flyers. A number of civilians stood interspersed among the officers—Boeing contract employees, who were considered part of the wing. A scattering of wives. A few husbands. More than one local who was checking out the Friday night action.

The convivial atmosphere in the club didn't arise from alcohol. Everyone knew a DUI would end a career faster than failing to show for a mission. What permeated the air in the club was more a sense of companionship, an unspoken sharing. This gathering, and ones similar to it in Officers' Clubs or wing shacks around the world, reinforced the subtle bond that people in uniform never overtly addressed but always felt.

The men and women who wore the 552d Wing patch on their left sleeve averaged over six months of temporary duty a year. Their TDY's took them regularly to Iceland and Turkey and Saudi, as well as Panama. They logged more flying time each year than most officers saw in their initial five- or six-year commitment. Their mission was unique in the Air Force, and they celebrated that uniqueness by gathering when they could.

Usually the activities in the Casual Lounge helped Brenna throw off the stress and strain of the preceding week. But tonight, she couldn't seem to relax in the company of other men and women who shared her vocation. Despite her sense of kinship with the people around her, despite her pleasure in the company of the man beside her, she couldn't shake the image of pain-filled brown eyes in a white, haunted face.

"You've got to let it go, Brenna."

Buck's low comment was almost lost amid the hoots and catcalls as a young lieutenant took to the dance floor. He began a loose-limbed, rolling electric slide with a woman in jeans so tight they

61

creased in every nook and cranny of her well-endowed body.

Brenna toyed with her beer. As the noise settled around them like a blanket and wrapped them in a measure of privacy, Buck returned to the conversation they'd been having before the crud match preempted their attention.

"You can't blame yourself because you didn't know one of the ninety-plus instructors assigned to your squadron well enough to realize he was on crack."

"I should have," Brenna replied, her lips settling in a grim line. "I should have taken the time to get to know him better. I shouldn't have let wartime exercises and academic reviews and paperwork eat up so much of my time."

Buck snorted. "The Air Force runs on paper. We use more paper than jet fuel. Everyone in the wing who wants one has a personal computer, but we're still up to our tender parts in paper."

"I shouldn't have lost sight of what makes my squadron run," she insisted stubbornly. "Not paper. Not computers. People."

"Brenna, stop it. You're a good commander. A damn good one. You take care of your people. Your squadron has the lowest discipline rate in the wing, and the highest promotion rates."

"It also has a dead instructor. One with a wife who doesn't accept what her husband seems to have become, any more than I want to."

Buck leaned toward her, studying her troubled

face. "This is about the Line of Duty Determination, isn't it?"

She traced a slow pattern in the wet tabletop, not answering.

"Did you complete it?"

Brenna drew in a slow breath. "Yes. I finished the interviews this afternoon."

"Didn't they help?"

The image of Sanderson's lean, cynical face filled her mind. "No," she responded with a grimace. "They didn't help."

"So?"

She met Buck's eyes across the small table. "So I found Sergeant Andrew Lang's death not in the line of duty."

"It was the only thing you could do," he said quietly.

She nodded, but his reassuring words didn't lessen her uncharacteristic sense of inadequacy.

It was done, Brenna told herself. The investigation was completed, the X placed in the only box it could be placed in, the form signed.

Now all she had to do was dress in her blues the day after tomorrow, drive to Seiling, and attend Andrew Lang's funeral. Then maybe she could banish two pairs of eyes from her mind once and for all—one brown and filled with despair, the other a mixture of green and brown and hard, flat anger.

Chapter Four

Arms resting on her swollen stomach, Janeen stared down at the paper-wrapped parcel held loosely in her hands.

"You want me to do it, Janey?"

Her momma's voice dragged at her, pulling her from the swirling pit of her thoughts. She lifted her head and stared blankly at the woman seated on the bed beside her. For a few moments, Janeen couldn't remember why she was back in her old bedroom, surrounded by the bright, flowered wallpaper and gauzy curtains she'd picked out years ago.

"Why don't you let me take care of this, honey?"

Janeen's gaze settled on her mother's face, noting the white lines of strain adding to the familiar wrinkles around her mouth.

"No," she replied slowly, "I'll do it, Momma."

"You sure?"

"I'm sure."

Sighing, her mother rose and dusted away the bits of pale green chenille that clung to her dark skirt. She hesitated, then lifted her hand to stroke her daughter's hair. She'd done the same when Janeen was just a youngster who'd come running to her with scraped knees or some new grievance against her brothers, who delighted in tormenting their pesky little sister.

"I guess there are some things a woman's got to do alone. I just never thought I'd see my daughter preparing her husband's things for his burial."

Her hand came around to caress her daughter's cheek. The skin of her palm felt dry and a little cracked, like old, much-used leather. Janeen tilted her head, pressing against it, drawing in the strength and resilient toughness. After a few, silent moments, Betty Wilson left.

Janeen sat unmoving on the wide, double bed. Despite her assurances to her mother, she wasn't sure she had the courage to open the parcel that had been delivered just this morning. Brown paper crackled as her fingers clenched on the outer wrapping.

The muted, distant roar of a tractor drew her eyes from the package to a window beaded by moisture from the muggy August heat. Her daddy was working the last quarter-section, she knew, preparing the ground for the winter wheat he'd plant next month. The land didn't wait, not for birthings or buryings, her granddad used to say.

Janeen wished she could be out there with her father, riding in the high, glassed-in cab. She'd often accompanied him as a child, and had learned to maneuver the huge vehicle herself as a teen. She couldn't count the hours she'd spent wheeling and turning and fighting to keep the rows straight as acre after acre of red-brown soil churned under the blades.

She desperately needed the antidote of hard, sweaty, physical labor now. Maybe a long day in the brutal sun would help dull her feelings. But she couldn't climb up into the cab, not as big and clumsy as she was, any more than she could blanket the pain.

She stared at the slanting rays of sunlight streaming through the window. Dust motes danced in the air, the inevitable legacy of the winds that constantly swept across the plains and stirred up the plowed land. Janeen followed one tiny reddish swirl as it floated on a sunbeam, thinking numbly that she and her momma would have to dust the whole house again before their friends and neighbors gathered here tomorrow . . . after the funeral services. The minuscule cloud of dust floated up, then sideways. It settled at last on the table beside a bright-patterned, overstuffed armchair. The fine particles drifted onto the framed pictures displayed on the table, diminishing the glare from their glass fronts.

As if it were a magnet, one large, wood-framed photo drew Janeen's eyes. It was of Andy and her brother, Bobby. They were laughing into the camera, their hair plastered to their foreheads. Sweat and mud stained their black and gold football uniforms. Bobby held up two fingers in a V. Andy had his arm looped over his friend's shoulders. Seiling High School had just won their first game of the season, and everyone knew it was going to be a great year. The wide grins splitting the two seniors' faces and the leashed power in their lean, rangy bodies echoed that sentiment.

It *had* been a great year. Janeen's throat closed with the memory of a time that now seemed to belong to another life. Seiling had gone on to win the state championship for its division. Bobby and Andy had both been courted by scouts from several big universities, with offers that were still talked about in the Shamrock Cafe, where a crowd of regulars gathered for coffee in the mornings. The discussion at the Shamrock always centered on the weather or the football team's prospects.

After that year, that heady, exciting year, Bobby had accepted a starting position at the University of Nebraska. But Andy had decided to stay in Oklahoma and go to OU, even though it meant he wouldn't be starting. The folks at the Shamrock had shaken their heads, wondering why their star running back would accept second-string. Even Janeen had wondered, until the October night she turned seventeen.

He wanted to stay close to home, Andy had told her that night, so he could come back to Seiling on weekends. So he could watch her, and wait for her, and take pleasure in just seein' her grow into her sweaters. She could almost see his slow grin when he'd told her that. Feel the heat that had rushed through her blood that crisp, autumn night. She'd thrown herself at him then, wanting him so bad she burned with it. As she'd burned secretly for years with wanting him.

He'd laughed and cuddled her and kissed her until she was breathless and dizzy and wet between her legs, but he refused to love her like she wanted to be loved. Not that night. Not in the back seat of his car. They'd wait, Andy insisted, till she was out of school and knew for sure that he was the one she wanted in life. And then he'd love her so sweet, she'd never want anyone else.

"Damn you!"

Janeen rubbed the heels of her hands against her dry eyes, shutting out the photo, trying to shut out her memories.

"Damn you, Andrew Lang!"

How could he do this to her? How could he make such a mockery of all those whispered words of love? All those promises? How could he die like that?

It hurt. It hurt so bad. Even after five days and five long, endless nights, it still hurt so much Janeen wanted to scream. She'd run the gamut from shock to disbelief to denial to fierce anger and a soul-deep embarrassment at the thought of Andy, her Andy, being found like that. But overlaying all was the pain.

In her heart, Janeen still didn't believe it. Something deep inside her still rejected what her mind was forced to accept. For days the battle between her heart and head had raged. The seesawing emotional swings were tearing her apart. If it wasn't for the baby, she'd curl up on this old chenille spread and stop trying to reconcile the Andy she knew and loved with the man she was burying tomorrow. She'd just lay here and wait for the sounds and the scents and the heat of August to wash over her. Wait for sleep . . . or for whatever came to ease the pain.

But she couldn't just lie down and sleep. She had the baby to think of. And she had Andy's funeral to get through.

Dry-eyed, fighting the waves of hurt that washed over her with every breath, she stared down again at the paper-wrapped parcel. Andy's personal effects, the officer who delivered them yesterday had said. The belongings he'd had with him the night he died.

The Air Force had provided a complete new uniform for the burial. The lieutenant had even taken care of having the stripes sewn on and a duplicate set of ribbons made up. Mrs. Lang didn't need to worry about that, the young officer had assured her. But maybe there was something in this package that she'd want her husband to have with him . . . in the casket. The lieutenant had stumbled over the words.

Her hands trembling, Janeen reached out and pulled at the brown paper.

Perspiration trickled down between Brenna's breasts. The green canopy that sheltered many of those gathered for Sergeant Lang's funeral provided some shade, but not enough to combat the sweltering heat. Under the jacket of her dress uniform, her blouse stuck to her back. Her dress hat, with its embroidered silver thunderclouds across the dark blue brim, rested heavy and hot on her forehead.

As the senior Air Force representative, Brenna sat in the front row of folding chairs, next to the family. The Reverend Brewster's words, eloquent in their simplicity, added to the guilt that had nagged her since signing the Line of Duty Determination.

This spindly, calm-faced minister had known Sergeant Lang as a boy, had seen him grow from youth to man. No matter what happened in a bar in Panama, Andy Lang would always be the towheaded youngster who helped pass the collection plate at the First Baptist Church on Sundays. The college student who came home to Seiling on weekends to help build the new church annex. The man whom this minister joined in holy wedlock to Janeen Wilson on a bright summer day not much different from this one.

Brenna let her glance roam the crowd spread out on either side of the bank of chairs. The men stood bareheaded in the heat, their faces red, their hands clasped in front of them. She recognized three men who could only be Janeen Lang's brothers standing shoulder to shoulder in tight formation, their faces grim. The Wilson family resemblance showed in their broad foreheads and tawny hair.

The women present at the small, white-fenced cemetery were mostly seated. Dressed in their Sunday best, they fanned themselves slowly with the printed pamphlet that bore a picture of Staff Sergeant Lang in his blue Air Force uniform.

A military Honor Guard stood in a double rank at parade rest a few yards beyond the flag-draped coffin. Brenna hoped the eight men and women in dark blue berets, spit-shined boots, and creased white neck scarves remembered to keep their knees bent. She'd seen more than one tough cadet keel over at the Academy, having locked his knees and slowed his circulation during a long formation. This group looked like they knew what they were doing, however.

The minister finished, and Brenna held her breath as the Honor Guard leader murmured a low command. The eight airmen snapped to attention, then marched forward at a slow, measured cadence. Retrieving the American flag from the coffin, they stood in two lines, the bright flag held chest high between them. The commander took one end. Folding it into a triangle, he tucked the edges in, then folded the flag once again. He repeated the process until the river of red-and-white-striped silk was contained within the field of blue stars. Brenna and the others watched as he approached Janeen Lang, his arms crossed, the flag secured tightly against his chest.

She looks so different, Brenna thought, studying the widow's pale face. Older. Harder. As though grief had planed all the softness from her features.

Her hair was drawn back in a thick French braid that hung down between her shoulders, its golden sheen discernible even in the canopy's shadow. She wore a full smock in a deep, gunmetal gray over a black skirt. And her eyes when she looked up to accept the flag were flat and dry.

For a moment stillness hung over the sun-baked cemetery, broken only by the whir of locusts in the grass behind them. Then the silvery notes of a bugle floated across the air, sounding the final farewell to a soldier.

Dry-eyed, Janeen Lang clutched the folded flag and stared out across the jumble of headstones toward the plowed fields beyond.

After the last note of Taps had faded, Brenna joined the line filing past the family. Sergeant Lang's parents were both dead, but the grief that ravaged his in-laws' faces told her he'd been well loved. She murmured her condolences, then stood face to face with the young widow.

"I'm sorry, Mrs. Lang," she began. "If there's anything I can do . . . ?"

The inadequacy of the words made Brenna wince inwardly. What more could she do for or to this woman? She'd brought her the news of her husband's death. She'd signed the damn form, labeling his death not in line of duty.

Janeen summoned a small smile. Brenna's heart twisted at the visible effort it took.

"Are . . . Are you coming back to the house, Colonel? You and the Honor Guard? The neighbors all brought food, more than we could eat in a week."

Brenna started to shake her head, thinking of the two-hour drive back to Tinker and the work she hadn't been able to attend to these past few days.

"I'd like to talk to you," Janeen said in a soft, hoarse voice. "Later. After . . ." Her eyes drifted to the open grave site. She took a deep, steadying breath. "After the funeral."

"Of course."

Brenna stepped out of the way. The others shuffled forward in a slow, steady stream. The entire town must be here, she thought, and half the neighboring community as well. She went over to give the Honor Guard a few quiet words of praise before they disbanded, then waited quietly while the population of Seiling paid their last respects to Sergeant Lang.

A half hour later, Brenna watched Janeen Lang make her way through the crowd that had gathered at her parents' home. The young widow carried a heaping plate, which she set down untouched on a side table filled with knickknacks and scattered farm magazines. After a murmured exchange with a solemn-faced couple, she joined Brenna and the gangly thirteen-year-old who'd been peppering her with questions about the Air Force. The boy, one of Janeen's nephews, offered to get them both fresh iced tea. For a few moments, the two women stood isolated alone together among the swarm of people eddying through the rooms of the spacious home.

"Thanks for staying, Colonel Duggan."

"Please, my name's Brenna." The long, desperate hours she'd shared with Janeen had put them both beyond the barriers of rank.

Janeen rolled the name in her easy Oklahoma drawl. "Brenna. That's pretty, like something soft and sugar-coated, fresh out of the oven."

"I doubt if many of the men and women in my squadron would agree that's an accurate assessment of my personality," Brenna replied with a smile.

"I guess not." Tilting her head, Janeen looked up at the older woman shyly. "Andy told me you were tougher than any six men he ever worked for. But fair and ready to stand up for your people. He liked that. He liked you."

"Thank you for telling me."

Some of Brenna's guilt at having failed Sergeant Lang lessened slightly. At least she knew that he trusted her enough to come to her for help . . . if he'd wanted to.

"Are you going to stay with your folks for a while?" she asked.

"For a while. Till the baby's born, anyway."

"I'm sorry I couldn't work it so you could stay in quarters."

Only Brenna would know how many hours of agonizing internal debate it had cost her to sign that damn form and deny Sergeant Lang's widow the right to extended housing benefits.

"You did what you thought was right." The younger woman's voice held no hint of blame. "Anyway, I wanted to come home. I *needed* to come home."

The muted intensity of her words made Brenna glance at her in concern. "Are you all right?"

Janeen nodded slowly. "Yes. I am now. I wasn't for a while. I . . . I kind of lost touch with Andy for a few days, and it scared me."

How remarkable that she had the strength to admit her fears, Brenna thought. Her admiration for Janeen Lang's courage racheted up another notch.

"It scared me bad. But last night I walked out to the old homestead, the one my great-grandaddy's folks built after they moved out of their sod hut. The old place has been deserted for years, and the barn roof's fallen in, but I've always felt at home there. That was my hidey-hole when I was little. Where I used to sneak to when I didn't want to help Momma with the chores."

She looked out one of the windows, a secret, faraway look shimmering in her eyes.

"That's where Andy and I made love for the first time. There, in the barn, with the clouds all puffy above us and the meadowlarks singin' in the trees by the creek."

The stark lines bracketing her mouth eased. Janeen sighed, bringing her gaze and her mind back to the present.

"All these doubts, Colonel . . . Brenna . . . all these hurtful thoughts I've had. I put them behind me last night. I could feel Andy there, in that barn. I . . . I can feel him here now. I saw him in the boy the minister described. I heard him in the memories his friends shared with me these past few days."

Brenna had seen him as well, although not with the intensity his widow had. No one would ever see Sergeant Lang as she had seen him.

"I suppose I'll never understand what happened down there in Panama," Janeen said, resting her hands on her stomach. "I just know it wasn't Andy. Not my Andy."

Brenna felt an ache well in her throat at the way Janeen Lang spoke her husband's name. Her own brief marriage had never produced the love she heard in this woman's voice. Even at the start, when Brenna and Mac had confused lust with love and shared the excitement of their fast-paced careers, they'd never been as close as she sensed Janeen had been to the mate she'd chosen.

"Anyway, I just wanted you to know that," Janeen said with another of those small smiles that were so painful to watch. "Oh, and I wanted to show you this."

She dug in the pocket of her gray smock and pulled out a rumpled scrap of paper. "I found it in Andy's wallet, behind the picture he . . . behind my picture. Do you know what this number is?"

Brenna eyed the string of scribbled characters. "A phone number maybe?"

"Maybe," Janeen said doubtfully. "Someplace

overseas, where they use letters and numbers together?"

"Could be. May I?"

Brenna took the scrap of paper, frowning slightly. The numbers could be anything. A code for the combination to Sergeant Lang's mailbox on base. Digits from a lost laundry stub. A bet for one of the endless, unauthorized football pools that floated around the squadron.

"Do you think this number could have something to do with what Andy was doing in that bar?" Janeen asked hesitantly.

Dave Sanderson's cynical words echoed in Brenna's mind. If the shaggy-haired Customs Agent was to be believed, there wasn't any big mystery about why the sergeant, who'd been away from home for nearly a month, was in a place like the Purple Parrot.

"No," Brenna replied. "No, it's probably just something he jotted down to remind himself of a bet, or a future flight or something."

"Would you take it back to the base? Ask the other crew members? Maybe it doesn't mean anything at all, but I'd ... I'd like to know."

"Mrs. Lang ..."

"Janeen."

"Janeen, I ..." Brenna swallowed her protest. If this tiny scrap of paper meant so much to Sergeant Lang's widow, the least she could do was make a few inquiries. "Sure. I'll ask around. If anyone recognizes it, I'll call you."

"Thank you."

*   *   *

Brenna needed far less time than she'd anticipated to identify the scribbled numbers. During the long drive back to Tinker, she mulled over a dozen different possibilities before the most obvious one clicked. As soon as she got back to her office, she called Buck and invited him to meet her that evening for dinner.

Hurrying home only to change some hours later, she met Buck at their favorite restaurant. While he munched on short-rib appetizers, she dug through her purse for the scrap of paper.

"What do you think this number is?"

Licking barbecue sauce off his fingers, Buck held the buff-colored paper up to the light by one corner.

"Looks like an aircraft tail number."

Satisfaction pulsed through Brenna, and a faint glimmer of excitement. "That was my guess, too. One of ours?"

After his wife's death, Buck had earned a private pilot's license and become an avid flier. He spent every week he wasn't with Brenna whizzing around the Midwest in one of the Tinker Aero Club's planes. If anyone would recognize this tail number, he would.

"It's not one of the club's, if that's what you mean. I know all those tag numbers."

"So it could be from anywhere. Anywhere in the United States," Brenna amended.

Having spent half of her military career glued to a scope-tracking aircraft moving through the skies, she knew that specific prefixes were used to identify the country where the plane was registered. But she wasn't sure what the rest of the sequencing meant.

"Can you tell from this combination where this plane is based?" she asked.

"No, you can pick whatever numbers or letters you want when you apply to register a plane, as long as they're preceded by that 'N.' The FAA will assign any combination that's not already taken."

"So the 'MD' at the end doesn't necessarily mean the plane's registered to a doctor?"

Buck put the scrap of paper aside and picked up a long, blackened rib. "Nope. Those letters could be anything. Someone's initials, a favorite expression, anything."

"Great," Brenna grumbled, tucking the paper back into the pocket of her shorts. "It'll probably take me twenty phone calls to track down the office that issues these numbers."

Buck grinned at her over the succulent meat. "If you're nice to me, I can cut the number of those calls down considerably."

"How nice is nice?"

Waggling his brows, he sent her a wicked leer. "Verrrrrry nice."

Brenna grinned back, acknowledging the invitation in his eyes. A corner of her mind wondered why she didn't take him up on that invitation. Buck Henry was laid-back and undemanding, a comfortable companion and a true friend.

That was the problem, she acknowledged with

sudden, rueful insight. She was at the point in her life where she should be willing to settle for comfort and companionship, but she wanted more. She wanted a man to look at her with something other than playful lechery in his eyes.

Unbidden, the image of another pair of eyes leapt into her mind. Dave Sanderson's narrowed gaze had been anything but playful. His hazel eyes had held a derision he hadn't bothered to disguise, and a cynical disregard for her authority. At first. When she'd torn into him, they'd fired with a leashed anger.

Yet throughout their confrontation, Brenna had sensed, had felt, something even more disturbing in the way he looked at her. It wasn't anything overt, anything she could take him to task for. But his gaze had raised prickly sensations on her skin wherever it lingered. Irritated anew at the man's lack of cooperation and at the way he'd gotten to her, Brenna sat back against the Naugahyde booth.

"I promised Janeen Lang I'd check these numbers out," she told Buck, the laughter fading from her voice. "I'd appreciate your help."

He set down his half-eaten rib. "All you have to do is call the FAA Aircraft Registry office. It's right here in Oklahoma City, over at the FAA Center at Will Rogers Airport. Tell them it's official business. They should be able to bring the registry number up on their computers."

Brenna nodded, too disturbed by the memory of her clash with Sanderson to regain the easy mood she and Buck had enjoyed earlier. She let him take the lead in a one-sided conversation while they finished their meal.

By three o'clock the following afternoon, Brenna was even more disturbed about Dave Sanderson than she'd been the night before.

The FAA identified the "N" number easily enough. It belonged to a Beechcraft King Air, a twin-engine turbojet registered to a man named Anthony Petrocelli, of Dallas, Texas. When the FAA official let fall that the King Air was the favorite choice of former military sky jockeys, Brenna called a friend at the Air Force Military Personnel Center in San Antonio, Texas.

Vince Wilbanks, sentenced to a tour of duty as Director of Rated Officer Assignments—a result of his recent promotion to colonel—promised to run a check of the computer base. Sure enough, an hour later Vince called back and announced in his distinctive Rhode Island twang that Lieutenant Anthony J. Petrocelli had once flown Air Force AC-130 Spectre gunships.

"I remember this guy now. He was a regular wild man in the Special Ops community. Went by the tag 'Mad Dog,' and really lived up to his name."

Brenna's pulse jumped. Mad Dog. MD.

"Almost got court-martialed over some aerial stunt he pulled during an exercise," Vince went on, unaware of the tension he'd generated at the other end of the line. "Instead he ended up getting decorated for heroism."

"Just your typical Air Force pilot," Brenna remarked dryly. "What did he do that was so heroic?"

"He was copilot on a gunship that took a SAM during the Grenada invasion. The aircraft caught fire and exploded, but the entire crew managed to get out alive. The aircraft commander and Mad Dog kept the burning plane in the air long enough for everyone to hit the chutes."

She could hear the sound of papers being shuffled over the line.

"Petrocelli was cited for extraordinary airmanship, along with the aircraft commander, a Captain Sanderson. They bailed out at the last minute, and the explosion sent parts of the plane ripping through their chutes. Both got bunged up pretty bad, I heard."

Brenna's heart pounded against her ribs. "Vince, that Captain Sanderson—was he Dave Sanderson, by any chance?"

"You got it in one, kiddo."

Her swift, indrawn hiss went unnoticed as Vince rambled on. "Best I can recall, Sanderson's injuries resulted in some damage to his spinal column. He couldn't fly anymore, at least not as a pilot. He retrained into . . ."

"AWACS," Brenna supplied.

"Yeah, that's right. Flew on AWACS for a while before he separated from the Air Force. Didn't you ever run into him? I thought you back-enders all knew one another."

"I was pulling an instructor tour at the Academy during Grenada, remember? I was out of circulation for almost four years."

"Oh, right. And Sanderson separated while you were at the Academy. I lost track of him after that. Someone said he was piloting bug-smashers for a small charter airline."

"He's flying with us again, Vince. As a Customs Agent. In the back end of our birds."

"No shit?"

"No shit."

Wilbanks signed off a little later. For long moments, Brenna stared at the ragged-edged piece of paper on her blotter. Then she pulled her Rolodex toward her and flipped through it.

Twenty minutes later she was seated across from Special Agent Richards in his sunlit office. Unlike most military work areas, this one boasted no squadron plaques or colorful memorabilia from past tours. The man's office was as anonymous as he was, Brenna thought.

Steepling her fingers, she waited while he copied the numbers meticulously into his black notebook. That done, he tucked his book into his inside jacket pocket and nodded at the scrap of paper.

"May I keep this, Colonel?"

Brenna bit her lip, not sure why she was so reluctant to see the scribbled note disappear.

"I suppose so. Mrs. Lang didn't ask for it back.

Why do you want it? For handwriting analysis or something?"

Richards permitted himself a half smile. "Nothing so esoteric. I just want to have it photocopied and placed in Sergeant Lang's file."

"Placed in his file? That's it?"

"We'll check out the tail number, of course."

"I've already done that," Brenna said impatiently. "It belongs to a Beechcraft King Air owned by this Mad Dog Petrocelli."

"We'll check out Mr. Petrocelli, as well."

"Why do I get the feeling you think this is a waste of time?"

"Nothing in a death investigation is ever a waste of time," Richards responded evenly. "I agree that it's coincidental Sergeant Lang had the tail number of a plane belonging to an acquaintance of Mr. Sanderson in his wallet. But there's no evidence to connect this piece of paper with his death."

"There has to be a connection. I'm sure of it."

His dark eyes searched her face. "What do you think it is?"

"I don't know," Brenna admitted, frustration adding an edge to her voice. "I just have this gut feeling that there's more to Lang's death than I've been able to determine."

"Let me check this out, Colonel Duggan. If there's a connection, we'll find it. If there isn't . . . well, we'll get back to you, either way."

Chapter Five

Squadron business absorbed Brenna for the next few days. With August fading fast into September, the 552d Air Control Wing was caught up in the Defense Department's annual effort to stretch tight funds until the new fiscal year began October first. Even then there was no guarantee Congress would authorize and appropriate the required funding by the deadline mandated by law. All of which meant that Brenna had to constantly shift her diminishing training dollars between classroom hours and simulator time to meet the students' scheduled objectives.

She was in the middle of a long, involved review of the contract for operation of the flight simulators when Special Agent Richards called. Asking her staff to wait outside, Brenna closed her office door and took his call.

"There isn't any connection between Sanderson, Petrocelli, and Lang," he reported, wasting little time on polite preliminaries. "At least none that my people could find. Sanderson says he's kept up a loose contact with his old flying buddy, but it's pretty sporadic. He says he never passed on to Sergeant Lang any information about Petrocelli, or vice versa."

Richards paused, then gave a chuckle. Brenna's brows rose at the sound. It was the first time she'd heard anything even vaguely resembling amusement from the OSI agent.

"This guy Petrocelli is quite a character."

"So I've heard."

Richards related that two agents had interviewed Petrocelli, who ran a flourishing import-export business out of Dallas. Flamboyant and cocky, the man admitted to being involved in a few revolutions, various entrepreneurial side ventures, and more than one orgy in his time, but none that included a Staff Sergeant Andrew Lang from Tinker Air Force Base.

"According to his statement, he's never heard of Lang, although he did mention that he was always open to contact with enterprising young business associates. Said he'd been looking for an Oklahoma distributor for the goat-skin bomber jackets he buys at cut-rate prices in the Philippines and sells for an exorbitant profit at military bases throughout the States. He'd asked a few friends to spread the word. His guess was that someone might have passed Lang his aircraft number, which is as easy a way to track him down as his phone number."

Brenna hung up a few moments later, dissatisfied and disappointed. Dammit, why couldn't she put this business with Sergeant Lang behind her? Only this morning she'd interviewed his replacement, a sharp, experienced technical sergeant from the 964th flying squadron who was only too happy to trade his imminent rotation to Turkey for a stateside instructor position. Her chief of academics had finagled an extra slot for the new man at the Instructor School at Kessler Air Force Base in Biloxi, Mississippi. In the meantime, the other instructors were covering Lang's student load. So why was Brenna so hesitant to call Janeen Lang and end her involvement with both the widow and her dead husband?

Maybe it was this searing, late-August heat, she thought with a flash of irritability. It affected everyone, draining and demanding, like an uninvited guest who arrived for a weekend visit and stayed a month. She tucked a damp, curling tendril of hair back into the smooth twist pinned to the back of her head.

And maybe it was something else again, she admitted with ruthless honesty. Maybe it was the fact that a certain hard-eyed Customs Agent had gotten under her skin. As prickly as poisonous oak, he'd raised a sweep of tiny, irritating blisters in her subconscious that she couldn't seem to shake. Too many times in the past few days Brenna had caught herself scanning the people who strolled through the corridors, searching for a glimpse of the man.

She didn't know why she watched for him.

He'd been less than cooperative during the interview in her office. His terse, clipped responses to her questions hadn't given her any real answers, any more than Richards had.

The Air Force considered the matter closed, Brenna reminded herself. The Line of Duty Determination was done. Sergeant Lang was laid to rest. Richards's call had been Brenna's last link to the case. Once she relayed to Janeen that those numbers she'd found in her husband's wallet had no apparent connection to his death, Brenna could get back to squadron business.

She should call Janeen now. Bring the matter to closure.

Her hand hovered over the phone. With a sigh, she realized that she couldn't end it. She had to give it one last shot. Instead of calling Janeen, she buzzed her admin clerk.

"Yes, ma'am?"

"Do me a favor, Pete. Go over to Ops and get me a copy of the aircrew schedule for the next few days."

"Local or overseas?"

"All of them."

Two days later Brenna walked into the aircrew briefing room on the second floor of the red brick Operations Building. Twenty or so military men and women occupied the rows of chairs, while two men stood at the back of the room. One wore the round, black-and-white-checkered patch of the 963rd Airborne Air Control Squadron on the sleeve of his green flight suit. The other sported the royal blue and gold Customs Service patch.

Sanderson's sun-bleached brows knit as Brenna walked to the podium. She didn't indicate she was aware of his presence by so much as a glance, but she felt his eyes on her with every step. Those damned eyes, part brown, mostly green, hiding far more than they revealed. Maybe she'd see something in them during the next twelve hours that would answer her questions.

"For those of you who don't know me," she told the assembled group, "I'm Lieutenant Colonel Duggan, the 552d Training Squadron Commander. I'll be taking Major Kline's place as Mission Crew Commander for tomorrow's flight."

Few crew members showed any surprise at the unexpected modification to the schedule. Changes occurred too frequently to occasion much more than a raised eyebrow or two. Medical problems, family emergencies, or conflicting Air Force requirements could and did often sideline a crew member.

"All right, let's get to it."

Stepping aside, she nodded to the aircraft commander. Captain "Tank" Beardsley took his place at the podium.

"This is the mission planning brief for flight Hotel-six-Mike-eight-four-zero. Our scheduled surveillance area is the southeastern sector, in support of an Air Combat Command exercise."

He pressed the podium button and a map of the southeastern United States and the Gulf of Mexico filled the screen. The various aircraft that would participate in the exercise showed up as different-colored dots on the slide.

Brenna didn't need to refer to posted information. She'd studied the mission profile thoroughly before coming to the planning briefing.

"We'll be controlling F–16s out of Jacksonville and a flight of Navy F–18s out of Beauford. Plan on being on orbit five hours, with one refueling prior to return. We go into crew rest at 1730 hours today. Report to squadron tomorrow morning at 0530 for preflight briefings. Start engines is at 0730, wheels up at 0800 local."

A few of the crew members scribbled the times in their notebooks, but the older crew dogs simply tucked them away in their heads. A final schedule had been posted yesterday in the Scheduling Branch as a heads-up. The AC's confirmation of the times constituted official word that the mission was a go.

"Our primary objective is to ensure that the aircraft participating in the exercise are directed to their targets successfully. We have several secondary training objectives, including an upgrade check ride for the navigator, Major Palmer."

All eyes turned to the short, red-haired major who'd be in the hot seat, his every move watched by an evaluator from the Wing staff. Grinning, he gave the group a thumbs-up.

"Since we'll be flying in the southeast sector," Beardsley continued, "we have the corollary mission of counternarcotics air surveillance. Mr. Sanderson, from U.S. Customs, will be flying with us."

Deliberately, Brenna let her gaze roam the room. It lingered briefly on the tall, lean man leaning against the back wall. From this distance, she couldn't read the expression in his eyes. But the way one side of his lip curled downward told her that he wasn't particularly pleased to be flying with her.

Tough.

When Beardsley finished his briefing, Weather gave a forecast for the flight. Then Brenna stepped forward once again and addressed her mission crew.

"You can split up now to do your individual planning. I want you all back here at . . ." She glanced at her watch. "At 1230 hours for the summary brief. Any questions?"

She spent the rest of the morning in the Ops building, reviewing the mission objectives with the senior Weapons Director responsible for the men and women who controlled the attacking aircraft. Then she went over the scenario with the Air Surveillance officer, whose people would watch the skies for potential bad guys as well as for unknowns who strayed into their air space.

Brenna slipped into the role of Mission Crew Commander with a sense of anticipation. Although her job as Training Squadron Commander meant she now logged more time on the ground than in the air, the greater part of her career had been spent in operational assignments. She'd gained air combat experience during Desert Storm, flying twelve- and sixteen-hour orbits on AWACS launched out of Saudi Arabia. During those tense days and nights, she'd commanded a crew as they directed real sorties to real targets and protected allied aircraft from all-too-real bad guys. She remembered every one of those gut-clenching missions in the crowded skies above Iraq. As a result, she took each training exercise very, very seriously.

When the mission preplanning had been completed to her satisfaction, she dismissed everyone and sent them home for the required crew rest.

She rose well before dawn the next morning. Stretching, she fumbled her way to her dresser and pulled on a regulation white, crew-neck T-shirt. The soft cotton hung over her hips and skimmed a pair of decidedly unregulation blue silk bikini panties.

Barefoot, she padded to the kitchen for an infusion of caffeine to stir her sluggish blood cells. While waiting for the coffee to finish gurgling, Brenna turned on the built-in stereo system. Propping one hip on a tall counter stool, she listened while the soft strains of a country-western ballad drifted across the quiet kitchen. Since her assignment to Oklahoma, Brenna had become a convert to the music that was as much a part of the local ambiance as friendly smiles, slow drawls, and dust-covered pickups.

While the aroma of brewing coffee wafted

through the air, Brenna peered through the slanted plantation shutters, trying to gauge the weather outside. She'd bought this two-bedroom condo on the south side of the city because of its understated elegance and its wide-open view of a meandering creek and green, rolling hills.

She couldn't see much of the hills or the creek this morning, however. Just the black, twisted silhouettes of the cottonwoods that lined the stream's banks. A brisk wind whipped their branches, making them dance in the predawn darkness. A rumble of distant thunder punctuated the stillness, causing Brenna to mutter a silent hope that they could launch their aircraft before the forecasted storm broke.

Coffee in hand, she headed back to her bedroom and showered quickly. It took her less than twenty minutes to dry and pin up her hair and apply a minimum of makeup. Pulling on thick cotton socks to pad her high-topped, black leather boots, she stepped into her flight suit, referred to as the green bag by aircrew members. The resilient, fire-resistant Nomex material wrapped around her like a familiar, second skin. Tucking her squadron's black scarf around her neck, she stuffed her flight cap and wallet into zippered pockets.

She grabbed her car keys and the small "ditty" bag with extra cash and credit cards she always carried in case of unscheduled stopovers, then let herself out of the condo. A gathering sense of anticipation thrummed through her veins during the twenty-minute drive to the base.

The entire crew assembled in the squadron area for a final preflight briefing. The aircraft commander took roll call and conducted a short safety brief, then Brenna verified that there were no changes to the mission profile. After a weather update, she and the flight crew went to Base Ops to file the flight plan and check the weather. The rest of the mission crew descended on Alice's Restaurant, as the in-flight kitchen was called, to draw their box lunches.

"Think we'll get off before the storm closes in?" she asked as they strolled out of Base Ops toward the waiting crew bus. "It's looking pretty grim."

"No sweat, Colonel," the aircraft commander replied. "I can take these jets up in a blizzard and land 'em in a sand storm."

He'd probably done both, Brenna thought, hiding her amusement at the pilot's cocky confidence. Tank Beardsley was one of the wing's best.

As always, Brenna's first glimpse of the jet she considered her second home sent a spurt of pride and pleasure through her. A long, white-painted cylinder with U.S. AIR FORCE marching down its side in huge letters, the E–3 Sentry sat patiently on the runway. A massive black radar dish dubbed the Frisbee by the irreverent crew members sat atop two massive struts above the fuselage.

Developed by the U.S. as an airborne command and control center, AWACS had become the world's standard for management of the air battle. Britain, France, and Saudi Arabia had acquired their own AWACS over the years, and Boeing now produced specially configured planes for NATO. With its unique look-down radar capability, which screened out ground clutter and detected low-flying targets, AWACS had also become a major player in the war against drugs.

Over the years, the Colombian cartels had become more and more sophisticated in their delivery aircraft and evasion techniques. Drug pilots had made a science out of flying low and slow in an effort to slip into the U.S. under the land-based radars. As a result, the high-flying AWACS had become America's ace in the hole. The bad guys never quite knew who was looking down at them from the skies, or when.

The first, fat splats of rain bounced off the concrete apron as Brenna and the rest of the crew piled out of the bus and headed for the metal stair ramp. Juggling the black leather briefcase that held the classified mission "flyaway kit" in one hand and her ditty bag and headset in the other, she climbed the stairs and made her way down the narrow, windowless interior. The entire back end of the E–3 was crammed with tall racks of electronic equipment and desk-sized display consoles. The four-person flight crew, dubbed the "pointy-enders" by the mission crew members, headed for the cockpit.

Taking her seat at the Mission Crew Commander's console, Brenna began her preflight checklist. When she'd verified that all sixteen back-enders were strapped in, she buckled her own seat belt and monitored the exchange between the flight deck and the ground that presaged takeoff.

"Ground Control, this is Sentry Four-two. Ready to start engines."

"Roger, Sentry Four-two. You're cleared for engine start and taxi."

"Clear on number three engine?"

"You're clear on number three, forward and aft," the flight engineer responded.

"Starting number three—now. Four, three, two, one."

"You have positive rotation."

"Fifteen percent power, AC."

"You have ignition."

"Thirty-five percent power."

"Clear on number four?"

The pilot ran through the same sequence for all four turbofan engines. Soon the entire plane vibrated with the leashed power of nearly a hundred thousand pounds of thrust.

"Starting taxi checklist. Ready for takeoff, MCC?"

"Mission crew ready for takeoff," Brenna replied.

The overhead lights dimmed as the huge bird shuddered delicately, then began a slow turn. With no windows, the back-enders had only their own sense of direction and years of experience to tell them when the aircraft pulled off the parking apron and onto the taxiway. The headsets echoed the tower operator's takeoff clearance.

The pilot throttled forward, and the engines

roared to full power. Like a thoroughbred racer in the starting gate, the E–3 seemed to tremble with eagerness, straining to break free of its restraints. After a final takeoff announcement, the plane began to roll down the runway. Within seconds, it lifted smoothly into the air.

The mission crew spent most of the two-and-a-half-hour transit time to the orbit area preparing for the simulated combat. While the radar techs powered up the rotating radar dish and the communications specialists worked their radio and data links, computer personnel ran test tapes. The officers and senior enlisted personnel who would actually direct the jets during the exercise coordinated with the pilots and the ground control facilities involved. Like a head coach orchestrating a football team's movements, Brenna oversaw the entire spectrum of activities.

An hour after takeoff, she decided to stretch her legs. Unclipping her seat belt, she strolled down the narrow aisle to midship and accepted a cup of coffee from a radar tech who'd just poured himself one as well. Familiar with the thick, muddy concoction brewed up on these long flights, Brenna took a cautious sip. Across the rim of the cup, she caught an intent, assessing hazel stare.

Seated at a console two rows away, Sanderson had a clear view of the galley. And of her.

Shock shimmied down her spine at the force of those glinting, green-brown eyes. Her heart thumped unevenly as their gazes locked. For several long seconds, he didn't break the contact, nor did Brenna. It took a conscious effort, but she kept a look of cool disinterest on her face as she sipped the coffee.

She might have known a man like Sanderson would take that as a challenge. The planes of his face shifted slightly, subtly, until his mouth hovered just on the edge of a mocking smile. His gaze dropped to her throat, and then traveled with slow deliberation down the length of her body. When his eyes clashed with hers once more, Brenna felt as if she'd been stripped of every article of clothing she wore.

"Bastard," she murmured to herself as she turned away.

"Pardon, ma'am?" The radar tech bent to catch her words.

"Nothing." Angry at herself for having let Sanderson affect her so, Brenna dumped the remains of her cup into the small, stainless steel sink. "Guess we'd better get to work. It's going to be a long flight."

It was even longer than Brenna had anticipated. As she'd feared, most of the scheduled exercise had to be canceled due to weather. Although the storm front made close maneuvers by the supersonic fighters too dangerous for peacetime training, the AWACS crew could accomplish their corollary mission objectives.

The surveillance officers and technicians stayed glued to their screens, identifying and tracking the hundreds of dots that crossed their sector. The comm and computer techs kept the data links open via satellite transmissions. The evaluator scrutinized the navigator's every move. Several hours into their orbit, Brenna finally had a chance to work her own, personal objective. She observed Sanderson in action.

One of the air surveillance students picked up a "track of interest"—an aircraft heading toward the Florida coast. The young sergeant flagged the dot on his screen as an unknown by moving his cursor onto it and clicking, causing an amber cage to appear around the moving speck. Immediately, the AWACS' onboard computers plotted the plane's airspeed, altitude, and heading. When the digital information came up on the screen, the surveillance tech ran through a series of checks.

Moments later, he notified his instructor that the aircraft was flying low and slow and didn't have its transponder turned on to allow proper identification. In a sector rife with drug runners, that meant one of two things. Either the pilot was some amateur on his way home from a vacation in the Caribbean who didn't have enough sense to avoid the weather, or he was a pro hoping to use the turbulence to avoid detection.

Hearing the exchange, Brenna punched in the track number on her keypad. Immediately, the student's sector map zoomed up on her screen with the suspicious dot in dead center.

If no Customs representative had been aboard, the instructor would have directed the student to follow the track himself. But the whole purpose of the agreement between Customs and the Air Force was to put experienced counternarcotics agents aboard AWACS to work suspected drug traffickers. Accordingly, the instructor passed the track to Sanderson.

"Hey, Customs, I've got track four-two-eight-three on my screen. He's heading two-six-zero degrees at three thousand feet, moving at two-seven-six knots. We did a voice tell, with no response. It meets our parameters as a possible."

"Send me the arrow," Sanderson replied.

Brenna grimaced. Even over the internal communications net, his laconic drawl grated on her ears.

"Roger, Customs," the surveillance officer responded.

He handled the track smoothly. She'd give him that. He ran another series of checks with quick efficiency. A few moments later, the little dot on Brenna's screen flashed as Sanderson forced it up to a higher priority. At that point, he contacted JTF-4 via secure satellite commnications to request they run an intercept.

Charged with coordinating the land, air, and sea resources involved in counterdrug operations, Joint Task Force Four acknowledged the suspicious track and indicated that they'd launch two Navy jets out of Cuba's Guantanamo Base to intercept and ID the bird.

Now came the long wait for a visual identification.

Unaccountably annoyed by the smooth way

Sanderson had managed the operation, Brenna got up to freshen her coffee. She felt his gaze on her as she walked by his console, and ignored it. But she couldn't ignore the way his solid frame blocked her way when she turned around.

"Did I handle that track to your satisfaction, Colonel?"

So he'd guessed she was monitoring his exchange with the ASO and with JTF-4.

"If you hadn't handled it properly, you would have heard about it," she replied coolly.

"Yeah, I imagine I would have."

His gaze skimmed her face, settled on her mouth. To her intense annoyance, Brenna felt a flush heat her neck. She disliked the idea that this man could affect her, and disliked him knowing it even more.

His eyes met hers. "Why don't you just get off my ass, lady?"

The low, sardonic question didn't carry any farther than the small galley. Carefully, Brenna set down her mug, then lifted her eyes again to the face just a few feet from hers. The look she sent him would have sliced anyone else into thin strips.

"I'm MCC on this flight," she reminded him. "I'm responsible for you and everyone else in the back end. I'll damn well look over your shoulder or anyone else's if I feel the need."

The skin across his cheeks tightened. "I'm not talking about this flight and you know it. I'm talking about the little visit I had from a couple of

OSI agents, asking me about my friends. You sicced them on me, didn't you?"

"Yes."

"You want to tell me why?"

"Not particularly."

When he took a step forward, Brenna refused to flinch, refused to give so much as a centimeter. His scent registered on her senses, a potent combination of leather and coffee and the faint tang of a healthy male. Broad shoulders encased in green Nomex blocked the rest of the cabin, narrowing her view to the corded column of his neck. The angle of his jaw. The tight line of his mouth.

"What is it with you, Duggan? Why can't you let go of Lang's death?"

She tilted her chin. "He was my responsibility."

"Yeah, sure. I heard how you handled your responsibility to Lang."

"What are you talking about?"

"You couldn't bring yourself to find his death in the line of duty, could you? You couldn't give the man or his wife that much of a break, could you?"

Like a sudden, unexpected frost, icy fury crystalized in Brenna's veins. At any other time, with any other man, her innate sense of fairness might have recognized that her anger had its root in her own frustration over Lang's death. But recognizing her nagging sense of failure was one thing. Admitting it to this hard-edged, cynical man was something else again.

"I made the only finding I could consistent with

the evidence," she returned frigidly. "If you'll re-call, you didn't give me any reason to do otherwise."

"You played it by the book, didn't you, Colonel? You played it the way you ring-knockers al-ways do. Safe, and by the book. You couldn't stretch the rules, even for a member of your own squadron."

"Especially not for a member of my own squadron."

Disgust etched sharp grooves beside his mouth. "No, I thought not. You made your decision, and now you don't like it. Is your conscience bothering you? Is that why you're asking so many ques-tions? Or . . . ?"

"Or what, Sanderson?"

He hesitated, but Brenna wasn't letting him off the hook now. Not with matters stripped down to the wire between them. Not when he might let something, anything, drop.

"Or what? Spit it out."

He didn't reply for several seconds. When he did, Brenna couldn't believe what she heard.

"Maybe this case fascinates you for another rea-son, Colonel. Maybe you're into kinky sex. Maybe you're so turned on by how Lang checked out that you just can't let go."

She reeled back, gasping. "What?"

He shouldn't do this, Sanderson thought sav-agely. He shouldn't taunt her like this. But he had to get her off his tail. Ever since those agents had come knocking on his door he'd been in a cold sweat. Damn Petrocelli for being so careless. And damn this long-legged, silky-haired female for being so blasted stubborn.

He had to turn her off, had to deflect her inquiries before she brought the whole frigging house of cards tumbling down on his head. And on hers. The thought of Brenna Duggan being pulled into the danger that swirled around him like a deadly gas drove Dave to deliberate crudeness.

He leaned closer, until his breath mingled with hers. He could feel her warmth, see a pulse flutter in the creamy skin of her throat. Bracing a hand on either side of the galley wall, he caged her.

"Is that it, Duggan? Are you looking for someone to teach the kind of games they play in the Purple Parrot."

A stab of perverse satisfaction shot through him as her eyes widened in outrage. They weren't frosted with ice now. They didn't skim over him with barely veiled contempt. They were fixed on his face and blazing with fury. He felt a leaping response, low in his belly. Steeling himself against the sudden tightening in his groin, he dropped his voice to a low, suggestive drawl.

"If you've got a sick little itch, Colonel, I'll be glad to scratch it for you."

Her mouth rounded in utter disbelief.

The need to cover those open, tantalizing lips with his own slammed through Dave. Everything in him urged him to lean forward another inch. To satisfy the hunger that twisted inside his gut with every glimpse of this woman's shining, sable hair and slender curves. Viciously, he reminded himself where they were, and who she was.

She didn't remain at a loss for words for long. Eyes narrowed to glittering slits, she answered his challenge with one of her own.

"Have you ever heard the term 'sexual harassment,' Sanderson?"

The question was soft, dangerous, and purely rhetorical. Anyone in or associated with the military walked a narrow line these days to avoid a repetition of the Tail Hook scandal. Dave had attended his share of briefings and sessions on the subject. He also knew, however, that he couldn't give an inch right now or he'd lose the battle that had sprung up between them. Maybe the war.

"Yeah, I've heard of it. Why? Are you planning to sexually harass me, Colonel? More than you already have?"

"Me? Harass you? You're out of your mind."

The contempt in her voice stung more than he wanted to admit.

"Think so?" he drawled. "Then suppose you tell me why you've been shooting those sideways looks at me in the halls. Why you put yourself down as MCC for this particular flight. I admit I've been a little slow on the uptake, but I'm receiving your signals now, loud and clear."

She managed her own version of a sneer. It wasn't as well-oiled as Dave's, or as ingrained, but it got the point across.

"In your dreams."

If only she knew, he thought sardonically. If

only she knew just how many of his dreams she'd figured in lately.

"Get out of my way, Sanderson. Now."

Christ, she didn't stay off balance for long. The flat, unshakable note of authority that set his teeth on edge was already back in her voice. He didn't take that tone any better from her than he had from the others he'd knocked heads with during his less-than-spectacular Air Force career. In fact, he took it a whole helluva lot worse. Deliberately, he leaned forward until the front of his flight suit just brushed hers.

"Tell you what, Duggan. I'll stay out of your way, and you stay out of mine."

Then he levered himself upright, tipped two fingers to his forehead in a parody of a salute, and sauntered back to his console.

Chapter Six

By the time the flight landed some six hours later, Brenna's desire to nail Dave Sanderson to the wall had hardened to a cold, unshakable resolve. As she rode from the flightline to the mission debrief with the senior crew members, she forced her simmering anger to a back burner and concentrated on a plan of attack.

She could bring charges against him. Despite his taunt about her harassing him, Brenna knew damn well she could slap him with a half-dozen breaches of ethical behavior. Proving the charges would boil down to a matter of her word against his, of course, but her reputation would carry against Sanderson's.

As a woman struggling to succeed in a male-dominated military, she'd learned long ago that off-color remarks could lead to serious misunderstandings. As a commander, she refused to tolerate them. No one would accept that she had sexually harassed Sanderson. No one would believe she'd been coming on to him, or slanted him "sideways" glances in the hall, as he claimed.

Even though she had.

Dammit, she had.

He knew it. She knew it. And Brenna's conscience wouldn't allow her to deny it. The realization that he'd caught a few of those speculative glances only added to her determination to wipe that sneer off his face once and for all.

No, she wouldn't file charges against him. She wasn't about to conduct publicly what had suddenly become a very private war. Besides, she reminded herself with brutal frankness, she wasn't working only her own agenda here. There was Janeen to consider, and the nagging, unresolved questions about Sergeant Andrew Lang.

She would not allow any sign of her inner fury to show during the mission debrief—it would be unprofessional—but the skin on the back of her neck prickled whenever her glance swept the room and snagged Sanderson's. He stood in what was obviously his preferred spot at the back of the briefing room, arms folded across his chest, chin shadowed by a sandy stubble. He looked as scruffy as she felt after a twelve-hour flight.

When the debrief was over, Brenna picked up her crew bag and walked out of the room without a backward glance.

By ten o'clock the next morning she had rearranged her schedule on the basis of one quick phone call. By two that same afternoon, she was heading west on I–240.

It was too hot to put down the Miata's top, and Brenna was too preoccupied to enjoy the drive in any case. She paid scant attention to the towering Oklahoma City skyline looming to the north of the interstate and even less to the nodding, grasshopper-like oil rigs that sprouted in the most unlikely places. At the approach to Will Rogers World Airport, she exited on Meridian and headed north, away from the airport. A few hundred yards brought her to the access road that led to the Customs National Aviation Center—CNAC as it was known to the legion of people who worked surveillance. A high, wire fence and an armed guard at the entrance discouraged casual visitors to the sprawling, one-story complex.

When she pulled up at the entrance, a gray-haired guard tipped his hat. "Afternoon, Colonel."

Brenna returned his greeting and passed him her military ID. "I'm here to see Mr. Hendricks."

Tilting the green plastic card to ease the sun's glare on its surface, the guard scrutinized it carefully, then handed it back to her. "Mr. Hendricks is expecting you. Just check in with security at the front desk, and they'll page him for you."

He stepped into his booth and pressed the button that activated the yawning iron jaws of the gate. With a word of thanks, Brenna drove through.

She'd only been to CNAC once before, during

a tour of the facility for AWACS crews. Built as part of the nation's increasing efforts to combat air shipment of illegal drugs, the center's huge command post monitored the operations of seventeen operational aviation field units. It also served as headquarters for the agents who flew aboard AWACS.

Just moments after Brenna stepped into the vestibule, a small, wiry man with a bald head fringed by wild, bushy red hair burst through the door opposite her.

"Hey, Duggan! You're looking good, woman!"

"Wish I could say the same for you, Thud," she replied, laughing in protest as he swooped her into a rib-cracking bear hug.

A former Air Force helicopter pilot, Terry "Thud" Hendricks had been stationed with Brenna at the time of her divorce. He'd earnestly and repeatedly offered his services to help her get through the bittersweet pain and regret. Although she'd refused his offers, Brenna had kept in touch with the incorrigible chopper pilot over the years.

Upon his retirement from the Air Force, he'd gone to work for Customs flying HH–60s, the deadly Blackhawk helicopters used to interdict drug smugglers. Brenna had been delighted when he'd married a criminal attorney with a razor-sharp mind and a devious sense of humor, and even more delighted when the unlikely couple had moved to Oklahoma City upon Thud's assignment to CNAC.

While she struggled to regain her breath from

his enthusiastic hug, Thud threw a companionable arm around her shoulders. "Have you dumped that wimpy Intel officer you've been dating yet?"

"You mean the one who broke your body tackle during that 'touch' football game at your house and left you facedown in the dust?" she replied. "The one your wife says is a combination of Robert Redford and the Incredible Hulk, all rolled into one?"

He grinned. "Yeah. That one."

"Nope."

Chuckling, Thud handed Brenna a visitor's badge, then inserted his own into the security control system. As she followed him down the gray-tiled hall to his cubbyhole of an office, he brought her up to date on his wife's latest practical jokes.

Shaking her head at their antics, Brenna took the chair wedged into the narrow space between the desk and the wall.

"So how's business, Thud?"

Squeezing himself into the chair behind the desk, the chopper pilot propped one booted foot on its lower drawer. His green flight suit stretched taunt across a muscled thigh.

"Not as much fun as it used to be, kid. A few years ago, we didn't have to spend so much time looking for a bad guy. The skies were full of 'em. We'd just climb to ten thousand feet and take our pick. It was," he told her with a waggle of his red brows, "what we used to call in the Air Force a target-rich environment."

"Just the kind you like."

"Just the kind I like," he agreed. "Now, we've got so many sophisticated systems operational to protect our airspace, the bad guys can't penetrate it as easily as they used to. They've taken to landing their loads just south of the border and shipping them across in containers or on foot."

"You still get your share of busts, though. I heard you pulled a hot stop a couple weeks ago that netted big tonnage."

He grinned happily. "Yeah, that was a real shoot 'em up, too. Thank God I have to stay current in my aircraft and get out of the Headquarters to fly on occasion."

"Mmm."

He hitched a brow at her less than enthusiastic response. "Okay, you didn't drive out here to listen to me bitch about my low kill rate. So what's with this unexpected visit? Not that I'm not delighted to see you, of course."

"What can you tell me about Dave Sanderson?"

It was a measure of their friendship that Thud didn't ask why she wanted to know.

"Not much. We sky drivers don't have much contact with the guys who man the scopes, except when they hand us a hot track to take down. I see him around here occasionally, but we're not what you'd call buddies."

"Do you have any idea what he did before he signed on with Customs?"

"I heard a rumor he was free-lancing somewhere down south, but nothing specific."

"Ever hear his name mentioned in any connection with dopers?"

Thud raised one reddish brow. "No. Why?"

"Sanderson was with a member of my squadron who died under questionable circumstances."

"How questionable?"

When she sketched the gruesome details, he whistled. "Sounds like Lang was flying solo on that one. Why do you think Sanderson had anything to do with the kid's death?"

"I don't know," Brenna admitted, trying without success to keep the frustration from her voice. "Something about the guy doesn't ... doesn't sit right with me."

"Well, from the little I've seen of him, I'll agree he doesn't exactly have the kind of disposition you'd want to wake up next to in the morning. Maybe that's why his wife hit the sauce so much."

Brenna swallowed. "His wife?"

Why was she so surprised that the man who'd propositioned her in such a crude manner yesterday had a wife tucked away? So he didn't wear a wedding ring? He radiated the kind of dangerous magnetism that attracted otherwise intelligent females when it should have sent them running in the opposite direction. Despite her personal antipathy for the man, Brenna had to admit he was all male. He wouldn't be the first man to indulge in a little recreational sex on the side while his wife ...

"Guess I should say his ex-wife."

Brenna let out a slow breath. "His ex? So he's divorced?"

"He was. His ex-wife is dead."

The reply was casual. Too casual. Brenna had known Thud too long to miss the subtle nuance in his voice. She leaned forward, her heartbeat accelerating. "You know something about him, don't you? Something about his dead wife? Or about their divorce?"

"Hey, I just heard it was rough. You know about that, Brenna. You've been there."

She didn't buy his too-pat answer. A team player herself, she knew how members of an organization closed ranks when an outsider started asking questions about one of its own ... even if that outsider was an old friend. Terry Hendricks knew something. She could see it in his eyes.

"Rough, like how?"

Obviously reluctant, the chopper pilot studied the tip of his boot.

"Come on, Thud. You know whatever you tell me won't go anywhere else unless it has some bearing on my sergeant's death. What about Sanderson's divorce? How was it rough?"

His shoulders shifted under his flight suit. "She was an alcoholic."

"What?"

"His ex-wife was an alcoholic. Suzy prosecuted her on a manslaughter charge after she ran down a six-year-old."

"Good God!"

"She and Sanderson were divorced by then, but

he stood by her at the trial. Even testified that his long absences when he was in the Air Force contributed to her condition. Said she'd started drinking years ago, and he hadn't been there to help her when she needed him."

Pity pulled at Brenna, and something else she refused to acknowledge. She wasn't ready to admit Sanderson might have good reason for some of his rough edges.

"What happened to her? His wife?"

"She got two years, most of it suspended, and mandatory treatment in a facility somewhere in eastern Oklahoma. The first weekend she was out, she drove her car into a bridge abutment."

"By accident?"

"On purpose." Thud's mouth twisted. "She left a note, blaming everything on Sanderson."

Brenna left CNAC shortly after that.

Thud didn't have or wouldn't share any more information about Sanderson. All he knew of Mad Dog Petrocelli were the wild stories she'd already heard, none of which established any connection between him and Sergeant Andrew Lang.

As Brenna drove back to Tinker with the wind in her face, Dave Sanderson's shadowed past ate at her. All right, she admitted, *everything* about the man ate at her. He refused to fit into any of the categories her neat, orderly mind wanted to squeeze him into.

He'd been decorated for heroism, then pissed away a promising Air Force career.

He'd divorced an alcoholic wife, then publicly shouldered the blame for her condition.

He'd drifted for years, then landed a job with Customs that any one of a hundred former AWACS back-enders would kill for.

Why? Brenna wondered. Why had he returned to flying, and to a military establishment he'd thumbed his nose at years ago? Unless . . . She gripped the wheel. Unless he was still thumbing his nose at it. Unless he had a reason of his own for wanting back in on the counterdrug surveillance action. A reason connected to those years he'd spent in Central or South America.

The thought shocked Brenna, and made her realize how close she'd come to losing all objectivity about Dave Sanderson. Frowning, she took a mental step back and regrouped.

Okay, the man irritated the hell out of her with his too-long hair and mocking drawl. And true, he'd gone out of his way to shock and infuriate her during those tense, heated moments in the galley yesterday. She shouldn't let her personal dislike for the man goad her into unfounded accusations.

Wheeling her car into her reserved parking space, Brenna sat for a moment, thinking. Then she grabbed a notepad and her flight cap from the seat beside her and stepped out into the lung-sucking heat. Her heels clicked on the sidewalk as she headed for the windowless brick building that housed the 662d Computer Group.

A quick scan of her ID cleared Brenna through

the security checkpoint and she headed for the stairs. She knew her way around the ground floor, which contained the many simulators her people trained on, but the second floor belonged to the white-coated technicians who worked with banks of humming mainframes. These innocuous-looking units weren't much larger than a typist's desk, but were capable of thousands of calculations per second. The 552d computer geniuses used them to develop, test, and maintain the sophisticated detection and tracking systems used by AWACS.

After the scorching heat outside, the cool air in the controlled-temperature building raised goose bumps on Brenna's arms. Shivering, she made her way through the canyon of computers. When at last she found the office she sought, a short, pudgy civilian with silver-framed glasses perched on the end of her nose glanced up in surprise.

"Brenna! What are you doing here, girl? Hey, don't tell me you're finally going to let me send someone over to show you how to use that toy on your desk?"

Brenna assumed a wounded expression. "I know how to use that toy, as you call it. I just, um, need to find some time to practice on it."

A rich chuckle filled Carol Houston Reeve's cluttered office. The woman had a doctorate in computer systems integration from the University of Alabama and held the highest-paid civilian position in the Wing. She was also a divorced mother of two and one of the few people within Brenna's circle of friends who enjoyed life to the fullest.

She had her eye on husband number three, a major who'd just reported in a couple of weeks ago and was still slightly stunned after his first date with the brainy, brawny woman.

"Honey," Carol drawled, "if you have to 'practice' on a personal computer any six-year-old could operate blindfolded, you might as well turn it in. Beats me how you pass your check-rides. Even Mission Crew Commanders have to be able to operate a trackball."

Brenna refused to be drawn into the familiar, bantering discussion that had grown from her frank admission that she still hadn't figured out how to program her VCR.

"I need a favor, Carol."

The other woman didn't blink. "You got it."

"Would you run the crew schedules for the last three months? I'm interested in any flights that included both Staff Sergeant Andrew Lang and a Customs agent who flies with us, Detection Systems Specialist David Sanderson. Here, I jotted down their social security numbers for you."

Carol took the slip of paper and peered at Brenna over the top of her glasses. "That'll take all of five minutes."

"Well, there's more."

"I figured."

"I'd like you to pull me the tapes for those missions where the two men flew together."

"Baby, you haven't got a vault in your office big enough to store all those tapes."

"Well, I was hoping you'd run the tapes through a screen on one of the mainframes."

"What kind of screen?"

"All I'm really interested in is any interaction between Lang and Sanderson. Any communications between them during flight. Couldn't you write a filter that will delete everything else on the tapes?"

Carol's penciled brows rose. "You don't want much, do you?" She pointedly refrained from making any reference to the work stacked on every horizontal surface in her office.

"I'll make it worth your while," Brenna promised. "How about I keep the kids at my place Friday night so you can work your wiles on that helpless major?"

"Done!" Carol waved a beringed hand and shooed Brenna away before she could change her mind. "Outta here, I've got work to do!"

Craftily deciding to kill two birds with one stone, Carol wrote the screen, ran the master tapes, then captured the requested data on floppy disks. Appearing unannounced at Brenna's office the next afternoon, she presented the floppies with a flourish and proceeded with a crash course on how to use the new, Air Force–issued PCs for something other than reading electronic mail. When Brenna clicked on the right icon the first time and the screen showed a neat row of files, Carol gave a little grunt of satisfaction.

"Each file contains a separate mission," she

stated, tapping a brilliant scarlet nail against one of the icons. "When you open the files, you'll see that I've flagged Staff Sergeant Lang with the designator Alpha One. Sanderson is Bravo One. All you have to do is scroll through the file to follow their communications."

"I've got it," Brenna replied confidently, maneuvering the mouse.

"No, you've got *them.* Six different disks, with a total of ten gigabits of data in each."

Brenna's hand stilled on the plastic trackball, and she threw her friend a doubtful look. "Is that as much as I think it is?"

"More," Carol drawled, patting the stack of three-inch-square disks. "These little jewels will keep you busy at least until Friday night, and then you'll have my little jewels." She slid her glasses down her nose and eyed Brenna. "If you'd tell me what it is you're looking for, maybe I could do another screen."

"Believe me, if I knew what I was looking for, I'd tell you."

"Well, good luck. Call me when you get stuck."

When, Brenna noted wryly, not *if.*

Despite Carol's seeming lack of confidence in her abilities, she managed to open the first file easily enough. Her heart began to beat a little tattoo as the screen filled with the language of surveillance.

It took Brenna several days to work her way through the stack of computer disks, sandwiching them in between the other demands on her time.

Of the six flights where Sanderson and Lang happened to be on the same crew, two were dedicated, twelve-hour-long antidrug flights. The other four were training missions in the southeast sector, with the Customs agent aboard because of the dense drug traffic in that area.

Brenna concentrated first on the dedicated drug missions. On the first flight Lang had picked up a number of suspicious tracks that he flagged in the system. Of those, only two failed to respond to the identification codes built into the computer tapes. Those two he passed to Sanderson to work. Which he did, competently. The man tended to exercise his own judgment a bit too freely for Brenna's taste, but in each instance the results had borne out his decision to flag or not flag a track as suspicious.

Her jaw set, Brenna began to scan the other missions. She scrolled through the screens, taking notes. Looking for holes. Searching for mishandled tracks.

She'd almost given up on finding anything when a familiar aircraft tail number flashed on the screen.

It was late, well after midnight. Brenna had put in a long day and an even longer night with her branch chiefs, reworking training schedules to fit the year-end crunch of available simulator hours. The halls were quiet, with only a faint echo of a local country-western radio station drifting through the stillness. She wanted nothing more than to go home, strip off her uniform, pour herself a glass of wine, and indulge in the luxury of a long, steaming bubble bath.

A wry smile tugged at her lips as she worked the PC mouse with one hand. Something was seriously wrong with this picture. Here she was, thirty-six years old, at the peak of her physical and sexual prime. Yet she was spending her evenings with a computer and contemplating a bubble bath with a sort of sensual anticipation.

A niggle of guilt worked its way through the separate layers of concentration she devoted to the screen and to her thoughts. This was the third night in a row she'd turned Buck down for dinner or a movie. He'd chided her good-naturedly about her long hours and made her promise to call when she had an evening free. She needed to make up her mind about Buck, she acknowledged, clicking the mouse to bring up another screen. He deserved better than this haphazard, not-quite relationship. He needed someone who—

The initials "MD" leaped out at her. Brenna's fingers froze on the mouse. There it was. The tail number of an aircraft flying low and slow across the Yucatan Peninsula heading for the Texas border.

Her heart hammering, Brenna read the script that scrolled onto the computer screen. The unfolding scenario was one she was familiar with, one she'd participated in many times.

A Navy P–3 Orion circling above the Caribbean on a routine patrol had picked up the track first. When it moved out of his range, he passed it to the AWACS to work. Lang flagged it as a TOI, a "track of interest" and ran a series of checks. In accordance with procedures, he then handed it to the Customs agent.

After taking the hand-off, Sanderson initiated a voice check with Joint Task Force Four. Some moments later, JTF–4 came back on line and signaled that civilian authorities had verified the plane's flight plan. Still, given its location of origin and route, they recommended Sanderson track it for any deviation. If the plane was carrying drugs or any other contraband, it would in all likelihood touch down at an isolated airstrip to off-load before continuing to its prefiled destination.

Sanderson monitored the TOI for some time. At one point, he notified JTF–4 of a minor deviation, but told them he was going to watch it a while yet before forcing it up to a higher priority. Moments later, the radar shut down in preparation for an aerial refueling.

"Damn!"

The E–3 had to take on fuel at least once during a twelve-hour mission. When it did, Big Bird lost his eyes. In this particular instance, it had lost sight of Mad Dog Petrocelli.

Brenna chewed on her lower lip as she scrolled back to reread those few lines. MD's plane had deviated from its flight plan by only a few degrees, too few to tell if the drift was due to pilot carelessness or an unscheduled change in destination. At that point, Sanderson had the option of following it longer to see if it corrected the drift or labeling the track "suspicious." He'd chosen to watch it, then lost it completely when the radar shut down.

He'd made a judgment call, using proper parameters, Brenna admitted grudgingly. The same call she and the other senior officers who flew AWACS made every day. On every mission, hundreds of planes passed through their sector. Many drifted far more than this one had, then made midcourse corrections. She couldn't fault Sanderson for deciding to watch this particular track a little longer . . . as much as she wanted to!

Shoving back her chair, she curled a hand around her neck and rotated her head to work out the kinks. Frustration left a bitter taste in her mouth as she stared at the screen. She could almost feel Sanderson's presence in the empty office, hear his mocking voice.

Give it up, Duggan.

Get off my ass.

Her mouth as tight as the tendons in her neck, Brenna yanked at the edge of her desk and pulled herself back into position before the screen. She had only the rest of this disk and one more to go through. She'd finish them both tonight. If there was any other link, however slight, between Sanderson and Lang and this Petrocelli character, she'd damn well find it.

There wasn't.

Heavy-eyed and more frustrated than ever, Brenna admitted defeat just as the sun painted the first pale gold streaks across the eastern sky. She shoved her rumpled blue blouse back into the waistband of her skirt. Dragging her purse and flight cap out of the desk drawer, she left the squadron.

Cool, predawn air whipped through the open car windows as she drove to her condo. The air revived her, and momentarily cleansed her mind that now seemed fixated on two men, one alive and one dead.

It was time to get a grip. She'd done all she could, followed every possible lead and come up with little more than she started with. She had to let this business with Sanderson and Sergeant Lang go. She had to put it to rest.

She'd grab an hour's sleep, shower, and get back to the squadron. Then she'd call Janeen Lang.

Chapter Seven

"I'm sorry, Janeen. There doesn't seem to be any connection between your husband's death and those numbers."

Despite the colonel's sympathetic tone, her words left Janeen feeling infinitely weary. She pressed the phone into her cheek for a moment and fought against a wave of desolation.

"What were they?" she asked when she could trust her voice.

"An aircraft tail number. The plane belongs to an individual by the name of Anthony Petrocelli."

"Is he in the squadron?"

"No. He's former Air Force, but now runs a Dallas-based import business. It appears he has his finger in a lot of enterprises." The colonel hesitated. "There's a rumor he was looking for someone in Oklahoma to distribute products for him. Could your husband have been thinking about earning some extra money?"

Janeen struggled against her crushing disappointment. Only now did she realize how much she'd hoped, prayed, those scribbled numbers and letters would somehow explain the unexplainable.

"Andy did say that we needed a new car with the baby coming," she replied dully. "But he never said anything about taking on another job."

"I'm sorry."

"I . . . I guess it was a long shot."

"I guess it was. Are you all right?"

"I'm doing better. I even manage to sleep a few hours at night now."

A small silence stretched between them, as though neither could bring herself to cut the last tie that bound them.

"If there's anything you need, anything I can do . . ."

"Thanks, Col . . . Thanks, Brenna."

The receiver slid into its cradle with a soft click. Resting her head against the high chair back behind her, Janeen felt as though she'd been abandoned. She and Andy both.

Come on! She hadn't been abandoned. The colonel had done all she could. She'd sounded really disappointed that those scribbled numbers didn't mean anything.

But she wasn't anywhere near as disappointed as Janeen was herself. That scrap of paper had been her last hope, her last chance to prove Andy hadn't shamed himself. And her. And the uniform he was so proud of.

As though they had a will of their own, her thoughts rolled back to the day Andy had first talked about leaving the University of Oklahoma and joining the Air Force. He didn't need to be playin' football, he'd told her that hot August afternoon, right after Iraq had invaded Kuwait and the President was talkin' war. Not when the Oklahoma National Guard had been called up and his friends were fixing to go get shot at.

She closed her eyes and saw imprinted on her lids a vivid portrait of Andy when he'd first come home from basic training—all spit-shined and so close to bald that he looked like a fuzzy-headed bear. A smile curved her mouth as she remembered how he'd growled low in his throat and told her he was hungry as a bear, too, after six weeks without her.

At her insistence he'd worn his Air Force uniform to the Shamrock Cafe the first morning he was home. The regulars had all let their coffee cool in the chipped mugs and their eggs congeal into puddles of grease while they pounded him on the back. Although he'd made light of it, Janeen could tell he was proud of the single stripe he'd earned as an honor graduate. He'd finished at the top of his class from tech school, too, and was thrilled when he came back to Tinker for AWACS training.

That was in '90, she remembered, tracing a pattern over her belly to quiet the baby stirring within. When crew after crew of AWACS personnel deployed to Saudi as part of the big buildup in preparation for war with Iraq. When she finally convinced Andy to marry her.

He wasn't goin' off to the Middle East, not without a ring on his finger that branded him as hers, Janeen had decided.

He'd wanted to wait—just in case something happened, she was sure, though he didn't say so. But Janeen was all done with waiting. She took him out to the tumbled-down homestead where they'd first made love and peeled off his uniform. Button by button. Layer by layer. Until the smooth skin of his chest met her seeking hands. He'd stood before her, surprised but willing when she'd dropped to her knees.

Janeen's throat dried with the memory. Her fingertips tingled, as though they could feel again the smooth, shiny belt buckle. She was sure that if she just listened hard enough, she'd hear the purr of his zipper as she'd pulled it down. Her palms began to sweat, anticipating the feel of his hair-roughened thighs as she smoothed his pants down his legs. His strong, tanned legs.

She opened her heart and let herself remember everything. Feel everything. See everything.

How her fingers had trembled when they reached for the waistband of his cotton briefs. How his had dug into her hair, holding her away.

She'd smiled at him then, a woman's smile of wanting, and he'd groaned and guided her to him. He'd tasted salty, she recalled with a silent moan. Salty and velvety and hot and incredibly wonderful.

He'd gripped her hair, his fingers tugging painfully at her scalp. Hers had spread to cup his rear.

His tight, muscled rear that dimpled in one cheek, she'd discovered to her delight. She'd stroked him with her tongue, teased him with her lips, loved him with every particle of her being.

And when he'd groaned once more and tried to pull away, she wouldn't let him. Her nails had curled into his flesh, the smooth hot flesh of his buttocks, holding him in place. Her mouth had shaped him, suckled him, sent him over the edge. Then he'd tumbled down beside her and tugged off her clothes and . . .

A ragged sob tore at Janeen's throat. She crammed the back of her hand against her mouth, biting into the tendons to keep the sob from breaking loose.

Andy.

Oh, Andy.

The grandfather clock in the hall donged once, twice, three times. Janeen heard the sound through a wash of pain. She sat still, willing her tears not to spill. Waiting for the aching need between her legs to subside.

She didn't stir from the big, overstuffed chair until the clump of her father's work boots sounded on the back steps and a murmur of cheerful conversation drifted to her from the kitchen. Slowly, like an old woman who's forgotten how to command her body's movements, she pushed herself out of the chair.

When she entered the kitchen, her father was drying his hands on a terry cloth towel.

"Hi, Janey. Did you get some sleep, honey?"

"No, this grandchild of yours wouldn't sit still long enough to let me sleep." Nor would her memories.

Her father tossed the cloth aside. "He's just like his father. Andy never could sit still for very long."

Janeen met his pale gray eyes, faded by age and years in the sun, and managed a smile. "No, he couldn't. But you shouldn't be so sure you're getting a grandson. Grandma Wilson says the way I'm carrying it, low like this, it's probably a girl."

"She ought to know," her mother threw in from across the kitchen. "She birthed nine babies herself and guessed right on most of ours."

With her father's arm around her and the yeasty scent of fresh-rolled biscuits filling her nostrils, Janeen felt the last, lingering tension at her core fade. It would come again, she knew, when she lay in the darkness with her memories. But she could live with it. And with them. She was learning to live with both.

She took a knife and a bowl of okra over to the kitchen table. Lowering herself into a spindle-backed chair, she began slicing off the tough tops. "Momma, is Cissy still in Dallas?"

"Your cousin?" Her mother bent to slide the tray of biscuits into the oven. "I think so. Why?"

"Oh, nothing. I just thought I'd give her a call. I haven't talked to her in a while."

"She was real sorry to have missed the funeral. Her mother said she was overseas, stuck in Japan or Hong Kong or somewhere. As many years as she's been with that company, you'd think she could put her foot down and not have to go jetting off to those outlandish places all the time."

Janeen hid a smile. From the time her cousin had been in ponytails, she'd dreamed of shaking Seiling's dust from her heels and seeing the world. Well, she'd done that, all right. Cissy had been to parts of the world even Andy hadn't been to. She'd also gathered a lot of friends in the process, both at home and abroad. People who knew other people in international trade. People who just might know this Anthony Petrocelli.

Janeen felt a little nervous about calling Cissy, especially since Colonel Duggan—Brenna—told her that Air Force investigators had already talked to Mr. Petrocelli. But she owed it to Andy to make one last call. She owed it to the memory of that proud, grinning young airman who had walked into the Shamrock Cafe beside her, his shoulders squared and his future bright. She owed it to herself.

Janeen's call to her cousin produced an unexpected result. It appeared on the doorstep to her parents' house not three days later.

Waddling through the house in answer to the ring of the doorbell, she pulled open the front door.

"Mrs. Lang?"

"Yes?"

She put up one hand to block the afternoon sun

and eyed the man who stood on the other side of the screen door with some reserve. Since the funeral a number of men had called at the house. She had to fend off insurance agents, financial planners, and once, incredibly, a computer salesman who touted the advantages of on-line dating services for widows.

But this man didn't look anything like a computer salesman. Not with that extravagant, outrageous handlebar mustache and those dark, piercing eyes. He wore ostrich-skin boots that Janeen guessed cost more than Andy had made in a month, well-worn jeans, and a crisp white shirt with sleeves rolled halfway up his muscular forearms. Although not much taller than Janeen herself, he bristled with a barely leashed energy that gave the impression of both height and strength. A huge gold nugget ring flashed on one finger when he raised a hand to tip his straw Stetson.

"I beg pardon for this intrusion, ma'am. I hope I'm not catching you at a bad time."

She kept the screen door between them. "It depends on what you want to catch me for."

White teeth gleamed under the bush on his upper lip. "Well, I just came to talk to you, Mrs. Lang, but then again, ol' Mad Dog was never one to miss an opportunity. If you're available for anything else . . . ?"

The glinting laughter in his black eyes robbed his words of any offense. Despite herself, Janeen felt her own lips twitch in response. "No, I'm not available, Mr. . . . . ?"

"Petrocelli." He pulled a card out of his shirt pocket. "Tony Petrocelli."

Janeen stood rooted in surprise for long moments before she opened the screen door and stepped outside. Hesitant and more than a little nervous, she took the card he offered. The discreetly embossed printing gave only his name, post office box, and telephone number, but when she turned the card over as the fine print at the bottom instructed, the bold script conveyed a much different message.

Tony "Mad Dog" Pretrocelli
Purveyor of used cars, land, whiskey, manure,
fly swatters, racing forms, and bongos.
Airplane driver. As yet undebarred attorney,
and entrepreneur extraordinaire.
Wars fought. Tigers tamed. Revolutions
started. Bars emptied. Virgins converted.
Governments run. Uprisings quelled. Orgies
organized.

According to the fine print at the very bottom of the card, Mr. Petrocelli also preached and led singing for revival meetings. All of the above services, the card announced, were available for a negotiable fee.

Janeen gave a sputter of laughter. "You're just like my cousin described you."

"The delectable, doe-eyed honey with the silver blond hair? The one with the smile that could make a man forget where he left his horse? That cousin?"

She nodded. "That cousin. Cissy told me she, uh, ran into you at a convention in Dallas."

"Quite a coincidence how she bumped into me at that trade fair. Must've been, oh, three, four thousand people there."

Embarrassment heated Janeen's cheeks. "Well, I . . . I did ask her if she knew anyone who might know you. I didn't mean for her to track you down herself."

"Oh, honey, every man dreams of being tracked down by a woman like that."

His wicked grin brought another bubble of laughter to Janeen's throat. So much for her clumsy attempt at sleuthing, she told herself wryly.

Petrocelli hooked his thumbs in his belt loops and rocked back on his heels. "I've had a steady stream of folks asking me questions about your husband. So I figured I'd just come on up here and see what this is all about. Answer any questions you might have, face to face."

"I . . . uh . . . thank you, Mr. Petrocelli."

"Tony, please. Or Mad Dog if you're so inclined, although the folks who call me that usually have one hand wrapped around either a throttle or a bottle."

Janeen hesitated, then gestured toward the door. "Would you like to come inside? I don't have a bottle handy, but I can fix you a glass of iced tea. I would like to talk to you 'bout Andy."

With her folks gone into town, the big house echoed emptily as she led her unexpected guest to the kitchen. His Stetson in one hand, Petrocelli looked around approvingly as Janeen poured them both huge glasses of sweetened tea. She took the glasses to the kitchen table, then gave a small sigh of relief as she lowered her bulk into the chair he held steady for her. Strangely, she didn't feel embarrassed by her awkwardness.

"Must've been rough, losing your husband at a time like this."

She looked up to find sympathy in his eyes. A genuine sympathy, untainted by the discomfort so many people seemed to feel at any discussion of Andy's death. She felt a rush of gratitude for his acknowledgment of her loss and, more importantly, of her right to talk about it.

"It was rough," she agreed in a low voice. "It still is."

He took the seat opposite her, laying his Stetson to one side. "I wish I could help you, Mrs. Lang, but . . ."

"Janeen."

He nodded. "Janeen. But I never met your husband. I don't know why he had my plane's tail number in his wallet."

"Maybe . . . maybe he wanted to talk to you about work."

"Could be. I'd mentioned to a few folks that I was looking for a distributor in the Oklahoma City area for some of the products I import."

"That's what Brenna ... That's what the colonel said."

"The colonel?"

"From the base. My husband's squadron commander."

"What else did the colonel say?" he asked, leaning back in his chair to hook one ankle over the other.

Janeen gave a small, frustrated sigh. "Nothing. Oh, only that you fly into Oklahoma City occasionally."

"That's true. Maybe your husband planned to meet me at the airport one day and talk to me about becoming a sales rep."

"Maybe."

"Didn't he mention anything about it? About me, or my plane?"

"No."

Petrocelli chewed on one corner of his mustache for a while. "Damn, I wish I could help you, but I just don't know how."

Gathering her courage, Janeen met his steady gaze. "Have you ever been to the Purple Parrot, in Panama City?"

"Can't say as I have. I usually hang out in Josephine's when I'm down south. The beer there is halfway cold, and the women ..." He stopped abruptly.

Her nails cut into her palms. "And the women?"

Uncrossing his ankles, he leaned forward and reached out a hand to cup her chin. Too startled at the unexpected intimacy to draw back, she raised wide eyes to his face.

"The women are gorgeous, but they wouldn't hold a hair's lick of interest to a man who had you to come home to."

Her face hardened, muscle by muscle.

Petrocelli winced. "Aw, hell, I'm sorry. You're thinking that he didn't come home, aren't you? Well, maybe he didn't. But don't think about what's in that autopsy report, little girl. A report like that makes things look a whole lot worse than they are."

Janeen jerked her chin out of his hold. "How did you know what was in the autopsy report? Did they tell you? Good Lord, did they tell everyone?"

Her flare of anger took him aback. His black eyes lost their sparkle and went flat and dark, like unpolished obsidian. In that instant, he bore little resemblance to the joking, jovial man he'd presented on the porch.

"I'm ... I'm sorry," she said with a little shake of her head. "I didn't mean to snap at you. It's just that I hate the idea that people know about ... About ..."

His mouth lost its hard edge. "I understand. Look, those fellas who came to see me didn't tell me anything. But I've got a lot of buddies in the flying business, and when people started asking me questions, I asked a few, too."

She looked away, biting down on her upper lip to still its quivering.

"If it helps any," he told her, "my sources told me your husband wasn't a regular customer at the Purple Parrot."

To her shame, Janeen snatched at that tiny bit of information like a stray mongrel would grab at a half-eaten hamburger it found on the road. Brenna had told her the same thing, had said that the other men indicated Andy usually didn't go bar-hopping while he was on temporary duty. Hearing it confirmed from another source both reassured her and made her more desperate than ever to know why he went to that awful place the night he died.

"It helps," she told the man opposite her quietly. "It helps."

"Good."

She should get up, Janeen thought. She should thank him and escort him to the door. But the weight of her fecund body held her in place. That and the tenuous link Tony Petrocelli had to Andy.

She studied him from beneath her lashes, noting how the fading afternoon sunlight gave his curling hair a blue-black sheen. How the band of his Stetson had left a faint imprint on his forehead. How his mustache almost covered a tiny white scar at one corner of his mouth. She wondered if that scar was a result of one of the improbable occupations listed on his card.

"Tell me about yourself. About . . ." She searched for one of his less provocative lines of work. "About the singing you lead at revival meetings."

His rich laughter rolled back the shadows in the kitchen. "Well, sweet thing, you'll hardly believe it, but my father was a minister. He had all us boys belting out hymns before we could walk. Of course, our favorite musical pieces were the ones we learned from sneaking in the back door at Red Lucy's Saloon and Supper Club in Upper Moose Springs. That's in Wy-Oh-Ming, you know."

The ache in her chest lessened enough for a small smile. "No, I didn't know."

He shook his head sadly at her ignorance. "No doubt you were confusing it with Lower Moose Springs. Montana," he added with a grimace.

"No doubt," she replied gravely.

"I remember this one particular song . . ."

For the next hour, the conversation ranged from saloon songs to favorite foods to some of the more unbelievable aerial maneuvers Tony swore he'd put his plane through. In the manner that Janeen had come to associate with all flyers, he talked with his hands. Palms facing outward, he arced and banked and swooped through the air, totally defying all laws of gravity.

Twice she rescued his glass of tea, long ago diluted by the melted ice, just before it toppled over. Once she had to excuse herself to relieve the pressure on her bladder. Tony picked up his running monologue as soon as she returned, seeming content to sit with her in the quiet kitchen as though he didn't have a dozen deals to work or contacts to make.

For the first time in weeks, Janeen relaxed.

Slowly. Imperceptibly. With each smile he drew from her, she felt less old. Less weary. She knew he was exaggerating his tales just to amuse her. Or at least, she thought he was. When it came right down to it, she didn't really care.

Her parents returned in the middle of one of his improbable stories. If they were surprised to find Janeen entertaining a stranger in the kitchen, they didn't show it. With in-bred courtesy, her mother offered Tony fresh tea, which he accepted, and her father pressed him to stay for dinner, which he declined. He left soon after, and Janeen shared with her parents edited versions of some of his more outrageous tales.

Only later that night, as her gaze fell on the picture of Andy beside her bed, did she feel a sharp stab of disappointment. Despite everything, she'd hoped that Petrocelli would know something. That he'd provide her with some clue, some snippet of understanding about what happened. She curled up on her side, thinking maybe she should give up trying to make sense out of his death. Just trust her instincts and forget all the official reports and documents.

A small frown settled between Janeen's brows. Petrocelli had mentioned the autopsy report. She remembered being given a copy of Andy's death certificate, and some sort of summary medical report, but she was sure she hadn't seen the autopsy report. Maybe she wasn't supposed to.

No, she was Andy's wife. Had been his wife, she corrected with a catch in her chest. She might need the autopsy someday for . . . for something official. Unable to let go, Janeen decided that she'd call tomorrow and see about getting a copy.

She tried Brenna first, only to learn the colonel was in the simulator that day doing a recertification. Then she got hold of the young officer who'd served as the estate officer appointed by the Air Force to help her handle Andy's affairs. He made a few calls, then directed her to the Hospital Administrator's office.

If a certain snippy receptionist hadn't rubbed her the wrong way, she might have given up after the first call to the hospital. The woman acted as though she had no right to inquire about her own husband, much less know the specific details of his death.

Thoroughly irritated, Janeen finally extracted the information that she'd have to go through the Freedom of Information Office, whatever that was. Gritting her teeth, she ploughed further into the bureaucratic maze. Four calls later, she angrily jotted down the address of the person on base who handled requests by "outsiders" for official Air Force information. That afternoon she dragged out her mother's battered old Smith-Corona portable and pecked out an official request for the autopsy report.

The response came back four days later, a form letter saying that she hadn't formatted her request correctly. That scratched her stubborn streak, the one Andy and her brother used to tease her about.

More determined than ever, she sat down and studied the form letter and accompanying pamphlet. She retyped her letter, checked it twice against the confusing instructions, then sent it off again.

Ten days later she received the report. Hands shaking, she turned the envelope over and over. A part of her didn't want to open it. Didn't want to destroy her fragile peace with Andy by reading this brutally clinical description of his death.

But another part of her, the part that needed to come to closure, forced her to unfold the closely printed pages and read them. Or try to. She didn't understand one word in five. They were all long, medical terms, unrecognizable except for a few. Those few caused her to feel sick.

After a debate with herself that lasted well into the night, Janeen drove into Seiling the next afternoon and pulled up at the small clinic that served the town and the surrounding farms. Pushing open the double-glass doors, she made her slow way down the hall to the nurses' station. The RN on duty looked up at her approach and smiled.

"You real busy, Margaret?"

"Not too busy for you, Janey. Are you here for the literature Saint Mary's was supposed to send down? I don't think it's here yet."

Janeen hadn't given a thought to the hospital in Enid where she'd go to deliver her baby. "No, I didn't come for the literature. I was wondering if I could talk to you for a few minutes?"

If there was one person she felt comfortable

showing the report to, it was Margaret Towers. A handsome, dark-haired woman with snapping black eyes and the prominent cheekbones that proclaimed her Cherokee heritage, Margaret had stitched the Wilson children's cuts, helped set their broken bones, and given Janeen her female exams from the time she first started her period.

"Sure thing, honey," Margaret replied. "Why don't we go into the lounge? I need a cup of coffee to keep me going."

The RN buzzed another nurse to cover the central desk, then led the way to the small, cheerful staff lounge. Both the cup of instant coffee she made for herself and the caffeine-free soft drink she provided Janeen went untouched as the older woman walked the younger one through the report, line by painful line. When at last they sat back, liquid compassion filled the nurse's black eyes.

"I'm sorry, Janey."

Her throat raw with the need to cry, Janeen tucked the folded sheets of paper back in her purse. "Me, too."

Strong, work-roughened fingers grasped her forearm. "I've seen a lot of things in my years here, honey. Things that sometimes don't make sense to me at the time. Maybe never make any sense. I don't try to understand them. I tell myself that the people I tend are just that, people. They have their strengths, their weaknesses. Their moments of glory and times of shame."

Unable to speak, Janeen nodded. The grip on her arm tightened.

"Andy loved you. I've never seen a boy as crazy in love as that one. Whatever moment of weakness he had there in Panama, he loved you."

"I . . . I know."

The nurse eyed her for a moment, then pushed herself to her feet. "You just come along with me, Janey Wilson Lang. We'll call Saint Mary's to tell them to get that literature down here pronto. Then I'm going to check you over real good."

Janeen took the strong, capable hand Margaret held out to help her up. As they walked down the hall, the nurse ran a professional eye over her bulging figure.

"What have you got left—six weeks? Seven?"

"Seven. I think. If we got the date right. I wasn't keepin' track of when we did and when we didn't . . ."

She broke off as Margaret's laughter echoed off the pastel yellow walls.

"More'n likely you *did* a whole heck of a lot more than you *didn't,* so there's no telling for sure when this little one's going to make an appearance. Doc Turner will be here tomorrow. I'll get him to go over your records again, and I'll give you a call every so often, just to see how you're doing."

To Janeen's surprise, Margaret called the very next evening. She took the receiver from her mother, wondering if the doctor had found something of concern in her records.

"Janey, you got that report handy?" Margaret asked abruptly.

"Report? Do you mean the autopsy? It's upstairs. Why?"

"I need you to check something in the report."

"What?"

"Didn't it say that Andy had puncture wounds in his left arm, from the needle?"

"I think so."

"Check that, okay? And call me right back."

It took Janeen some moments to climb the stairs, pull the report from the file where she'd buried it, and scan through the closely typed pages. Her bedsprings sagged as she leaned forward and reached for the phone. Punching Margaret's number, she blinked in surprise when the nurse answered on the first ring.

"What does the report say?"

"Hold on . . . Here it is. 'Evidence of two puncture wounds, corresponding to needle marks, in the skin above the basilic vein, left anterior forearm.' "

"Left? It says left?"

"Yes. Why?"

"Andy was left-handed, wasn't he?"

"Yes."

"I thought so. I remembered setting his broken arm when he was sixteen or seventeen. He came back every day for weeks, begging to have the cast off, saying he couldn't eat right-handed without slopping all over himself, couldn't write, couldn't even drive his car."

"I don't understand, Margaret. What are you saying?"

"Honey, I've stuck a lot of veins in my time. And I've taught a whole bunch of folks how to stick themselves to take insulin or vitamins or whatever. But never, in all the years I've been nursing, have I known a left-handed person who could stick himself in his left arm. Or vice versa."

"But what does that prove?"

"Maybe nothing. I just think it's pretty strange that a boy couldn't get a forkful of mashed potatoes from his plate to his mouth with his right hand supposedly used it to shoot dope."

Chapter Eight

At the sight of the figure seated in her outer office, Brenna halted in midstride.

"Janeen! What are you doing here?"

The younger woman smiled hesitantly. "I came to talk to you. If you have time."

"Of course. Come on into my office."

Crossing to her side, Brenna held out a hand to help her rise. "Want some coffee?"

"No, I'm not supposed to have caffeine. But if you've got a caffeine-free diet drink of some kind, that would be great."

"Sure. Have a seat while I dig something out."

Brenna pulled two soft drinks from the small fridge tucked behind the carved teak screen that was a memento of a short tour in Korea. Popping a couple ice cubes into tall mugs emblazoned with her squadron's patch, she poured the sodas and carried them to the round table.

Janeen took the fizzing drink with a murmured word of thanks. Sensing that the young woman needed to work up to whatever it was that had brought her across more than a hundred miles of Oklahoma roads, Brenna asked about the baby, then about her folks. While they chatted, she studied her unexpected visitor.

This woman was far different from the one who'd opened her front door to Brenna four, almost five, weeks ago. Then, Janeen's wide brown eyes stared at her with a gathering fear. Her curling mane of honey-colored hair had been mussed from sleep and framed a face gone white with a foreknowledge of what was to come.

Now, her hair tumbled in soft waves about her face, and she met Brenna's gaze with an expression that was at once hesitant and yet determined. If bluish smudges still stained the skin under her eyes, at least the stark lines that had grooved the skin beside her mouth on the day of her husband's funeral had eased.

After a few moments of idle chat, Janeen eased into the reason for her visit. "Thanks for seeing me like this. I probably should have called first, but ..." She twisted the shoulder strap of the purse she clutched in one hand. "But I wasn't sure I would come. It was harder than I thought, walking into the squadron."

Brenna could only guess at the courage it must have taken for her to enter the building where her husband had worked. The sight of so many uniformed personnel busy with their normal routine had to cut deeply. The world hadn't suddenly stopped for them, as it had for her, and tilted crazily on its axis, never to be quite right again.

But she had come. For all her fragile appearance, Janeen Lang was bred of tough stock. Curious, Brenna watched while she dug into her purse and pulled out a few folded sheets of paper.

"I wanted to talk to you about the autopsy report. Have you seen it?"

"Yes."

She'd seen it, and ached at the dry, desiccated description of what was once an instructor assigned to her squadron. A smiling young husband.

The papers whispered as Janeen unfolded them slowly, her fingers shaking. "I didn't understand some of the medical terms."

"I wasn't too sure of some of them myself. But I can certainly call and get answers to whatever question you might have." Brenna wiped her tongue over dry lips. This wasn't going to be easy. "What do you need explained."

"This . . . this report says Andy injected cocaine into his left arm."

"I know. I questioned the investigators myself about that."

The velvety brown eyes opposite her widened in surprise. "You did?"

"I did. I thought only heroin users mainlined. Most coke users sniff it or cook it up into crack and smoke it. But . . ." Brenna lifted her shoulders. "Shooting up is supposedly faster and gives a more powerful high."

The widow grimaced. "God, those words are so awful. Like the stuff you hear on TV or in the movies. Shooting up. Mainlining. Autoerotic death. I never dreamed those kind of happenings would invade my safe, snug little world."

A rasp of painful laughter tore from Janeen's throat. "Oh, I knew kids in high school who smoked grass. I even tried it once myself, but I never told Andy. He was so straight, so involved in sports he never even touched a cigarette. He didn't, Brenna. He didn't!"

"I believe you."

And she did. But the Andrew Lang who played football at Seiling High and at the University of Oklahoma had died, naked, with a rope knotted around his neck and cocaine swimming in his blood.

"He didn't inject himself down there in Panama, either," Janeen continued desperately. "He couldn't have. He was left-handed, you know."

"No, I didn't know."

"He was. He could hardly do anything with his right hand. Not write. Not throw a ball. Not even steer a car. He sure as heck couldn't ..." Her lip curled. "He couldn't shoot up with it."

The papers crackled as Janeen spread them out on the desk. Her hand shaking, she pointed to a phrase underlined in red.

"Look at what it says here. Puncture wounds in the left anterior forearm."

Frowning, Brenna noted the underlined passage. Then she glanced up, reluctant to articulate the thought that sprang instantly into her mind.

Janeen put it into words for her. "You think one of those women in the bar helped him, don't you?"

"One of the women, or whoever sold him the hit. It could have been anyone."

"But the investigation said there was no one with Andy. It said he was alone when he died, which was just moments after the cocaine entered his bloodstream."

"Just because no one admitted to being with him doesn't mean no one was there," Brenna replied gently. "They wouldn't have wanted to become involved."

"I know." The younger woman's chin lifted. "But if the investigators could make a mistake about this, maybe they made mistakes about other things, too. Tony said he'd heard Andy didn't go to places like the Purple Parrot regularly. Maybe—"

"Tony who?"

"Tony Petrocelli."

Brenna stared at her, stunned. "You spoke to Petrocelli?"

"He came to the house a week or so ago. Said he wanted to meet me, since so many people had been askin' him questions about my husband."

"And he thinks the investigators made a mistake?"

Brenna's mind whirled with the possible implications. Maybe this Mad Dog knew more than he'd admitted. Maybe he knew something about . . .

"No, he didn't say that exactly. He just said that everything isn't always the way it sounds in these reports. And that . . . that I should trust my own instincts." Her outstretched fingers curled, wadding the autopsy report into a tight, crumpled ball. "Every instinct in my body tells me Andy wouldn't do the things this report says he did."

"Oh, Janeen . . ."

What could she say? Brenna thought hopelessly. What could she possibly say in the face of this desperate need to believe?

"The investigators made one mistake," the younger woman insisted doggedly. "Maybe they got other things wrong as well. Maybe Andy had business in the Purple Parrot that didn't have anything to do with ropes and drugs and such. Maybe . . . Maybe he didn't go into that back room voluntarily."

Her eyes begged Brenna to doubt, just for a moment. To question. To give Andy one more chance.

The fact that her desperate words echoed Brenna's own vague, half-formed suspicions decided the matter. Rising, she motioned Janeen to keep her seat.

"Sit right here."

She crossed the short distance from the conference table to her desk in four quick strides. After flipping through her Rolodex, she punched the OSI commander's number into the phone.

"This is Lieutenant Colonel Duggan at the 552d

Training Squadron. I'd like to speak to Mr. Richards, please."

Her nails drummed on the polished surface of her desk until Richards answered. When he did, she wasted no time on polite exchanges.

"Could you come over to my office for a moment? I have someone here I'd like you to talk to. Mrs. Lang. Mrs. Andrew Lang."

Brenna sensed immediately that Richards didn't like the idea of Janeen challenging the results of the official investigation. Although he listened to her politely and took detailed notes, his eyes held no hint of friendliness or sympathy. When she finished, he promised only to review the police reports and get back to Colonel Duggan.

Janeen's color faded a bit at his less than encouraging tone, but she managed a small smile as she pushed herself to her feet.

"Thank you. I'll wait till I hear from the colonel, then."

Asking Richards to sit tight, Brenna escorted her to the door. They stood together for a moment in the hallway.

"How long do you think it will be before we hear anything?" Janeen asked.

"I'm not sure. A few days, maybe. A week at most. They'll have to contact the people in Panama and ask them to review their findings. I'll stay on them and let you know as soon as they have anything."

"Thank you. I . . . I just want to know the full story."

"They may not be able to find anything more," Brenna cautioned. "Especially after all this time."

"But at least they'll ask. At least there's some doubt about what happened."

"Yes, there's some doubt."

Resting one hand against the door frame, she watched Janeen make her way down the tiled corridor toward the double-glass doors at the far end. A couple of students gave her a friendly, if impersonal, greeting. An instructor rounded a corner, then stopped in surprise. After a moment, he stepped forward.

When Janeen lifted her head and returned the man's greeting with a determined smile, Brenna felt a swell of admiration for the younger woman. This had to be hell for her. Coming here, running into men and women who knew the circumstances of Andy Lang's death. Yet she refused to let those circumstances shame her. Or her husband. Her grit sparked an answering determination in Brenna. Heading back to her office, she closed the door.

Special Agent Richards's face settled into tight lines as she related the information she'd learned from Thud about Dave Sanderson's ex-wife. If Richards knew about the woman's alcohol problem and subsequent suicide, he didn't say so. Nor did he comment when Brenna gave him an expurgated version of her confrontation with Sanderson aboard the AWACS. He jotted the information down in his ever-present notebook, then rose to leave.

"So when do you think you'll have something?" she asked, annoyed by his uncommunicative attitude.

"You'll hear something soon, Colonel."

Soon turned out to be the very next morning.

Pete stuck his head in her office, interrupting a meeting with the major who headed the curriculum for Battle Staff Directors. "The boss wants to see you, ma'am."

"General Adams?"

The chief clerk nodded. "His exec just called. Said to come right over."

"Did he mention what the boss wants to see me about?"

"No, ma'am."

"Okay, buzz him back and tell him I'm on my way."

Brenna dismissed the major and grabbed her small, leather-bound "brain book," which contained every possible current statistic concerning her squadron. Settling her flight cap onto her forehead at a precise angle, she left her office.

A spurt of Canadian air had chased away the searing heat and washed central Oklahoma in blessedly cool, crisp sunshine. As Brenna returned the salutes of the military personnel she passed, she breathed in the scent of the climbing clematis vine that rooted so stubbornly in the inhospitable red soil around the squadron. The light, flowery fragrance was one of the unexpected pleasures of an Oklahoma fall.

Crossing the street to the wing headquarters, she searched her mind for the reason behind this unexpected summons. The boss probably wanted to see her about training funds. That was the hot topic on this last day of the fiscal year, with Congress still dithering over next year's budget. Luckily, she knew to a dollar how much it would cost to continue current training levels, and had worked up detailed contingency plans to scale back if the budget wasn't passed. Mentally reviewing those plans, she headed for the low, one-story building sunk down within sheltering earthen banks. The ultramodern facility housed the command post that monitored the wing's activities worldwide, as well as most of the headquarters staff. The commander's office was just inside the front entrance.

After a friendly exchange of greetings with the receptionist, Brenna strolled over to the Exec's desk. A pilot who'd paid his dues during Desert Storm, Captain Hargrove was sharp, efficient, and well-liked within the wing. He stood at her approach and waved her toward the inner sanctum.

"Go right in, ma'am. The boss is waiting for you."

Not only the boss, Brenna saw as soon as she entered a cavernous office decorated austerely and elegantly in shades of gray and Air Force blue. Another man was seated in one of the high-backed leather and oak chairs in front of the general's desk, a civilian. He rose at her entrance and turned.

She stopped a few paces inside the door and snapped General Adams a salute. "You wanted to see me, sir?"

"Yes, Duggan. Come in."

Brenna had often thought that General Robert "Rock" Adams came closer than anyone else she knew to epitomizing the idealized, Steve Canyon image of an Air Force officer. His precisely creased blue uniform molded a lean, trim body. Black hair winged with silver added to an unshakable air of authority. A graduate of the Air Force Academy, he'd flown F–100s in Vietnam, logging over two hundred combat missions. Having served on the air staff and at Combat Air Command headquarters, he knew how to work the system to get the job done.

On a more personal level, he could greet by name every man and woman in the wing, and most of their spouses. His leadership style often took him out to the alert facility in the middle of the night to shoot the breeze with the crews. Just as often, he could be found up on a maintenance stand with one of the wrench-benders, checking out a sick bird. He was ruthless when it came to safety, and on those rare occasions when he was riled, could put his colonels in a brace with a few well-chosen words.

To a person, the men and women of the wing admired and respected him. A few, like Brenna, hoped to follow in his footsteps someday. The ratings he gave her on her last efficiency report indicated that it might be a possibility.

Somewhat to her surprise, his gray eyes were cool as he returned her salute, then gestured toward a dark-suited civilian with thinning, reddish-brown hair.

"This is Mr. Jerry O'Halloran, from the U.S. Customs Service Office of Internal Affairs."

Brenna shook the man's hand, her heartbeat accelerating. Obviously, she hadn't been called in to the general's office to talk about training funds. Internal Affairs was Customs's equivalent to the Air Force's Office of Special Investigations. Richards must have been busy since their talk yesterday.

General Adams nodded to the chairs in front of his desk. "Sit down, Mr. O'Halloran, Colonel Duggan."

Tucking her slim skirt under her thighs, Brenna took a seat. Excitement thrummed in her veins. Excitement, and the hope that she'd finally have something positive to relate to Janeen Lang.

Not one to beat about the bush, the general plunged right into business. "As you're probably aware, Internal Affairs is responsible for investigating allegations made against one of their employees."

"Yes, sir."

"Mr. O'Halloran is here to discuss your suspicions you relayed to Special Agent Richards yesterday about one of their Detection Systems Specialists."

"Not so much suspicions as questions. In relation to Sergeant Lang's death."

General Adams pinned her with a hard look. "I understood the case on Sergeant Lang was closed. As I recall, you interviewed Sanderson, among others, before you found Lang's death not in the line of duty."

"Yes, sir. Since that time, certain . . . discrepancies have come to light that I wanted checked out."

"Such as?"

Briefly, Brenna outlined what appeared to be Sergeant Lang's uncharacteristic behavior at the Purple Parrot, the scribbled aircraft tail number his wife had found in his wallet, and Janeen Lang's conviction that her husband didn't inject himself, as the autopsy and investigative report concluded.

"That's it?"

When Brenna hesitated, O'Halloran leaned forward. "We understand that you also made a trip out to CNAC, asking questions about Mr. Sanderson's personal life."

Brenna met the hint of accusation in his voice head-on. "Yes, I did."

"You exceeded your authority there, Colonel."

"I don't agree. As Sergeant Lang's commander, it's well within my authority to check out every aspect of his death. Including the backgrounds of the men he spent his last hours with."

O'Halloran notched a brow at her cool rebuttal. "We do a thorough background check on all our employees, particularly those in sensitive jobs. We're well aware of the circumstances leading to the former Mrs. Sanderson's suicide. They have no bearing on Dave's performance or his credibility."

"Does your background check explain the connection between Sanderson, Petrocelli, and Lang?"

"There is no connection, according to your own agents."

"I'm not satisfied with that."

The general intervened. "I'm afraid you'll have to be. You're not a trained investigator, Duggan. Nor is Mrs. Lang. She's a grieving widow who is, understandably, looking for any thread, any excuse, to soften the circumstances of her husband's death."

Surprised at his lack of support, Brenna chose her words carefully. "With all due respect, sir, it appears the circumstances warrant another look. The OSI investigation stated that Sergeant Lang injected himself in the left arm. Given the fact that he was left-handed, that's a physical impossibility. That's also a pretty significant discrepancy in the investigation."

"So it is," Adams conceded stiffly. "The Chief of Investigations at OSI Headquarters called me this morning to discuss it. He confirmed that the locals had control of the scene for some time. They interviewed and released all those still in the bar. No one admitted then to being with Lang when he died, and no one's likely to come forward now. It's entirely possible that someone else helped Lang shoot up, but the OSI doesn't feel that there are sufficient grounds to reopen the investigation."

"But ..."

"No buts, Colonel. This is coming from the top."

An instinctive protest rose to Brenna's lips. With some difficulty, she swallowed it.

"What's more," he continued, "there's nothing in your suspicions to warrant an investigation of Mr. Sanderson. Unless and until you discover specific evidence of wrongdoing, you'll cease your unofficial queries into his activities. If you do find something, Customs will work it through their own channels. Understood?"

Across the wide expanse of his desk, his eyes locked with hers.

"Understood, Colonel Duggan?"

"Yes, sir."

"That's all."

The setting sun had begun to paint the sky a mixture of swirling red and purple when a shrill ring jerked Dave Sanderson's attention to the phone booth beside his parked truck. Shoving the door open, he stepped out of the pickup and lifted the receiver. He'd been waiting for the prearranged call.

He listened intently, his eyes narrowed on the color-filled horizon beyond the busy truck stop. The spectacular sunset didn't register on his consciousness, however. All his attention was riveted on the speaker's voice.

"It's done. The investigation has been turned off."

"It damn well better be. We can't afford any more screwups."

"Relax. I'm telling you, it's taken care of."

"Anyone who relaxes in this business is liable to end up dead," he snarled. "Like Andy Lang."

"Hey, it was a chance in a million the kid tumbled to what was going down. Who would've expected him to follow up on that track on his own?"

"Dammit, I should have! When he asked me why I hadn't forced it to a higher priority, I should have expected him to do some digging. The kid was smart."

"Yeah, well, it's done, buddy. It's done."

Dave's jaw worked as he stared unseeing at the distant horizon. "Yeah," he said after a moment. "It's done."

"So when are you going to make the next pass?"

He shook his head. Just like that, they turned from yesterday to tomorrow. From the last move to the next in this deadly game of betrayal and greed. It was the only way to play it, he knew. The only way to survive.

"The October schedules should be out by the end of next week. I'll find a way to take a rotation as soon as I get my hands on one. And Petrocelli?"

"Yeah?"

"Stick to the plan this time."

"Roger-dodger."

"I mean it, Mad Dog. No more unscheduled trips down south like that last one to meet with our customers. I can't cover for you again."

"No sweat, old buddy."

With his partner's breezy assurances ringing in his ears, Dave replaced the receiver. Unconsciously, he reached for the cigarettes he'd given up years ago. Swearing, he yanked open the door to his pickup and slid into the driver's seat. Hands on the wheel, he sat unmoving for a few moments. While the blazing sun sank into the now purple horizon, Dave retraced in his mind the crooked road that had brought him to a truck stop on the outskirts of Oklahoma City—a road that wound through eleven years in the Air Force, almost as many years in his own private hell, two years now with Customs, and four months in the pay of the most powerful drug cartel in South America.

A road that was about to take another sharp twist. The gut-level, animal instincts that had kept him alive the past four months sensed the change coming. And it scared the hell out of him.

Damn Duggan for refusing to let go of Lang's death. She had no idea what she was poking and prying into. She couldn't know how close she skirted to the same whirling vortex that had sucked him in and destroyed Andy Lang.

Even if she did know, he thought, it wouldn't deter her. Not Lieutenant Colonel Brenna Duggan of the silky brown hair and narrow, tunnel vision of right and wrong. If she caught even a whiff of this miasma, this foul-smelling cesspool that swirled all around him, she'd be on his ass even more than she was now.

His mouth curved sardonically. The idea of

Brenna Duggan on his ass or on any other available portion of his anatomy sent a sharp, lancing shaft of heat through his belly.

Christ, he couldn't seem to let go of her, any more than she could let go of this business with Lang. Somehow the woman had broken into the compartments of his mind he'd kept sealed for too many years. The compartments labeled attraction. Companionship. Maybe even relationship.

No, what he wanted from Brenna Duggan went beyond attraction and didn't have anything to do with companionship. And he sure as hell wasn't looking for anything as tame as a relationship. Methodically, Dave listed a few of the things he did want from her.

Like the sound of her breath hot and panting in his ear.

The feel of her sweat-slick body under his.

The taste of her bare skin on his lips and tongue.

And that was just for starters.

He figured his chances of getting any of the items on his little list ranged from zero to somewhere around minus two hundred. Even if his disastrous marriage hadn't proved how little he had to offer a woman, he couldn't afford to tangle with someone like Brenna. Not in her position. Not now. Not ever.

Twisting the key in the ignition, he shoved the truck into gear and drove toward a twilight that was slowly sinking into black, unrelenting night.

Chapter Nine

This time, Brenna couldn't bring herself to deliver the bad news to Janeen over the phone. Not after the desperate pleading she'd seen in the younger woman's brown eyes. She decided to drive to Seiling that afternoon, hoping the two-hour trip would give her time to sort through her own inner turmoil before she added to Janeen's.

Oklahoma's brief taste of fall hadn't lasted. By the time Brenna guided her Miata along the state road that cut across Oklahoma's rolling wheat lands, heat rose in shimmering waves from the asphalt. On either side of her, acres of newly planted fields lay baking in the sun. The furrowed, red-brown earth whizzed by unnoticed as she played and replayed the scene with General Adams in her mind.

No one had given her a direct order like that in years. Although she'd swallowed any further protest, saluted smartly, and left, her boss's flat, uncompromising directive had singed her pride as much as her professionalism. Adams was often terse and to the point, but to her knowledge he'd never cut off one of his squadron commanders without any discussion like that.

Okay, maybe she had stretched the limits of her authority by going to see Thud Hendricks at CNAC. Maybe she had been grasping at straws when she voiced her half-formed suspicions about Dave Sanderson to Special Agent Richards. Maybe she was 180 degrees off course here.

And maybe she wasn't.

Sanderson's mocking hazel eyes danced before her. Jaw tight, Brenna recalled how he'd all but pinned her against the galley. How his body had hovered just inches from her own and his sharp, masculine scent had tugged at her senses. To her profound disgust, the vivid memory of his nearness even now triggered some primitive, instinctive response deep in her belly.

She slapped a hand against the steering wheel. Damn the man, and damn her growing conviction that he deliberately laid on that insolent, half-sneering grin every time he sauntered into her vicinity. She was becoming more and more convinced that the taunting way he stripped her with his eyes every time they clashed was as much for effect as for . . .

For what? Dammit, for what?

The question nagged at her for most of the long, dusty drive. By the time the Wilsons' two-story stone house came into sight, Brenna still hadn't found an answer, except the obvious one, of course.

Maybe he wasn't putting on any front. Maybe he was just the unpredictable, mocking, thoroughly rogue male he appeared to be. The kind of man any woman with half a lick of common sense would walk a wide path around. The kind, she acknowledged cynically, that every woman itched to tame. Her included.

From the first moment he'd sauntered into her office, ten minutes late for their interview and not the least repentant, she'd wanted to put him in a brace like some raw, untrained recruit, rip him apart, and put him back together as the kind of professional she admired and respected. When she finished with Sanderson, there wouldn't be much left of his flagrant, in-your-face independence. Or whatever it was that made her nails curve into her palms and her pulse start drumming an irregular beat whenever she was around him.

Good Lord! Her festering, perverse sort of fascination with the man had dug deeper into her psyche than she'd realized. She was crazy to believe, even for a second, that she could curb his arrogance. Or harness the lazy, lambent fire in his eyes when he let them roam so slowly and so deliberately from her face to her throat to her . . .

A spark of heat streaked through her belly, shocking Brenna. And sobering her. For the first time, she was forced to admit that her reaction to Sanderson was rooted in more than just dislike. As much as she'd like to deny it, he generated a whole host of conflicting emotions in her. Buried somewhere among them was a burning awareness of him as a man.

Okay! Okay! She could handle that. If she looked at the matter rationally, she could understand why she might be attracted to Sanderson on some subliminal, purely physical level.

She was a normal, healthy woman in her prime. She worked mostly around men all day. Trim, fighting-fit men. She experienced her share of subtle sexual urges, which she ruthlessly suppressed given her position and her natural fastidiousness. She wasn't the kind of woman to indulge in tacky little grab-and-grunt sessions behind a locked office door or risk entanglement with someone in her chain of command.

Besides, she'd learned the hard way that physical attraction wasn't enough, not for her. She wanted more. She wanted it all. Unadulterated, old-fashioned lust. Mind-bending passion. And a love that tempered them both into something enduring, something ... Something like what Janeen and Andy Lang seemed to have found.

A regret she hadn't experienced in years feathered through Brenna's heart as she thought of the man she'd planned to spend her life with. Her marriage had been short and sweet, a passionate joining of two people who gradually came to find more excitement and stimulation in their work than in each other. She'd thought she loved Mac. Had been sure of it during those first, heady days of courtship and spiraling sexual desire. But when they ended their marriage some years later, her pride had hurt more than her heart.

Why hadn't their love lasted? Why hadn't it found a bedrock to cling to during the long separations, during the endless exercises and deployments? Why hadn't it taken root and flourished, as had Andy and Janeen Lang's?

The young couple had endured as many separations as Brenna and Mac. Yet their love had formed the foundation of their lives. Despite the circumstances of Andy Lang's death, despite the evidence to the contrary, those two people had shared something Brenna and her ex-husband never came close to.

Maybe she and Dave Sanderson were more alike than she wanted to admit, Brenna thought with a sudden, hollow feeling. They'd both failed at marriage, had both skirted around another permanent relationship, and now seemed to generate some kind of warped, knife-edged tension in each other that was part active dislike, part purely primitive sexual awareness, and completely wrong.

When the flower-edged dirt drive leading to the Wilson house came into view some moments later, Brenna gave herself a mental shake. She needed to pull herself together before she faced Janeen. To put Sanderson out of her mind, and shake off this sudden preoccupation with a marriage that had dissolved years ago.

She needed, she reminded herself tightly, to drape the cloak of officialdom around her before she told a young widow that the United States Air Force saw no reason to reopen the investigation of her husband's death.

By the time she'd pulled into the shade of the tall elms that formed a windbreak around the two-story stone house, Brenna had herself in hand. She hoped.

Janeen took it well, better than she had anticipated. Once more, Brenna caught a glimpse of the hard core of red clay earth beneath the younger woman's sunflower soft exterior.

Janeen listened without speaking, sitting as straight as her advancing pregnancy would allow on a spindle-backed kitchen chair. When Brenna relayed that the Air Force didn't feel there were sufficient grounds to reopen the investigation, her ringless, swollen hands curled into fists on the blue-patterned plastic tablecloth.

"I'm not giving up."

"Janeen . . ."

"I'm not. I won't."

Her coffee-brown eyes gleamed with a fierce, determined light. As it seemed to in times of stress, the young woman's accent deepened.

"This isn't just for me anymore. Or even for Andy. The closer I get to my time, the more I want our baby to come into a world where she can be proud of her daddy. I want her to know he didn't die like they say. Like that report says, shot all full of dope and doin' those disgustin' things to himself. The report's wrong, Brenna. I know it is."

"There's no evidence to support that."

"It's wrong. It has to be wrong. I doubted Andy at first, after readin' that report. I even hated him for a little while. But I knew him. I knew him the way a woman knows a man. The way a wife knows her husband. He was my best friend as well as my lover, and I'm tellin' you he didn't shoot dope and he didn't . . . didn't do those kind of things."

Reaching across the table, she covered both of Brenna's hands with her own.

"Can't you help me?" she pleaded. "Isn't there anything you can do to *make* them take another look?"

As she stared into Janeen's pleading eyes, Brenna felt a small, almost imperceptible shift inside her chest. Only later, when her world had tilted at almost as sharp an angle as Janeen's, did Brenna realize that the tiny movement, the subtle realignment of her thoughts and emotions, represented the first crack in her loyalty to the Air Force.

Always afterward, she would wonder why she didn't hear a rending groan, or feel the earth quiver as a fissure opened in what had always been solid ground beneath her feet. There should have been some sound, some physical manifestation that marked the movement in her planes of existence.

Never before had she doubted herself or the institution she'd dedicated her life to.

Never again would she be sure of either.

In that moment, she realized that everything now narrowed down to a single choice. Between this young woman's unshakable belief in her husband, and the evidence that labeled him unworthy of that belief. Between her own confused doubts about Sanderson, and the bureaucracy's insistence she put those doubts aside. Between what she'd been ordered to do, and what her heart told her she should do.

Even with the doubts that suddenly shook her, Brenna knew immediately the choice she would make. She wouldn't jettison her professional scruples or a lifetime of discipline. She'd been given a direct order. She couldn't voice her own unfounded suspicions in violation of that order.

But she could, and damn well would, provide Janeen one last avenue of recourse.

"Do you still have the copy of the regulation governing Line of Duty Determinations? The one I gave you when I briefed you on the impact of the finding?"

Janeen's pale brows drew together. "I think so. It's upstairs, in the file with all of Andy's other papers."

Brenna measured each word carefully. "You might want to take a look at it. I don't remember the exact paragraph, but I know there's a provision in the regulation that applies to dependents of deceased military personnel who lose their benefits."

The younger woman withdrew her hands and sat back, her jaw set stubbornly. "I don't care about those benefits. You said I'll continue to get medical care until after the baby's born. I've got everything else I need, and have a little money in the bank for when the baby comes. Momma and Daddy will help me until I find a job and—"

"Listen to me, Janeen. The regulation allows the dependent who's been denied benefits to formally request a reinvestigation."

"It does?"

"It does. You have to submit the request in writing, and there's a time limit. Forty-five days, I think."

"Forty-five days?"

Brenna did a quick mental calculation. "Andy died on the nineteenth of August. This is the end of September. You still have time."

"Who do I send it to?"

"I'm not sure. The regulation will tell you. The person who directed the Line of Duty, I'd guess."

"Who's that?"

Brenna's hesitation was so slight, she might have simply been drawing in a breath. But in that fleeting instant, the fissure beneath her feet seemed to widen even more.

"General Adams."

"The wing commander?" Janeen's forehead wrinkled as she struggled to understand the system. "Wasn't he the one who approved your findings? Why would he let me challenge them, if he already approved them?"

"In the event of a challenge, the matter goes to a higher authority for review."

"It does? To someone above General Adams?"

Telling herself that the bitter taste in her throat was absurd, Brenna nodded. She wasn't betraying her boss, a man she'd always admired and respected, by simply reminding Janeen of a right that was hers by regulation.

Excitement gleamed in the young woman's eyes as she planted both palms on the table and pushed herself up. "I'll go get that regulation right now! Will you help me write out the request while you're here?"

Brenna rose as well, guilt and regret and a nagging sense of loss tugging at her heart.

"I can't. That would constitute a conflict of interest, since I was the determining commander." She chewed on the inside of her cheek for a moment, then continued slowly, reluctantly. "You might want to consult with an attorney about it."

"One of the lawyers at the base legal office? They'll still see me?"

"They will, but . . ."

Oh, God, Brenna thought. She'd taken the first step down a path she never dreamed she'd follow, and now she couldn't seem to get off the damned thing. It stretched far into the distance, bleak and empty.

Janeen tilted her head. "But?"

Brenna couldn't do it. She couldn't take the next

step. She couldn't suggest that military lawyers might not be the best ones to consult when challenging a military finding.

A civilian attorney wouldn't understand the process, she rationalized. A civilian would take too long and charge too much just learning how to file the request. Janeen couldn't afford to pay those kind of legal fees, despite her assertion that she was set financially.

Shaking her head, she gathered her purse and prepared to leave. "Nothing. I'd better get back to the base."

They were halfway to the door when the younger woman stopped suddenly. Gasping, she clutched at her stomach with both hands.

Brenna whirled. "What? What is it?"

When Janeen raised her head, her cinnamon brown eyes sparkled with unshadowed joy.

"It's the baby. She's just letting me know she's awake and wanting to play."

Relief slagged through Brenna. "Good grief, you scared me half to death."

While her heart resumed its regular beat, she watched Janeen's blunt-tipped fingers caress the distend mound of her stomach, soothing the rambunctious child within.

"You keep calling the baby 'her.' Do you know for sure it's a girl?"

"No, not for sure. But Grandma Wilson thinks so, and she doesn't miss her mark very often."

The two women resumed their slow progress toward the front door.

"When are you due?"

"The end of next month. That's what the doctor says anyway."

Pushing open the screen door, Janeen followed Brenna out onto the front porch. With a wry smile, she shifted her hands from her stomach to the small of her back and arched against the pull of the baby's weight.

"Next month seems like forever. Or it did. At least now I've got something to keep me busy for a while. Thanks for telling me about the regulation."

Digging her aviator sunglasses out of her purse, Brenna slid them on. "It may not change anything."

"Maybe not. But I've got to try."

"I know."

With a final good-bye, she slipped on her flight cap and walked toward the dust-streaked Miata. Funny, she thought, rummaging in her purse for her keys. Here she was, smack in the middle of nowhere, with no one to see or care whether she observed proper military etiquette. Yet she couldn't even walk the few yards to the car without putting on her cover.

Maybe she hadn't traveled as far down that path as she had feared.

The thought sustained her on the long, dusty drive back to the base.

Janeen wasn't sure just what motivated her to contact her brother that afternoon and ask if he knew a good lawyer.

She could have called Tinker and talked to one of the attorneys who'd helped her sort through things after Andy's death. The folks at the base would have known just what she needed to do. But something in Brenna's face, or maybe in her voice, had snagged Janeen's attention. Maybe it wouldn't hurt to get an outside opinion, she concluded. Maybe a civilian lawyer would have a fresh perspective on the investigation.

An officer with the Oklahoma Department of Corrections, her brother Bobby knew his way around the judicial system. When he understood what kind of legal advice she needed, he recommended several good attorneys. He also told her he'd call and talk to them first, to make sure they didn't give her a runaround.

Most likely he wanted to make sure they gave her a discount on the fee, Janeen guessed with an inner smile. Her brothers were as protective of her as Andy had been, but in this instance she didn't mind one bit.

The attorney she finally chose to handle the matter specialized primarily in criminal cases, but she was so down-to-earth and easy to talk to that Janeen made an appointment to see her the next day. With the lawyer's help, she filed the request for reinvestigation on the third of October, just a few days under the forty-five-day deadline.

Her lawyer called Tinker three days later to make sure the letter had been received. Some faceless official assured her the request had been logged in and would receive prompt attention. A week went by, then ten days. When the attorney called again to check the status, she was directed to the Office of the Judge Advocate General at Air Combat Command in Virginia, the 552d Wing's higher headquarters. Disgust colored the attorney's voice when she updated Janeen over the phone later that day.

"What a goat-rope! I must have made half a dozen different calls before I finally found the office that's working the request, and the only thing they'd tell me is that it's being staffed. In nonmilitary parlance, that means the thing's buried in the slow, grinding wheels of officialdom."

"But they promised us a quick turnaround."

"Apparently quick doesn't mean the same thing to the Air Force as it does to the rest of the world. All they'd say is that they're drafting up a recommendation for the Reviewing Official."

"Wouldn't they at least tell you what they're recommending?"

"No, they wouldn't."

Janeen twisted the phone cord nervously. "I don't understand why not."

The other woman gave a very unlawyerlike snort. "This is one of those inexplicable phenomenons that occur whenever any big institution is challenged. I've seen it happen so many times, and not just with the military. Whenever an outsider questions their system, the bureaucracy closes ranks."

Hurt prickled through Janeen. "I'm not an outsider. I'm a military widow. The system is supposed to work for me, too."

"I know that, and you know that, but we have to face reality here. You've challenged an official military determination, one that was endorsed by a general. You're questioning his judgment and the judgment of the officer who made the determination."

Janeen hadn't revealed to anyone, even her attorney, that the determining officer was the one who'd explained how to challenge the decision. She might not understand all the nuances of this "system," but her common sense told her that Brenna had put herself out on a limb by suggesting she exercise this provision of the regulation.

"I'll keep the pressure on," the lawyer assured her. "They've already labeled you a troublemaker, so we might as well ride that horse for all it's worth."

The offhand comment took Janeen aback. "They think I'm a troublemaker?"

"No one said it in so many words, of course, but anyone who challenges the system by definition is causing trouble."

"But I'm not trying to cause trouble."

"Hey, don't worry about it. That's what litigation's all about. Questioning. Challenging. Making waves."

"I . . . I guess so."

Janeen sat by the phone for long moments after

concluding the conversation with the attorney. Unseeing, she stared at the faded print of a spring bouquet on the far wall.

A troublemaker? Was that what she now was to the Air Force? A troublemaker? The little prickle of hurt she'd felt earlier expanded, swelling into a sudden wave of panic.

If she made too much trouble, would they cut off her benefits? The ones not linked to the Line of Duty Determination?

The thought of losing the medical coverage she was entitled to until after the baby's birth sent a spear of fear through Janeen. She didn't have a job, hadn't planned to even look for one until a few months after the baby was born. Her folks' insurance didn't cover her. The hospital costs would wipe out the money she'd set aside to pay her way and the baby's until she could start earning for them both.

Surely, surely they wouldn't take her medical benefits away!

Her hand shaking, Janeen reached for the phone again, intending to call Brenna. Before the call went through, more rational thought prevailed.

She was acting like some silly, frightened little kid. The Air Force had been good to her, she reminded herself sternly, replacing the receiver. Everyone at Tinker had gone out of their way to help her during those first days after Andy's death. She shouldn't jump like a gun-shy bird dog just because her lawyer thought someone at higher headquarters considered her request a challenge. Or feel hurt and shivery scared, like she was standing all alone in front of some huge Goliath, without even a pebble for her slingshot.

She'd wait. She'd wait until she heard something through channels, as Andy used to say.

If she closed her eyes, if she laid her head back against the wall and listened with her heart, she could almost hear him saying it.

Everything in the Air Force had to go through channels. Like the time his flight pay got screwed up and he put a request in—through channels— to straighten it out. Took forever, but the back pay finally came through in a big, fat lump sum. They'd gone out and bought a new TV with it.

He was good at that, Janeen remembered, easing into memories that held less pain for her these days.

Andy was good at straightening things out. He never got frustrated, never lost his patience. But he sure as the dickens wouldn't let go of something once he got hold of it. He'd just grin that lopsided grin of his and tell her they'd work it out, whatever it was.

Folding her arms across her stomach, Janeen closed her eyes. The last of her panic faded. In its place, the determination that had so recently taken root in her heart put up new, stronger shoots.

We'll work it out, Andy.

I promise you, we'll work it out.

Chapter Ten

Caught between her loyalty to the Air Force and her uneasy sense of responsibility to Janeen, Brenna initiated her own discreet inquires into the status of the request for reinvestigation.

She discovered easily enough that Sergeant Lang's widow hadn't sought counsel from Tinker's Office of the Judge Advocate General. Instead, she'd submitted her request to General Adams through an off-base attorney. The package had been staffed on base, then forwarded to Air Combat Command for final decision.

The fact that no one from the wing or from higher headquarters had contacted her, even by phone, puzzled Brenna. As the original determining officer, she had fully expected to be consulted about her decision before a recommendation went from General Adams to higher headquarters.

Curious, she put in a call to Air Combat Command's Deputy Judge Advocate General at Langley AFB in Virginia. Rather tersely, he informed her the determining officer's coordination wasn't required. The request would receive due consideration, and she should work any further queries through her base legal staff. Irritated by both his tone and his unspoken message to butt out, Brenna tried to put the matter out of her mind and attend to the press of squadron business.

Despite her best efforts and a grinding work schedule, guilt continued to nip at her. She worried that she'd set Janeen on an expensive course of legal action, one she couldn't afford. That she'd raised false hopes, which would only be shattered again. And in the quiet reaches of the night, Brenna felt a growing sympathy for the widow's impossible quest.

Her silent frustration on Janeen's behalf accumulated with each passing day . . . and with every glimpse of Dave Sanderson at a flight crew briefing or sauntering through the halls. More and more, Brenna found herself watching for a pair of broad shoulders or a head of shaggy, too-long light brown hair. Whenever she caught sight of either, a new familiar combination of irritation, suspicion, and tension gripped her.

When almost a week went by without any sign of Sanderson, Brenna decided to check his whereabouts. Strolling into Wing Scheduling early one morning, she nodded to the crew dogs screening the rosters for their upcoming flights, then asked the clerk to pull up Detection System Specialist Dave Sanderson's status.

"Can do, ma'am. What do you need to know?"

"Just his flight schedule for the next few weeks."

"That's easy," Sergeant Davis replied. "He's sitting alert at Howard until ... um, end of next week, I think. Wait a sec, I'll verify the date"

"He's at Howard?"

Davis nodded absently, his fingers flying over the keyboard. "Yeah. He went down with the changeover crew for the alert bird last week."

"I don't remember seeing his name on the rotation schedule."

"He switched with another one of the Customs guys at the last minute. Said the other guy wanted to go on vacation or something."

Unexpected schedule changes occurred all the time, Brenna reminded herself. Just because Sanderson had rearranged schedules to take a three-week rotation in Panama was no reason for this feeling of vague unease.

"Said the long days in the alert shack didn't bother him," the clerk continued conversationally while he waited for the right schedule to come up on his screen. "Hey, the man's a bachelor, isn't he? He probably doesn't mind the days because he enjoys the nights off with those hot little senoritas in the ..."

Catching sight of Brenna's raised brow, Davis suddenly realized he was treading on treacherous ground. Swallowing the rest of his off-color remark, he gave the screen his undivided attention.

"Here it is, ma'am. Mr. Sanderson left last

Wednesday with the change-out crew, and is due back on the twelfth of October."

"Thanks, Davis," Brenna replied, her eyes thoughtful.

As she walked to her office, General Adams's words echoed in her head. He'd ordered her to back off, to let Customs Internal Affairs handle the matter if and when she found specific evidence of any wrongdoing on Dave Sanderson's part. Which she hadn't.

Fine. She'd backed off. Except for tracking Janeen's request for redetermination, she'd ceased her unofficial inquiries into Sergeant Lang's death. But maybe, just maybe, she might find something specific and suspicious behind Dave Sanderson's sudden willingness to sit alert for three weeks in a small, stuffy alert shack at Howard Air Force Base.

She flew out of Tinker the next morning on a four-day training mission to Panama. She needed the flight time, she told the senior instructor whose place she took. Which was true. Chained to their desks by a thousand routine and several hundred not so routine tasks, squadron commanders chronically ran short of air time, and Brenna was no exception. Only too happy to stay at home for his son's third birthday, the major passed her the mission planning kit with a grin and a hearty wish for a good flight.

She kept busy during the long trip to the Caribbean monitoring the performance of several captains in upgrade training to Senior Weapons

Director. During every lull in the activity, however, her thoughts returned to the man who seemed to have taken up permanent residence in her mind.

Maybe Sanderson just wanted to pull in the few extra dollars the three-week temporary duty would earn him. Maybe, as the scheduling clerk had hinted, the man had a taste for the women who catered to the U.S. aircrews at places like the Purple Parrot.

Disgust curled Brenna's mouth before she remembered that Sanderson hadn't stayed at the bar the night Lang died. Although he'd already pushed the twelve-hour bottle-to-throttle prohibition for crew members and busted his crew rest, he'd left with the others. If he had a preference for the kind of women who frequented places like the Purple Parrot, he hadn't indulged it that night, at least.

Unbidden and completely unwelcome, a curiosity about the kind of woman Dave Sanderson did prefer snaked into her mind. What had his wife been like before a fatal dependency on alcohol destroyed her? Who had he turned to since then? Where did he spend his nights?

Brenna had looked up his address in the squadron records, had verified that he lived in an apartment on the north side of Oklahoma City. She'd also dropped casual, offhand questions about him to other crew members before General Adams had ordered her to cease her inquiries. No one knew much more about his personal life than Thud

Hendricks had. He was good for a few beers after a long flight, could match the other crewdogs' more outrageous stories with one or two improbable tales of his own, and otherwise stuck to himself.

With any luck, Brenna thought grimly, she'd know more about Dave Sanderson when she returned from Panama. A whole lot more.

The E–3 landed at Howard Air Base in the Canal Zone at four-fifteen in the afternoon. Sweltering tropical heat wrapped around the crew like a wet blanket the moment they deplaned. After a short ride to the red tile-roofed operations building, they conducted the mission debrief.

While the rest of the crew waited for the buses that would take them to their assigned billeting, Brenna strolled into the Ops Center. The people who managed the alert assets knew her by sight and by reputation. Within moments, she'd ascertained Sanderson's status.

He'd pulled a solid week of alert and had just come off alert for a twenty-four-hour stand-down. Her timing couldn't have been more perfect. What's more, he was staying at the Hotel Plaza Paitilla in downtown Panama City, where her crew would also stay.

Most of the time, the Tinker aircrews enjoyed being billeted off-base on overseas missions. It gave them a chance to hit the shops and enjoy the local sights . . . among other things. Since the Panama Invasion in 1989, however, many locals' feelings had swung from relief at having Noriega taken out to a sullen and increasing resentment against the U.S. for interfering in their affairs. More than one crew bus or passenger car with U.S. plates had been caught in the protests and riots that still occurred in the Canal Zone on a regular basis. Six months ago, two U.S. Army troops had been pulled out of their vehicle and beaten.

Although things had settled down lately, the bus driver who chauffeured Brenna and her crew to the Paitilla kept the radio on to listen for news of any disturbances en route. In the process, he treated his passengers to an earsplitting concert of pounding, Latin-flavored reggae. The music assaulted Brenna's ears as the bus wound through a dismal stretch of suburbs known as El Currio, abounding with dilapidated stucco huts, open-fronted bars, shattered streetlights, and shockingly explicit graffiti.

When El Currio gradually gave way to a more established residential area, Brenna breathed a little easier. Relaxing against the seat, she let her gaze roam the narrow, hilly streets lined with two-story white houses. Wrought-iron balconies, lush greenery, and brilliant red and pink hibiscus gave the area a quiet, tropical beauty. Then the bus topped a hill, and she caught a glimpse of a turquoise blue bay in the hazy distance. Like a delicate filigree necklace, the soaring Bridge of the Americas arched above the sparkling waters.

Within moments, the driver turned onto Avenue Balboa and headed for the white, curving high-rise that dominated the east end of the bay. When he pulled up outside the Hotel Plaza Paitilla's revolving glass doors, attendants in the cool, sensible white shirts that were the traditional dress in Panama helped the crew offload their luggage.

After checking in, Brenna reconfirmed their scheduled flight time tomorrow afternoon, which meant they all went into crew rest at two a.m. That gave them plenty of time to eat and have a drink or two at one of the local cantinas, if they were so inclined.

Smiling, she declined a general invitation to dinner. Her plans for the evening centered on a lukewarm shower, an ice cold beer, and tracking down Dave Sanderson, not necessarily in that order. She'd think about dinner later, after she'd figured out just what she'd do when and if she located her quarry.

As it turned out, she got her shower, but no cold beer and no dinner.

After a restorative session under pulsing streams of water, she pulled on a sleeveless green cotton blouse and a silky skirt in a jungle pattern of greens and blues that tied sarong-style at her waist. Taking the pins out of her hair, she ran a brush through the dark brown strands until they swung in a smooth, curving fall that just brushed her shoulders. Anxious now to get on with the business that had brought her here, she applied a minimum of makeup, strapped on a pair of flat-heeled sandals, then grabbed her black Coach shoulder bag that served her both in uniform and in civvies. A quick inventory confirmed that it held her wallet, a copy of her aircrew orders, and an extra fold of bills tucked into the zippered compartment. Since U.S. dollars were almost interchangeable with the Panamanian balboa, she hadn't needed to exchange any currency.

The thought darted into Brenna's mind that she ought to take some kind of a weapon with her. She had no idea if she'd spot her quarry tonight or where he might lead her if she did, but . . .

She glanced around the hotel room speculatively. Aside from the heavy brass lamp on the low table beside the sofa, she didn't spot anything useful. Since there wasn't any way she could conceal that lamp in her bag or on her person without garnering a few strange looks, Brenna shrugged and fastened the flap of her purse. If she was lucky enough to track Sanderson down tonight, she'd just have to rely on her training and her assessment of the situation before she plunged ahead with . . . with whatever.

She almost choked when she stepped out of the elevator and spotted her quarry moving through the lobby in that hip-rolling stride of his. She only saw him from behind, but there was no mistaking the sun-streaked brown hair that curled at the neck of his white shirt. Or the shoulders that strained its seams.

Brenna didn't stop to think. She sure as heck

didn't stop to assess the situation. Adrenaline pumping through her veins, she hurried across the palm-filled lobby in pursuit. Just inside the revolving door she stopped and watched Sanderson fold his rangy frame into a cab.

Frowning, she pushed at the glass door. Given the tortuous city streets, following one of the kamikaze taxi drivers who wove through them at breakneck speed would be a real challenge. While an attendant signaled to a taxi waiting in the rank, Brenna kept her eyes on Sanderson's vehicle as it pulled out of the hotel's curving drive. It braked at the entrance to the street, waiting for an opening in the traffic, and she felt a leap of excitement. One of its rear lights was out.

"Do you see that cab?" she asked, sliding into the back seat of her taxi. "The one with the broken taillight?"

"*Sí, señora.*"

"Follow it. But not too closely. I don't want him to see us."

Inured to the foibles of *touristas*, the driver shrugged, pulled down the meter flag, and shoved the gearshift into drive. They left the Plaza Paitilla with a squeal of threadbare tires.

Keeping some distance behind Sanderson's cab, her own went careening down Avenue Balboa with the total disregard for pedestrians or oncoming vehicles displayed by taxi drivers all over the world. Brenna clutched at the armrest as they swerved through traffic, then swung right onto a major side street. A few moments later, the single taillight ahead of them flashed, and Sanderson's cab rolled to a stop at the entrance to a narrow street lined with tourist shops, restaurants, and bars.

Brenna urged her driver to pull over half a block behind and made a mental note of their location. *Calle Rosa*, according to the enameled street sign tacked to a stuccoed wall.

"I'll get out here," she said, fumbling in her purse for her wallet as she watched Sanderson saunter down the narrow, busy street.

"Are you sure, *señora*?" The driver stretched an arm across the back of the seat and twisted around. "This part of town is not so good."

No kidding!

But Brenna had seen worse areas. There were a few square blocks of Washington, D.C. she wouldn't stroll through, even in the bright light of day. During one rotation to Turkey, she'd gotten lost in a part of Izmir she didn't want to ever set foot in again. But the side streets of Panama City on a hot, steamy night emanated their own particular menace.

It wasn't that they were deserted. Just the opposite, in fact. This early in the evening, throngs of men wearing gauzy white Panama shirts and women dressed in everything from tight, leopard-skin leggings to colorful cotton skirts filled the narrow lanes. Among them, Brenna caught glimpses of obvious foreigners. U.S. servicemen stationed in the Zone, she guessed, and sailors from the ships of every flag that waited to transit the Canal. And of course, there were the children. Sharp-eyed, quicksilver street creatures who catered to the pleasure-seeking night crowds and hawked everything from chewing gum to drugs.

Streets like Calle Rosa abounded in every port in every corner of the world. Brenna had been down one or two of them in her more reckless youth, but always in the company of other crew members. She hesitated with one hand on the door handle, her common sense battling the driving need that had brought her here in the first place.

The sight of Sanderson strolling off into a hazy twilight pierced by flashing neon bar signs decided the matter. Passing a fold of bills to the driver, she slipped out of the cab.

Immediately, the sounds and scents of Calle Rosa assaulted her. Music from the discos drummed on the night air. An occasional burst of adult laughter vied with the high-pitched shouts of children trying to draw customers into various establishments. The mouthwatering aroma of charcoal-grilled pork and fried plantain drifted out of the restaurants.

Telling herself that the sudden, hollow feeling in her stomach was due as much to hunger as to tension, Brenna wove a path through the slow-moving crowds. She kept to the inner edge of the sidewalk, prepared to pop into a doorway if the tall figure ahead of her gave any sign of turning around. She felt a little silly, like an amateur James Bond, and more than a little nervous.

Halfway down the Calle Rosa, a small, grubby hand clutched at her skirt.

"*Señora!* Hey, *Americana*! You come in here, to my uncle's restaurant."

Her eyes on Sanderson's back, Brenna shook her head at the dark-haired child. "No, not tonight."

"Yes, yes! It is good, this restaurant. And very clean." Tenacious, he tugged at her skirt. "Come inside, *señora*."

The blue and green jungle print fabric parted, baring most of Brenna's thigh. Annoyed, she pulled at the material caught in the boy's determined fist.

"Not tonight, *muchacho*."

A wolf whistle pierced the night behind her, followed by a ribald comment in Spanish she only half understood. The boy hung on, not about to let go of a potential customer, and sent her a wide-eyed, soulful look.

"But the *ceviche* my uncle makes, it is the best in Panama City! He uses only the freshest fish, soaked all day in the lime, and serves it with the onions and the chilies. You will like it, *señora*. come inside."

"Some other time."

The unmistakable whip of authority in Brenna's voice had intimidated older and brawnier males than this one. Blinking, the boy loosened his hold.

He tossed a very adult comment after her as she hurried on, but Brenna ignored it. Her whole being was focused on the street ahead, and the absence of a certain pair of broad shoulders.

Damn! Sanderson must have turned off onto a side alley while she'd been distracted by the child.

Hurrying forward, she peered down one narrow street and saw nothing but shadows. The next alley offered a few dark windows and the dimly lit entrance to what looked like a disco at the far end. Turning, Brenna swept Calle Rosa once again in both directions. When she caught no sight of her quarry, she took a single step into the narrow alley, then stopped.

This was crazy. If she'd seen one of her troops about to plunge down a dark street, alone, in this part of the city, she would have berated his lack of sense and sent him back to the base immediately. For all she knew, this web of back streets was off-limits. She could be risking her career as well as her personal safety if she took another step.

She hesitated a second too long.

Without warning, a hard hand closed around her upper arm and spun her into the shadows. In the space of a single heartbeat, she was slammed back against the wall and pinned in place by a dark, looming presence.

Immediately, instincts honed by a string of self-defense courses and months of Air Force survival training kicked in. Without thinking, without hesitating, Brenna brought up her knee.

Her attacker parried the thrust with a vicious curse and a twist of his lower body that dug his hips into Brenna's and left her gasping. Ducking, he barely managed to avoid the balled fist she aimed at the soft, vulnerable cartilage in his nose.

Anticipating her next move, he jerked his head back, away from the forehead Brenna tried to smash into his face. While she was still off balance from the move, he caught her wrists and shoved them behind her back. Thrusting a knee between hers to keep her from twisting free, he brought her up hard against his body.

"Are you out of your goddamned mind?"

Panting, incensed by the intimate hold, Brenna turned a furious face up to his.

"No, but . . . you are! I'm going to have your head . . . on a platter for this attack, Sanderson."

The brutal grip on her wrists tightened, pinioning her against the unyielding wall of his chest. She couldn't move, could hardly breathe.

"Attack?" Derision deepened his voice to that mocking drawl she hated. "Is that how you want to play this one, Duggan?"

"I'm . . . not playing."

"No? Sure looked to me like you were doing something pretty close to it back there on the street."

"What are you talking about?"

"Christ, woman, I couldn't believe it when I turned around and saw you flashing your legs, like some fifty-peso whore trolling for customers. What are you trying to do, give the locals a little competition?"

"Let me go."

"I ought to. I sure as hell ought to. It might be

fun watching you turn that Arctic stare on the sleazers who roam these streets. And watching them ignore it while they rip off the half skirt you're wearing."

She dragged in a shallow, furious breath. "You're the only sleazer who's bothered me."

"I don't think you even know what bothered is, lady. Maybe I should show you."

Her skirt rode up her legs as his knee moved against her. Crudely. Intimately.

"You bastard."

He smiled then. A small twist of his lips that sent fear feathering down her spine. Fear, and something else. Something that made her feel twisted and sick and filled with disgust. For herself. For him.

"What are you doing here, Duggan?"

Brenna barely heard the soft, dangerous question over the pounding of her heart.

"Tell me."

The dim light cast his face in shadows, but his eyes held a feral gleam that told her he wasn't going to let her go until he got an answer.

"I was following you."

The admission surprised him. Good! Surprise was just about the only weapon Brenna had left in her arsenal right now.

Eyes thinned to glittering slits, he stared down at her. "Why?"

"Because I think you know more than you told me about Sergeant Lang's death. Because I don't trust you."

His rock-hard body tensed, and Brenna felt the movement along every raging nerve.

In that moment, she understood how much it was costing him to hold back. His muscles shivered with the force of their leashed power. His heart slammed against hers. He could hurt her so easily, could degrade her far more than he had. But he held himself, and her, in check.

"I told you before to get the hell off my tail, Duggan. I'm telling you again, for the last time."

The need to shatter his control pounded through her. She knew it was dangerous, sensed she was playing with a fire that might consume them both. But she wanted to, *had to*, push him one more inch, one more . . .

"Or what?"

The breathless taunt hovered between them like a single, shared heartbeat. For a long moment they were locked together, unmoving, unspeaking. Then he lowered his head until his mouth was a whisper away from hers.

"Or this."

When his lips came down on hers, they were as hard as the rest of his body. And as powerful. And far more skilled than Brenna had dreamed they would be.

With searing honesty, she acknowledged that she'd goaded him into this kiss. A tiny part of her ached to respond. The rest of her was shamed by that flicker of need.

She didn't struggle, but she refused to yield. If she'd been thinking with anything near her normal lucidity, she would have realized that Sanderson would view her lack of response as simply another challenge.

Transferring both of her wrists into one hand, he wrapped the other around her neck. A thumb slid under her chin and tilted her head. His mouth slanted over hers. Taking. And, damn him, giving.

When he lifted his head, Brenna didn't move. Her breath rasped on the night, as uneven as his. He stared down at her through narrowed eyes, then released her.

Folding her arms across her waist to hide the trembling in her hands, Brenna leaned back against the wall. The shattering kiss had consumed her stark fear of moments before. She wasn't quite sure what was left.

"You're showing your age," she got out on a note of dripping scorn. "That kind of heavy-handed technique went out with bell bottoms and sideburns."

To her astonishment, his mouth curved. "It went out long before that, Duggan. I guess I'm a throwback or ..."

She snorted derisively.

"Or you stir some atavisitc urges in me I never knew I had," he finished.

"And you've never learned to control your urges, have you?"

"No, I haven't. Maybe you'd better remember that."

"Go to hell, Sanderson."

"I'm on my way," he said softly. "God knows, I'm on my way."

While Brenna stared up at his shadowed eyes, he raised a hand and brushed a thumb across her lower lip. This time his touch was so gentle, so tender, that she drew back in startled surprise.

Her involuntary movement seemed to pull him from some distant plane. The familiar, mocking gleam she detested lit his eyes, and he cupped her chin with less gentleness than before.

"The problem is, Duggan, I'm thinking seriously about taking you with me."

"What makes you think you can take me anywhere?"

"Don't kid yourself, lady. You're hot for it, as hot as I am."

She slapped his hand away.

The sound of flesh on flesh ricocheted through the dark alley and ripped apart the shaky cease-fire that had sprung up between them.

Chapter Eleven

Brenna had had enough.

Enough of his overdone, macho sexism. Enough of his deliberate attempts to intimidate her. Enough of her confused, gutless responses to both.

With the sound of the slap still echoing between them, she lifted her chin and invoked the authority that was as natural to her as breathing.

"That's enough, Sanderson," she ordered in a cool, calm tone of command. "I'm getting tired of these pathetic displays of hyperactive testosterone."

For a moment, she wasn't sure if she'd gotten through to him. He didn't back off, didn't give her the space she so desperately craved. Then the lips that had wrought such dark, sensual magic on hers just moments ago curved.

"Pathetic, huh?" he asked with just a hint of laughter.

"Pathetic. Do us both a favor and call a halt to these big, bad caveman tactics. First, they're becoming repetitious. Second, they don't work with me. Third, they're not going to divert my attention from—"

"All right, all right. I get the picture."

"Good. Just keep it in mind while we focus on the real issue here, and that's the connection between you and this Mad Dog Petrocelli and Sergeant Lang."

"We've already been down this road. Give it up, Duggan. You signed the LOD. That's the end of it."

"That might have been the end of it, except Lang's widow wasn't satisfied with the results. She's requested a redetermination."

His eyes narrowed. "Since when?"

"Since a week ago. Her request is buried under a stack of papers in some lawyer's in-basket right now, but it's in the system."

The news that Janeen wasn't giving up didn't appear to sit well with him. Frowning, he plowed a hand through his hair. Brenna immediately pounded home the small advantage her bit of news gave her.

"Your friend Petrocelli might have charmed Janeen Lang with his flamboyant, outrageous tales, but she's tough, a lot tougher than she looks. And she believes in her husband. She's not going to give up."

The hand he'd half lowered froze in place for several long seconds. Before her eyes, he seemed to harden, to take on a menacing intensity. When he stepped toward her, Brenna felt the ground she'd just reclaimed slip away.

The man who'd held her so roughly a few moments ago had infuriated her and disgusted her, then thoroughly confused her with his unexpected gentleness.

This one frightened the hell out of her. He didn't touch her, didn't constrain her in any way, but Brenna felt the threat emanating from every line of his taut body.

"You want to run that by me one more time, Duggan? The part about my friend, Petrocelli?"

There wasn't any hint of laughter, rueful or otherwise, in his voice now. It was cold and low and raised the hairs on her arms.

"Tell me, Duggan," he said softly. "Tell me about . . ."

"Hey, man!" The slurred voice boomed out of the darkness from a few feet away. "Looks to me like the lady don't want your business."

Sanderson turned, and Brenna edged to one side to peer around his solid form. A hulking young man with no discernible neck and the distinctive haircut of a U.S. Marine stood at the entrance to the alley, weaving unsteadily from side to side.

A second voice as fuzzed as the first broke the stillness. "Jesuz, Walters, what the hell are you doin'? C'mon, lez get back to the ship."

Ignoring the unseen speaker, the brawny young man squinted into shadows. "Hey, she's American! You an American, lady?"

"Move on, Marine."

At Sanderson's low warning, the grunt looked from Brenna to him, then back again.

"This guy botherin' you, lady?"

A hand tugged at his arm. "For crissakes, Walters, this ain't none of our business."

The big Marine's lip curled as he planted both feet wide and measured Sanderson from head to toe. "Maybe I'm makin' it my business. Maybe I don't like seein' some long-haired wuss come down heavy on a lady, s'pecially an American lady."

"I think you'd better listen to your friend, pal."

Walters bristled at the soft menace in Sanderson's voice. Yanking his arm free of his buddy's hold, he staggered into the alley. "How 'bout you take your advice and stick it up your ass, *pal*? Better yet, I'll do it for you."

His threat would have carried a lot more weight if he hadn't tripped over his own feet. Suddenly, Brenna decided she'd had all the bristling male she could take for one night. She wasn't about to let this well-intentioned if belligerent young grunt take on Dave Sanderson. Despite the kid's bull-like size, he was falling-down drunk. Even sober, she doubted he'd be a match for the man who had countered her own skilled moves so easily.

Besides, there wasn't any reason to prolong this farce. Wherever Sanderson had been heading when he'd started down the Calle Rosa, he wouldn't go there now. Not while she was anywhere in the vicinity.

She needed to fall back and regroup. She needed to understand what she'd said that had caused Sanderson to suddenly freeze. She had to get her confused thoughts in order before she confronted him again. Next time, she promised silently, she'd choose the meeting ground. And they'd play the game by her rules.

"I'm Lieutenant Colonel Duggan, with the 552d AWACS wing," she told the Marines crisply. "I appreciate your offer of assistance, but it's not necessary."

The two men gaped at her for several long seconds, then the shorter one wagged his head from side to side.

"I never seen no lieutenant colonel with legs like that."

Ignoring Sanderson's mocking half smile, Brenna tugged the twisted fabric of her skirt into place and brushed past him. Three long strides brought her to the entrance to the alleyway.

"I was just heading back to my hotel. Would one of you help me flag down a cab?"

"Duggan . . ."

She threw a look over one shoulder.

"We haven't finished this little discussion."

"No," she replied, "we haven't. I'll let you know where and when we'll continue it."

She'd let him know!

Dave remained motionless as the sound of her footsteps and the heavy, unsteady tread of the two Marines faded. A whistle pierced the darkness of the alleyway. Brenna murmured something, then Walters mumbled in response. A car door slammed. Gears ground out a protest as they were forced into drive.

Christ! *She'd let him know!* What did it take to shake this woman?

He'd felt the imprint of her body on every level surface of his skin, had come closer to losing his control tonight than ever before in his life. She, on the other hand, had folded her arms, sent him one of her patented don't-hand-me-that-crap looks, and told him to get real.

If he hadn't felt her flicker of response, so quickly and ruthlessly suppressed, Dave might have been convinced Lieutenant Colonel Duggan was the cold, emotionless commander he needed to believe she was. But he'd felt it, and wanted more.

Despite the danger, despite the sheer stupidity of it, he'd let himself explore that tiny quiver. Let himself touch her. For just an instant, he'd let the feel of the pulsing, satiny smooth skin sink into his soul.

If she hadn't drawn back, if she hadn't dropped that offhand remark about Petrocelli, he might have taken the next step and forgotten all about the specter that hung over them both.

At the thought, a trickle of cold sweat rolled down between his shoulder blades. What the hell had happened? Why was Duggan still on his case? Petrocelli had assured him the colonel's unofficial inquiries had been turned off. And what was this crap about Mad Dog and Janeen Lang?

Warning indicators pinged like crazy in his mind. There were too many surprises popping up, too many questions swirling around unanswered. His instincts urged him to abort this mission, to walk out of this dark alley, grab a taxi, and bolt back to the hotel.

He took a step, then jerked to a halt. He couldn't back out now. There was too much riding on this contact. Too many months of careful planning. Too many nights in a cold sweat. Too many deaths.

Faces floated before him in the darkness. Kristine's, tear-soaked, ravaged by the alcohol that had been her solace and his destruction. Andy Lang's, smiling as he worked with his students, then puzzled as he listened to Dave's explanation for the way he'd handled that damned track.

And Brenna's. Christ, Brenna's. Her silky cloud of dark hair framing her face. Her full mouth set. Her eyes frosted with blue ice as she cut his feet out from under him with a few well chosen words.

No, he couldn't back away now. He'd have to go in blind and trust the instincts that had kept him alive this long. They'd have to carry him through one more night, until he could get some answers to his questions.

Rolling his shoulders to break the stranglehold of tension that gripped them, he left the alley and joined the motley throng on Calle Rosa. A five-minute walk brought him to another side street. A flashing neon sign halfway down the street displayed a female shape, hips rocking from side to side and breasts bare.

The moment Dave stepped inside the club, cigarette smoke as thick as a San Francisco fog grabbed at his lungs and triggered the craving that never left him. Cursing, he dropped the hand he'd lifted toward his shirt pocket and threaded his way through the tables to an empty one in the corner.

He ordered a tequila from a bored waitress in a skin-tight wrap of pink Spandex. Legs outstretched, he let his gaze settle on the dancer on the postage stamp–sized stage. Ignoring the hoots and calls of encouragement from the men seated around the stage, she moved in a slow, erotic rhythm totally at odds with the pulsing beat of the canned music. She was higher than a moon shot, Dave thought, his eyes drifting from her face to her lush breasts, then down over wide hips banded by a skimpy red thong that ran between her legs.

High, and new to the business, Dave decided. Her skin wouldn't retain that golden hue for long, or her mouth that private, pouting half smile. She'd be on her knees within a few months, offering to perform any act, any service, to get the money for her next hit. God, how he hated this place and what it could do to people.

His fingers curled around the shot glass the waitress sloshed down before him. With a quick toss, he put away half the cloudy tequila. White fire burned a path down his throat and steadied the nerves that had been jumping like ants on a hot sidewalk since he'd left the alley.

That had been Kristine's favorite excuse, he remembered grimly. Her nerves were shot. The only difference between them, she'd screamed at him, was that one drink worked for him and she needed two or three. Deliberately, he shoved all thoughts of his ex-wife out of his mind and focused on the girl moving slowly in the haze of smoke.

He was still nursing the second half of his drink when a slender, mustached man in Reeboks and a T-shirt hailing the victors of the last World Cup soccer championship strolled up to the table.

"Do you like the girl?"

Dave lifted an indifferent shoulder. "I've seen worse."

"This one is special."

"They all are."

"No, no, I swear. She's still fresh. But expensive, my friend. Very expensive."

Tilting his head, Dave gave the man a casual scrutiny. He'd never seen the Panamanian before, which didn't surprise him. He hadn't recognized any of his previous contacts, either. The people he was doing business with were too smart and too good at their trade to use the same underlings more than once.

"How expensive?" he asked.

The man pulled out a chair. "You can afford her, my friend."

"I'm not your friend. How much?"

A few moments later, they agreed on the price. If Dave hadn't been coiled so tight and fighting not to show it, he might have felt a spear of pity for a girl whose body could be sold to a stranger for less than the cost of a good steak.

He didn't feel any pity, however, or any sense of anticipation. Giving the girl a slow, assessing look, he reached into the top of his black leather jump boot and extracted a fold of bills. Without speaking, he shoved them across the table.

The other man slipped the bills into his pants pocket without bothering to count them. Nor did he check to see if the piece of paper he'd been sent to collect was tucked inside them.

They both knew it was. Dave wouldn't be here otherwise.

"There is a room at the back of the bar," the Panamanian said, rising. "I'll send the girl there after this dance."

Dave curled his hand around his glass. "Later. I haven't finished my tequila."

"As you will."

Shrugging, the contact turned and strolled through the haze-filled room. He kept one hand in his pocket, jingling the loose change. Yet Dave knew the Panamanian had that fold of bills in a tight, sweaty grip. His life would be worth a whole hell of a lot less than the glassy-eyed dancer's if he lost the sheet of paper concealed inside the bills to the pickpockets who swarmed like mosquitoes through this part of town.

Dave's fingers tightened around the shot glass as he watched the T-shirted figure disappear into a blue-gray haze of smoke. It was done. He'd made the pass. Within an hour, two at most, the most powerful drug cartel in South America would have in its possession the AWACS schedule for the next two weeks.

Not that they'd do anything with it. Not yet. According to Mad Dog, he and Dave were still on probation. The big guys didn't quite trust them. They'd test this information first, send a few small shipments. If the flights slipped through AWACS' net and the shit hit the street, fifty thousand dollars would appear in the account Mad Dog had opened in a bank in Grand Cayman.

And Dave would pass another schedule.

Assuming he lived that long, he thought cynically. One slip, one false step, and there wouldn't be enough of him left for fish bait. His new business partners played rough, and they played for keeps.

Which meant he had to get Duggan off his back, and fast. She didn't know anything yet. She couldn't, or he would've heard about it. But she was keeping him in a sweat, in more ways than one. She and Mad Dog.

Bending his elbow, he took a swallow of the tequila and slanted a quick look at his watch. An hour, he figured. He'd be back at the hotel within an hour. Then he'd make some calls and find out what the hell his partner was up to.

Dave walked through the lobby of the Plaza Paitilla some fifty minutes later. Stale cigarette smoke filled his pores, and the empty, apathetic smile of the dancer snaked through his mind. He felt wired and edgy and restless.

Maybe if he'd taken what the girl had offered in that throaty, slurred voice, he wouldn't be so tense right now. But he'd known even before he opened the door to the stuffy back room he wouldn't use the dancer to gain the release his body craved. She'd been floating so freely in her own universe by then, she hadn't noticed either his presence or his departure.

Stabbing the elevator button, Dave leaned a forearm against the marble-faced wall and waited impatiently for it to arrive. In the short interval, he tried to convince himself that he'd left the girl out of weariness, or pity, or distaste. But he knew damn well what had drawn him out of that back room.

She was probably pacing the floor of Room 551 right now, as wired by their earlier confrontation as he was. The helpful desk clerk who'd verified Duggan's room number a few moments go had offered to ring it for him, but Dave had declined. He had to get himself under control before he confronted Lieutenant Colonel Brenna Duggan again.

The thought of going head to head with her

again sent a spear of heat into his belly. Muttering a curse, Dave stabbed the elevator button again.

She'd let him know. When she was ready to continue their "discussion," *she'd let him know.*

Dave shook his head. Duggan still didn't understand that she wasn't setting the rules in this particular game.

The elevator doors pinged open. A few moments later, he shoved his card key into the lock and entered the chill of his air-conditioned room.

He'd left the drapes open earlier, and the wall of windows at the far end of the room now framed a spectacular vista. Far across the dark bay, the lights of the Bridge of the Americas spanned the night sky. Like glittering strands of diamonds, they hung suspended against a backdrop of black velvet.

The sharp beauty of the view pulled at Dave. The bridge at night was like the woman two floors above, he thought. All long, clean lines. A superstructure of hard steel framed against clouds of soft darkness. Shoving his hands in his pockets, he crossed to the window and waited for the call he knew would come.

The shrill of the phone shattered the stillness just moments later. As soon as Dave answered, Petrocelli jumped in.

"Did you make the pass?"

"Yeah, I made it."

His partner gave a slow hiss of satisfaction. "Good. No problems?"

"Not with the pass."

The deliberate response sparked a sudden tightness at the other end of the phone. "With what, then?"

"Duggan's down here."

"Shit!"

"That about sums up how I felt when I turned around and found her tagging me tonight."

"Did she see anything?"

"Give me a little credit."

"Yeah, yeah. What the fuck is she doing there? I thought we'd turned her off."

"You thought wrong. About Duggan, and a few other things, apparently."

Silence descended, sharp and crystalline.

"Like what?" Petrocelli asked after a moment.

"Like Mrs. Lang." The anger Dave had held in check since Brenna had dropped her little bombshell exploded. "Why the hell didn't you tell me you'd gone to see Lang's wife?"

"Hey, I was just checking the woman out."

"I warned you before about flying solo, Petrocelli."

"Look, she was asking all kinds of questions about me. I figured I'd let her see how charming and debonair ol' Mad Dog really is, and in the process find out what she knew. Which is *nada*. She's safe, Dave. Soft as butter, but a whole lot sweeter." A chuckle drifted over the line. "I wouldn't mind spreading a little of Janeen Lang on my toast in the mornings."

Dave cursed viciously under his breath. Petrocelli had always been as cocky as a banty rooster, and just about as hardheaded. In their Air Force days, Dave had flown cover for him too many times to count while he talked or battled his way out of a tight spot. He was still flying cover for him, only the spots were a whole hell of a lot tighter now.

"Mrs. Lang's not as soft as you seem to think," he shot at Petrocelli. "She's asked the Air Force to take another look at her husband's death."

"Yeah, I heard about that. Don't sweat, there are still a few folks at Langley who owe me for past favors. The request is buried under a pile of cases somewhere. It won't come to anything."

"Duggan seems to think otherwise."

"Duggan again! That female is starting to get on my nerves, big time."

Dave smiled grimly into the darkness. "Mine, too."

"We're gonna have to do something about the bitch."

His smile flattened, then disappeared. "Back off, Mad Dog. She's suspicious, but she doesn't have anything."

"She's getting too close."

"Back off, I said!"

The barked command produced a silence that stretched for several seconds.

"Don't try to pull rank on me, big guy," Petrocelli replied after a moment, his voice low. "We're in this together. And we're flying without any parachutes this time. Neither one of us can bail out if this baby blows up in our face."

"Do you think I don't know that? I'm the one down here taking all the risks, remember?"

"You knew what we were getting into when we started this game," Mad Dog shot back.

"Yeah, I knew."

"It'll be worth it in the long run. You know it will."

Maybe. Dave wasn't so sure anymore. He hadn't been sure of anything in a long time, he realized wearily. Not since Kristine. Not since Lang. But he was in too deep to turn back now.

"Look, I'll take care of Duggan." He rubbed the back of his neck, wondering how he was going to manage that particular trick. "You just make sure Mrs. Lang's request doesn't see the light of day for a long, long time."

"Consider it buried, buddy." The bluff heartiness was back in Petrocelli's voice. "Consider it dead and buried."

Dave let the receiver drop. Too restless to sleep, he turned his back on the view and headed for the bathroom. Maybe a shower would help.

It didn't.

He dried off, slung the towel around his neck, and switched off the lights in the bathroom, plunging it and the bedroom beyond into darkness. He hadn't bothered to turn on a bedside lamp, preferring to heave the drapes open to the nightscape.

Naked except for the towel around his neck, he walked into the bedroom. The clean, clear lights of the bridge shone like a beacon in the darkness. Following a narrow path of moonlight, he crossed to the windows.

Dave had no idea how long he stood there before he caught the slither of sound behind him. He didn't move a muscle, but every one of his senses slammed into high torque as he tried to identify the soft whisper.

It wasn't the click of a silencer. He knew that.

Or the snicker of a knife blade cutting through the air. He'd heard that often enough.

Or even the twist of the plastic seal on a liquor bottle. Thanks to Kristine, he could pick that sound out in the middle of a hurricane.

Preparing mentally and physically to launch himself across the room at this unknown threat, Dave pivoted on the ball of one foot.

The shadowy figure seated in the bedroom's only easy chair swung one leg in a casual arc. The silky fabric of her skirt swished at the movement. As Dave stared at her in disbelief, her soft, mocking drawl filled the darkness.

"Nice view, Sanderson."

Chapter Twelve

In the past few months, Dave had perfected a near mastery over his reflexes. He'd managed to control his reactions in a few situations he'd never experienced before, and in a few more he hoped he'd never experience again. Still, it took everything he had to reply casually to the woman surveying him with cool amusement.

"Hello, Duggan. How'd you get in?"

"The desk clerk gave me a key."

"Accommodating guy."

"Isn't he? He seemed to think we'd missed some sort of an assignation. Said you'd asked for my room number earlier. He was only too happy to help us connect."

"Is that why you're here? To connect?"

"Watch it, Sanderson," she said gently. "Your testosterone is showing." Her gaze slid down his body. "More or less."

Despite the fact that his heart was still thumping from a combination of tension and shock, Dave felt a rumble of laughter deep in his chest. Shaking his head, he dragged the towel from his neck and wrapped it around his hips.

"Doesn't anything ever throw you?"

"Not for long."

"I'll keep that in mind."

"You do that."

Leaning his shoulders against the wall, he folded his arms across his chest. From this distance his unexpected guest wasn't much more than a patchwork of pale shadows, dimly illuminated by the moonlight streaming over his shoulder. A smooth curtain of dark hair partially obscured her face. One long leg continued to swish back and forth with maddening nonchalance. With some effort, Dave tore his eyes from that curving ribbon of white.

"I take it you're here to continue our . . . discussion."

"Since you go back on alert tomorrow, this seemed like as good a time as any."

"What if I tell you I've decided we don't have anything more to discuss?"

"No good, Sanderson."

Dave didn't miss the steely resolve beneath her light response. Shrugging, he gave her a mixture of truth and his own iron resolve.

"You took me by surprise there in the alley. I didn't like the idea of you following me. I liked the idea of Mrs. Lang requesting another investigation into Sergeant Lang's death even less. But

I've had time to think about both since you marched off with your Marine escort."

And he'd had time to talk to Petrocelli. He still wasn't happy about the recent sequence of events. Although Mad Dog swore he'd turned his own peculiar brand of charm on the young widow and soothed her doubts, Dave suspected her request for redetermination somehow sprang from Petrocelli's trip to western Oklahoma. The request was buried, however. Petrocelli would see that it stayed at the bottom of someone's in-box until time blurred the circumstances of Andrew Lang's death even more.

"And?" she prompted.

"And," he replied with deliberate callousness, "I decided it wasn't any of my business if Mrs. Lang wants to wallow in her own pain. Another investigation won't answer her questions any better than the first one did. Obviously, you think so, too, or you wouldn't be down here tagging after me."

He could see that he'd struck a nerve. Her crossed leg stilled, and a tense little silence descended. With the ruthlessness of a predator probing the weaknesses in his prey's defenses, Dave zeroed in on the reasons behind her foolhardy stroll down the Calle Rosa.

"You've kind of put yourself out on a limb here, haven't you, Duggan? You wrapped up your part of the official investigation all nice and tidy when you signed off on the LOD, yet you're still poking and prying. Making phone calls. Changing flight schedules. Following me to the Calle Rosa. Are you doing all this on your own, or do you have some backing for these little extracurricular activities?"

When she didn't answer, he gave her a small, nasty smile. "I didn't think so. You can't keep on me like this, and you know it. You'll have to put up or shut up pretty soon, lady. Make some kind of formal charge, or get off my back."

Steepling her fingers, she rested her chin on their tips. "All right, let's come at this from another direction. Suppose this doesn't have to lead to a formal charge? Suppose we work together, instead of against each other?"

"Suppose we don't."

"If you're keeping something back about Andy Lang and your friend Petrocelli, tell me. Help Janeen Lang know that her faith in her husband wasn't misplaced. In return, I'll do what I can to help you if those answers implicate you in any way."

The urge to give her a kernel of reassurance to take back to Lang's widow gripped him. Dave steeled himself against it. There was too much at stake. Too many lives involved, his included.

"There aren't any answers, Duggan, trust me."

She pinned him with a long, cool look. "I want to trust you. God knows why, but I want to. Give me a reason to."

Her voice carried to him through the shadows, low and urgent with the offer of a truce between them. More than a truce. A trust. Dave fought the overwhelming desire to meet her halfway.

"I can't."

"Can't? Or won't?"

He might have known she wouldn't give up. Her silky skirt whispered as she rose and moved toward him. The moonlight spilling through the windows illuminated her more clearly now. Her skin gleamed opalescent in the light, and her hair brushed her shoulders in a sable swirl that made Dave fist his hands to keep from reaching out.

She was so close he could smell the subtle combination of shampoo and lotion and woman that was hers alone. Hear the skip in her breath. See the dark smudge of lashes around eyes that pulled at something in him he'd thought long dead. He hardened his voice and his heart against it, and her.

"What is this, Duggan? Rule number twenty-seven in the commander's handbook? Look after the troops and keep them out of trouble, even if you have to visit their bedrooms in the middle of the night to do it."

She ignored his biting sarcasm, or had become inured to it. "Are you in trouble?"

"Jesus, let it go."

"Let me help you. Whatever it is that's got you twisted into this tight coil, let me help you with it."

The simple offer got to him as nothing else could have. She'd been on his case for weeks now. Their every contact had begun as a small skirmish and quickly escalated into pitched battle. Although he knew damn well she suspected him of withholding information, or worse, the sense of responsibility she lugged around like a suitcase forced her to take this reluctant step. That, and the indefinable attraction sizzling between them.

She'd tried to deny it, but the sexual pull was there.

He'd tried to subdue it, but every time he caught a glimpse of her, it grabbed at his chest ... among other parts of his body.

It hovered between them now like a shimmering curtain, waiting for one of them to push it aside and reveal what lay behind.

Against every grain of common sense, Dave decided to take one, small look behind that curtain. Lifting his hand, he curved a palm along her cheek. Her skin was cool to his touch, and smooth, and so soft he ached.

"The only way you can help me is to turn around and walk out of here. Now. Before I do something we'll both regret in the morning."

He was right. Brenna knew he was right.

If she reached up and covered his hand with hers, she'd regret it, probably long before morning. If she turned her head a few inches and pressed her lips to the palm cradling her cheek, she'd hate herself for it.

She didn't trust him. She didn't even like him. And she wanted to brush her fingertips across the broad planes of his chest more than she'd ever wanted anything in her life.

The impulse tore her apart. For a few breathless moments, she felt as though she were splintering into separate halves, each warring with the other. Her rational mind fought to subdue irrational instincts. A lifetime of rigid discipline clashed with her body's spiraling needs. The officer in her struggled to keep the woman in line.

Then the hand nestled against her cheek slid lower and threaded through her hair to curve around her neck. He brought her closer, and fierce anticipation streaked through her.

"We're playing with fire here, Duggan."

This was insane, her mind screamed. Irrational. Illogical. A violation of her self-imposed standards that allowed no fraternization with other crew members, especially not with one she couldn't bring herself to trust. Yet every second he looked down at her with that mocking challenge in his eyes, a heat too long repressed crept through her veins.

"I know," she whispered.

Her hands splayed against his bare chest, burrowing through the soft, springy hair. His muscles jumped under her fingertips, giving her a heady sense of power that was more potent, more intoxicating, than anything she'd ever felt with a man.

She wanted him. She didn't trust him. Didn't understand the demons that drove him. Yet she wanted him with a searing intensity that blurred rational thought and left her with a single need.

And he wanted her. It was there, behind the mockery and the challenge and the guarded watchfulness in his eyes. Behind the seeming casualness of his hold.

Tomorrow, she told herself fiercely. Tomorrow, she'd sort out this tangled mess. Tomorrow, she'd rail against this idiocy, just as he would. Tonight, she just wanted to touch him. And taste him. And satisfy the dark, liquid urgency he generated within her.

"I let you walk out of that alley, Brenna. I'm fast reaching the point where I'm not going to let you walk out of this room."

Much later, she would wonder whether she would've pulled back if he called her "Duggan" in his usual, sarcastic way. Whether she might have exercised the caution that was so much a part of her nature, and salvaged at least a little of her pride. But the husky sound of her name on his lips stilled the last shrill protest and gave her a quiver of hope. For a foolish moment, Brenna let herself believe they might both find something they hadn't been looking for in each other's touch.

Slowly, she slid her palms upward. His flesh was warm under hers, despite the chill of the air-conditioning. More than warm. Flushed. Hot. Giving in to a desire so strong she ached with it, she leaned forward and brushed her lips across the taut skin of his shoulder.

He didn't move. Didn't react, other than to tighten his body even more. But his very rigidity added to her sense of power.

She was establishing the rules here. She was setting the pace. For now. Every instinct she possessed told her Sanderson wouldn't remain passive for long. With the unpredictability and danger than simmered just under his skin, he'd explode. But she, and she alone, had the power to trigger that explosion.

All she had to do was set the spark to his fuse. She curled her arms around his neck. Her fingers tangled in the too-long mane. Craving the feel of his body against hers, she arched into him. Triumph soared through her as he twisted his hand in her hair at the back of her neck and anchored her head for his kiss.

His mouth came down on hers with the same driving force he'd used in the alley. And with the same skill. Slanting his head, he molded her lips, shaping them to fit his.

His scent surrounded her, a spicy blend of soap and shampoo and heated male. Brenna drank it in, as eagerly as she took in the taste of his mouth on hers. Elbows bent, arms locked around his neck, she drew herself up on her toes and matched his hunger with hers.

His other arm banded her waist, dragging her even closer. The friction of her body against his dislodged the towel draped around his hips. It slid down and landed at their feet.

Through the thin layers of her clothing, Brenna felt his erection rock hard against her belly. Every one of her muscles leaped in response. Heat arrowed through her womb, so intense she had to drag her mouth from his and lean back in his hold, gasping. The movement canted her hips even more into his.

He sucked in a quick breath, then brought the hand curled around her neck down over her shoulder. When he tugged at the first button on her blouse, Brenna knew he could feel her heart hammering against her breast. Unbidden, his jeering words from the alley rose to taunt her. He was right, she thought on a wave of shame. She was as hot for it as he was.

As quickly as the thought came, she shoved it away. She'd deal with her shame and her guilt later. At this moment, her only focus was the man staring down at her as he freed the last of the buttons and pushed her blouse aside.

His hand cupped her breast in its thin covering of silk and lace. Brenna bit down hard on her lower lip, willing herself not to moan when he lifted and shaped and stroked her.

"Nice," he murmured, bending to brush his mouth across the mounded curve. "Cool and smooth and very nice. Just like the rest of you, Duggan."

His teeth nipped her tingling flesh, and Brenna closed her eyes for a few seconds. Then the need to be an equal player in this dark, sensual game asserted itself. Smiling, she slid her palms along the muscles cording his upper arms.

"Nice," she whispered. "Hard and a little rough and very nice. Like the rest of you, Sanderson."

He lifted his head, and his hazel eyes narrowed

on her face. "It could get rougher. I'm not real good at slow and easy."

She caught his meaning instantly. He wasn't talking about what was happening between them at this moment. Brenna knew she wouldn't pull away. Not when they'd come this far down a path that could lead anywhere. Not with his hand on her breast and his hard shaft probing her stomach.

"I'll show you," she promised. Her hands glided down his arms to his belly. "I'll show you slow."

"Duggan . . ."

"And easy." Her fingers closed around him. "And sweet. I'll show you sweet."

He was smooth satin and ridged steel. Hot blood and bone-hard flesh.

"And very, very nice," she whispered.

True to her promise, she kept it slow and sweet . . . for as long as she could. Enclosed in a warp of exquisite exploration and mounting passion, she lost track of time. The feel of his hot flesh in her hand excited her as much as it did him, and narrowed her world to the small circle of moonlight and shadows that surrounded them. With each harsh breath he drew, Brenna heard him come closer to the flash point. With each kiss she planted on his chest and his chin and his mouth, she felt his fuse shorten.

The explosion she'd both wanted and feared came moments later.

Shoving her hand aside, he stripped off the rest of her clothes and swept her into his arms. They hit the bed in a tangle of arms and legs. His weight was heavy on hers, his body hard and urgent. She parted her legs and he found the slickness between her thighs. Probing, pressuring, thrusting, he primed her as she had him just moments before. Brenna arched against his hand, gasping.

His mouth took the small gasp and turned it into a ragged, panting moan. When he pulled back some time later, she was wet and hot and ready.

"Are you using anything?" he asked harshly. "Do you have any protection?"

"No."

Through heavy, half-closed lids Brenna caught the expression on his face. Disbelief ripped through her. "Oh, God! Don't you?"

He shook his head, and she gave a groan of sheer frustration.

He swept a hard hand over her sprawled, vulnerable body. "I guess we'll just have to improvise."

The glint in his eyes both excited and alarmed her. "Maybe ... Maybe we'd better not. I mean, I'm not sure ..."

His slow, predatory grin took her breath away. At that moment, Brenna understood that what she felt for this man went beyond lust, beyond desire. She was drawn to the darkness in his eyes, and to the danger in his soul.

"I'm sure," he told her, his smile lethal. "Very, very sure. Trust me, Duggan."

She groaned again, then closed her eyes as he

bent his body and brought her hips up to his mouth.

Moments, or maybe hours later, she climaxed in an explosion of white light and searing red heat.

Hours, or maybe moments later, he followed her over the edge.

The first streaks of purple tinted the darkness outside the windows when Brenna slid Dave's arm off her chest and eased out of the tangle of sheets. She dressed slowly, the languor in her body at odds with the emotions already battering at her mind.

She'd expected to feel regret and shame and disgust when her flush of sensual satisfaction faded. What she hadn't expected was this gathering sense of disappointment.

Although she'd gone into Sanderson's arms with her eyes open and her illusions on hold, some hidden corner of her heart had foolishly believed they both were looking for more than just a physical release. The expression on his face now told her otherwise.

Naked, he sprawled amid the sheets, one arm bent under his head as he watched her with lazy, careful eyes. He'd mingled his sweat and his body with hers, but obviously nothing else. Brenna's disappointment became a nagging little ache.

"I warned you, Duggan." The mocking edge was back in his voice.

Cursing herself for letting her thoughts show on her face, Brenna buttoned her blouse. It took some

effort, but she managed to inject a cool nonchalance into her reply.

"So you did."

"When are you going home?"

"Why?" she returned, sliding her skirt around
her hips. Her fingers fumbled with the ties.

The question seemed to throw him for a moment. He slanted her a narrow look, then he
swung his legs over the edge of the bed and
grabbed at a pair of slacks tossed over a nearby
chair.

Brenna's fingers froze on the ties. God, he was
magnificent, and so damned arrogant.

He tugged on the pants with the lithe movement of a jungle cat, all sinewy grace and sleek,
rippling muscles. Disgusted at her gripping
awareness of his body, she bent to pull on a sandal. The sweep of her hair curtained him from
view.

"Look," he said gruffly, "I have to go back on
alert tomorrow."

She pulled on the other sandal. "And?"

"And ..."

His hesitation added to Brenna's nagging little
ache and ripped at her pride. Straightening, she
shoved a hand through her tangled hair to get it
out of her face.

"And what, Sanderson? Do you want me to
come out to the alert shack so we can lock the
door to the crew room and have another ... discussion? I don't think so."

The stinging reply tightened the planes of his

face. For a moment, she feared ... hoped ... he might take a step toward her. Instead, he lifted a shoulder.

"Suit yourself."

Her ache flowered into hurt, but she lifted her chin and met his look head-on. "The next time we have anything to discuss, you'll have to come to me."

An expression that could have been surprise or satisfaction or anticipation flickered across his face. In the dim light, Brenna couldn't quite tell.

"Is there going to be a next time?"

Despite her hurt, she couldn't lie to herself, and she wouldn't lie to him. "There could be," she said slowly. "But not like this. Not with so many unanswered questions between us. Not with Janeen and Andy Lang looking over our shoulders."

She sensed rather than saw his withdrawal, and berated herself for expecting anything else.

"Then I guess we're at an impasse," he said at last.

For the life of her, Brenna couldn't hear any hint of regret in his voice. "I guess we are."

She groped for her black leather purse. Lifting the flap, she fumbled inside for a moment, then tossed the card key the desk clerk had given her onto the end table.

"See you around, Sanderson."

Chapter Thirteen

The moment she closed the door to her own room, every emotion Brenna had anticipated when she'd walked into Dave Sanderson's arms came crashing down on her. Guilt, shame, and regret shoved aside the last remnants of physical pleasure. They were followed almost immediately by disbelief at her incredible stupidity.

She'd thought she could separate those few hours of passion into some isolated chamber of her mind. She'd been sure of it when she'd run her palms up Dave's arms and answered the challenge in his eyes.

Now she knew better.

Tossing her purse on the bed, she stripped off the clothes she'd pulled on just moments ago and headed for the shower. Stepping into the tiny cubicle, she leaned her shoulders against the tiles and let the lukewarm streams of water sluice over her. Despite the stinging splash against her body, she could feel Sanderson's imprint on every surface of her skin.

God, how naive she'd been to think she could sleep with the man and walk away unscathed. Her fingertips still tingled from the remembered feel of his roped muscles. Her thighs ached from unaccustomed stretching. If she wiped her tongue along her lips, she was sure she'd taste the salty tang of his skin.

Yet as she turned her face up to the streaming water, Brenna knew she wouldn't touch or taste him again . . . unless he came to her as she'd stipulated, which wasn't likely. Not if the expression in his eyes when she'd walked out the door of his room was any gauge.

It was just as well he had to go back on alert and she had a long, grueling mission ahead of her, she told herself wearily. Unless she made a special trip to the alert facility, she wouldn't see Sanderson again before he got back to the States next week. Maybe by then, she'd have convinced herself that last night wasn't the disaster her heart told her it was.

Eleven hours later, her flight touched down at Tinker. Brenna deplaned with her tired crew and conducted a mission debrief before dispersing.

A cool fall breeze teased at her face and hair as she left the Ops building and headed across the street to her private parking spot. Tossing her crew bag in the trunk, she stopped by her office to glance through the "hot" items her admin clerk had placed in a neat stack on her desk.

When Brenna drove home some hours later,

weariness pulled at her like a slow, dark tide. She put down the top on the little red Miata, hoping the crisp evening air would revive her. From long experience, she knew she needed to stay awake a few more hours yet to get her body clock back on a nonflying schedule.

Her two-bedroom condo had a closed-in, musty odor. After depositing her purse and crew bag on the kitchen counter, Brenna picked up her hot line to let the Command Post know she was back in quarters. That done, she opened the wood shutters to let in the last of the sun and turned on the ceiling fan to stir the air.

What she needed, she decided, was a cold drink, a long, hot bath, and a good night's sleep.

The first item on her list she took care of immediately. She kept a bottle of Chardonnay chilled in the fridge for postflight wind downs. The second item would have to wait until she'd sorted through her mail and messages.

Wineglass in hand, she walked into the bedroom. In short order, she rid herself of her boots and the blue scarf tucked into the neckline of her flight suit, then stripped off the green Nomex bag itself. Wearing only her regulation white cotton T-shirt over lacy panties, she padded barefoot into the living room.

Sipping at the wine, she picked through her accumulated mail. Nothing but junk and an ever-increasing assortment of catalogs greeted her. Brenna smiled at the eclectic collection. She could understand why half the clothiers in the country had put her on their mailing list. She rarely had time to shop and had taken to ordering by phone the splashy, colorful clothes she preferred in contrast to her uniforms. But she couldn't understand why Williams-Sonoma and The Gourmet Kitchen would think a woman who hadn't cooked a meal in two years would be interested in their goods.

Tossing the catalogs aside, she dug in her desk drawer for a paper and pencil, then punched the play button on her answering machine. As usual in this electronic age, she found a far greater number of messages waiting for her on the recorder than in the mail.

Absently, she listened to a message from her mother reminding her to send her only nephew a birthday card. Charley was ten, and Brenna hadn't gotten his birthday right yet.

Buck came on next, inviting her to a promotion party on Friday. At the sound of his cheerful voice, Brenna's smile slipped. The guilt she'd held at bay during the busy flight home came rolling back.

Although she and the stocky, handsome intelligence officer hadn't made any commitments, their relationship went deeper than a few casual dates. The fact that Brenna had given Dave Sanderson what she hadn't been able to give this warm, considerate man made her feel a little sick.

The next message only added to her disquiet. After a long beep, a soft Oklahoma accent filled the quiet living room.

"Brenna, this is Janeen Lang. I, uh, just wanted

to tell you I haven't heard anything about the request I filed yet. It's been almost a month now. My attorney says we're being stonewalled. I . . . Well, I may file a petition in a civil court to force the Air Force to act."

She paused, obviously uncomfortable with conveying news such as this into a recorder.

"I hope you don't think I'm bein' disloyal or a troublemaker or anything, but I'm not going to give up. I just wanted to let you know you may be called as a witness, you bein' Andy's commander. I'm sorry. I don't want to cause you any trouble, not after all you've done for me. I hope you understand."

There were more messages after that, but Brenna barely heard them. She'd discovered several new emotions to add to the others she'd have to come to grips with before she saw Sanderson again.

Betrayal headed the list. Listening to Janeen's nervous, determined voice, Brenna had felt a lurch at the pit of her stomach, as though she'd been caught sleeping with the enemy.

Failure ran a close second. She wasn't used to failing at anything. Her brief marriage had been an exception to an otherwise outstanding string of successes. As a high school student, she'd excelled in athletics as well as academics. Her years at the Academy had only honed her competitive edge. Once commissioned, she'd worked hard to earn both early promotions and this prized command billet. She knew she was on track for another promotion, this time to full colonel. In her professional life at least, she'd scored only wins. Now, she couldn't shake the bitter feeling that she'd failed both Sergeant Lang and his wife.

Abruptly, Brenna tossed down the pencil and reached for her wineglass. She wouldn't betray Janeen again, she promised grimly. Or herself.

This impasse with Sanderson had to end sooner or later. Neither she nor Janeen could rest now until their questions were answered. But the way it would end depended a great deal on when ... and *if* ... he came to her.

The end came crashing out of the night less than a week later, in a manner Brenna could never have anticipated.

This time, the call from the command post didn't jerk her from sleep. This time, she was wide awake, but no more prepared for the disaster Sergeant Adkins laid on her than she'd been on the night Sergeant Lang died.

When her beeper started pinging, she was at the Officers' Club celebrating the promotion of four very happy new majors. The selectees had combined their celebration with the wing's traditional Friday night occupation of the casual lounge. Buoyed by the boisterous spirits of the soon-to-be majors, the noise in the lounge had climbed to deafening levels. Country western music wailed from the juke box, the combatants engaged in a crud match at the pool table shouted and whistled, and every so often a wild cheer went up from the men clustered around the large screen TV in one corner of the room.

Brenna toasted the beaming officers when appropriate and listened with half an ear while Buck Henry filled her in on the latest wrangle with headquarters over a levy for intel assets to support an upcoming exercise. Caught up in her own thoughts, she didn't realize he'd finished until she glanced at the handsome man beside her and caught his speculative gaze.

"You want to talk about it, Brenna?"

"About what?"

"Whatever's made you so distant lately."

His quiet reply spurred her guilt. Mindful of General Adams's order, she couldn't discuss her growing conviction that there was more to Andy Lang's death than the brutally terse facts in the official report. Nor could she articulate her lingering suspicions about Dave Sanderson. Even without the general's order hanging over her, she couldn't tell Buck about the hours she'd spent in Sanderson's arms or her unshakable fixation with the man.

He was back from Panama. She'd ascertained that much, although she hadn't seen him around the wing. He'd built up a good chunk of comp time during his three weeks on alert, so she hadn't really expected to run into him immediately after his return. Yet every glimpse of a royal blue and gold Customs patch started her stomach churning and heat streaking through her veins.

Why didn't Buck cause these reactions in her?

Brenna wondered in mingled resentment and frustration. Why didn't her nipples tighten when he looked at her? Why didn't her heart start to pound some irregular, primitive rhythm?

Shaking her head, she shoved aside her own confused feelings and forced herself to think of Buck's. He was a generous friend. A good man. He deserved far more than she could give him.

"We do need to talk," she agreed. "Maybe we should go somewhere quiet and have dinner?"

He toyed with his beer, his relaxed slouch at odds with the intent expression on his face.

"Dinner sounds good, but I don't need soft lights and undisturbed quiet to hear what you think you have to tell me. I see it in your eyes, Brenna. I've felt it in your slow withdrawal these past weeks."

"Buck ..." She hesitated, searching for the right words.

"It's okay," he told her, his voice low and steady over the noise that swirled around them. "You don't have to explain. If I didn't learn anything else from my wife's death, I learned that I can't force things to happen if they're not meant to. I couldn't spare her the pain and suffering she went through, and I can't make you love me."

Brenna leaned forward, her throat tight. "I do love you, but ... but not the way you want me to. You're my best friend."

His mouth twisted for a moment, then he set his beer aside. Curling a hand over her arm, he squeezed it gently.

"Friend is good. I can settle for that. But I hope you find more than friendship with someone, Brenna. Life's too short and too uncertain to face it alone."

She nodded, unable to speak over the constriction in her throat. Her hand covered his, and for a few moments they drew from each other's strength. Then he smiled and reached for his flight cap.

"Now about that dinner . . ."

The sharp ping of a beeper cut him off. Glancing down at the pager clipped to the waistband of her crimson silk slacks, Brenna recognized the digits marching across the liquid crystal display immediately. She shoved back her chair.

"It's the Command Post. I have to call in."

He nodded, settling back in his seat. "I'll wait for you here."

Guilt, a wretched sense of relief, and waves of noise followed Brenna into the hall. Jamming the receiver against her right ear to block out the music and laughter, she dropped a coin in the slot and dialed the Command Post.

"Five-fifty-second Command Post. Sergeant Adkins here."

"This is Colonel Duggan. I got your page."

"Glad you called in, ma'am. I just got a call from a Mr. Paul Wilson. Sounded kind of urgent."

"Paul Wilson?" She drew a blank. "Who's he?"

"A civilian, no connection to the base. He said you know his daughter, Janeen."

Frowning, Brenna leaned into the half booth to

cut some of the noise. "Yes, I know his daughter. What's the message?"

"She fell down some stairs. She's in Saint Mary's Hospital in Enid."

"Oh, my God! Is she all right?"

"According to Mr. Wilson, she's okay, but they're not sure about the baby. They're watching to see if they need to do a C-section."

"Oh, no! It's too early!"

"Wilson says she's holding on. And she's asking for you."

"Did he leave a number where he could be reached?"

"Yes, ma'am."

"Call him back and tell him I'll be there in . . ." She glanced down at her watch and calculated the distance to the northern Oklahoma city. "I'll be there in an hour."

She made it in forty-five minutes.

Declining Buck's offer of company on the trip, she snatched her purse and the red silk bomber-style jacket that matched her slacks from her chair, then rushed out of the Officers' Club. As soon as she exited the front gate of Tinker and hit the westbound ramp to I–40, Brenna opened the Miata up. Thankfully, the traffic around the city was light, which wasn't unusual on Friday nights during football season when a good portion of the population of Oklahoma poured into high school stadiums across the state.

Turning off I–40 at El Reno, she followed State

Road 81 straight north. Vast, purple-shaded open spaces whizzed by, broken intermittently by the lights of small towns. The speedometer inched to the right, and only Brenna's iron discipline kept her from pushing it all the way over. She wouldn't be any comfort to Janeen if she ended up in the bed next to hers.

Once she hit Enid's city limits, she located the hospital with only one quick stop for directions. The Miata's tires squealed as she wheeled into the parking lot and rammed the gear shift into park. Rushing into the brick building, she scanned a wall-mounted directory, then took the elevator to the fourth floor.

She found Paul Wilson pacing the floor of a waiting room decorated in soothing shades of mauve and gray. Janeen's father looked anything but soothed, however. His short, salt-and-pepper hair stood up in spikes, as though he'd shoved a hand through it repeatedly, and his leathery face was drawn into tight lines.

Two other men stood at the window. Brenna recognized Janeen's brothers from the funeral and the tense young woman beside them as a sister-in-law. They all turned at the sound of her footsteps in the hallway.

Paul Wilson came forward to meet her, his low-heeled work boots thudding hollowly on the tile. "Thanks for coming, Colonel Duggan."

"How's Janeen?"

"She's in the labor room, with her mother. They gave her something to stop the contractions, and she was doing okay for a while, but . . ." He swallowed heavily. "But she started bleeding a few minutes ago. If she doesn't stop, they'll have to take the baby."

"I'm so sorry. What happened?"

One of Janeen's brothers stepped forward. He was older than his sister by some years, but the family resemblance was unmistakable in his honey-toned hair and brown eyes. Where Janeen's eyes were soft and doelike, however, his glittered like hard agates.

"We were at the game," he told Brenna. "The Seiling football game. My son's playing this year, and Janey didn't want to miss his first time starting."

A spasm of pain crossed Paul Wilson's seamed face. "Danny's wearing Andy's old number," he mumbled.

Brenna swallowed and forced aside a swift resurgence of her shame and sense of having betrayed Janeen and her husband. This wasn't the time to indulge in bitter self-recrimination. Her whole focus was on the young woman who lay in a bed not far away.

"Janey got up a couple of times to go to the bathroom," the younger Wilson continued. "She didn't like using the Porta Potti, so she went across the parking lot to the gym. My wife went with her the first time, but Janey said she didn't need any help the last time."

The younger woman beside him shook her

head. "I'll never forgive myself for letting her go alone. If the baby's . . . if . . ."

Her husband laid his arm across her shoulders and squeezed her to his side. "It's not your fault, Mary. It's not anyone's fault. She fell, that's all."

"We had just scored a touchdown," Janeen's father put in. "That must have been when she fell, because no one heard her scream or cry out. We sort of got caught up in the game, and didn't miss her for a while. Then Mary went looking for her and found her at the bottom of a short flight of stairs, unconscious. By the time we got her to the hospital, the contractions had started."

Brenna dug her clenched fists into the pockets of her bomber jacket. Janeen didn't need this. On top of everything else, she didn't need this.

"She'll be okay, won't she? She and the baby?"

"I hope so," her father replied, his eyes bleak. "The doctors say this bleeding isn't a good sign."

"Is . . . is she awake now?"

Paul Wilson nodded. "Sort of. The medication gives her the shakes and makes her woozy. She's been drifting in and out for the past hour, and asking for you."

"For me?"

"I told her you were on your way."

Her heart jackhammering against her ribs, Brenna hurried down the corridor to the labor room. Unsure what to expect, she pushed the door open slowly.

The room was bathed in soft shadows and scented with disinfectant and something flowery.

Janeen lay in a wide bed with her head slightly elevated and her eyes closed. An IV tube snaked from one arm to the plastic pack suspended above her head, and wires ran from her mounded stomach to several flickering monitors.

Brenna hesitated, not wanting to wake her, but Mrs. Wilson slewed sideways in the chair beside her daughter's bed and saw her standing in the doorway.

"Come on in, Colonel," she called softly. "Janey's been askin' for you."

As Brenna approached the bed, Janeen's eyelids fluttered up. Her brown eyes were confused, almost dazed. Sweat sheened her face, and deep, white lines bracketed either side of her mouth.

"Janey, honey," Mrs. Wilson crooned softly. "It's Colonel Duggan."

With a visible effort, Janeen focused on the figure behind her mother. A wave of tremors shook her from head to toe.

"Momma. I . . . I want to talk to Colonel Duggan." Her hoarse whisper barely carried above the hum of the monitors.

"I know, honey, I know. But just for a minute, okay? You've got to rest, like the doctor said."

Still shaking, Janeen nodded.

The older woman patted her daughter's hand, then rose and turned to Brenna.

"They gave her magnesium sulfate to relax her uterus and stop the contractions. It makes her shake. The doctor says all we can do is try to keep her quiet and hope the bleeding stops."

"I understand."

Moving to the bed, Brenna took Janeen's trembling hand. Her heart aching at the new crisis in this young woman's life, she offered what little comfort she could.

"If you need any special care, you or the baby, the Air Force will cover it. Just don't worry."

"Brenna . . ." Janeen's fingers clutched at her hand. "I didn't fall."

Confused, Brenna stared down at the pale, sweat-dampened face. "But I thought . . ."

"I didn't fall." The raspy whisper hung on the air between them. "Someone pushed me."

Shock held Brenna utterly motionless.

"It was dark," Janeen whispered, her whole body shaking. "I didn't see anyone. But . . . someone pushed me. I'm sure of it." Her hand gripped Brenna's in a clawlike hold. "If anything happens to me . . . or to my baby, promise me you'll help my lawyer."

"Janeen . . ."

"Promise me!"

Chapter Fourteen

Brenna would always think of that night as the point where the malevolent forces swirling around her gathered the speed and destructive power of a tornado and cut an indelible swath through her life.

She was still standing beside Janeen's bed, stunned by her whispered revelations, when the younger woman groaned and arched her back. While Brenna watched, horrified, Janeen's full lips stretched in a rictus of pain that seemed to last for an eternity. She fell back to the bed, panting and shaking more than ever.

"Call . . . my momma. The . . . doctor."

With her free hand, Brenna scrabbled for the call button clipped to the pillow and punched it repeatedly. When she straightened, her stomach plummeted at the red smear on the sheet bunched around Janeen's legs. The stain spread with terrifying speed, like a fast-forward video of a crimson rose unfurling its petals.

"Promise me, Brenna." Janeen's viselike hold tightened painfully. "Promise me!"

Tearing her eyes from the dark stain, Brenna met her pleading stare with a grim, determined one of her own.

"I promise."

The door flew open at that moment, and events became a blur of determined faces, pale blue scrubs, and frantic activity.

Brenna didn't try to pry loose the excruciating grip on her hand. She didn't think she could, even if she'd wanted to. Moving as far out of the way as Janeen's hold would allow, she watched while the doctor examined the young widow. When he announced that the placenta had abrupted and they'd have to do an immediate C-section, she silently echoed Janeen's cry of dismay.

After she'd been lifted onto a gurney, Janeen uncurled her fingers, one by one. Hand throbbing, heart hammering, Brenna watched the medical team wheel her out of the labor room. She trailed behind them more slowly and joined the others in the waiting area.

While the various members of the Wilson clan paced or huddled or talked among themselves, she claimed a quiet corner near the windows. Her chaotic thoughts bounced wildly from the drama she'd just participated in to Janeen's stunning assertion. Surely she'd been mistaken! No one would deliberately shove a pregnant woman down a flight of stairs!

Unless ... Oh, God, unless this accident had

something to do with the message Janeen had left on her answering machine last week!

Wrapping her hands around her middle to hide their sudden trembling, Brenna replayed that brief message over and over in her mind. Janeen had said she wouldn't give up. She'd mentioned filing a petition in civil court to force the Air Force to act on her request.

Could this accident have anything to do with the petition? Did someone push Janeen to stop her request for a new investigation? Did everything lead back to Andrew Lang's bizarre death?

Brenna's initial disbelief gave way to doubt, then to a sick feeling of certainty. The blood drained from her face when she recalled how she'd set aside her suspicions for those few hours in a darkened hotel room in Panama. How she'd held out a tentative olive branch to Sanderson. Offered to help him. Told him she'd wait for him to come to her.

Guilt crashed over her in waves. All this week, she'd sat on her duff. Watching for Sanderson. Waiting for him to take that first step. Doing nothing to help Janeen. While Brenna played her games with the Customs agent, Sergeant Lang's widow had plowed ahead on her own ... and taken the consequences.

Blindly, Brenna stared out the darkened window. Shame at her unknowing complicity in this horrible accident ate at her soul. Only when one of Janeen's brothers approached with a container ot coffee did a fragment of common sense force its way through the sick disgust clawing at her chest.

While the scalding liquid burned a line down the back of her throat, she reminded herself that she didn't *know* whether Janeen's accident was anything more than that, an accident. She wasn't *sure* Sanderson was involved in Andrew Lang's death. She had no proof, other than her own vague suspicions . . . and the hard look in his eyes whenever she got too close.

Even as she formulated the rational arguments, her bruised and battered instincts refuted them. She had only to compare the sardonic expression on Sanderson's face when she'd left him in his hotel room to the agony in Janeen's eyes tonight to know that she would keep her promise. Whatever it cost and whoever it implicated, Brenna would see that the request for redetermination went through.

When a tired doctor in blue scrubs walked into the waiting room some time later, Janeen's family stood and waited grimly for his news. Brenna hung back, not wanting to intrude. She didn't realize her hands were shaking until coffee sloshed over the sides of her cup. Setting the cup down, she swiped her hand on the back of her slacks and gave all her attention to the tense group clustered around the doctor.

"Your daughter delivered a baby girl," he told Paul Wilson. "Janeen lost a lot of blood in the process. It was touch and go with her for a while, but she's in recovery now and doing fine."

"And the baby?"

"The baby has some respiratory problems. We've got her on Survanta, which allows the lungs to relax and expand, but so far she's showing little ability to breathe on her own. She's in the Neonatal Intensive Care Unit."

"Is she going to be all right?"

The doctor's brown eyes held no promises. "We'll be watching her closely."

Soft golden dawn painted the sky outside the waiting room windows when Brenna checked in with the Command Post. Sergeant Adkins promised to relay to her squadron and to the command section that she was in Enid and would remain there indefinitely.

At her request, he also promised to check the current duty status of Detection Systems Specialist Sanderson. She hung up, feeling slightly sick and hoping that Dave was in the air when Janeen went tumbling down those stairs. It wouldn't prove anything, of course, and Brenna still intended to take Janeen's allegations to the general as soon as she returned to the base. But in the secret recesses of her soul, she prayed those allegations proved unfounded.

It was almost noon before she saw Janeen again, and then only for a few moments. The young woman's blond hair was limp and her face pearl white. Surrounded by her family, Janeen sent Brenna a weak smile and asked hoarsely if she could stay a little while.

Realizing her life was now inextricably bound to the young woman in the hospital bed, Brenna nodded.

Later that afternoon, she rented a room at a motel across the street from St. Mary's and went to clean up. Several of Janeen's family members offered to put her up, but she didn't want to give them the added burden of a guest to worry about. Besides, she was too restless to do more than take a quick shower and grab something to eat before returning to the hospital. The steam from the shower erased most of the wrinkles from her red silk slacks and matching bomber jacket, as well as the white stretch tank top she wore underneath. After refreshing her makeup from the meager supply she carried in her purse, Brenna hurried back to the hospital.

Before heading for Janeen's room, she lingered for a long while at the window of the Neonatal ICU. The pathetic scrap of humanity in a clear plastic incubator wrung her heart. Tubes and wires were strung from the baby to the instruments clustered around her. She lay still, eyes closed, her tiny chest rising and falling with the help of the respirator.

She was so small, so helpless. So innocent of whatever had brought her to this desperate condition. Tears stung Brenna's eyelids as she watched a nurse stroke the baby's back and jiggle its tiny fingers in a vain attempt to stimulate a response. The infant didn't move, didn't flutter an eyelid.

Brenna's fingers curled against the window in

choking frustration. This was a situation she couldn't control. A circumstance she couldn't influence. All her training and years of taking charge counted for nothing in this silent battle between one small infant and death.

At that moment, Brenna would have given everything she possessed in exchange for a single movement from the small, still form.

The scuff of slippers on tile alerted her to another presence in the empty hallway. Blinking back her incipient tears, Brenna edged aside while Janeen shuffled up, accompanied by her mother on one side and a nurse on the other. She walked bent over, pushing an IV stand before her. Her shining, newly washed hair fell forward in soft waves to frame a scrubbed face.

Mrs. Wilson gave Brenna a tired smile, then murmured that she was going to visit with her husband for a little bit. Patting her daughter's back, she left her standing beside Brenna at the nursery window. The nurse hovered at her other side until a call from a coworker drew her away for a moment. Alone in the empty corridor, Brenna and Janeen stared in silence at the unmoving infant in her plastic cocoon.

"They call it 'Failure to Thrive Syndrome,' " Janeen said quietly. "I guess that's as good a term as any."

Brenna's throat ached. "I've been watching her for a while. She's not going to give up. She's . . . she's stubborn."

The ghost of a smile feathered across the pale face beside her. "Just like her daddy."

"And her momma."

Janeen's tentative smile faltered. She turned awkwardly to face Brenna, still hunched and clinging to the IV stand.

"And her momma," she repeated. "I won't give up on this business 'bout Andy, Brenna. I don't know if . . . if my fall had anything to do with my request. I can't prove I was pushed. I'm not even sure myself anymore. Everything's so blurred, and all I can think of is the baby right now. But whatever happens, I won't give up."

Brenna's hand covered the small, blunt tipped one gripping the metal stand. "I'm sorry you've had to fight your battle alone. You won't be alone any longer."

"I wasn't alone. I had my folks with me. And Andy. But having you here helps. A lot. You and the baby." Her brown eyes drifted to the tiny form in the incubator. "I'm going to go in and hold her for a while. Do you want to come with me?"

Brenna glanced into the brightly lit ICU doubtfully. "Will they let me?"

"I think so. Yes, I'm sure they will . . . if we tell them you're her aunt." She hesitated, then sent Brenna a look of shy inquiry. "Would you? Be a sort of honorary aunt, I mean? I'd like you stand beside me at her baptism. I don't know what faith you hold to, but in ours, standing up with a baby means you promise to help her find the Lord."

The tears Brenna had forced back only moments before prickled her lids. "I'd be honored."

The hours that followed were the longest of Brenna's life. Day flowed into night, then dragged interminably into day again. Together, she and Janeen watched the baby's battle for every breath.

The shy, timid wife whose whole life to that point had been defined by the man she'd loved drew upon a bedrock of strength and religious faith to sustain her. The Lord wouldn't take her baby, she maintained with unflinching conviction. Not now. Not after He'd taken Andy.

Hour after hour she occupied a rocking chair beside the incubator, careful not to disturb the tubes and wires as she held her child in her arms and crooned to her. Once, while Brenna was donning scrubs in preparation for another visit to the Infant ICU, she overheard Janeen carrying on a gentle, one-sided conversation.

The young mother sat in a circle of light from the heat lamps beside the incubator, her hair a halo of spun gold. Smiling, she curled a finger under the baby's minute hand and held it up to the light, commenting to her husband on the tiny perfection of their child.

Brenna stood motionless, the hospital gown pulled halfway up her arms. With all her soul, she wanted to believe that Andrew Lang was there beside his wife, smiling down at his baby. Long forgotten precepts of her Irish Catholic upbringing drifted through her mind. It didn't take a great leap of faith to believe that Andy could see and hear and feel his wife's love for him and their child.

Brenna remained still until Janeen finished her quiet communion with her husband. Humbled by the younger woman's unshakable faith, she tugged on the robe with trembling fingers and joined her.

Janeen smiled at her approach. "I've been thinking 'bout her name," she said softly. "If you don't mind, can I give her yours as a middle name?"

Brenna swallowed the lump in her throat. "I don't mind at all."

"Andrea Brenna Lang. Kind of a tongue-twister for such a little bit of a thing, but pretty, don't you think?"

"Very."

As much as she hated to leave her child, even for a few hours, Janeen's body demanded rest to recuperate. Along with the other Wilson women, Brenna took turns watching and holding the baby during her mother's brief absences. Nervous and awkward at first, she learned to lift and cradle the baby without disturbing the tubes and wires.

She was holding her namesake when the baby opened her eyes for the first time. It was late, well after midnight, and the nursery lights had dimmed except for the heat lamps over the incubator. Brenna was humming an old lullaby that she'd dredged up from some corner of her memory when she felt the small form in her arms stir. It was more of a halfhearted twitch than a real effort to shift her arms and legs, but the faint movement stopped Brenna in midrock.

Not daring to breathe for fear she'd miss another ripple of movement, she stared down at the tiny, wrinkled face still tinged with blue at the nostrils and lips. The lips pursed once. Twice. Then egg shell–thin eyelids lifted.

For a timeless instant, they stared at each other. Blurred blue eyes focused slowly on crystal blue ones that suddenly swam with tears.

"Are you awake, sweetheart?" Brenna murmured through the ache in her throat. Her finger stroked one wrinkled cheek. "Are you awake, and ready to meet your momma?"

Leaving Janeen surrounded by the tight-knit security of her family, Brenna walked out of the hospital some hours later, filled with relief and unshakable determination.

Surprised to find the sun beating down on the parking lot with unrelenting brightness, Brenna stood at the entrance and tried to remember what day it was. Sunday. No, Monday. Monday morning. A quick glance at her watch told her she could make it home, take a quick shower, pull on a uniform, and arrive at the base in time for the general's weekly staff meeting.

To hell with the shower and uniform, Brenna decided as she crossed the shimmering asphalt with long, purposeful strides. What she had to say to General Adams couldn't be said at a staff meeting and it couldn't wait. Not any longer.

At any other point in her life, Brenna would have used the drive back to Tinker to rehearse what she wanted to say to her boss. She'd long ago trained herself not to walk into a situation unprepared. But with every dusty mile, her euphoria at the baby's tentative grasp on life gave way to a growing anger and disgust with herself for caving in the last time she'd faced her boss.

By the time she wheeled into her parking space at the base, grabbed her purse, and covered the short distance to the headquarters complex, she had moved well beyond caution and any regard for military protocol. The cool dimness of the headquarters momentarily blinded her after the bright light outside. She stood just inside the entrance, waiting for her eyes to adjust. When they had focused enough for her to catch a glimpse of herself in the one-way window that shielded the Command Post, she raked a hand through her tangled hair, drew in a deep breath, and pushed open the door to the Command Section. Brushing past the receptionist's desk with a brisk nod, she strode up to the executive officer.

"Is the general in?"

Captain Hargove scrambled to his feet and eyed her loose hair and bright civilian clothes with some surprise. "Yes, ma'am, but he's ..."

"I'd like to see him. Now."

The exec's sandy brows shot up, but he replied politely. "He's got the chief of maintenance in with him. They're going over the reliability stats for last month."

"I'll wait."

"We've got a staff meeting in a few minutes," he pointed out.

"This is important, Rooster. I'll wait."

The Gulf War veteran sent her a searching look, then reached for the phone. "I'll tell the boss you need to see him."

If General Adams was perturbed at having his conference with the chief of maintenance cut short or the least bit surprised at Brenna's rumpled appearance, he didn't show it.

"What's going on, Duggan?" he asked with his customary directness, motioning to one of the chairs in front of his desk.

Brenna ignored the gesture. "I've just left Janeen Lang. Staff Sergeant Lang's widow."

"I know who she is. The Command Post briefed me on her accident. How is she? And the baby?"

"Janeen's recovering from an emergency C-section. It's still touch and go with the baby."

Pity softened the general's knife-blade features. "Poor woman. I'm glad you were with her. She's had a rough time in the past few months. First her husband, and now this."

"I'm glad I was with her, too, sir, but you need to know she doesn't think her fall was an accident."

"What?"

"She believes someone pushed her down those stairs. She doesn't remember exactly what happened. It was dark. She didn't see anything. But she's sure she felt a push."

General Adams rose with a swift economy of movement. He was taller than Brenna by some inches, and wielded infinitely more authority. But this time neither his impressive physical aura nor his rank daunted her.

"Why would anyone want to harm Mrs. Lang?"

"Perhaps to stop her request for a redetermination of her husband's death."

His gray eyes sliced into Brenna with cutting intensity. Before he could comment, she continued in a fierce rush.

"Janeen has no proof. She's not sure there's any connection between her fall and her request. But she believes someone pushed her, and her baby almost died!"

The general's brows snapped together, but Brenna couldn't tell what he was thinking behind that hard-as-steel exterior. Knowing there was no turning back now, she plunged ahead.

"I've made a few calls. I know Mrs. Lang's request is buried at headquarters. I told her I would see that it received immediate attention."

Adams didn't reply for long moments. When he did, his tone left Brenna in no doubt where she stood.

"You overstepped your authority, Colonel."

During the long hours in the Neonatal ICU, the chasm that had first opened under Brenna's feet in the Wilsons' kitchen had widened. It was now an impassable gorge.

"I don't agree."

His gray eyes narrowed to slits. "You're close

to stepping over the bounds here, Duggan. You'd better back off and think about what you're doing."

"I took the first step across the line weeks ago, and didn't have the courage to take the next. My cowardice almost cost Janeen her life and her baby."

A muscle ticked in the side of her boss's jaw. "If Janeen Lang was pushed, I'll damn well find out why. But I'm not having my hand forced on this, or on anything else. You had no authority to involve yourself in her request for a redetermination and I'm telling you again to back off."

Looking him straight in the eye, Brenna laid her career on the line.

"If you won't help me ensure that Mrs. Lang's request gets an impartial, thorough review, I'll go over your head. As high as necessary. And if the Air Force tries to stonewall me, as it has Janeen Lang, I'll go to the press."

Adams leaned forward, his fingertips pressing against the desk. "You're flying too close to the ground, Duggan," he said softly. "Pull up."

"No, sir."

He straightened slowly. The silver stars on his epaulets caught the light, their glitter matching the hard sheen of his eyes.

"You're confined to your quarters for twenty-four hours, Colonel Duggan. During that period, I'll consider whether to bring charges against you for insubordination and refusal to obey a direct order."

Although the expression on his face had warned Brenna of what was coming, the words still hit her like a falling wall. It took everything she had not to flinch.

"Yes, sir."

"Report to me at ten o'clock tomorrow morning. I'll let you know my decision then. Dismissed."

Brenna's arm was half lifted in a salute before she remembered she wasn't in uniform. Without another word, she dropped her arm, spun on one heel, and left.

Chapter Fifteen

The officer who reported to the Command Section at ten o'clock the following morning bore little resemblance to the windblown, fiery woman of the day before.

Her dark brown hair was swept back into its customary smooth coil. The rows of ribbons on her blue service jacket anchored a polished, nickel-plated Weapons Director badge and shiny wings. Her blue skirt hung without a wrinkle, and the glossy sheen on her black pumps would have been the envy of any gawking doolie at the Academy.

If Brenna's outer appearance had changed, however, her inner determination had not. The twenty-four-hour interval between her stormy interview with General Adams and the phone calls she'd made to St. Mary's hospital to check on the infant who clung so precariously to life had only strengthened her resolve. In her mind, Janeen's quest to find answers to her questions about her

husband's death had become inextricably inter-
woven with her daughter's struggle to breathe.
Brenna no longer stood on the periphery of either battle.

When she entered the commander's outer office,
the executive officer stood. His carefully neutral
expression told her more clearly than words the
gravity of the situation she now faced.

"The general is waiting for you, ma'am. I'll tell
him you're here."

Thankful that General Adams wasn't the kind
of man to play power games and keep her cooling
her heels in the outer office, Brenna used the few
moments while the exec announced her to steel
herself for what was to come. She didn't expect
fireworks or angry recriminations. That wasn't the
general's style. But she knew his way would scar
far worse, and far more permanently.

When Captain Hargrove returned the receiver
and nodded to her, Brenna squared her shoulders
and walked into the commander's office. She
halted a few paces from his desk and lifted her
right arm in the beginning of a salute. At that
moment, she caught sight of a second man standing off to the right. Her arm froze halfway up,
then slowly dropped.

Stiff with disbelief, Brenna met Dave Sanderson's intent stare. For an unguarded instant, she
spun back to a darkened hotel room in Panama.
A bed spilling tangled sheets onto the floor. A
male body heavy and urgent on hers.

She flushed hot with the memory, then as

quickly went ice cold. Thrown completely off stride, she struggled to understand just what the hell he was doing here.

He looked even more disreputable than usual, if that was possible. Several days' growth stubbled his jaw, and his fawn-colored hair badly needed a trim. His white cotton shirt clung to his chest in damp patches, and dusty jeans rode low on his hips. He wore the boots Brenna had last seen tossed beside a bed in the Hotel Plaza Paitilla, and an expression on his face that lit small, incendiary fires under her skin.

A week ago, she'd let herself believe the fierce glint in the depths of his hazel eyes hinted at some need, some spark of humanity. A week ago—even a few days ago—she might have made another foolish attempt to meet that need halfway. After her hours in the Neonatal ICU, she no longer had any desire to reach out to him at all.

Turning her back on him, she faced the general. "What's going on? What is Sanderson doing here?"

She didn't know if it was the sheer gutsiness of her questions or her less than respectful tone that lifted the general's brows. She didn't really care. While she waited for an answer, Sanderson moved into the circle of her view. Although her nerves jumped at his sudden nearness, Brenna pointedly ignored him.

But she couldn't ignore the quick look the two men exchanged. It was just a sideways glance, a brief flicker of the general's eyes toward the man beside her. Yet the brief glance rocked Brenna back on her heels. The floor seemed to tilt as a possibility she hadn't considered until this moment shoved its way into her mind.

Oh, God! Had General Adams stepped into the same quicksand that sucked at Dave Sanderson?

No, she thought desperately. Not this man. Not the leader she'd tried to model herself after. The commander who set the standard for everyone in the wing. The sense that nothing in the world was quite what it seemed assaulted Brenna, and she knew she wouldn't carry the same set of illusions out of this office she'd carried in.

Leveling her a look that would have curled her toes in any other circumstances, Adams answered her with acidic brevity.

"Sanderson's here because I want him here, Duggan." He gestured toward one of the high-backed chairs in front of his desk. "Sit down."

Whatever was coming next, Brenna needed to be on an equal footing with these two men when it hit.

"I'll stand."

Adams regarded her in frozen silence for long moments.

She felt her palms dampen, but refused to drop her eyes or her chin.

"Suit yourself," he replied at last, his gray eyes flat with the promise that this would be remembered.

A tightness wrapped around Brenna's chest. The sense of being caught in a vise almost overwhelmed her. She could feel Sanderson watching her. Every exposed surface of her skin itched with awareness of his presence at her side. Yet she didn't dare take her eyes off General Adams as he leaned forward, palms flat on the desk.

"You asked what's going on. I can't tell you, not all of it. But I've been cleared to inform you that Detection Systems Specialist Sanderson is part of an Interagency Special Task Force."

Brenna didn't move, didn't respond. For a few seconds, she didn't breathe.

General Adams's brusque voice cut through her frozen stillness. "He was assigned to this wing for a specific purpose."

She dragged in a shallow breath. "Which was?"

"To set himself up as a source for AWACS flight schedules."

Brenna felt as though she was watching a video of a glass window being broken in reverse. With agonizing slowness, the shards began to reassemble into a whole. The opaque picture they formed made her feel sick.

"A source for AWACS flight schedules," she repeated slowly. "I see."

"Do you?" Sanderson's fierce question brought her head around.

"I think so. You sold the schedules, didn't you? In Panama."

"Yes."

"At places like the Purple Parrot."

His face tightened. "Yes."

Brenna didn't allow herself the luxury of anger

at the way she'd been used. That would come later. Nor would she admit that a huge part of her wanted to cry with relief. That *might* come later. At this moment, her only concern was for the woman and infant she'd left in St. Mary's Hospital.

"So where . . . ?" She wet her lips. "Where does Sergeant Lang fit into your operation? Was he part of this Special Task Force?"

She knew the answer before the words were out of her mouth. Sanderson didn't look away, and didn't try to soften the blow.

"No."

Which meant, Brenna realized instantly, Andrew Lang was either an innocent victim or playing his own deadly game. Sanderson must have seen the question in her eyes.

"As far as we know," he told her tersely, "Lang wasn't on the other side. We think he just stumbled onto something that made him suspicious. He followed me to the Purple Parrot that night. I had to abort my contact, and tried to shake the kid off."

"But he wouldn't shake."

"No."

"He stayed after you left, trying to find answers to his questions."

"We've suspected all along his death wasn't accidental, but . . ."

He broke off with a small, frustrated lift of one shoulder, and a glacial coldness crept through

Brenna's veins. Spacing each word with care, she finished for him.

"But you didn't want to jeopardize your entire operation by investigating it."

"That's right."

She thought of all the responses she could make to that flat, emotionless statement. Only one made it past her slowly gathering fury.

"You bastard."

Her words were low and savage in their icy contempt. Above the rough stubble darkening Sanderson's cheeks, the skin stretched taut across his bones as the muscle in his jaw flexed.

As much as anything else in this filthy business, Dave had come to hate the way Brenna could bottle her fury and retreat behind that frigid, impenetrable wall. He wanted her to lash out at him. To singe him with her anger and the searing heat he now knew burned at her core. He wanted anything, everything, from her, except this icy scorn.

Despite the urgency of the message that brought him rushing back to Oklahoma only hours ago, his pulse had kick-started the moment she'd entered Adams's office. In the few seconds before she'd noticed his presence, Dave had mentally stripped every uniform item from her body, yanked the pins out of her hair, and feasted on the woman he'd joined with in a wide, sheet-tangled bed at the Plaza Paitilla.

She couldn't know how much it had cost him to watch her drop that hotel key on the table and walk out of his room. How he'd had to clench his jaw against the urge to call her back.

And he hoped to hell she'd never know how he'd jerked around at every sound during the next few days in alert shack, hoping she'd stride in and do exactly what she'd sworn she wouldn't. He'd gone from tense to rock hard every time he thought about her locking the door to the crew room and insisting they have another intimate discussion.

The days since his return from Panama had been the longest of Dave's life. Not even the years he'd spent in hell with Kristine measured up to the raw, blistering agony Brenna had put him through this past week.

He wanted her as he'd never wanted any woman before. All of her. Not just the liquid, searing passion she'd wrapped around him during their stolen interlude in Panama. And not the guarded truce she'd offered despite her own doubts and suspicions. He wanted her courage, and her strength, and her integrity. He wanted the intrinsic worth of the woman who would hold out a hand to him even though she wasn't sure he deserved it.

Then, he couldn't take her hand. It was too dangerous for both of them.

Now, he looked down into her eyes and knew it was too late. The faint hope that she might understand and accept his role in Andrew Lang's death slid away.

''The decision not to reveal the circumstances of

Sergeant Lang's death was painful, but necessary," General Adams said heavily. "We felt it would deepen Sanderson's cover if the people he was doing business with thought they'd protected their source."

Dave's gut clenched at the disgust that coursed over Brenna's face as she swung around.

"You felt it was necessary?" She choked a bit over the words. "Excuse me, sir, but *you* weren't the one who had to notify Sergeant Lang's wife. *You* didn't watch her being torn apart by doubts about herself and her husband. *You* didn't sit beside her hour after hour while she counted every one of her baby's heartbeats on a monitor."

General Adams hadn't survived two wars without learning how to take a few hits. His granite eyes didn't waver.

"I won't explain my actions to you."

"No, sir. But you might try explaining them to Mrs. Lang. If she lives long enough to hear any explanations. Whoever pushed her down those stairs could very well decide to try a more direct approach."

"A full security detail was dispatched to Saint Mary's Hospital five minutes after you left my office yesterday morning," Adams said acidly. "Mrs. Lang and her baby are under constant surveillance."

"Does she know why?"

"No. She's only been told that you reported her suspicions about the accident and they're being investigated."

"Wonderful."

"Careful, Colonel," the general warned. "Mrs. Lang's safety is why Dave Sanderson is here. And your concern for the woman's welfare is the only reason you're not facing a battery of charges right now. That, and your pigheadedness."

Her chin lifted.

Adams heaved an exasperated sigh. "Dammit, Duggan, do you think I'd let anyone get away with insubordination?"

"I wasn't aware that I've gotten away with anything."

"You put your career on the line for Mrs. Lang's safety. That's not insubordination in my book. That's taking care of your troops, and by extension, their families. The only matter that concerns me now is Mrs. Lang. I want you to tell Sanderson what you know about her accident."

Still angry over the months Janeen had suffered, Brenna wasn't ready to unbend. "I don't know anything more about it than I've told you," she replied stiffly.

Dave stepped into her line of sight, forcing her to meet his gaze. "Why would someone push her down those stairs? What did she say or do related to her husband's death that we don't know about?"

"She's talked to a lawyer ..."

"We know that."

"... about filing a civil suit," Brenna continued coldly.

"What kind of a civil suit?"

"A petition to require the Air Force to move on her request for redetermination."

"Jesus!"

A thousand possibilities flashed through Dave's mind, none of them helpful. He'd have his contacts run a check on the lawyer, try to find out who she might have talked to. But he knew damn well the chances of turning up a connection were slim at best. Anyone could have picked up this tiny thread of information and unthinkingly relayed it to the wrong person. Or ... His breath snagged in his throat. Or to the right person.

He stared down at the woman before him, one corner of his mind recording the spike of her sable lashes and the coldness in her eyes, while another spun in a direction he didn't want to follow.

No! Christ, no!

Despite his instinctive denial, Mad Dog's promise of a week ago echoed in his ears.

Consider it buried, ol' buddy. Consider it dead and buried.

Sweat trickled down Dave's neck as he remembered the bluff heartiness in his partner's words. And the desperation behind them. Forcing himself to meet Brenna's still accusing stare, he framed the next question carefully.

"Did Mrs. Lang talk about this civil suit to anyone besides you and her lawyer?"

"I don't know. Her family, I'm sure. Maybe some friends."

"You mentioned before that she'd been in contact with Tony Petrocelli. Do you think she might have told him about it?"

"I told you, I don't know. We didn't even talk

about it, really. She just left a message on my machine a few days ago. I . . ."

She stopped abruptly, an arrested expression in her clear blue eyes. Frowning, she looked from Dave to the quiet, watchful general, then back again.

"He's at the middle of all this, isn't he? This Petrocelli character?"

"I'm just asking, Duggan."

"He keeps cropping up in the most unexpected places," she said slowly. "The note with his aircraft tail number on it. His unannounced visit to Janeen. The track Sergeant Lang passed you."

Startled, Dave frowned down at her. "How the hell did you know about that track?"

"I ran a screen of all missions you and Lang flew together and reviewed the tapes. I saw the TOI he passed you. The one with MD's tail number pinned to it."

His stomach turned over. All this time, she'd held his life in the palm of her hand and hadn't known it.

"Have you told anyone else about that track?"

"Have I blown your cover, you mean?"

"Look, Duggan," he shot back, "this isn't just my ass we're talking about. There are a half-dozen people out there with their lives on the line right this minute, and several hundred more trying to keep billions of dollars in cocaine from hitting the streets. This operation is a lot bigger than both of us, so don't play the smart-mouthed commander with me. Just tell me if you've talked about that track to anyone else."

The tension in him was a living thing. It reached out and grabbed her, wrapping its coils around her until she answered in the same angry clip.

"No, I didn't talk about it to anyone."

"Are you sure?"

"You didn't mention it to Janeen Lang?" General Adams asked. "She's got to have some reason to push this redetermination so hard."

Like an ice floe breaking off a glacier, the anger Brenna had held so long in check splintered free. Her eyes flashing cold fire, she swept both men a look of utter scorn.

"You still don't get it, do you? Either of you. Janeen doesn't need any reason to pursue the redetermination except her belief in her husband. I didn't tell her a thing, because I followed orders and unwittingly took part in a cover-up that makes me sick. But I'm going to tell her something. I'm damn well going to."

"You can't," Dave countered abruptly. "Not yet."

"Just watch me."

He stepped forward, crowding her against the edge of the desk. "The hell you will. This whole operation is teetering on the edge, and I'll be damned if I'll let you compromise it any further."

She flung her head back to meet his eyes. "Janeen has a right to know what's going on! For her own safety, as well as her peace of mind."

"I just need a little more time. A few days. A week at most. We'll keep Janeen under protection until then."

Her expression told Dave more clearly than

words that she wouldn't yield. For a wild instant, the primitive male urge swept through him to use whatever force it took to overcome her resistance. He wasn't sure what held him back—the last shreds of his civilized veneer or the absolute certainty that Brenna would leave him writhing on the floor from a knee to the balls if he tried.

"*Maybe* you can protect Janeen," she conceded, her voice low and biting. "But can you breathe life into her baby?"

He didn't have an answer for that. There wasn't one.

"You've got to tell her!"

When he didn't reply, disgust etched fine lines on either side of her mouth.

"You've been down in the gutter too long, Sanderson. You're as callous as the scum you deal with."

"Yeah, I guess I am."

"You know," she said slowly, ice coating every word, "for a crazy moment in Panama, I thought I might be able to help you."

Dave had made a lot of mistakes in his life. He came close to making another one right then. Just in time, he squelched the urge to promise her another shot when this was all over. She was the only clean, decent thing that had come into his life in longer than he could remember, and he needed the help she'd offered him more than she could ever imagine.

But he couldn't promise her anything, and he wasn't ready to ask for anyone's help, even Brenna's. He moved back, feeling old and tired and as dirty as she had pegged him.

"I guess you thought wrong. Just keep what we've discussed in here to yourself. Until I give you the authority to do otherwise."

Her eyes frosted with contempt, she turned her back on him. Ramrod straight, she faced the general.

"Am I dismissed?"

Adams regarded her intently for several seconds, then nodded.

Neither man moved until the door closed behind her. Then Dave released the air trapped in his lungs and turned to the general.

"You know her better than I do. What do you think she'll do?"

"From what I've observed in the past few minutes," Adams responded dryly, "you're far better acquainted with Colonel Duggan than I am. Frankly, I have no idea what she'll do. I'd be disappointed in her if I did."

Dave raked a hand through his hair. "That doesn't leave me a whole lot of options."

In fact, he thought as he walked out of the headquarters into the crisp brightness of the October morning, Brenna had left him with damn few options. He didn't like what he had to do at this point any more than he suspected she would when she found out about it.

Chapter Sixteen

Damn him!

Brenna slammed the door to her condo with a violence she'd never let herself display anywhere else. She was still seething from the incredible session in the general's office that morning. She'd been forced to bottle up her fury all day long as she attended to her squadron duties and tried to decide just what the hell to do next, but she gave it free rein now.

Tossing her uniform jacket onto the kitchen counter, she kicked off her shoes. The tiles were cool and smooth under her nylon-clad feet, in marked contrast to her mood as she crossed to the fridge and yanked out a bottle of chilled mineral water. She was too dry for a soft drink, and too angry for anything as sweet as the Chardonnay.

Damn him!

All this time, Sanderson had let her spin and twist in the dark, like some dumb spider dangling at the end of a loose thread. For two months, he'd kept his secrets. For two months, he'd stood back while Janeen Lang turned herself inside out over her husband's death and Brenna questioned her judgment and her loyalty to the Air Force.

Damn him all to hell! *And* the powers behind him in this special operation. In their collective wisdom and need for secrecy, they'd refused to assuage one woman's grief, or another's doubts.

Twisting off the bottle cap, Brenna splashed the sparkling water into a tumbler. Her fingers shook as she lifted the glass to her lips.

A few weeks ago, she might have agreed that covering up the details of Sergeant Lang's death was a small price to pay in the battle against a greater evil. Out of respect for a higher authority, she might have swallowed her indignation at being told to back off of an investigation involving a member of her own squadron.

But she couldn't swallow her anger or her indignation any longer. Not after watching Janeen's private grief and painful doubts. Not after holding Sergeant Lang's baby in her arms. Setting the glass aside, she reached for the phone and punched in the number that was now burned into her memory.

"Neonatal ICU."

"This is Brenna Duggan. I wanted to check on the Lang baby. How's she doing?"

"There isn't much change in her condition since your last call, Colonel, but we've had a few hopeful signs. She's breathing on her own a little more. The doctor thinks we might be able to take her off the respirator soon." Hope shone through Brenna's anger like sunshine through storm clouds.

"And Mrs. Lang?"

"She's doing fine. She's taking a shower right now. Shall I have her call you when she's done?"

"Yes, if you . . ." Brenna stopped. What she had to say to Janeen couldn't be said over the phone. "No, just tell her that I'll be there in a couple of hours. I need to talk to her."

Replacing the receiver, Brenna glanced at her watch. It was a little after six. She had time for a quick shower and change, then she'd grab a hamburger at a drive-through on her way out of the city. Maybe by the time she'd made the hour-long odyssey to Enid, she'd have figured out just what she was going to tell Janeen.

A half hour later, she sped through the darkening countryside. Having traveled these long stretches of deserted road between Oklahoma City and Enid several times now, Brenna paid scant attention to the shadowed landscape whizzing past. The thin, ivory-colored wool sweater she'd pulled on with her taupe suede skirt provided just the right amount of protection from the night air whipping through the convertible's windows. Just in case the temperature dropped later, she'd thrown a Pendleton blazer in a muted, coffee-and-cream plaid into the back seat. Even now, after a solitary half hour of driving, her thoughts still chased around and around in her head like laboratory mice scurrying around on a track wheel.

She didn't know the exact classification of Sanderson's Special Task Force, but suspected it carried at least a "secret" label. So whatever she told Janeen tonight would stretch the limits of security classifications . . . if it didn't directly violate them.

Brenna had never knowingly violated a directive or an order in her life. She'd come close, by hinting to Janeen about the provision in the regulation that allowed for dependents to request a redetermination despite the general's order to back off. And she'd stood toe to toe with her boss yesterday and told him she was going over his head if he didn't support Janeen's request. But this was the first time she'd contemplated a deliberate breech of security.

The prospect made her feel slightly nauseated, but no less certain. The decision to press on with the request for redetermination at this point belonged to Janeen Lang, and to no one but her. One way or another, Brenna was going to make sure she made an informed choice.

Absorbed in her own thoughts, she didn't pay any attention to the cars that flew by her at infrequent intervals on the otherwise deserted road. Nor did she give the vehicle that crept up behind her Miata any particular thought until its high beams suddenly blazed in her rearview mirror.

Startled, Brenna squinted into the mirror and made out what looked like the silhouette of a pickup. Glancing down at the speedometer, she realized that she'd slowed for the last curve and hadn't resumed cruising speed. She pressed down on the accelerator, irritated with herself for her inattention to the road.

To her annoyance, the truck behind her speeded up as well. She cursed under her breath, in no mood for road games. Slowing again, she waited for the other driver to pass. The road stretched dark and empty for endless miles ahead. The idiot riding her bumper had plenty of room to pull around.

Her heart gave a funny little lurch when the shadowy vehicle matched her slower pace and stayed right on her tail. Its headlights dimmed, then flashed. Narrowing her eyes against the glare, Brenna peered into the mirror once more. She couldn't distinguish anything except the outline of the cab.

Swallowing, she gripped the leather-wrapped wheel and searched the dark horizon. A few faint lights gleamed far off to the west, but she had no idea whether the farm they represented was accessible from this road or another. Her heart now thumping erratically, she depressed the accelerator.

Like a sleek, racing greyhound, the low-slung Miata pulsed ahead. Brenna shivered in relief when the truck fell back, then swallowed again when it started to inch forward. Sweat bonded her palms to the leather as she took a firmer grip on the wheel and pressed down on the gas pedal.

Although her eyes were glued to the road

ahead, her mind raced with the same frantic speed as the car. It could be a drunk behind her. Or some high school kid out for a little fun. Or someone just wanting to prey on a woman driving alone at night. Or . . .

She clenched her jaw.

Or it could be the same unknown person who'd shoved Janeen Lang down a flight of stairs.

The rushing night lashed at her face and hair and teared her eyes. Blinking desperately, Brenna scanned the deserted road ahead for a sign that would tell her how far she was from the next town. Nothing appeared, except a long, rolling rise. She shot up the low hill, praying an all-night convenience store would appear on the other side. Or a brightly lit farmhouse. An intersection with a major highway. Another vehicle. Anything!

The Miata flew over the hill's crest, and Brenna's stomach plummeted at the inky emptiness beyond. She threw another look in the rear mirror. Fear grabbed at her throat, then spiraled into panic as the truck came barreling over the hill. Its headlights spiked the black sky before lowering to pin her in their harsh wash.

She tromped the gas pedal flat to the floor. The Miata took a small leap forward. Over the smooth throb of its engine, Brenna heard a grind of gears, then a gathering roar. The truck pulled out of the lane behind her and nosed along her left fender. Her heart slamming against her ribs, she kept her eyes glued to the road ahead and the gas pedal jammed to the floor. A narrow curve loomed just anead, one she remembered from her previous trip. She wasn't sure she could take it at this speed, but she didn't dare brake with the pickup nudging her tail like this.

With a whimper of sheer terror, she swung the Miata into the turn. The little sports car tried valiantly to cling to the road. Its tires screamed a protest as centrifugal force pulled it across the tarmac. Brenna threw herself sideways to fight the drag and hung onto the wheel. At the last minute, she slammed on the brakes, hoping she could spin away from the truck on the wide, flat shoulder.

The desperate maneuver almost worked. Her car swung clear of the other vehicle and twisted around. But its momentum was too powerful for Brenna to stop the spin and point the hood in the opposite direction. The little Miata made almost a complete circle and skidded to a stop with its nose just a few feet from a ditch.

A cloud of choking dust enveloped the vehicle immediately. The thick grit added to the fear clogging Brenna's nose and throat as she scrabbled for the expandable metal baton she kept under her seat. Before her frantic fingers could find the heavy weapon, the car door was wrenched open. A hard hand wrapped around her upper arm, dragged her out of the car, and spun her against the Miata's fender.

In a blinding instant of sheer terror, she took in a black T-shirt stretched taut across a broad chest, a neck corded with fury, a square chin. Brenna barely had time to register the fact that the chin was now clean shaven and not stubbled with shadows, as it had been in the general's office that morning, before Sanderson's bellow thundered above the whine of his truck's engine and the blood roaring in her ears.

"Are you nuts! You could have killed us both with that crazy stunt!"

"*Me?*" The single syllable spiraled into a screech. "I wasn't the one playing touch tag at a hundred miles an hour!"

Still trembling and more frightened than she ever wanted to admit, Brenna shoved at his chest. The futile attempt to push him away resulted in an inarticulate snarl and a movement that bent her back against the warm car.

"I just about lost it when you spun around like that!"

The instant Dave shouted the words at the woman he'd followed through the night, he recognized their truth. The few seconds the red Miata had twisted through the blackness had played across his mind again and again. He was certain Brenna had lost control of the car, and feared he'd lost her.

In that heart-stopping moment, all the guilt, all the pain, all the self-blame he'd heaped on himself in the years since Kristine's death had coalesced into a single, driving fact. If Brenna survived that death spiral and he got his hands on her, he'd never let her go.

Now that he had her, however, he couldn't decide what the hell to do with her. His heart hammered with a combination of fear and fury, and she wasn't in much better shape. In fact, he decided with a bolt of savage satisfaction, the cool, collected, always-in-control Colonel Duggan looked every bit as shaken and enraged as he was.

There wasn't any trace of ice in her blue eyes now. They blazed up at him with unleashed rage. Her hair was a windblown mass of dark, tangled silk, and her breath came hot and fast in uneven pants that lifted her breasts under the clinging sweater. Her fingers were curled into claws that made Dave tighten his grip on her upper arms as he lashed out at her.

"Why the hell didn't you stop when I flashed my lights?"

"Oh, sure!" she shouted, shoving at his chest again with both fists. "Like I'm going to stop out here! In the middle of nowhere. With some jerk climbing right up my ass."

Her choice of words almost sent him over the edge. "Watch it, lady. This particular jerk's about a half a hair away from doing just that."

"You try anything with me, Sanderson, and I swear I'll . . ."

"You'll what? Court-martial me? Not hardly. If anyone's going to be answering for their conduct tonight, it's you."

She didn't give up easily. Dave had to give her that. Tossing her head back to get her hair out of her eyes, she glared up at him.

"You're full of it."

"I must be full of something," he fired back.

"Why else would I be chasing after you like this, trying to stop you from doing something you'll always regret?"

"You don't have any idea what I'm . . ."

"Dammit, Brenna, I know exactly what you're doing! I put a tap on your phone a half hour after you walked out of the general's office this morning. I picked up your tail before you turned off I–40."

Her mouth opened, then closed, then opened again.

If it weren't for the inarticulate little noises she made at that moment, Dave might have been able to pull back. But the incoherent sputtering was so unlike Brenna, so different from her usual, unassailable dignity, that something inside him shattered into tiny pieces.

Softening both his tone and his hold, he tried to find a path through the anger and distrust that swirled around them, as thick and as suffocating as the road dust.

"Brenna, listen to me. Please. I know you're furious. I know you despise me for what Janeen Lang's gone through these past months. You can't hate me any more than I hate myself for that, but I had to do it. Just as I had to tap your phone, and come after you tonight."

Her mouth snapped shut.

Dave waited for her to say something. Anything. But the only sounds that came back to him were the distinctive whine of the engines, one deep-throated and powerful, the other well-oiled and plaintive.

As he stared down into her pale face, his crushing need of a few moments ago came back with blade-sharp clarity. He couldn't let her go. Whatever it cost him, he couldn't let her go. Not this time.

Hiding a desperation he only half recognized in the deep rasp of his voice, he drew her up, into his heat.

"You told me in Panama I had to make the next move. I just made it. I came after you . . . as much for my sake as yours."

She stiffened her palms against his chest. "It's too late. It was too late when someone shoved Janeen down those stairs."

"I'll find him. I swear, I'll find whoever was behind that."

He knew. In his gut, Dave knew who had engineered the tragic accident. The one man he counted as friend. The only one who'd stood by him during the years he'd wallowed in bitterness and self-recrimination. The knowledge ate at him like acid dripping on bare, unprotected metal.

He'd deal with Mad Dog. Soon.

In the slicing glare of the pickup's headlights, Brenna saw the face above her tighten into stark planes. The desolation that darkened his eyes came and went so quickly, someone else might have missed it. But she knew this man well enough now to recognize his pain for what it was. The brief glimpse into his being sliced through the tumult of her own wild emotions. Out of the swirling tides that pulled her in a thousand different directions, she grasped at a single, shattering truth.

He needed her as much as he wanted her. He had no one else. Only her. He didn't like the idea. That was obvious from the taut line of his jaw. He'd come to her furious with himself and with her. But he'd come.

No one had ever needed her before, Brenna realized with searing honesty. Not like this. Not at such a basic, elemental level. Not her former husband. Not Buck Henry. Not even Janeen Lang.

The young widow's love for her husband, and now for her child, formed the bedrock of her existence. The bond that had formed between the two women since Andrew Lang's death touched only the periphery of Janeen's central core. She would understand, Brenna thought with a flash of insight. Janeen had understood all along what only now became clear to her.

What bound a man and a woman went beyond reason. Beyond rational explanation. It was shaped by what she saw in Sanderson's eyes at that moment. And molded in the hopeless need to respond that trickled through her like water seeping through a crack in a dam. The trickle gathered force with each passing second, until Brenna could only rest her forehead against his chest and give a muffled groan.

"Damn you, Sanderson."

A ragged breath rattled through his rib cage,

and one of his hands left her arm to curl under her chin. Tilting her face to his, he shook his head.

"I want something better than that, lady."

"That's about all I'm capable of at this moment."

His eyes searched hers. "Oh, no, Duggan," he said softly. "I think you're capable of a whole lot more. You held out your hand to me once."

"Right," she huffed. "And look what it got me."

A slow grin softened the stark planes of his face. "As I recall, it got you all tangled up in some sheets."

She'd seen that crooked grin and the sudden glitter in his eyes before. Several times. Once at twenty thousand feet, with her back pressed against a stainless steel counter in the belly of an E–3. Once in a narrow alley off the Calle Rosa. And once in a darkened hotel room. Each time she'd fought the flicker of response that predatory look sparked in her. This time, she didn't even try.

"So it did," she whispered.

With a growled warning, his hand moved to her hip. "I don't think you can convince me to go slow and easy this time, Brenna."

"What makes you think I want slow and easy this time?"

Excitement eddied along her flesh as he rode her skirt up her thighs and bared them to the night air. A litany she'd probably repeat many times in the weeks or days or hours she'd have with this man sounded in her head.

This was crazy.

This was insane.

They were in plain view. On the shoulder of a state road, for God's sake!

She was a lieutenant colonel in the United States Air Force . . . for the moment, anyway. She'd been prepared to face charges of insubordination, but the thought of being caught and having to explain a compromising situation like this boggled Brenna's very straight, very disciplined mind.

Then Sanderson hooked a thumb in her panties and shoved them down, and she knew she'd risk being caught in situations far worse than this for the touch of his hand on her body and the feel of his mouth on hers.

With an inarticulate sound, he lifted her onto the Miata's hood. Neither one of them thought of protection now. Or improvisation. Or compromise. Their joining was hard and fast and furious. Brenna gasped as sensation after sensation bombarded her. The hot car hood under her bare buttocks. The cold night air. The thrust of his sex into hers. The tangle of tongues and teeth and greedy lips.

He tore her sweater over her head, or she did. The front fastening on her bra gave under his hand, or maybe hers. Dragging his head down with both hands, Brenna took his mouth.

They were both panting when he lifted his head. His hands were hard and urgent as he slid her bottom across the hood, impaling her fully. He held her hard against him, his hips slamming into hers. She locked her legs around his waist, matching every lunge with a thrust of her hips.

Then he bent to take her nipple in his teeth, and Brenna cried out at the exquisite little pain. Planting both palms on the vibrating car hood, she arched her back to give him easier access to her breasts. The muscles in her legs and her thighs and her belly strained as she pulled him again and again into her slick flesh.

She didn't know who climaxed first. She was so lost in the spasms of sensation that convulsed her core and stung her nipples that she barely heard him call her name in a harsh, unrecognizable voice.

Answering his call took all her strength. Her arms shook as she hooked them around his neck, lifted herself, then pushed her hips down hard onto his.

Their bodies locked together. And, for a moment out of time, their separate beings joined.

Chapter Seventeen

"Brenna."

Sanderson's deep voice barely penetrated the cloud of sensual satisfaction hazing her mind. Languorous and replete, Brenna refused to move.

The shoulder under her cheek shifted. A hand came up to stroke her hair. "We need to talk."

"No," she mumbled, burrowing her nose deeper in the warm, salty flesh of his neck.

"We have to."

"I know, I know. But not yet."

God, not yet! She couldn't handle talking yet. Not with her breasts flattened against his chest and the soft, fuzzy hair arrowing down his middle causing all kinds of delayed reactions to her sensitized nipples.

"Well, I wouldn't mind passing the rest of the night with you plastered against me like this, you understand," Sanderson drawled, still stroking her hair. "But then my rear isn't planted on a car fender and available for inspection by any and all passersby . . . like the one coming over the hill behind you."

Brenna jerked up her head and threw a quick glance over her shoulder. In the distance, headlights speared the night sky, then descended in a slow arc as an oncoming vehicle swept down the hill toward them.

With a small squeak, she unwound her body from his and slid off the car. The night air danced on her sweat-slick skin as she grabbed for her scattered clothes. Frantically, she shook the dust from her thin wool sweater and pulled it on. Stepping into her skirt, she yanked it up and began searching for her shoes and underwear. She found one loafer near the Miata's back tire and her bra in a puddle of dust.

Sanderson had removed far fewer articles of clothing, she noted with a mixture of amusement and pique. He certainly needed less time to pull himself together. While she stuffed the bra in her skirt pocket and searched for her other shoe, he zipped up his jeans, tucked his T-shirt into his waistband, and moved to his pickup. Opening the driver's door, he retrieved a small, black bundle.

He was back at her side by the time the other car came to a rolling stop some distance away. Engine idling, it hunched in the darkness like some big, inquisitive bug. Brenna squinted into the glare, but couldn't make out the driver.

As seconds passed with no sign of movement in the other vehicle, her exasperation at almost being caught naked in the middle of Nowhere,

Oklahoma, feathered into a tingling sense of un-ease. Instinctively, she edged closer to Sanderson.

He leaned a hip against the Miata, one hand resting casually against the cherry red fender, the other out of sight at his side. With a nonchalant twist of his shoulders, he placed most of his body between her and the other vehicle. Brenna noted the protective movement and tucked it away for future consideration.

The driver's side window of the car whirred down. "Are . . . ? Are you all right?"

Brenna's shoulders sagged in relief at the sound of a wavery, feminine voice.

"We're fine," Sanderson called out. "The lady had some car trouble and I stopped to help. We've got her running again."

"Do you need me to call a tow truck or the police?"

Brenna admired the courage of a woman who would stop to help on this deserted stretch of road, and the common sense that kept her in her car with the engine running.

"We've got it under control," she replied, step-ping out of Dave's shadow. "Thanks for stopping, though. I really appreciate it."

"You sure you don't need some help?"

No, she wasn't sure about that at all. But a stranger couldn't provide the kind of help she needed to get through the next few minutes.

"We'll manage. Thanks again."

"Well, if you're sure . . ."

His muscles knotted with a tension that had become second nature, Dave watched the taillights of the woman's car dwindle to two indistinct blurs. Rolling his shoulders to loosen their wire stiffness, he slid his Smith & Wesson 9mm into its leather nest at the small of his back. The weapon was standard Customs issue, normally carried only by personnel on the law enforcement and apprehension side of the house. Dave had carried one day and night for the past four months. He'd exchanged its twelve-round clip for a high-capacity staggered stack of fifteen Teflon-coated hollow-point bullets that would do serious body damage in a close-up skirmish. He wouldn't want to pit the handgun against a high-powered rifle or assault weapon, however, which their seeming Good Samaritan could easily have been carrying.

Cursing himself as ten kinds of a fool for dallying with Brenna in this isolated, exposed spot, he turned to find her watching him. Her expression was thoughtful and very cautious.

Dave swore again under his breath. Regret slashed through him—for the vanished intimacy of a few moments ago, and for the wariness in her eyes.

"We have to talk," he said again. "But not here. I'll follow you back to Oklahoma City, to your place."

When he reached down to open the Miata's door, she shook her head. "I'm not going back to Oklahoma City. Not yet."

Frowning, he straightened. "I thought we talked about this."

"As I recall," she replied dryly, "we shouted about it a bit."

The car door slammed shut. "You can't go on to Enid, Brenna. You can't do something you know you'll regret later, when this is all over."

She lifted her chin, every inch the cool, composed woman who both fascinated Dave and irritated the hell out of him. Frustration rose in jagged edges as he wondered how the devil she could pull off that regal air when her hair looked like it had been combed by the rotor blades of a chopper, her cream-colored sweater bore a boot print on one breast, and her lips were still red and swollen from his kisses.

"I'll probably regret a lot of things that have happened lately," she said calmly, "but going to see Janeen tonight is not one of them."

Spreading his legs, he hooked his thumbs in his belt. "I can't let you do it."

One sable brow arched. "What are you going to do? Knock me out and toss me in the back of your truck?"

"If I have to."

She didn't blink. "I know you're trying to protect me as much as your mission, but I'm fully prepared to face the consequences of my decision."

Things had gone too far between them for Dave to let her think he was protecting her for any lofty, idealistic reasons. He'd left altruistic behind years ago, and had never been into noble.

"If you want to flush your career down the

tubes, that's your decision. But this isn't your decision to make. I told you before, my ass is on the line here."

"I won't compromise your operation."

"Dammit, Brenna, I'm not talking about the operation. I'm talking about lives. Mine, and a lot of others."

"Tell that to Janeen Lang. She's the woman who tumbled down a flight of stairs, remember? The one who lost a husband to your operation."

He didn't flinch. He wasn't even sure he could anymore. Taking a half step closer, he laid himself as bare as he dared.

"Look, I know sorry doesn't carry any weight at this point, but I am. I'm sorry as hell about Mrs. Lang and her baby and even sorrier about Andy Lang. They got caught up in something dirtier than you can imagine and almost out of control."

"So did you, evidently."

Dave steeled himself against the flicker of compassion he saw in her eyes.

"So did I. But don't make the mistake of thinking I'm in this out of any misguided sense of patriotism or burning desire to right the wrongs of the world."

"So why are you in it?"

"Because I didn't have any choice," he replied with brutal honesty. "I hit bottom, rock bottom, a few years ago. In one of my less brilliant moments, I took a charter from a supposedly upright and outstanding citizen who just happened to be selling illegal arms south of the border. The Mexican government detained me for several months, but eventually the Feds extricated me. We cut a deal, and I've been working for Customs ever since."

She shook her head. "I'm not buying that. You're not the kind of man to be roped into doing something you don't want to do. You never have been, if your military record is anything to go by."

He shoved a hand through his hair. "Believe what you want. Just understand that I can't let you go to Enid."

"Fine. Don't *let* me go. Come with me."

"Didn't you hear anything I said? I can't."

"Yes, you can. You have to. You need to talk to Janeen. You need to lay to rest the ghost who's haunting us both almost much as he is her."

"Brenna, for God's sake—"

"No, Dave. For your sake. For mine and Janeen's. And Andy Lang's."

He stared down at her, wondering how the hell she managed to see everything in such stark black and white. Everything in his life had been a dim, murky gray for so long, he'd forgotten any clarity existed.

"Well?" she asked when he hesitated for a fraction of a second too long. "Do you want to take your pickup or my car?"

After a silence that stretched forever, he admitted defeat. Mouth tight, he gestured toward the truck.

Too smart to let any sign of triumph show on

her face, Brenna bent and extracted her keys from the Miata. Its engine rattled a last time, then stilled. The sway of her slender hips as she moved toward the pickup grabbed at Dave's groin. He allowed himself the pleasure of watching her, thinking that he and Lieutenant Colonel Duggan were going to have one very long, very private discussion when they got back from Enid. She had the passenger door half open when he called out to her.

"Brenna."

She turned, leveling him a look that said she was done with arguments. It was her best commander look, one Dave knew all too well. Bending down, he retrieved a scrap of lace and nylon that lay almost under the sports car's front tire.

"We've still got some long stretches of dark country road ahead," he said, dangling the fabric from one finger. "If you want me to keep my hands on the wheel, you'd better put these on."

He almost lost it when she strolled back to him, gave him a very private, very uncommander-like smile, and stuffed the panties into her skirt pocket.

"Let's get it in gear, Sanderson."

When they arrived at St. Mary's Hospital an hour later, Dave still hadn't decided just what he could or should tell Janeen Lang. He knew only that he wouldn't let Brenna compromise herself or his mission. If anyone was going to talk to the widow about her husband tonight, he was.

He followed her down a long, brightly lit

fourth-floor corridor. When a woman in street clothes stepped from behind the nurses' station and stopped them, Brenna blinked in surprise.

"We're just going to visit a patient," she explained.

"May I ask who?"

"Mrs. Lang. Janeen Lang."

"I'm sorry, she's not receiving visitors."

"But . . ."

Brenna broke off, suddenly remembering that General Adams had said he'd dispatched a full security detail to guard Janeen. Digging in her purse, she pulled out her wallet and flipped it open to show her military ID.

"I'm Lieutenant Colonel Duggan, Commander of the 552d Training Squadron. Mrs. Lang's husband was a member of my unit."

"Sorry. Our orders are family only."

Frustrated, Brenna looked to Dave.

He weighed the possibility of using the orders as an excuse to take her home, but the determined set to her mouth told him she wasn't leaving.

"Let me make a quick call," he said, moving to the nurses' station. A moment later, he held out the receiver.

After a brief exchange, the guard hung up.

"You can go on back. Mrs. Lang is in her room."

Another guard was posted outside the door Brenna led them to. After confirming their status with the woman at the nurses' station, he stood aside.

Brenna rapped her knuckles softly on the wood-paneled door. At the low-voiced reply, she pushed it open a few inches, then walked in. Dave followed more slowly, steeling himself for what would come.

He expected anger. Tears. Recriminations.

What he hadn't expected was the shining joy in Janeen Lang's eyes as she lifted her head and greeted Brenna.

"She started breathing on her own a few hours ago, and now she's sucking! Look, Brenna, she's sucking!"

Dave stood rooted to the floor, completely out of his element as Brenna dropped to her knees beside Janeen's chair and exclaimed over the tiny, fuzz-covered head nestled in the crook of her arm.

"Oh, God, she is! She is!"

She laughed in delight as a miniature fist batted the air, then pushed at her mother's breast.

Watching the intimate tableau, Dave was struck by how different the two women were. One was tall. Slender. With a mane of dark chocolate hair that managed to look sleek despite the fact that it was windblown and tangled.

The other still carried signs of her pregnancy in her rounded face, which was framed by a tumble of honey-blond curls. Even seated, she appeared short. And so damn young. Hardly more than a girl.

She'd spent her few years as a wife wrapped in her husband's arms and absorbed in his life, if the little Dave had heard about Janeen Lang was correct. In contrast, Brenna had carved a successful career for herself out of a profession dominated by men and still subtly resistant to women in some areas.

Yet in that moment, they met on an equal plane. Dave saw the same strength in both women, and a fierce, untrammeled joy in the child that overrode any differences in age or character or profession.

The wrenching doubts he'd harbored during the past hour about telling Janeen Lang anything sifted through the sieve of gut-instinct and left him with a sense of certainty. This woman was far stronger than he or anyone else believed. She could be trusted to keep to herself whatever he told her in confidence.

Hands in his pockets, he watched silvered tears trail a shining path down Brenna's cheeks. She sniffed noisily, then reached for a hospital wipe from the box on the low table beside Janeen.

"I told you she'd make it." Janeen's soft voice was vibrant with triumph.

Brenna angled her head away and blew her nose. "So you did," she mumbled.

"She's tough. Just like her daddy. And her auntie." Tenderly, Janeen palmed the baby blond fuzz. "Aren't you, Andrea Brenna Lang?"

Dave barely managed to stifle an involuntary groan. Good Lord! There'd be another Brenna out there in fifteen or twenty years, organizing the world to her own particular specifications.

Janeen planted a kiss on the baby's crown, then glanced up with a shy, inquiring smile.

"Are you Brenna's friend, the lieutenant colonel she told me about? Did you come with her to see the baby?"

Without having to think about it more than a half second, Dave realized that he did *not* like the idea of Brenna having a "friend." Frowning, he tried to figure out just when the hell he'd transitioned from wanting to tumble her into his bed to wanting to keep her there for the foreseeable future. On a more or less exclusive basis.

She returned his frown with a bland smile that set his teeth on edge and waited with Janeen for his reply.

"No, Mrs. Lang," he said deliberately. "I'm not Brenna's 'friend.' I'm not quite sure what our relationship is at this point, but I certainly wouldn't label it friendship."

The younger woman blinked. Glancing from Dave to Brenna and back, she formed her own opinions and kept them to herself. His reluctant respect for her ratcheted up another notch. She wasn't as soft as that shy exterior would lead a stranger to think, not by a long shot.

"I didn't come specifically to see the baby," he continued, his grimace sliding into a rusty smile. "But I'm glad I got a chance to meet the lady. She's, ah, . . . beautiful."

Janeen's laughter drifted across the room, as low and rich as the summer breeze rippling the tassels on a field of wheat.

"Well," she replied in her rolling drawl, "she's still a little blue around the gills and more wrinkled than my daddy's shirt back after a church meetin' in the middle of July, but you're right. She's beautiful."

Shifting the baby to her other arm, she folded the hospital gown across her breasts and returned Dave's smile with a grin that kicked at his gut. From where he stood, she shone with a feminine, totally sensual beauty.

"Would you like to hold her?"

Dave took a hasty step back. There was no way he wanted responsibility for that fragile snip of humanity.

"No. Uh, thanks. I'm wearing too much road dust to handle anything now."

Brenna lifted a brow, but refrained from commenting that he hadn't worried about road dust or anything else when he'd handled her a short while ago.

"Here, I'll take her."

She eased the child into her arms with a competency that made him wonder where she'd gotten her proficiency training. Brushing a knuckle down a red, wrinkled cheek, she rose.

"This is Dave Sanderson, Janeen. He's a U.S. Customs agent who flies aboard our AWACS on certain missions. He was with Andy the night he died."

Janeen's brown eyes widened, then slewed sideways to capture Dave's.

Cradling the baby carefully, Brenna walked to

the door. "I'll take Andrea back to the nursery while you two talk."

Dave shot her an exasperated glare as she sailed out of the room. He still hadn't quite figured out how he was going to broach the subject of Andrew Lang's death with his widow, but he sure as hell hadn't planned to just stomp into it with both boots and no backup.

But when he slid a chair up and sat down beside her, he realized that Brenna's approach was the only one Janeen would accept. She'd long ago passed the point of hesitancy or awkwardness or subterfuge. She deserved the truth.

Dave only wished he knew it himself.

"Tell me about that night," she said, gripping her hands together in her lap. "Tell me about Andy."

Chapter Eighteen

They left St. Mary's a little before midnight. The drive back to Oklahoma City lacked both the drama and the explosive sexual energy of the trip up. A more subtle tension permeated the pickup's cab this time, no less sexual, but far less frenetic.

Dave seemed reluctant to discuss his session with Janeen, and Brenna didn't push him. For the time being, she was content to wedge one shoulder against the door frame, rest her head on the high seat back, and watch him through half-closed lids.

In the shadowy darkness, he was all hard angles and lean, uncompromising edges. His hair still tickled the back of his neck in a way that snagged her unwilling attention whenever she saw it. Brenna tried to visualize him in one of the buzz-cuts popular these days. To her surprise, the mental image of Dave Sanderson in a neat crew cut didn't appeal to her half as much as it once would have.

Smiling to herself, she ran her eyes down his shoulders and sinewy arms, lingering for long moments on his hands. The memory of those square-tipped fingers rough and urgent on her waist as they lifted her onto the Miata's fender returned in a rush. Her stomach muscles contracted involuntarily, and she wondered just where in the world the two of them would go from here.

They'd reached a new stage in their undefined relationship tonight. Like Dave, Brenna wasn't exactly sure how to label the feelings that swirled between them. Whatever she felt for him, it held none of the comfortable give-and-take of her friendship with Buck Henry. Nor did it contain the seeds of permanency and happy-ever-after that had characterized her early passion for her ex-husband. True, those seeds hadn't sprouted and flowered into the kind of enduring love Janeen and Andy Lang appeared to have found. But the potential had been there in the beginning, at least.

Dave Sanderson, she sensed, lived only for the moment. He refused to talk about his past, or even acknowledge its impact on his present. Given the kind of activities he was involved in, she suspected he didn't look too far into the future either. If happy-ever-after was part of his personal agenda, he didn't give any evidence of it.

Was it part of hers?

Brenna shifted on the hard seat, troubled by the realization that the future she'd always assumed for herself had somehow dissipated into the mists surrounding Sergeant Lang's death.

She'd put her career on the line several times now. To her surprise and considerable relief, General Adams hadn't torn her to shreds for threatening to go over his head. She wasn't as sure what he'd do about her deliberate decision to tell Janeen about the Special Task Force.

Of course, she reminded herself, she hadn't told Janeen anything. Sanderson had.

She gave the silent man beside her another assessing look. He came across as so hard. So tough and uncaring. Yet he'd refused to allow her to destroy her career, then he'd compromised his own by speaking with Janeen.

She wasn't sure how much Dave had shared with the young widow. When Brenna had gone back to say good-bye, Janeen had been alone, staring out the window. Her back to the door, she stood with her arms wrapped fiercely around her middle. She hadn't moved, hadn't responded at all to Brenna's hesitant farewell. Not wanting to intrude, she'd left Janeen with her memories.

Sanderson had given them back to her. For that alone, Brenna would always . . . What? Love him?

She chewed on the inside of her lower lip, unwilling to label the intense, confused emotion this man generated in her. She was no nearer to defining it when his deep voice ended the stillness between them.

"You looked like you knew what you were doing when you handled that baby."

With a start, Brenna realized that the man she'd opened herself to so intimately on more than one occasion knew even less about her than she knew about him.

"I haven't had any of my own," she returned with a small smile, "but that doesn't mean I don't know which end is up."

"Why didn't you? Have any of your own?"

"Never found the right time in my career, I guess. Or the right man to have them with." She tilted her head, studying his shadowed eyes. "What about you, Sanderson? Do you have children?"

"None that I know of."

She wasn't letting him off that easy. He'd started this conversation, after all. "Why not?"

He kept his eyes on the road and his hands loose on the wheel, but Brenna caught a ripple of movement as a muscle tensed alongside his jaw.

"It never seemed like the right time for us, either."

"I know about your wife," she said softly.

"No, you don't. You can't."

"So tell me."

He was silent for so long, Brenna didn't think he intended to answer. Dark, purpled scenery whizzed by unseen as she held her breath, waiting, hoping.

"It's a familiar story to someone in the military," he said at last. "Kristine liked the idea of being married to a man in uniform, but hated the long absences that went with it. I resented the guilt she heaped on me every time I came home. After a while, I stopped coming home."

"That's when she started drinking?"

His hands tightened on the wheel. "No, she'd been hitting it pretty hard all along. But it got worse, a lot worse, after I got banged up punching out of a plane and couldn't fly in the front seat anymore. I cross-trained as a Weapons Director and ended up in AWACS."

"Which meant you were gone almost six months out of every year."

"Yeah, during the quiet years." His knuckles showed white against his tanned skin. "I quit the Air Force then and tried a nine-to-five job, but . . ."

He shrugged off the bitter years she knew had followed.

"But you and your wife had grown too far apart," Brenna finished for him. "I've been there."

She rested her head against the door frame, not pushing, but hoping he'd continue. This was the first time he'd allowed her so much as a glimpse behind the solid concrete wall he'd built between himself and the rest of the world. When he only stared ahead at the dark road, she stifled her disappointment and directed her questions from his past to a present they both shared.

"So where does Petrocelli come into the picture?"

A muscle ticked in the side of his jaw.

"You have to tell me about him, Dave. I want to know how he plays in this scenario."

Suddenly, the quiet sharing of a few moments ago was gone. Tension strung wire taut through the cab as the man beside her reached for his shirt pocket, then cursed and dropped his hand back to the wheel again.

"Mad Dog's my partner," he told her, reluctance audible in each word. "We flew together in the Air Force, and he pulled me out of the pit I'd dug for myself after my marriage and career went south."

"By getting you involved in some of his cock-eyed moneymaking schemes?"

"They weren't all cockeyed. Some of them actually paid off. Like the air charter service we started in Brownsville with one single-engine Cessna. We'd built up to a fleet of six aircraft when the roof caved in on us."

He kept his eyes on the road, but Brenna suspected that he saw more than an empty stretch of Oklahoma in the blackness before him.

"That was when I got busted. I'd hauled a load of oil-drilling equipment to Ciudad Juárez. Unfortunately, I discovered the pipes were stuffed with illegal arms at about the same time the Mexican government did. I ended up in a ten-by-twenty cell with four other sweaty prisoners who didn't particularly cotton to *norte americanos*."

"Did Petrocelli set you up with that load?"

"No."

Brenna blinked at the flat, unequivocal reply. "How do you know?"

"Because I was the one who took the charter, and Mad Dog took a bullet in the gut trying to get me out of Ciudad Juárez."

She sat up, detecting far more in his voice than she suspected he wanted her to hear. His fierce response held echoes of loyalty. Long years of friendship. The kind of bond that could only be forged in danger. And a tight, almost desperate edge.

"What happened then?"

"I told you. The Feds stepped in. I cut a deal to provide information against the arms dealer, and went under cover for Treasury. Customs recruited me shortly after that. A few years later, I recruited Tony."

"So he's part of this Task Force?"

"He's one of the pivotal players."

Brenna bit her lip. She wanted more, and he knew it. Yet she couldn't ask him to compromise himself and his mission any more than he already had.

As if sensing her dilemma, his mouth curled into the mocking smile she hated. For a moment, the old Sanderson sat beside her, the one who chose the rules he'd follow.

"What's the matter, Duggan? Are you having trouble fitting Tony and me into nice, neat boxes labeled 'good guy' or 'bad guy'?"

"Yes, I am. So why don't you tell me which box he fits into?"

He'd tell her, Dave thought savagely, if only he knew. At this moment, though, he had a bagful of questions and no answers. Avoiding any attempt to label the complex character of Anthony Petrocelli, he stuck to the irrefutable facts.

"Mad Dog kept up the charter service after I left. We used his 'business' contacts to set me up with the right people ... the people who can pay the kind of money I'm asking for a copy of the AWACS schedule. He's in and out of Central America all the time, which might look suspicious to anyone outside the Task Force."

"So that's why you covered for him when Sergeant Lang passed you that track?"

"Yes, that's why I covered for him."

It all came back to that track, Dave thought bitterly. That damned track.

Like a grainy, poorly made porn flick, those moments in the belly of the AWACS replayed in his mind. Andy Lang had arrowed the amber dot and flagged it as a TOI. When Dave spotted the arrow and the accompanying information that ID'ed the aircraft, his fingers had frozen on the trackball. Even after all these weeks, Dave could recall every moment he'd tracked Mad Dog's plane across the Yucatan, cursing his partner for this uncoordinated trip and wondering how he'd cover for him if he deviated from his flight plan or made an unscheduled stop. When the radars shut down in preparation for refueling, relief had rolled through Dave in waves. He'd wallowed in that relief until after the mission terminated and they'd completed the debrief.

Then Sergeant Lang stopped him in the hall and asked why he hadn't forced the track up to a higher priority, given its point of origin and suspicious speed. During sleepless nights, Dave still saw the doubt that crossed Lang's face at his deliberately offhand response. Doubt that led ultimately to a staged meeting outside the Purple Parrot.

It all came back to that track. And to Petrocelli's blithe assurances that he'd gone south to line up contacts for the next sale. Not for the first time in recent weeks, Dave searched his soul for the reason his partner had timed his trip home to coincide with AWACS' scheduled shutdown.

Maybe Mad Dog had brought back more than the names of a few contacts.

Maybe he'd been making a little profit on the side by hauling a few loads of his own.

Maybe . . .

"There's my car."

Brenna's quiet observation pulled him back from the insidious doubts that ate at his gut. He nodded, slowing as the headlights illuminated the bright red sports car.

"Well, at least it's still in one piece."

The pickup rolled onto the shoulder and slowed to a halt. For a few quiet moments, they faced each other in the dim cab. Dave took in the lines of weariness etched on either side of Brenna's mouth and abandoned his plans to invite himself in when they reached her place.

"I'll follow you back to the city."

Nodding, Brenna dug in her purse for her car keys. "Where do you live?"

The casual question threw him. "On the north

side, not far from Wiley Post Airport," he replied guardedly.

"Good. That's closer than my place on the southeast side. When we hit I–40, you take the lead and I'll follow you."

Looks like the lady wasn't worried about invitations, Dave thought with a small, inner smile. Crossing his forearms on the steering wheel, he allowed himself the simple pleasure of watching her walk to her car. Despite the weariness that rode on his shoulders like a weight, he felt himself harden at the sight of her clean lines and long, lithe curves.

He was tired, bone tired. He desperately needed time to think, to work through his doubts and gathering suspicions before he spelled them out for the task force coordinator. Yet he knew that when they reached I–40, he'd hit the accelerator and take the lead.

He had no idea what waited for him with the daylight. A few hours ago, he wouldn't really have cared. Now, he couldn't let go of the idea of waking to sunshine with Brenna in his arms.

The apartment complex Dave lived in had been constructed in a fake Tudor style that was popular in the fifties and sixties and looked so out of place in Oklahoma. As Dave turned into the cluster of dark, silent buildings, his headlights picked out heavy timbers placed at geometric angles in peeling white stucco.

He'd lived there for almost six months now ...

two while he recertified to fly aboard AWACS and four while he established his "credentials" as a embittered loser who would sell Big Bird's flight schedules to the highest bidder. The location as much as the run-down character of the complex suited him and his cover perfectly.

He pulled into a parking slot, cut the engine, and climbed out of the pickup, then waited while Brenna parked her little toy beside him. He took her arm, as much to give himself the pleasure of touching her as to guide her over the cracked sidewalks.

His apartment was on the second floor, which Dave had chosen deliberately. The narrow flight of stairs leading up to the landing would slow down a concerted rush on his front door. The second story was high enough to give him a good view of the stark, unlandscaped parking lot below, but not so high he'd break anything vital if he had to drop out of a back window.

Unobtrusively, he kept his body between Brenna and the door as he fitted his key into the cheap lock. Security had wanted to install all kinds of high-tech safety and listening devices, which Dave had refused. He didn't plan to invite the scum he did business with back to his place for a friendly beer and an evening of male bonding, but neither did he take unnecessary chances. Nor did the men he dealt with. As he'd anticipated, his apartment had been thoroughly and competently searched shortly after he passed the first AWACS schedule to the contact Mad Dog had set up in Panama.

Once inside, Dave swept the apartment with a quick glance, searching for signs of unauthorized entry that only he would identify. Finding none, he turned and discovered Brenna doing a sweep of her own. She didn't appear impressed with the worn, pea-green carpet, rented furniture, and unadorned walls.

"Nice place," she commented dryly, tossing her shoulder bag onto the Formica counter that separated the kitchenette from the living area.

"It suits my needs."

"Are your needs really so basic?" she teased.

"Some of them are."

A smile that was three parts weariness and one part promise curved her mouth. "Yes, I guess they are."

"Brenna . . ."

"Let's not talk. Not now. It's too late, and I'm too tired." She slid her arms around his waist and laid her head against his chest. "Just hold me."

"My pleasure," he murmured.

He should check the phone for messages. He ought to call in and let his controller know he was back. Instead, he closed his eyes and stroked the bumps of her spine. He'd hold her, just for a little while, then check in.

He should have known holding wouldn't satisfy either of them for very long. Soft stroking led to pressing. Lazy murmurs became husky whispers of pleasure. His breath deepened. Hers shortened. She lifted her head, and his descended.

"Given the choice," he told her some moments later, "I think I'd rather hold you naked."

She leaned back in his hold. "Given the choice, I'd rather you were horizontal when you did it. Let's go to bed."

For the first time, Dave regretted his lack of interest in physical comforts. "I haven't gotten around to acquiring a bed. I just use the sofa."

Twisting in his arms, Brenna eyed the orange and green flowered couch with obvious misgiving. "Do you think it will hold us both?"

"Why don't we find out?"

Leaving clothes strewn in their wake, they did an awkward, erotic waltz across the room. Halfway to the threadbare sofa, Dave heard a sudden pinging.

Not recognizing the sound, he reacted instinctively. Shoving Brenna behind him, he spun around and dropped into a half crouch. Muscles tensed, eyes straining, he searched the living room for the source of the muted sound.

It came again, a soft ping-ping.

"That's my beeper," Brenna said breathlessly. "It's in my purse."

Dave willed his nerves to stop jumping around under his skin like live electrical wires. Straightening, he turned and saw that the laughing, aroused woman of a few moments ago had disappeared. Frowning, she started toward her purse.

"I don't suppose you can ignore it?" he asked, knowing the answer.

"No, of course not. It's probably the Command Post. Or it could be Janeen. I left her my pager number and told her to get in touch with me if . . . if anything changed."

Digging in her black leather purse, she extracted the beeper and glanced at the dial display.

"It's the Command Post. I have to call in."

Without asking or waiting for permission, she pulled the instrument on the chipped Formica counter toward her, punched in a number, and tapped her nails impatiently on the counter while she waited for a response.

"This is Colonel Duggan. Were you trying to reach me?"

She listened for a moment, then her brows arched in surprise. "Now?"

Lifting her wrist as if to check the time, she realized that her watch was buried somewhere in the pile of clothing strewn across the living-room floor.

"All right. Tell him I'm on my way."

She hung up, still frowning, and began to retrieve her clothing. Dave hunkered down beside her to sift through the small pile.

"General Adams wants me to report to wing headquarters. Immediately."

"What's going on?"

"I don't know, and the Command Post controller wouldn't say."

Dave retrieved his shirt, then rose and strode

across the room to discover two messages on the answering machine beside the phone.

The first included a mumbled "sorry, wrong number," and a hang-up. The second was a prerecorded solicitation inviting him to participate in a special discount phone service.

A frown very similar to Brenna's creased his brow. In the four months he'd spent under cover, the Task Force Coordinator had only "invited" him to call in a couple of times. Once, he recalled grimly, was when Jerry O'Halloran wanted to know just why the hell a certain Lieutenant Colonel Duggan had gone out to CNAC to check up on him.

"Wait here," he told her.

She nodded, intent on pulling herself together and reporting in to the base. Dave dialed a safe number, only to learn O'Halloran wasn't there, but the agent in place passed him a succinct, coded message.

Brenna was tugging a comb through her hair when he returned to the living room a few moments later, fully dressed. Her arm stilled when she caught the expression on his face.

"What's going on?"

"I don't know any more than you do at this point." He dug his keys out of his pocket. "Let's go. I'll follow you to the base."

She pushed the comb back into her purse, slung its strap over her shoulder, and headed for the front door. "Thanks, but I don't need an escort."

"Look, I'm not being chivalrous. I've been instructed to report to Tinker, too."

She paused with one hand on the door. "I suppose this is about our trip to Enid," she said slowly.

"Could be."

"If I were a betting person, I'd say a whole truckload of crap is about to hit the fan."

"Something's about to hit," he replied grimly. "Let's go find out what."

They arrived at wing headquarters to find it ablaze with light. Her stomach churning, Brenna lifted the phone to identify herself and Sanderson to the Command Post controller. He buzzed them in, then directed them to the Command Briefing Room.

To her surprise, she discovered that a classified briefing was in progress, and that she'd been cleared for access. She offered the fatigue-clad airman posted at the door her ID card, as did Sanderson. After verifying their identities against a security roster, the guard stood aside for them to enter.

Brenna had attended countless staff meetings and briefings in the huge, oak-paneled room lined with squadron plaques and pictures of the wing in operation. As she and Dave stood at the back of the room, she swiftly identified the uniformed personnel seated around the oval table. They represented an abbreviated staff, clearly only those with a need to know.

The chief of operations occupied his usual seat, as did the chief of maintenance. Major John "Duke" Woodward, the wing's focal point for counternarcotics operations, sat halfway down the table next to Buck Henry. The intelligence officer gave Brenna a private smile and Sanderson a thoughtful, assessing once-over.

Several civilians were also seated around the table, Brenna noted, recognizing instantly the one seated to General Adams's left. He'd been present the morning the general had called her in and ordered her to cease her inquiries into Dave Sanderson's activities.

A perverse and very human pleasure darted through her at the civilian's scowl when he spotted her and Dave standing side by side. Obviously, he didn't like the fact that his agent appeared to be siding with the enemy. Her secret satisfaction faded considerably, however, as the general's high-backed chair swung around and she saw a similar expression on his cast-iron features.

Adams informed his staff there'd be a five-minute break, then rose and started toward the latecomers. A question from his exec delayed the general momentarily and gave O'Halloran the opportunity to approach alone.

After a tight-lipped nod to Brenna, he focused his attention exclusively on Dave. "Where the hell have you been?"

"I went for a ride."

At the laconic reply, a slow flush crept up

O'Halloran's face. Brenna wasn't surprised that the two men appeared to rub each other the wrong way. Despite his loosened tie and wrinkled gray suit, O'Halloran exuded a take-charge air. Dave Sanderson wasn't the kind of man who let himself be taken charge of.

"I went to Enid," he continued deliberately. "To see Mrs. Lang. I decided it was time someone talked to her about her husband."

"Dammit, Sanderson, you had no authority—"

He broke off at the general's approach. Swiping a hand over his thinning, reddish-brown hair, O'Halloran made a visible effort to control his temper.

General Adams raked Dave over with a piercing look, then shifted his attention to Brenna. Despite her determination to remain cool, she felt herself redden as he took in her scrubbed face, hastily combed hair, and less than pristine ivory sweater.

"The security detail guarding Mrs. Lang reported that you were with Sanderson tonight."

The acid in his voice could have stripped paint from a plane's fuselage.

"Yes, sir."

"They also reported that you left the hospital with him a little after midnight."

"Yes, sir."

He flicked a pointed glance at the row of clocks set into the wall above the opaque screen. To her relief, he chose not to comment on the fact that the Command Post hadn't been able to raise her at her quarters some five hours later. This wasn't the time or the place to explain what she was doing at Dave Sanderson's apartment.

Evidently Adams thought so, too. His voice brusque, he proceeded to throw Brenna completely off balance.

"Since you're so damned determined to involve yourself in this operation, Colonel, I got approval for you to be read in as part of the Task Force. You'll be briefed on our wing's involvement after we get through here."

Brenna's jaw sagged. For several seconds, she could only stare at the whipcord-lean man opposite her. Then she gave him a broad, thoroughly unprofessional grin.

"Thank you, sir."

O'Halloran's sour expression told her he wasn't happy about the general's decision. Ignoring him, she nodded toward the assembled staff.

"What's going on?"

"Southern Command intelligence has pieced together evidence of sizable cocaine shipments in transit from processing centers in Colombia to dispersed airfields in Panama, Guatemala, and Belize. The guess is that the stuff's being readied for imminent transshipment to the States."

Adams's rigid features relaxed. For an instant, his steel-gray eyes took on the gleam of a hunter who'd just spotted his prey.

"We've been requested to identify additional assets for possible deployment to the Western Atlantic."

"This could be it," O'Halloran put in, addressing himself to Sanderson. "The big haul we've been waiting for."

"Maybe," Dave replied slowly.

"If the shipments are as big as Intel estimates, the bastards are just waiting for a hole in the sky to push their planes through," O'Halloran continued in a fierce rush of satisfaction. "You're going to give it to them, Sanderson. All wrapped up in a nice pink bow. You leave tonight, as soon as you get hold of Petrocelli to set up another contact."

Brenna went still. Across the few feet separating them, her gaze locked with Dave's. Despite the hours she'd spent in his arms, she couldn't penetrate the flat sheen shielding his hazel eyes.

His jaw tight, he turned to O'Halloran. "We need to talk."

Chapter Nineteen

"I do it my way, or not at all."

The unequivocal statement brought another flush to O'Halloran's fair complexion. Whirling, the Task Force coordinator paced the small office that had been turned over for their use.

"Dammit, Sanderson, we can't risk it."

Dave's temper inched closer to the edge. His tolerance for headquarters types was minimal at best. Granted, O'Halloran had spent a number of years in the trenches before being assigned to Customs Internal Affairs Division in D.C. And it was true that his detail to spearhead Customs' part in the Task Force had helped with the massive coordination effort required for the multiagency operation. Still, the man had made little effort to disguise his frustration with Dave's independent operation in the field. The two men had clashed more than once in the past four months, but had managed to bury their mutual antipathy in the pressure of their work. Dave's dislike came closer to the surface with each angry turn O'Halloran took about the room.

"We have to take Petrocelli out," the coordinator insisted.

"If we take him out now," Dave replied coldly, "there won't be any operation. Besides, we don't have proof that he's turned."

They *didn't* have proof, Dave repeated savagely to himself. Only suspicions. A few unanswered questions. Years of friendship, of sweating through more tight spots than he wanted to remember, tore at him.

Then he remembered Janeen Lang's face when he'd left her at the hospital and knew that a few unanswered questions were too many. Involuntarily, he reached for his shirt pocket for his nonexistent cigarettes. Swearing viciously under his breath, he dropped his hand.

"I don't need proof to take him out," O'Halloran ground out. "Not with all that's at stake."

Dave made a last attempt to hang onto his temper. "Look, you're an Internal Affairs man. You of all people know things aren't always what they seem. We'd better tread carefully here."

O'Halloran spun around, his face red. "I don't need some Rambo field agent telling me how to do my job."

"And I don't need some hotshot headquarters type fucking up an operation that's taken months to put into action."

Animosity fed by weeks of nerve-shredding tension flared hot and high. The two men glared at each other, neither willing to back down. Then the hard-won experience that had led to their assignment to the Task Force reasserted itself.

Muttering something vaguely conciliatory under his breath, O'Halloran brushed a palm over his thinning, reddish-brown hair.

In turn, Dave reined in his own belligerence. "Look, Jerry, you know as well as I do that the people we're dealing with aren't stupid."

"No, whatever else they are, they're not stupid."

"If Petrocelli disappears from the scene just days before a major transshipment—one he helped set up—his 'associates' are going be suspicious as hell."

"I know."

"If you expect me to make a pass, we need him to set it up."

"I know, dammit. I know."

Dave forced himself to ask the next question. "How much does Tony know about the intelligence reports we heard tonight?"

"Nothing, yet. I was waiting for you to get here before I contacted any of the others."

"Then I say we play the scenario out."

Dave's words came slowly, each one weighted with a gut-deep reluctance to set up a man who'd taken a bullet trying to spring him from a Mexican prison cell.

"I'll call Tony and tell him there's been a change in the AWACS schedule. He arranges the contact.

I go in. I make the pass. Then, if we're lucky, we take down a whole sky full of dopers."

"And if we're not? If the dopers suspect something and don't move the stuff?"

"Then we take down a bad agent."

O'Halloran eyed him for long moments. Finally, he exhaled heavily.

"All right, we'll play it your way. For now. But it's your ass if this whole thing blows up in our faces."

"So what else is new?"

O'Halloran reddened, but chose to ignore the sarcastic response. "Here's where we are so far. Adams has directed his people to put together a revised flight schedule. It'll show a curtailment of training missions due to an urgent requirement to support NATO and the Bosnian crisis ... leaving a big hole in the sky in the southeast sector beginning tonight."

"Convenient."

And believable, Dave acknowledged silently. Half the wing was gone at any one time in support of some far-flung world crisis or another.

"We've got a C–21 standing by," O'Halloran continued. "Your gear's already on board. If anyone asks, you're hitching a ride south to switch out with Larry Ramirez. His kid's in the hospital with a severe allergic reaction to a bee sting. The reaction's under control, but no one else needs to know that."

As excuses for a change out went, it was as good as any. Despite his antipathy for headquarters types, Dave had to admit the man didn't waste time.

"The only thing left to do is for you to get hold of Petrocelli and arrange the pass," O'Halloran concluded. "You know where he is?"

"Not exactly."

Given their separate covers, Dave and his partner were rarely in the same city, let alone the same country, at the same time. In pursuit of his various business interests, Mad Dog roamed constantly throughout the southwestern U.S. and Central America . . . which made him so perfect for his undercover role.

Dave's gaze dropped to the tan phone sitting on the desk. Feeling a hundred years old, he reached for the receiver.

There wasn't any answer at the number he dialed. He hadn't expected one. Security had discovered months ago that Mad Dog's home phone south of Dallas was wired. That hadn't surprised anyone, given the resources of his Central American business associates. Security had left the listening device in place and set up a safe drop number.

Dave left a brief message, stating only that there'd been a change in the AWACS schedules and he'd taken advantage of Larry Rameriz's recall to carry the revised schedule south. If Mad Dog could arrange a contact, he'd pass it. If not, he'd eat the damn thing and be home in a few days.

When Dave hung up, O'Halloran grunted and moved toward the door.

"Just so you know, Sanderson, I'm going to set a small army combing through Tony Petrocelli's personal assets and bank accounts in the next few hours. If he's turned, if he's taken so much as a single *centavo* from those bastards, I'll find it."

Dave made no comment. He knew damn well they wouldn't find anything. Mad Dog had a stake in too many off-the-wall enterprises and cash salted away in too many layered accounts to leave behind a trail he didn't want followed. The financial disclosure statement he provided every year as part of his security clearance update drove the auditors up a wall.

The big cartels possessed networks of financial contacts almost as extensive and far more ruthless than that of the United States government. If the big boys hadn't uncovered Mad Dog's connection to Customs, it was a pretty good bet Customs wouldn't uncover any connection to them.

Besides, if Petrocelli had turned, he hadn't done it for money. Tony made ten times his government salary from his various schemes and went through it all like water. He believed money was made to be spent, as fast and as flamboyantly as it had been gathered in.

All of which left Dave with the same unanswered questions: Why? And how? And when, dammit? When had he turned ... *if* he'd turned?

Before, or after, Andy Lang's death?

The questions ate at him as he followed O'Halloran into the hall.

The senior agent jerked his head toward the conference room. "You want to sit in on the rest of this intelligence briefing? I can have them hold the C–21 a little while yet."

Dave hesitated, glancing at the door to the briefing room. His part in the upcoming operation had narrowed to a phone call, a trip south, and a pass in some dark, noisy bar. He didn't need to know the details of the greater drama, which involved several foreign and domestic government agencies, a communications net that stretched across two continents, and a host of land, sea, and air assets. The less he knew, in fact, the less he could reveal to the wrong people. If he went back into the conference room, it would be for one reason only . . . because he craved another glimpse of a certain long-legged, silky-lashed lieutenant colonel.

Dave doubted Brenna would even notice him if he did return. She'd be all business now, absorbed in the intricacies of the coming operation. Despite her civilian clothes and the tangle of dark hair brushing her shoulders, she'd project that air of cool, unshakable competence she pulled around her at will.

In a deliberate mental exercise, Dave contrasted that Brenna with the one who'd joined her body to his on the hood of a little red sports car, with the engine still hot beneath her skin and her mouth hungry on his. That was the image he wanted to take with him, he decided with a small, tight smile.

O'Halloran turned, impatience stamped on his face. "Well?"

"You go on in. I'll catch my plane."

When the last briefing finished, the lights in the conference room came back up. Brenna rose with the others and stood at attention while the general departed. Then she went in search of Dave.

She didn't find him, but did spot O'Halloran in conversation with the Director of Operations outside the Command Post. As soon as the two men had finished their conversation, she cornered the Customs agent.

"Where's Sanderson?"

"He's gone."

"Gone?"

"He left a half hour ago for Panama."

His clipped responses irritated Brenna, but they didn't sting nearly as much as the realization that Dave had left without any word to her.

"I see."

The frost in her voice pierced O'Halloran's shell. He blinked and remembered belatedly that they were supposed to be on the same team. Passing a hand over his scalp, he grudgingly gave her a little more information.

"He had to leave right away. We had a C–21 standing by to take Sanderson to Howard. He'll check in at the alert facility, then head downtown to get some sleep. We're trying to set up a contact for him tonight. With any luck, things will start popping soon after that."

The explanation helped. A little. Brenna told herself it was foolish to wish he'd delayed long enough to say good-bye to her. He had a mission to perform, just as she did. Still, his abrupt departure left a hollow feeling in the pit of her stomach.

Impatience worked its way back into O'Halloran's face. "Look, I have to get out to California. I'll be at Customs' Domestic Air Interdiction Center. It's at March Air Force Base, just outside—"

"I know where it is."

"Yeah, well, you can reach me there if you need me."

Not likely, Brenna thought. Her mouth tight, she watched him push open the glass doors. Then she snatched a quick look at her watch and dismissed O'Halloran completely from her mind. She had more pressing considerations to occupy her— like her role in this Task Force. So far, it had been limited to listening and learning.

All indications were that things might start breaking tonight. Based on the intelligence gathered from a number of sources, Southern Command believed a major attempt to penetrate U.S. borders was imminent. SOUTHCOM had requested a backup AWACS, which Tinker had agreed to launch and put on orbit in the Western Atlantic. Contrary to the schedule Dave would pass that showed a hole in the sky, there'd be two sets of eyes looking down. With the Navy and Customs assets that would also be on alert, backed up by land-based radars and powerful aerostats, they'd throw a net so tight over the southeastern sector a mosquito couldn't slip through.

Brenna wanted a part of that action.

If she moved fast, real fast, she could get home, change into her flight suit, and make it back in time for the mission planning brief for the backup AWACS.

First, however, she had to get the chief of scheduling to tag her as the Mission Crew Commander on this particular flight. That shouldn't take much doing. A short-notice tasking like this one was a chore to fill. Pigeonholing the harried major in his office, she got right to the point.

"I want this flight, Mac."

He put down the phone he'd just jammed between his ear and shoulder and beamed at her. "Bless you, Colonel."

There were plenty of qualified MCC's available, of course, but yanking the senior folks out of bed before dawn and pulling them back to the base for a mission planning brief in less than an hour didn't tend to improve scheduling's popularity.

"I owe you one for this."

"I'll collect next Friday night," Brenna promised with a grin. "And I'm talking the gold label stuff here, not bar stock."

"You got it."

She left headquarters not long after that, wondering if her designation as MCC would stick. General Adams didn't get involved in selecting or approving crews for routine missions. This one was anything but routine, however. Despite the fact that he'd gotten approval for her to be read in as part of the Task Force, Brenna still felt as though she was walking a tightrope with her boss. She'd gone head to head with him twice now, and neither experience was one she wanted to repeat in this lifetime.

When she arrived home a half hour later, she found a number of messages waiting for her on her answering machine. To her relief, none were from the chief of scheduling or from General Adams. After a quick call to St. Mary's to check on Janeen and the baby, she headed for the bedroom, stripping as she went.

Within fifteen minutes she was showered, blown dry, and minimally made up. Stepping into her green bag, she pulled up the front zipper and tucked the black 552d Training Squadron scarf around her neck. Her fingers flew over the lacings of her boots. Snatching up her flight cap, ditty bag, and car keys, she was out the door once more.

By the time she pulled into her parking slot at the base, Brenna felt as though she'd run the Boston Marathon. Dragging in a deep breath to slow her galloping heart, she walked up the pebbled walk to the two-story red brick Ops building.

The mission prebrief ate up her fast-depleting store of energy. Since the primary focus of this mission would be counternarcotics, the crew was more heavily weighted with air surveillance techs and officers than a routine training mission. To take advantage of the added air time, however, scheduling had loaded the remaining consoles with students. The extra eyes and hands would be useful if the skies got as crowded as Intelligence expected.

Dawn streaked the sky by the time the hastily assembled crew left the base to go into crew rest. Brenna made this trip back to her condo at a considerably more sedate pace than the trip into the base. Once home, she stripped down to her underwear, adjusted the blinds to shut out the morning light, and flopped down on the bed.

With a groan that was part pleasure, part aching weariness, she threaded her hands together under her head and waited for sleep to claim her. But as tired as she was, sleep took a backseat to the worry that had hovered at the edges of her mind for the past few hours. With the intense concentration necessary for mission planning behind her, the worry now moved to center stage.

Swallowing, Brenna closed her eyes and tried to keep the hollow feeling in her stomach from blossoming into full-fledged fear. Dave knew what he was doing. He'd been a key player in setting up this whole operation, or so the briefer who'd given her a quick rundown on the Task Force concept, scope, and operating parameters had told her.

Sanderson had dealt with the contacts Petrocelli set up before. He'd passed several schedules to establish his credibility as a source. If intelligence was right, he'd more than succeeded. The number of loads being readied for transshipment at airfields scattered all across Central America indicated significant imminent activity. All signs pointed to a major attempt to penetrate U.S. airspace.

They'd take them down. Customs and DEA and FAA and DOD would work in concert with their counterparts in Mexico and Guatemala and other Central American nations to take them down. All of them, or a damn good number of them. The dopers would know they'd been set up, of course, which meant Dave Sanderson wouldn't be passing any more AWACS schedules in the future.

Just what he would be doing was an interesting question.

Brenna concentrated on that particular question until she realized that speculating about Dave's future wasn't any more conducive to sleep than worrying about his present. She didn't have any input into the latter, and didn't have a clue how much she had into the former.

She wasn't even sure whether she wanted to play in Dave Sanderson's future, or let him play in hers. The explosive physical desire that blazed between them couldn't sustain itself. There had to be more. There had to be need. And respect. And commitment.

The seeds of the first two were there. Dave's need went as deep as hers, although he might not be ready to admit it yet.

Respect she had to work on a little. She still hadn't quite forgiven him and the others involved in their collective decision to let Janeen suffer such private pain. But at least he'd gone with Brenna to St. Mary's and faced up to the consequences of that decision.

Commitment ... well, commitment represented the absolute unknown on both sides of the equation. Was she any more ready to commit to a relationship than Dave was?

The thought of trying again, of commingling her life with another's, made Brenna groan a second time and flip over onto her stomach. Did she want to risk another emotional investment? With someone like Sanderson? Did he?

The answer to that one had to wait until he got back from Panama.

If he got back from Panama.

Andy Lang hadn't.

Oh, God.

By sheer strength of will, Brenna forced down a wave of sudden, paralyzing fear. She had to get some sleep. She couldn't let herself think about Dave walking into some place like the Purple Parrot tonight to meet a contact set up by Mad Dog Petrocelli. And she flatly refused to dwell on the possibility that he might not walk out.

Dragging the pillow over her head, she surrounded herself in smothery darkness.

A little before six p.m., she was back at the base. A quick conference with the wing's liaison to the Special Task Force confirmed that General Adams had received a call from Jerry O'Halloran. The message was brief, stating only that Dave Sanderson was in place in Panama and a contact had been set up for eight o'clock tonight.

Two hours, Brenna thought grimly as she made her way to the Ops building. Dave would make his contact in two hours. The hollow feeling in the pit of her stomach came back with a vengeance. She had to take several deep breaths before joining the stream of crew members heading into the briefing room.

As she entered the wedge-shaped, flag-lined room, everyone came to attention. At Brenna's nod, the burly aircraft commander stepped to the podium.

"Listen up, folks. This is the final brief for flight Lima-Echo-Mike Seven-Two-Two. We'll start with roll call."

Brenna glanced at each crew member as he or she responded. She knew them all by sight and more than half from personal contact. They represented an excellent mix of skills and experience, given the task ahead.

Her heart skipped a beat at the sight of the man wearing a blue and gold Customs patch. She'd flown with Bob Pierce several times and found him extremely competent. She'd also admired his strict adherence to military grooming standards, even in his civilian role. At this moment, though, she would've much preferred to see a head of shaggy, sun-streaked bronze hair and a pair of mocking hazel eyes above that blue and gold patch.

The roll call completed, the AC then ran

through a quick review of mission objectives, updated the weather, and posted the anticipated times for launch, transit to orbit, refueling, and recovery. When he finished, he stepped aside and Brenna moved to the podium.

"As you know, this mission has a specific counternarcotics focus, based on classified intelligence. If the Intel is accurate, the skies could get real crowded tonight."

Every man and woman in the room hoped so. Brenna could see it in their faces. This might not be their primary Air Force mission, but it was a real one, with real results.

"Consequently," she continued, "I want you to keep the chatter to a minimum when we reach our orbit. Any time you go out over the voice net, use proper comm protocol."

A low murmur told her that the senior crew members at least understood the implications of her admonition. Trading good-natured insults with other units was a time-honored method of relieving the boredom of long orbits. That Brenna would warn them to keep it professional tonight suggested strongly they wouldn't be bored.

After a quick safety briefing, she glanced around the small auditorium.

"Any questions?"

There were none.

A half hour later, Brenna and the rest of her crew boarded the huge, windowless E–3. Stowing the mission flyaway kit beside her console, she completed the pretakeoff checklist, then strapped herself in.

Within moments, the AC began the start engines checklist. A familiar, high-pitched whine filled the cabin as four massive engines revved up to full power, one after another. The E–3 shimmied and strained, waiting to be released from the chocks. When the tower gave the clearance for takeoff, the AC throttled back, slipped the big plane's leash, and headed down the taxiway.

While Brenna waited for the slow thrust of power that would send them down the runway and into the air, she closed her eyes. These would be the last moments she had to herself. Once the E–3 was in the air and the radars operational, she'd begin the supervisory and training tasks that came with her rank and position as Mission Crew Commander. For these few moments at least, she was alone with her thoughts.

In less than two hours Dave would walk into some bar and pass a thin, photocopied sheet of paper to the contact Mad Dog had set up.

Was he already awake? Had he been able to get any sleep, or had he tossed and turned, as she had? Had heat speared through his belly every time he remembered what had happened the last time he checked into a hotel in Panama?

She wanted him to remember. Every move. Every lick. Every stinging nip and drugging kiss and thrust of his thigh between hers. For a little while longer, at least, he had the luxury of remembering. Then he had to put everything else out of his mind and concentrate on his mission. Just as she had to concentrate on hers.

As the huge plane rolled down the runway, the ear-piercing whine of the engines spiraled to a deafening roar. Racks of equipment rattled. Stressed metal groaned. Cabin lights blinked. Then the E–3 lifted into the dusk.

Chapter Twenty

The room on the third floor of the Plaza Paitilla didn't offer as spectacular a view as the last room Dave had occupied at the same hotel. He could see only one span of the Bridge of the Americas, its white lights brilliant against the purple sky.

Turning his back on the deepening twilight, Dave reached for the white Panama shirt he'd tossed onto the bed earlier. As he shrugged it on, his eyes drifted to the empty chair in one corner of the room. Despite the tension clawing at his chest, his mouth crooked in a small smile. He didn't think he'd ever forget the shock of turning around to find a cool, collected Brenna checking out the view.

For the few moments it took for him to work the buttons on the soft cotton shirt, Dave let himself savor the memory of the explosive pleasure they'd found together that night. An intense desire to repeat the experience every night for the rest of his life rocked through him.

The rest of his life had to wait, he reminded himself, tearing his eyes from the empty chair. Until after he made this contact. And after he caught up with Mad Dog Petrocelli.

Where the hell was Tony?

Since he'd arrived in Panama, Dave had left two messages at Mad Dog's safe number, neither of which had been answered. Ordinarily, he wouldn't have worried about the lack of immediate response. He and Petrocelli both kept erratic schedules in their separate lives. Tonight, however, unease crawled over Dave's skin like a colony of fire ants.

His mouth grim, he rolled his shoulders to settle the Panama shirt over the holster he wore at the small of his back, then left the room. He was on his way through the lobby when the rack of Cuban cigars and American cigarettes behind the cashier stand in the gift shop snagged his attention. He stopped in his tracks, fighting against the craving that lurked just below the level of his conscious will. Then he swore and strode into the shop.

Moments later he was on his way to meet the contact Mad Dog had arranged.

The pulsing rhythm of a merengue grabbed at him while his taxi was still a good fifty yards from the entrance to Josephine's. The music grew in both volume and intensity as the cab pulled up outside the club. Passing the driver a clutch of American dollars, Dave climbed out of the taxi. After the close confines of the car, which reeked of stale perspiration and axle grease, even the muggy heat of the night was a relief. Rolling his shoulders once more to unstick his shirt from his spine, he stood on the street for a moment to get his bearings.

Josephine's was one of the better-class strip joints that catered to U.S. servicemen and the male half of the tourist populations. It sat squeezed between a darkened souvenir shop and a hotel conveniently situated to take the spillover trade from the club. Both the bar and the hotel did a booming business.

Inside the club, strobe lights pierced the smoky darkness in a constant, mind-numbing display of color. An avid crowd clustered around the stage where a small, incredibly ripe dancer performed her own provocative version of the merengue. A few customers more interested in participating than watching gyrated across the dance floor, more or less to the beat of the music.

Dave thought he recognized a couple of the men from Howard. One looked a little scared, as if he knew damn well that a dance with a woman in a place like this constituted a contract for the night. Refusal to follow through with that contract had been known to lead to screaming and scratching and biting, no small danger with the ever-present threat of AIDS. Given the awesome beauty of some of the Panamanian and Puerto Rican women who frequented Josephine's, however, a good percentage of its customers were willing to take the risks.

Eyes narrowed against the smoke and bursts of light, Dave made his way to the bar that ran the length of one wall. He wasn't in the mood to watch the dancers either on or off the stage. His contact would find him wherever he parked himself.

He was taking the head off his second beer when the moment came. After the hours of gut-twisting tension, the actual pass was almost anticlimactic.

"You have something for me, *señor?*"

The smooth, accented voice barely carried over the pulse of the music. Lowering his beer, Dave gave the man who claimed the bar stool beside him a disinterested glance.

This particular specimen appeared to occupy a spot a little higher in the food chain than the usual scum he dealt with. The Panamanian wore pleated white slacks and an open-necked shirt with a logo on the pocket identifying one of Miami's more exclusive men's stores. The pleats concealed the weapon strapped to his upper thigh, Dave guessed, which was reached through a slit in the pocket.

"What makes you think I have something for you?"

"No games, *señor,*" the Panamanian returned, his words all but lost in the pounding beat of a lumbata. "I'll go to the bathroom. You follow."

The idea of taking orders from a doper rubbed Dave exactly the wrong way.

"Tell you what, pal. You go piss." He tossed the pack of cigarettes he'd purchased earlier onto the bar. "And take this with you."

The Panamanian's eyes went flat and black for a moment. Then he pocketed the cigarettes and left without another word.

It was too easy, Dave thought cynically. Too damn easy for a man to sell out his country and himself. All he had to do was pass a pack of cigarettes with a folded piece of paper inside it to a sleaze who wore two-hundred-dollar shirts and traded in death.

Feeling bitter and restless and frustrated he lifted the dew-streaked beer bottle. It would take the dopers a few hours to study the schedule and decide whether to take advantage of that supposed hole in the sky. If they did, Dave wouldn't know about it. Not right away, anyway. His part in this phase of the operation was over.

The new phase, the one that involved only him and Mad Dog Petrocelli, would come next. Dave didn't know where or when or how they'd meet, but he knew he wouldn't shake the tension that prickled across the surface of his skin with every breath until it did.

It came far sooner than he'd anticipated.

As little as Dave liked the thought of sitting in an empty hotel room, he couldn't take the noise and the body wrapping at Josephine's. He left the club soon after the pass, still edgy and restless. The pounding music followed him down the street. So did a dark, late-model sedan.

Dave caught the flash of neon on its polished fender as it pulled out of the slow-moving traffic and nudged the curb beside him. His muscles tensed, but he kept walking.

The car inched forward, then stopped a short distance ahead of him. The rear passenger door opened and the same Panamanian who'd picked up the cigarettes stepped out. Dave noted that he kept one hand in the pocket of his pleated white slacks.

"My employer found your information of great interest."

"Is that so?"

The Panamanian's black eyes flickered. "Yes, it is so. He wishes to speak with you. You will get in the car."

Deliberately, Dave hooked his thumbs in his pockets and rocked back on his heels. The heightened situational awareness that had become second nature to him in the past months had already cataloged possible cover and various escape routes. This doper wasn't going to snatch him off the street . . . unless he let him.

"Now, my friend. We haven't much time, not if we're to use the information you gave us. And if we cannot use it, it is of no value to us, *comprende*?"

He understood all right. They'd taken the bait.

Fierce elation surged through Dave. Now all he had to do was get them to run with it.

"Yeah, I understand."

Slowly, Dave started for the car. He could still back out. He could listen to the warnings his mind was screaming. He could take this scum down, deal with the driver, and walk away.

Like he'd walked away from Kristine.

And from the Air Force.

And from Andy Lang that night at the Purple Parrot.

His mouth tight, he reached for the door handle.

"Before you get in," the Panamanian said softly, "you will give me the weapon you wear, yes?"

After the noise of the busy street, the silence in the sedan pulsed with quiet menace. The hulking driver didn't need any directions. Without speaking, he wove through the city traffic, then turned onto Boulevard Gaillard.

As they headed north on the broad thoroughfare, Dave caught the lights of Southern Command's headquarters atop the dark, rolling hills that constituted Quarry Heights. He smiled grimly to himself. SOUTHCOM's intelligence folks would be very interested to know he was speeding by them at this precise moment, en route to a meeting with one of the drug traffickers they hoped to take down tonight.

All inclination to smile faded, however, as the lights of the city fell away and the sedan picked up the Transisthmian Highway. It sped north, toward Colón, then turned off the highway onto a narrow, two-laned road. Within moments, the jungle closed in. Black. Impenetrable. Heavy with the scent of night-blooming flowers and rotting vegetation.

Just beyond a small village consisting primarily of cement huts, the driver slowed the sedan to a crawl. Shoulders hunched, he leaned forward and searched the darkness to the left of the road. When the headlights picked up a small reflector nailed to a straggling fig tree, he gave a grunt of satisfaction and swung the wheel. Spiky palmettos scratched at the car as it rocked over a bumpy track that only the driver could see.

Long before the first perimeter guard stopped them, Dave knew where they were headed. He'd flown into a good number of jungle airstrips during his years working charters, hauling everything from pigs to petroleum exploration rigs into sites as remote as this one.

He wasn't surprised when the sedan rattled to a halt at the edge of a long, narrow clearing some moments later. But his hand froze on the door handle when he spotted the aircraft parked at the end of the clearing, its fuselage gleaming in the lights provided by the trucks lined up beside it.

He didn't have to read the figures of the "N" number on its tail to recognize the Beechcraft King Air. It was one he'd flown in many times before.

Nor could he mistake Tony Petrocelli's stocky figure or flamboyant, handlebar mustache when he detached himself from the cluster of men around the plane and sauntered toward the sedan in the wake of another, taller individual.

Fighting to control the fury and instant, overwhelming desolation that slammed into him, Dave wrenched open the car door and stepped out. The next few seconds would determine whether he or Petrocelli would leave this clearing alive.

Dave was too far away to see Mad Dog's expression even if the straw Stetson hadn't shadowed his face. He didn't need to see it.

Tony stopped in his tracks. His body rigid, he stared at Dave. Then the white-suited businessman at his side urged him forward.

"Come, Petrocelli. You know this man, I think."

Nothing had ever thrown Mad Dog off course for long. Not even taking a bullet during a botched prison break. Mastering the emotion that held him immobile, he started forward.

"You know damn well I know him. He's my partner in this little enterprise."

Crossing the rough stubble, he stopped a few feet away from Dave. Under the brim of his hat, his black eyes glittered in the reflected light of the headlamps.

"What're you doing here, ol' buddy?"

Dave let the question hang on the hot jungle night for long, tense moments. "Ask your friends."

Petrocelli's mouth tightened at the mocking drawl. Turning to the man at his side, he made no effort to disguise his anger.

"What the hell's going on here?"

"We have decided that your friend should fly with you tonight. To verify the information he's passed to us, you understand?"

Dave placed the man's accent immediately. It was native to a mountainous region to the south, across the Colombian border.

"You haven't needed this kind of verification before," Mad Dog snarled.

"We had not so much at stake before."

The tips of Petrocelli's mustache twitched as his jaw worked. For once, he'd boxed himself into a nice tight corner that even he couldn't talk his way out of.

He couldn't expose Dave without exposing himself.

The knowledge should have provided Dave with some measure of satisfaction. Instead, it burned a hole as big as a fist in his chest.

"Look, Cardoza," Petrocelli argued fiercely, "you've already loaded me with twice what I usually take. I won't have enough fuel to make it to Florida if I have to haul an extra passenger."

"Two extra passengers, my friend." He gestured to the Panamanian standing beside Dave. "Stefan will also fly with you."

"Like hell he will! Not if you want me to deliver this load."

"You can refuel in the Bahamas. The airport on Inagua Island frequently handles such late-night flights."

Mad Dog's eyes narrowed to slits. "You son of a bitch, are you setting me up? I've already deviated from my flight plan to pick up this load. Making another unscheduled stop on Inagua will be like waving a red flag to anyone who might be watching."

"But no one is watching, according to the schedule your friend brings us. Is that not so, Sanderson?"

Forcing himself to ignore the intent stare of the man he once called friend, Dave shrugged. "No one's looking down from twenty-thousand feet. That's the only schedule I have access to."

"You know as well as we do there are still Navy patrols out there," Mad Dog insisted. "And land-based radars."

"This won't be the first time you have evaded the patrols and flown a load in under the radars," the Colombian returned. "If there is no AWACS circling above, you can make it. If you make it, the others will follow."

"Yeah? And what if I don't make it?"

Cardoza smiled politely. "Let us just hope that you do."

The moment Dave had been waiting for came just before takeoff.

The Panamanian was having a last-minute conference with his boss. Dave stood in the shadows beside the King Air while the truck drivers crammed the last container into the cabin. Only two of the six-passenger seats had been removed, he noted. Mad Dog hadn't planned on the load he was being forced to take on.

Swearing, sweating, all but spitting in his anger at the excess weight, Petrocelli swung out of the hatch and started toward the Colombian.

He stopped abruptly a few feet away from Dave, then closed the distance more slowly. The two men stared at each other, unspeaking. Then Dave uttered a single syllable.

"Why?"

Petrocelli didn't pretend to misunderstand. His response was as low and succinct as the question.

"For kicks. At first."

When Dave didn't respond, Mad Dog chopped the air with his hand. "Okay, so I got a high out of selling these dopers schedules to set them up for our sting, then using the same information to make a few runs of my own. I figured I could talk my way out of it if I got caught. Claim I had to prove my trustworthiness by taking in a few loads myself."

"And then?" Dave asked softly, knowing the answer but needing to hear it.

"Then . . ." Petrocelli rubbed a palm across his neck. "Then that goddamned kid picked up my track."

It always came back to that track, Dave thought starkly. One track in a hundred. One flight in a thousand.

"I know you tried to cover for me, Dave, but Lang wouldn't let go of it. He had my tail number in his log. Called down to Dallas, asked a lot of questions. By the time he followed you into the Purple Parrot, my . . . associates had already gotten nervous about him and his questions. Real nervous."

"So they shot him full of dope and strung him up like a skinned deer."

"I didn't know! I swear, I didn't know about it until afterward."

A week ago, Dave might have felt a shred of sympathy for the agony in Tony's hoarse whisper. Now, the memory of Janeen Lang's pain-filled brown eyes made him clench his fists to keep them away from Mad Dog's throat.

"You knew about Mrs. Lang, Tony. You knew about her request for redetermination. What do you know about her accident?"

Above the thick mustache, Petrocelli's face was as desolate as Dave had ever seen it.

"I was in too deep. I couldn't get out. These guys play for keeps, you know that. I had to tell them about Janeen. They said they were just going to scare her off."

Wetting his lips, he flicked a quick glance at the Colombian.

"That was the last straw for me, though. That woman and her baby. I'm not going back after tonight."

No, he wasn't, Dave promised silently.

"You don't have to, either," Mad Dog said in a low, tense rush. "With what I have stashed, we can live real comfortable in Mexico or the Caymans. Think about it. What have you got waiting for you in the States? An empty apartment with puke-green walls and a civil servant's salary?"

Dave knew exactly what he had waiting. A chance. A slim one admittedly, but a chance with a woman strong enough to hold her own against him and the rest of the establishment and honest enough to admit that she wanted him, despite her own doubts and his every attempt to turn her off.

Petrocelli stepped closer, desperation tearing ragged edges in his low voice.

"You don't like taking orders from those assholes at Customs any more than you did from the ring-knocking bureaucrats in the Air Force. We can—"

He broke off as the Colombian strolled across the uneven stubble. Regaining his poise and his bravado, he dusted his Stetson against his leg, then settled it firmly on his head.

"We're ready to roll, Cardoza. Unless you've got another hundred kilos or so you want to cram on board."

"You have sufficient. We will be most anxious to hear of your progress, my friend. Radio me when you leave Inagua. You have the frequency?"

"Yeah, I have it."

"Then I wish you good speed."

Smiling urbanely, the Colombian stepped back while Tony and Dave climbed aboard. Stefan settled into the seat behind Mad Dog and strapped himself in.

Ten minutes later, the King Air rattled down the rough clearing lit only by the trucks lined up on either side. Sweating profusely, Mad Dog shoved the power lever to full throttle.

The twin engines whined in protest at the heavy load. The tail wheel dragged in the grass.

"Come on, baby," Petrocelli ground out through clenched teeth. "Come on!"

A solid wall of darkness loomed ahead of them. From the corner of one eye, Dave caught the way Stefan pressed himself back against the passenger seat. The bastard didn't have either one of his hands in his pocket now. They clawed the armrests, the manicured fingers digging into the worn gray fabric.

His own fingers curved with the need to curl around the control wheel as the jungle drew closer. They rattled past the last truck, still dragging their tail. Dave felt the shrill reverberations of the protesting engines in every pore.

Now! Take her up!

As if responding to the silent command, Petrocelli eased back on the wheel. The King Air bounced, slammed back to the earth, then lifted into the blackness with a groan.

Chapter Twenty-one

"I've got one!"

The excited voice of a student surveillance tech spurted over AWACS' internal net. Her instructor answered in a more measured manner.

"What have you got, Boudreaux?"

Taking her cue from the instructor, the airman moderated her tone. "Uh, I've got track echo-two-one-zero on my screen."

"And?"

"And it meets the criteria for a possible suspect."

"Have you put some symbology on it?"

"Roger, AST."

"Send me the arrow and let me take a look at it."

The exchange came through clearly over Brenna's headset. Setting aside her coffee container, she toggled one of the switches on the left side of her console. Immediately, the student's sector map painted across her screen. A number of moving dots representing the air traffic in that sector appeared, but one stood out. It was caged by a flashing amber square.

Leaning forward, Brenna checked the data in the lower corner of the screen. From the airspeed, heading, and altitude, she saw that the aircraft associated with track was traveling on a course that took him from Panama toward the Bahamas. It was following an established commercial air route, but no commercial airliner flew that low or that slow.

"Have you checked the IFF history on this track?" the instructor inquired.

"Roger, AST. It's not squawking."

The fact that the aircraft wasn't emitting Identification Friend or Foe signals didn't completely rule out the possibility it was a legitimate flight. Some pilots in this part of the world just forgot to turn on their IFF transponder. Some deliberately shut it off, particularly when overflying Cuba, which tended to object violently to any penetration of its airspace by commercial liners from certain Western nations. Some, Brenna knew well, didn't want to be identified when flying through this drug-laden corridor.

Was this one of them? she wondered. Was this aircraft part of the wave Intel had predicted?

Contrary to the intelligence estimates, suspicious traffic had been light tonight. Strangely light. Maybe this was the beginning of the big push the Special Task Force was hoping for. Eyes intent, Brenna studied the symbology on her screen and listened to the exchange between the instructor and the student.

"All right, Boudreaux," surveillance tech advised calmly. "Let's pass it to Customs to work."

"I've got it," Bob Pierce replied. Like Brenna, the Customs agent two consoles over had been listening to the exchange. "I'm going to JTF–4 now to see what they know about this guy."

Reclaiming her coffee cup, Brenna took a sip of the muddy liquid. It would take a few moments for Joint Task Force Four at Key West to work the track. Their computers would sort through masses of information to determine whether anyone had filed a flight plan that matched the characteristics of this particular aircraft. Until JTF–4 got back to them, AWACS would watch it.

Brenna rose and stretched her tight muscles, then made her way back to the galley. Leaning a hip against the stainless steel counter, she poured herself a fresh cup of coffee. As she did, memories of another flight and another galley tugged at her mind. Even now, after all these weeks, her senses stirred when she remembered how Sanderson had caged her against the wall. She could see the mocking glint in his brown-flecked eyes as he told her to get off his case. Hear the cadence of his irritating drawl.

Where was he right now? If everything had gone as scheduled, he should've made the pass hours ago. Had he gone back to the hotel? Or was he still parked in some bar, checking out the local action? Brenna pursed her lips, not particularly caring for that thought.

Coffee in hand, she headed back to the Mission Crew Commander's console. When she pulled on her headset, she learned that JTF–4 had confirmed that the track met the parameters for a "TOI" and had decided to do a visual ID.

Brenna listened over the secure satellite communications as the admiral responsible for all military assets assigned to drug duty in the Caribbean scrambled two Air National Guard F–15 Eagles sitting permanent alert at Howard. Within minutes, the jets were in the air and streaking through the dark skies toward the suspect. At that point, one of the weapons directors on Brenna's crew took over responsibility for guiding the friendlies to the target.

"Sentry four-five, this is Eagle six-six-three."

"This is Sentry four-five. We have you, Eagle."

"All right, AWACS, vector us in."

Guiding a jet aircraft traveling at .3 mach to an intercept with a plane traveling at one hundred and fifty knots was a little like pairing a speeding bullet with a hand-thrown water balloon. But that was what Brenna's people trained for, in war as well as peace. Hunching over the console, she watched while the weapons director brought the two jets in well above and behind the target.

As they approached the suspect aircraft, the lead pilot queried his wing man. "Ready for blackout operations?"

The second pilot confirmed that he'd turned off

all cockpit lights and donned his night vision goggles.

"Okay, wing, let's go splash some trash."

Brenna smiled wryly to herself. Most of these hotshot fighter pilots would love to swoop down and leave the bad guys bucking in their jet wash, if not blast them out of the sky with a heat-seeking missile. Contrary to the hyped-up chase scenes in action-adventure movies, however, most intercepts were done covertly from a safe distance. The goal was to identify the target, not let them know they were being watched. The last thing anyone wanted was for the suspect to dump his cargo into the ocean and hightail it back to his origination point. It was far more satisfying and effective to track him to his destination, then seize him, his cargo, his aircraft, and every bastard on the ground helping him unload.

"AWACS, this is Eagle six-six-three. We've got a visual. He's a King Air turboprop. Do you copy?"

"I copy, Eagle."

Static crackled over the radio as the fighters swooped off into the night, too far above the target for it to know it had been passed. While the jets made a rapid turn, Pierce transmitted the information to the other key players via secure data downlink. By the time the F–15s had come around, JTF–4 had confirmed that no craft matching that general description had filed a flight plan with this particular heading and asked for more detail.

"You're cleared to go in and get the tail number," Pierce relayed.

"Roger, AWACS."

Moments later, the pilot was back on the radio. "The registration is ... Hang on ... November-three . . . Correction, November-eight-eight-six-Mike-Delta. Do you copy?"

"Roger, Eagle, we copy. November-eight-eight-six-Mike-Delta."

"Jeez, these characters are flying low. The spray must be hitting them in the face. Think they're trying to sneak in under a few radars, AWACS?"

"That's my guess, Eagle."

Brenna hardly heard the easy chatter. Her heart pounding, she stared at the tail she'd jotted down in her log. N-8-8-6-M-D.

She'd seen that number before. Twice.

Once on a scrap of paper Janeen had handed her after her husband's funeral.

Once in Sergeant Lang's mission log.

Brenna didn't need JTF–4's confirmation to know the King Air skimming the waves below her was registered to one Anthony Petrocelli out of Dallas, Texas.

Some twenty-two hundred feet below and a hundred nautical miles west, Dave glanced at the King Air's altimeter and stifled an involuntary curse. He hoped to hell Petrocelli had kept his instruments well calibrated, or he'd send them smashing into the waves. Running without lights as they were, the blackness of the night was indistinguishable from the surface of the sea less than a hundred feet beneath them. With every gust of wind, the small plane dipped even lower.

This kind of flying took cool nerves and a lot of experience. Petrocelli had certainly logged enough hours in the air, but his nerves were exposed and raw right now. His cocky confidence had taken a direct hit when he'd first seen Dave in the jungle clearing. Since leaving Panama, it had evaporated completely. His hands were now so slick he could hardly hold onto the wheel, and sweat stained huge patches under the arms of his blue knit shirt.

He'd been dividing his attention between the altimeter and the fuel gauge for the entire flight. As heavily loaded as the plane was, even making it to Inagua was going to be close. Real close.

They'd been in the air for over an hour now. Given the assets dedicated to surveillance tonight, Dave guessed they were probably flashing amber on a half-dozen radar screens at this very minute. Without seeming to, he searched the sky above. The broken cloud cover hid all but a few scattered stars, but he knew Big Bird was up there. No doubt they'd run an intercept by now. If he'd been at the Customs console working this track, he sure as hell would've requested one.

The Howard alert birds would have checked them out before they were halfway to Cuba. The Eagles didn't have the legs to follow them all the way across the water, though. Chances were they'd already been handed off to a Customs Citation equipped with long-range tracking capability and a whole grab bag full of sophisticated surveillance goodies.

Dave wasn't the only one interested in the skies around them. Mad Dog twisted forward and peered up at the stars. The aircraft dipped dangerously with the movement. In the seat just behind him, Stefan grabbed at the armrests.

Dave braced a hand against the dash to counter the downward thrust. "Get the nose up!"

Cursing, Petrocelli leveled off.

The acrid scent of perspiration filled the small cabin, and Dave slanted a quick look at its source. Did Mad Dog suspect the revised schedule was a setup? If he did, he'd know they were being watched from above, and probably from behind. In other circumstances, he would have swung the King Air around in circles periodically to check his six. Tonight, he couldn't. The maneuver would take too much of his rapidly depleting fuel.

The corner Petrocelli had painted himself in was getting smaller and narrower and tighter by the minute. If the schedule was phony, he'd be burned the moment his wheels touched down. If it wasn't a fake and this flight slipped through to its final destination, he still had to contend with Dave. At this point, Mad Dog didn't know whether his old buddy would burn him or not.

He'd burn him, Dave vowed silently. To a crisp. For Andy Lang. For Janeen and her baby. For all the agents who put their lives on the line every day and didn't turn bad.

A few moments later, Petrocelli called over his

shoulder to the Panamanian. "We're approaching Inagua. I'm going to call back and let Cardoza know."

"Not yet."

"Look," he growled, "it's no skin off my nose. I'm getting paid in any case. But it's already after midnight. If your boss doesn't put his other assets in the air soon, they're going to run out of night before they reach their destinations."

"Not yet."

Mad Dog muttered something vituperous about Stefan's parentage under his breath and gripped the wheel with sweat-slick hands.

Dave stretched out his legs as much as the cockpit would allow. For all his seemingly casual slouch, his muscles were coiled tighter than a sidewinder and his throat burned for a cigarette. He'd give everything he owned for one drag right now . . . which admittedly wasn't a whole hell of a lot. He'd never been one to collect things.

For a few seconds, Dave allowed himself to recall the expression on Brenna's face as she'd glanced around his apartment. When he got back, maybe he should see about getting some better furniture. His surroundings didn't make much difference to him, but Brenna might eventually object to hotel rooms and car hoods and threadbare living-room sofas.

Dave didn't even question the fact that her comfort now figured as a consideration in his future. Assuming, of course, his future extended beyond this flight.

A quick look at the instruments told him they were about twenty minutes out of Inagua. Thirty max. Fifteen minutes on the ground to refuel, then they'd be back in the air, heading for an unknown destination along Flordia's coast.

Once they came within a hundred-mile radius of the U.S. coastline, Customs would have responsibility for the takedown. Citations and Blackhawk helicopters controlled by the Customs Domestic Air Interdiction Center would follow the King Air and swoop down on it as soon as it touched ground. Jerry O'Halloran was probably watching them right now on one of the big screens in the Riverside Center. Wondering what the hell was going on. Waiting for the surge of tracks Intel had predicted.

Inagua was a critical decision point, Dave knew.

If he'd been working this TOI under more normal circumstances, he would have recommended an apprehension on Inagua. He'd want to snare the bird in hand instead of taking the chance of losing it in the Florida swamps. Call in the Bahaman police. Back them up with Customs' assets. Have a whole welcoming committee waiting the moment the King Air touched ground. It would be an easy takedown in more normal circumstances.

But these were hardly normal circumstances. If the King Air got busted on Inagua, Cardoza would know the hole in the sky wasn't as big as they'd been led to believe. None of the other dopers would launch.

So don't blow it, Dave urged the silent watchers. Don't go for the easy prize. Don't jump the gun, O'Halloran. Not yet.

From the outside, the single-story facility on March Air Force Base near Riverside, California, appeared dark and quiet. So quiet, someone unfamiliar with its mission might wonder at the need for a high, chain-link fence topped with strands of barbed wire, armed guards behind bulletproof shields, and massive antennas on its roof.

Inside, however, Customs' Domestic Air Interdiction Center hummed with activity. In the operations room that formed the hub of the center, controllers wearing light blue shirts and navy trousers manned an array of consoles. Two huge back-lit screens measuring eight feet wide by six feet tall dominated Ops center, dubbed the "dark room" by the agents who worked there.

Jerry O'Halloran stared up at a flashing dot moving across one of the screens. He'd been at DAICC for twelve hours now. Watching the screens. Waiting for the movement Intelligence had predicted. Wondering why the hell Sanderson hadn't checked in after·making his pass.

Shoving back his suit coat, he planted both hands on his hips. His eyes narrowed as a tail number painted across the screen under the flashing dot.

"Who is he, Logan?"

The black man seated at the console next to him toggled a switch. Instantly, the display on the screen doubled in size, making the identification data below the flashing dot clearly legible.

"The registration checks to a King Air out of Dallas," Logan read. "It's owned by . . . oh, shit!"

A veteran of more than ten years in the counter-narcotics business, Logan had seen it all and then some. Despite the constant pressure inherent in juggling dozens of tracks at one time and orchestrating takedowns that involved a wide variety of Customs, DEA, and military assets, he rarely displayed emotion of any kind. His low exclamation made more than one head turn.

"That's Mad Dog Petrocelli skipping across the waves, or someone flying his plane," he muttered.

A silence descended over the huge room as one controller after another picked up the significance of the tag. Not all of them knew Mad Dog personally, but most of them knew he was involved in the Special Task Force in some capacity.

Logan swiveled in his seat and glanced up at O'Halloran. "The King Air's got just enough fuel capacity to make it from Panama to Inagua, unless he's rigged up an external pod or internal bladder. If he does, he could make it easily to any deserted strip along the southeastern coast."

"I know."

"Best I recall," one of the other controllers volunteered, "the airport at Inagua isn't much more than a couple of shacks. We could take him down there easily, without much collateral damage."

His eyes intent on the flashing dot, O'Halloran only nodded.

"The Citation out of Grand Cayman is already in the air," Logan reminded him. "If the Bahamians request it, I can have the Blackhawks on their way in the next five minutes."

O'Halloran swiped a palm across his hair. Where were they? Where was this flotilla of dopers Intel had predicted? What the hell was Mad Dog doing out there by himself? And where was Sanderson?

The sensible thing to do would be to take Petrocelli down at Inagua. But was it the smart thing? As Sanderson had argued so forcefully, taking out Petrocelli would make his contacts nervous. Real nervous.

"Want me to launch the Blackhawks?" Logan asked.

"Not yet. We'll wait."

Despite the quiet confidence in his voice, O'Halloran's mind churned with unanswered questions.

What was going on?

Where was Sanderson?

Gritting his teeth, Dave balled his hands into fists to keep from snatching at the wheel. It jumped in Petrocelli's hands like an angry cat as he fought to hold the King Air steady against the buffeting winds.

"Get on the horn and wake up the folks on Inagua," Mad Dog ordered tersely, rivulets of sweat tracking down either side of his mustache. "Tell 'em we want fuel and a fast turnaround."

His mind racing, Dave reached for the fat, two-ring binder wedged between the seats. If the surveillance aircraft were listening in to the right frequencies, maybe he could . . .

"I've already dialed up the frequency," Petrocelli snarled. "Just get 'em on the net! You know what to tell them to cover our track."

Lifting the hand mike, Dave pressed the send button. "Inagua approach, this is November-eight-eight-six-Mike-Delta. I'm on a flight plan from Panama City to Nassau. I've misjudged my fuel and am running a little low. Request permission to land at Inagua and take on some gas. Over."

For endless moments, only static cackled over the speaker.

Mad Dog risked letting go of the wheel to swipe the back of his hand across his forehead. "Dammit, where are they? Where the f—?"

"November-eight-eight-six, this is Inagua approach. You have permission to land runway zero-nine-zero. What's your current position? Over."

Another gust hit the King Air, lifting the right wing dangerously into the air. While Mad Dog fought the updraft, Dave braced himself against the instrument panel once again. Unobtrusively, he slid his hand downward. The faint clicking of the radio dials as he switched frequencies went unnoticed in the tumult of Stefan's shout and Petrocelli's cursing.

Pressing the send button on the mike to prevent incoming chatter, he waited until Petrocelli had righted the plane, then broadcast his own message over a frequency well-known in the counter-narcotics business as one favored by dopers.

"Roger Inagua approach. November-eight-eight-six will land runway zero-nine-zero. We're currently about twenty miles out. We'll only be on the ground long enough to take on fuel," Dave drawled, dragging out the transmission as long as he dared. "Please tell your fixed base operator to stand by. We'll only need a hundred pounds to get us where we're going. Correction, Inagua, that's three hundred and eight liters. Over and out."

The senior communications tech aboard Sentry four-five jerked his head up as the high-speed scanner at his console locked onto a frequency.

"... be on the ground long enough to take on fuel. Please tell your fixed base operator to stand by."

Instantly, the sophisticated computers aboard AWACS traced the signal. A small, tight smile played at the corners of the technician's mouth. The chatter was emanating from the TOI they'd been tracking. With the click of a switch, he broadcast the communication over AWACS' internal net.

"We'll only need a hundred pounds to get us where we're going. Correction, Inagua. That's three hundred and eight liters. Over and out."

The major at the console next to Brenna's leaned back in his seat, grinning.

"Only three hundred plus liters. Sounds like our

boys are loaded to the gills. Two guesses what they're hauling that's so dang heavy."

When she didn't respond, he swiveled around. His grin slipped, then vanished completely.

"Hey, MCC, are you all right?"

He sounded distant to Brenna, as though he were speaking to her through a tunnel. His voice competed with the one still echoing in her ears. Even crackly with static, she'd recognized the laconic drawl instantly.

The major leaned forward, concern leaping into his brown eyes. "Colonel Duggan?"

She blinked, seeing but not seeing his face. Shudders rippled through her, one after another. She gripped the edge of the console with both hands, as if to anchor her whirling thoughts and searing emotions.

Focus, Duggan! her mind commanded. *Focus! Do your job! Do what you're up here to do!*

She dragged in a deep breath.

"I'm fine," she said slowly in answer to the question in the major's eyes. Still, her fingers shook as she unbuckled her seat belt and made her way back to the Customs console.

"Did you copy that last transmission, Bob?"

Pierce nodded. "Sure did, Colonel."

"Did you recognize the person making it?"

His sandy brows rose. "No. Did you?"

"Yes," Brenna replied grimly. "Get me a SAT-COM link to Riverside, would you? I need to talk to Jerry O'Halloran."

"Roger, MCC."

Chapter Twenty-two

Brenna used the few moments it took for Pierce to hook up to the Customs' Air Interdiction Center to pull herself together. Still, her hand shook as she plugged her headset into a connector at the console next to his.

The moment he identified himself, Brenna recognized O'Halloran's voice. Even after being bounced off a satellite orbiting more than two hundred miles overhead, it hadn't lost its clipped quality. She drew in a deep breath.

"This is the Mission Crew Commander for Sentry Four-five. Are you following track echo-two-one-zero?"

"Roger, MCC. We're following it."

"We've just intercepted a voice transmission from that track. I recognized the voice of the person who made it."

"Identify the person, please." Sudden tension sharpened O'Halloran's words to a knife-blade finish.

"Detection Systems Specialist Sanderson."

Dead silence followed.

"Do you copy?" Brenna pressed the mouthpiece on her headset closer to her lips. "Customs, do you copy?"

"Roger," O'Halloran replied at last. "I copy. You're sure?"

"Believe me," she returned in a very close approximation of Dave's slow, deliberate twang, "I'm sure."

"All right, MCC. We'll take it from here."

Like hell they would.

"Do you want us to flag the track as a 'friendly'?"

O'Halloran hesitated, as though he still hadn't quite absorbed the implications of Dave's presence on an aircraft that met all the criteria for a TOI.

"No. Keep it suspect. We'll watch it all the way to its final destination."

"So will we, Customs. So will we."

Brenna had participated in some long, intense missions during her years in AWACS, particularly during Desert Storm. But this was the first time she'd had such an immediate, personal stake in the outcome of a mission.

With traffic as light as it was, her responsibilities to oversee the back-end operations didn't demand her entire concentration. As a consequence, she was able to follow the track's progress via her screen and by listening to transmission from the Customs Citation on its tail. What seemed like hours but was only minutes later, the King Air landed at Inagua and took on fuel. Then it took off again. Her eyes ˜glued to the screen, Brenna saw the amber blip change course slightly and head for the Florida Keys. Kissing the waves, the plane stayed low to avoid detection by land-based and high-altitude aerostat radars.

She would have followed it all the way in if, in the vernacular of the crew, the sky hadn't suddenly filled with snow.

Not ten minutes after the King Air's take off, a small mountaintop radar site jointly manned by U.S. and Colombian personnel painted a suspicious track. The track was filtered by JTF–4 and passed to AWACS.

"Okay, I'm flagging track foxtrot-four-four-seven," a surveillance tech notified the MCC. "He's a big guy, a 727, heading due north out of Colombia, not squawking and following no known flight plan. JTF–4's running an intercept on him now for a visual ID."

Moments later, another tech spotted a small plane that met the parameters for a suspicious track just off the Honduran coast.

Suddenly, the air inside the huge, windowless AWACS came alive with static-charged tension.

A third suspect flashed on a screen. Then a fourth.

In the next hour, a constant stream of communications flowed between the E–3 and the many agencies involved in detecting, identifying, intercepting, and tracking drug smugglers. Brenna stayed glued to her console, orchestrating the actions of the seventeen-person mission crew. To an outside observer, the intense activity in the aircraft might have looked and sounded like uncontrolled mayhem. To anyone who'd flown aboard AWACS, the action had both the precision and the excitement of a Super Bowl's television production control room. Every player knew his or her role, and the director knew them all.

Surveillance techs and officers hunched over consoles, working the suspicious tracks among the many routine flights that marched across their screens. Weapons directors vectored friendly aircraft in for intercepts and visual identification. Communications technicians humped to keep the voice and data links clear and open, while the computer specialists ran through the stacks of mission tapes that followed the tracks across the huge surveillance sector.

Whenever a break in the action occurred, Brenna switched screens to follow Sanderson's progress toward the Florida coast. She didn't know if Petrocelli or anyone else was in the King Air with him. She didn't know *why* he was in the King Air to begin with. But she suspected it wasn't by choice.

As track two-one-zero approached the Florida coast, a wide band seemed to squeeze tighter and tighter around Brenna's chest. She'd listened to and seen the tapes of a number of takedowns and knew darn well that apprehension was the most dangerous phase in the counternarcotics effort.

Desperate men suddenly confronted by law enforcement officials could and often did perform desperate acts to avoid arrest.

When Dave's plane was still some miles from the Florida shore, Bob Pierce came over the net. "MCC, this is Customs. Navy's just passed me a string of three suspects overflying the Gulf in loose formation. Can one of your people take them? I've got my hands full right now."

Brenna wrenched her eyes from track two-one-zero. "Roger, Customs. We'll take them."

If there was a landing strip or a ground crew anywhere in front of them, Dave sure as hell couldn't see them. Fists balled, he searched the heavy blackness. Not a single light illuminated the black stretch of scrub palms and marshy swamps below.

Frustration and fury emanated from Mad Dog in waves as he peered into the night. Dave could hear it in his voice, smell it in his sweat. Clamping the radio mike in a meaty fist, Petrocelli shouted into it.

"Where are you, you stupid bastards?"

Some moments later, a heavily accented voice replied. "Relax, man. We're almost there. Five minutes. Maybe ten."

The Panamanian in the seat behind Mad Dog leaned forward, peering into the impenetrable darkness that hung like a black curtain all around the plane. Dave wasn't surprised to see the subdued glow from the instrument panel reflect dully on the weapon in the Panamanian's hand. It was a .45, he noted dispassionately, with one of those fancy silver grips inlaid with a Mayan sun calendar.

"You set this up, Petrocelli," Stefan hissed. "Can you not trust these men?"

"I don't trust anyone in this business," Mad Dog snarled, "particularly not some pipe-heads off the streets."

Drug pilots had good reason not to trust the crew on the ground, Dave knew. They constituted the weakest link in air smuggling operations. The dealers usually rounded up fifteen or twenty illegal aliens, offered them fifty bucks and a few hits for a night's work, then trucked them out to the drop point. They'd fill the time waiting for the plane to arrive smoking dope and drinking. By the time the pilot started searching for his landing point, the ground crew was often so drunk or stoned, it was anyone's guess whether they'd even remember to turn on the truck lights. Apparently, this crew was no different.

Which meant the next half hour could get real tight. With an unreliable ground crew, a .45-wielding passenger getting more tense by the moment, and a pilot who didn't know whether or not he would be burned the moment he touched down, Dave estimated his chances of walking away from the King Air were just this side of nonexistent.

With infinite care, he angled his body slightly to the right. His first priority had to be the Panamanian. Stefan wasn't going to go down without a fight, and a .45 could do some serious damage in the close confines of the King Air's cabin. Dave knew Mad Dog was also armed, but the pilot would have his hands full for the few critical moments Dave needed.

He didn't even consider the possibility that the King Air had slipped through the surveillance net. He had to assume there was a Citation circling overhead, watching them on infrared, and two Blackhawk helicopters on their tail. The moment the King Air touched down and rolled to the end of the strip, one heavily armed Blackhawk would swoop in right behind him to block any attempt to turn and take off again. A two and a half million candlepower spotlight would blind the pilot while the bust team jumped out to take him down. The second Blackhawk would chase the ground crew, which usually scattered like frenzied rabbits at the first hint of trouble.

That was how it was supposed to work, according to the manuals. But Mad Dog Petrocelli was at the stick, and he didn't believe in going by the book any more than Dave did.

Jamming the mike against his mouth, Petrocelli shouted his fury at the ground crew. "If I don't see some lights in the next two minutes, I'm outta here. I'm dumping this shit in the Gulf and I'm outta here!"

"Hey, man. We're almost there. Hang loose."

"I'm making one circle, you understand me? One goddamn circle!"

Yanking the wheel, Petrocelli put the King Air

into a sharp bank. As they completed the turn, Stefan leaned forward. Both men searched the darkness, while Dave watched them.

Petrocelli swore in relief as a pinpoint of light appeared off to the right. A second light appeared, then others. Within moments, they'd illuminated a rough oblong.

Mad Dog lined up an approach. One corner of his mouth worked furiously, causing the tip of his mustache to twitch. Dave caught the movement . . . and the last, grim look the pilot gave him.

"What's behind me, old buddy? What's out there?"

"You're on your own on this one, Tony."

Afterward, Dave would always wonder whether Mad Dog knew. Whether he thought he could cut one final deal, talk himself out of one last mess. At that moment, however, he didn't have time to wonder about anything.

Everything happened too fast. The low, short approach and bumpy touchdown. The sudden panic among the ground crew as they heard not only the King Air's engines but the whump-whump-whump of the Blackhawk's rotors beating the night air. The sudden loss of visibility as the drivers slewed their vehicles around and tried to escape. Mad Dog's hands jerking at the power lever. Stefan's fury as Dave grabbed for his gun. The blue-white flash. The sound of the windshield shattering. The blood streaming into Dave's eyes as slivers of tempered glass flew through the cockpit like tiny needles of fire.

*　　*　　*

"Hey, MCC!"

Responding to the urgency in Bob Pierce's voice, Brenna cut off her communications with the Navy.

"The Blackhawks are on the net," the Customs agent told her. "They're taking down track two-one-zero."

Brenna's heart slammed against her ribs. "What frequency?"

Her hand shot out, clicking to the secure UHF frequency Pierce indicated. Instantly, a taut male voice jumped out at her.

". . . right wing's dragging the dirt! I don't know what the hell he's doing!"

"Maybe he's trying a short turn to get back in the air. Spray him with some raid!"

Brenna's breath sliced at her throat. No! she screamed silently. No! Don't fire on him.

"I won't need to use any beetle juice," the first pilot returned a second later. "The poor bastard's out of control. He's . . . Oh, hell! Back off, Two! Back off! He's flipped over. He's skidding right into one of the trucks."

In the instant of silence that followed, Brenna heard muted mutters as word of what was going down spread through the mission crew compartment. She felt her arm jostled as the major next to her reached out to switch to the UHF frequency. But nothing registered. Nothing penetrated except the voice coming over the net.

"Jesus, look at those flames!"

She closed her eyes, swallowing convulsively.

"Well, we've got one live one at least. He's dragging something out of the wreckage. Looks like a body."

"Yeah, and there's another 'bout twenty yards back. Must have been thrown out when they went over."

"Two down, one still moving."

"Roger, lead. Let's go in for the kill."

Sentry Four-five recovered at Tinker Air Force base sixteen and a half hours after launching. The crew laughed and talked among themselves as they gathered their gear and headed for the exit. For them, the mission had ended on a huge high. They'd tracked dozens of TOIs and had feedback on three takedowns already. Three kills, possibly more.

Standing beside her console, Brenna stuffed her log into her flight case with stiff, awkward fingers. She replied when spoken to by the passing crew members. Nodded when the aircraft commander asked if she wanted to conduct the debrief as soon as they'd swung by AWACS Ops to drop off the logs.

She moved and responded as if on automatic pilot, but her inner being—that part of her separate from her duties as MCC and her responsibilities as a senior Air Force officer—was frozen. She couldn't feel anything, hadn't allowed herself to feel anything, since the last transmission from the Blackhawks.

Two down.
One still moving.
Go in for the kill.

There'd been no direct communication after that, other than a brief message relayed through Riverside that there'd been some casualties and the site was secure. Brenna hadn't expected any more. Like the military, Customs wouldn't broadcast over an open net if one of its own had been killed or wounded. They'd have to go in. Identify the remains. Notify the next of kin.

Oh, God.

That was how this nightmare had begun so many weeks ago. With a late-night call from the Command Post and a drive through the night to notify Andrew Lang's next of kin. Brenna's nails dug into the hard sides of the case. They couldn't have come full circle! Not yet! Dear Lord, not yet!

She and Dave hadn't spent more than a few hours together at any one time. She didn't know what kind of music he liked, or if he listened to music at all. She had no idea whether he was a steak and potatoes man or a fast-food freak like her. She didn't know if his parents were still alive. If he had sisters or brothers. She knew nothing about him, except that he lit flames under her skin with his mocking smile and spun her out of control with his touch. And that he needed her. As much as she needed him.

Two down.
One still moving.

Her hands shaking, Brenna folded the flaps on

the flight case and twisted the locks. Her crew was waiting. She had to drop off her mission log. Conduct the debrief. Dismiss the crew and send them home to their families. They didn't know her private agony. She wouldn't have told them, even if she could. Not during a mission that demanded everyone's total and unwavering concentration.

Feeling as though everything alive had been sucked out of her, leaving behind an automan with programmed responses, Brenna walked up the narrow aisle toward the patch of watery gray outlined by the open door. As she stepped out onto the platform at the top of the metal stairs, a cold, fine drizzle drifted over her hair and face.

She stopped at the top of the stairs, disoriented. After sixteen and a half hours in a windowless cylinder of gray metal, her numbed mind struggled to adjust to daylight and to a world other than the fiery one that played and replayed without stop in her mind.

By the time she descended the stairs and made her way to the waiting crew bus, the heavy mist thickened into rain. The bus took them along a familiar route, one Brenna had traveled hundreds of times before. Eyes and mind turned inward, she didn't see the gray-painted tankers lined up in a neat row or hear the AWACS powering up its engines in preparation for takeoff.

Two down.

One still moving.

When the crew bus pulled up in front of the red brick building that housed AWACS Ops, Brenna grasped her flight case and stepped out of the bus.

The rain trickled down the neck of her green bag as she and the aircraft commander walked up the pebbled walk. They'd just reached the glass doors when tires squealed on the wet tarmac behind them. Glancing over one shoulder, Brenna saw the "552 ACW CC" designation on the license tag of the blue Air Force vehicle.

"Wonder what the old man wants?" the aircraft commander murmured.

The moment she saw General Adams's face, she knew.

He slammed the car door and walked toward them, heedless of the rain that darkened his light blue uniform shirt. As he approached, the numbness that had encased Brenna since the Blackhawk's last transmission shattered. Waves of fear built low in her chest cavity, spread through her lungs, grabbed at her throat.

This was how Janeen must have felt, she realized on a spiral of sheer animal panic. The night Brenna rang her bell. The night she opened the door to find the officials standing on her porch. She must have felt the same suffocating fear. The instinctive denial. The urge to weep and rage and scream.

Please, please don't let it have come full circle, she prayed in mindless desperation. It can't have come full circle.

She couldn't bring her body to attention, as the AC did. Couldn't raise her arm. General Adams returned the major's salute, but his eyes remained unwavering on Brenna's face.

"Sanderson's all right."

She didn't breathe. Her lungs refused to function. Her throat wouldn't open.

"He sustained third-degree burns," Adams continued. "And a bullet supposedly put a new part in his hair, but he walked away."

She stared at the lean, weathered face before her. Her mind processed his words. Her heart tried to absorb them.

"He's all right, Brenna," Adams said, his voice brusque with understanding. "I just got the word and drove out to meet your plane. I knew you'd want to know. He's all right."

"Yes, sir." The whisper was low and hoarse, but it was all she could manage.

"He's on his way back to Tinker right now. Should touch down within the next half hour."

"Yes, sir." She wiped her tongue over dry lips. "Thank you, sir."

"Brenna . . ."

"Would you excuse me?"

Without waiting for a reply, she turned and pushed open the glass doors. Blindly, she passed through flight ops. Her boots echoed on the tile floor, a slow thud at first, then a fast walk.

Suddenly, she broke into a run. Flinging aside the heavy flight case, she slammed both palms against the wooden door to the ladies' room. It crashed back against the hall, startling a little shriek out of the woman washing her hands at one of the sinks.

Her sides heaving, Brenna yanked open the door to one of the stalls and sank to her knees.

That was where Sanderson found her some time later. In the ladies' room. Her face streaked with tears as she splashed cold water on her face.

Thankfully, the woman who'd shrieked at Brenna's precipitous entrance had stayed with her while she heaved, then brought her a Coke to take the taste of bile from her mouth.

When the ladies' room door crashed once more, the hapless woman gave another small scream. Recovering quickly, she stepped in front of Sanderson.

"She's all right," she said, eyeing the newcomer warily. "She'll be out in a few minutes."

Boots thudded across the tiles. "Brenna. Sweetheart."

The hoarse, harsh whisper brought her head up. Tears still blurred her eyes, but she recognized the broad shoulders straining the seams of what had to be a borrowed flight suit. She was afraid to speak, afraid to loose her hold on the stool and dash the tears out of her eyes for fear the apparition before her would dissolve.

And apparition it was. The hair on one side of his head had been singed off. Where it wasn't blistered, his face was a mass of tiny cuts. The sun-bleached eyebrows Brenna had fantasized about more than once were gone. She stared at him helplessly, fresh tears pouring down her cheeks.

Dave's heart ached at the sight. This woman had reduced him to fury with a single glance from her cool blue eyes about as often as she'd stirred him to a fever of need. He'd seen those same eyes widen with fear in a dark alley, and glitter with passion in the middle of an Oklahoma night. He'd dreamed about them, imagined them soft and gleaming with an emotion he hesitated to put a name to. But he'd never thought to see them awash with tears. His heart aching, he held out his arms.

Racked by sobs, Brenna buried her face in his chest. "I th . . . thought you were dead. I heard the explo . . . explosion. I thought you were dead."

"It's okay, sweetheart," Dave croaked, his throat raw from the smoke and fumes he'd breathed. "It's okay."

"No!" she sobbed. "No, it's not! I thought you were *dead*!"

"I'm not dead," he whispered, stroking her hair with a bandaged palm. "I'm here. For as long as you want me."

"I thought we'd come full circle. I thought about Andy Lang. And Janeen."

"So did I." He cupped the back of her head. "So did I."

Locked together, they rocked back and forth. Brenna clutched at his flight suit. His arms held her fast against his chest.

He had no idea how long they stayed like that. It might have been minutes or hours before a hesitant, feminine voice dragged them from their small, private universe.

"Uh, do you need me to stay?"

Dave glanced at the woman who hovered beside them. "No," he said quietly.

She glanced uncertainly from him to Brenna. "Are you sure?"

"We're sure."

When the woman's footsteps had faded, Brenna dragged her head back. Dave's stomach knotted at the fierce expression that gripped her tear-ravaged face.

"I love you. I don't know why or . . ." She sniffled noisily. ". . . or when it happened, but I love you."

Still holding her with one arm, Dave dragged down the tail of the paper towel dangling just behind her left shoulder, yanked off a good length, and handed it to her.

"That's funny," he said as she blew her nose. "I know exactly when it happened with me."

She stared at him over the wad of paper. For long moments, he smiled down into wide blue eyes spiked with wet lashes. Then she lowered the tissue and drew in a shuddering breath.

"When did it happen with you? Exactly?"

"About five minutes after I walked into your office for the first time," he told her, his words sandpapery from the smoke. "When you informed me in your haughty-snotty commander's voice that you'd haul my ass in front of a flying review board if I didn't give you some straight answers."

Her dark brows slanted. "That was it?"

"That was it."

"My haughty-snotty commander's voice turned you on?"

"Among other things."

"Like what?"

Feathering a thumb across her cheek, he whispered a low, rough litany. "Like hair I wanted to dig my hands into. And eyes that flashed blue fire. And a mouth made for mine. And legs designed to drive a man to desperate measures."

Dave saw the wonder in her eyes, and the doubt.

"I know," he murmured hoarsely, his thumb soft on her cheek. "Even before I scorched off half my face, I didn't have much to offer a woman like you. Hell, I didn't think I had much left to offer *any* woman. But then you marched into my life and refused to march out. I want you, Brenna. I want you more than I've ever wanted anyone or anything."

It wasn't enough. He could see in her eyes that it wasn't enough. It had been so long since he'd said the words, he had to force them through his raw throat.

"I need you."

She could settle for two out of three, Brenna thought. She didn't doubt Dave respected her. And he'd now admitted his need. They could work on commitment together, she decided.

She lifted a hand, wanting to touch him as he was touching her to seal the bargain. The only spot marked by bloody cuts was the left side of his chin. To Brenna's consternation, her eyes filled again as her fingertips brushed the rough stubble. She couldn't remember the last time she'd cried, and couldn't seem to halt the tears now.

"I want you, too. More than I've ever wanted anything in my life."

He let out his breath in a long ragged sigh. "Let's get out of here."

The husky timber of his voice raised goose bumps on Brenna's skin. She managed a watery smile.

"We'll go to my place. I have a bed."

Epilogue

The First Baptist Church of Seiling wore a festive air. Baskets of mums stood massed on the altar, their gold and rust colors vibrant against the white cloth. A small choir robed in purple lifted their voices in a hymn of thanksgiving appropriate to the season. The tantalizing aroma of honey glazed ham and fresh baked bread drifted in from the church hall with each cold draft that snaked through the pews.

The first taste of winter had swept down unexpectedly from Kansas during the night, leaving the stubbled wheat fields visible through the windows covered with a blanket of glittering frost. Parishioners in wool jackets and colorful down vests filled the wooden pews.

At Janeen's request, Brenna had worn her blue dress uniform to the service. Her hair was swept up in a thick twist under her blue flight cap with its silver oak leaf on one side denoting her rank. Small diamond studs sparkled at her ears, and the accoutrements on her blue uniform gleamed in the bright morning sun. Shoulders straight, she stood beside Janeen at the front rail.

Brenna had never attended a Baptist worship service before, much less taken part in a baby's dedication. She rarely attended any kind of services at all anymore, having lost the fervor of her Catholic youth years ago. But the simple ceremony moved her to the depths of her soul.

While the pastor smiled in encouragement, Janeen peeled the fuzzy yellow blanket back from her daughter's face. The small bundle in her arms stirred, and a tiny nose wrinkled in protest at this disturbance.

"I promise to raise my daughter in a Christian home," Janeen said, her brown eyes shining. "And to give her all the love God gave me and her daddy."

The baby hiccuped, then came fully awake. A small fist pushed free of the blanket and waved in the air. Smiling, Brenna brushed the dimpled knuckles with one finger. Her namesake immediately clamped on to her finger and refused to let go. Above the hiccuping baby, Janeen's eyes met hers.

Things *have* come full circle, Brenna realized. Death has flowed into life. Pain into love.

Still anchored to the infant, she searched the small crowd until she found the man she sought. He sat in the back pew, well behind Janeen's relatives and friends. With a tie collaring his neck and his hair trimmed to a quarter of an inch all over his head to even out the ravages left by the crash, he blended in with the rest of the men present.

Almost.

Brenna's smile deepened. In the past month, she'd discovered a hundred reasons why Dave Sanderson would never blend into anything. He was too strong. Too unpredictable. Too explosively passionate . . . when he wasn't sprawled across her body, too lazy to move. He still hadn't decided whether he was going to take the desk job Customs had offered him in D.C. or continue to fly with AWACS. It depended on her, he'd said with a shrug, indifferent to his own future except where it touched hers.

She couldn't imagine wanting him any other way.

Over the heads of the congregation, Dave caught the smile on Brenna's face and tried to guess what had put it there. The simple exercise gave him a dart of pleasure. Strange. In the past few weeks, he'd discovered that Lieutenant Colonel Duggan's smile could stir him even more than her clear blue eyes and delectable body.

When the baby's gurgling cries drew the attention of both women, Dave's mind drifted back to a noisy, smoke-filled bar in Panama. For the first time, he recalled that night without a shaft of crippling guilt.

He filtered out the noise and the smoke and his gut-wrenching tension when he'd realized that Andy Lang had followed him to the Purple Parrot. Instead, he remembered how the tall, lanky staff sergeant with the easy grin had flipped open his wallet to pay for his beer, displaying the picture of his honey-haired wife in the process. The sergeant's gaze had lingered on the photo, and he'd responded with a smile to a question about the woman in the picture.

You were right, Lang. She's something special.

Dave sketched an invisible salute to Andrew Lang, then made a promise of his own. They'd watch out for Janeen and the baby. He and Brenna. Together.

If you enjoyed *Line of Duty*, be sure to look for Merline Lovelace's next military thriller, in which Colonel Julia Endicott, a high-ranking officer in the Pentagon, is about to get stripped of her hard-won duty and plunged into dishonor over an affair from her past. . . .

Turn the page for a special preview of Merline Lovelace's

DUTY AND DISHONOR

Available soon at bookstores everywhere.

When she answered the shrill buzz of her intercom that crisp December afternoon, Julia Endicott had no idea that the summons she received would change her life forever.

"Colonel Endicott," she answered distractedly, her mind on the press release she and her staff were preparing in anticipation of the media blitz over the latest round of base closures.

"The Vice Chief's exec just called," her secretary informed her. "General Titus wants to see you, ma'am."

Julia's lips curved into a wry grimace as she surveyed the crowd huddled around the mahogany work table in her Pentagon office.

"Right now, I suppose?"

Her secretary laughed. "When else?"

"Tell them I'm on my way."

Reaching for the leather-bound notebook she referred to as her "brainbook," Julia rose.

"General Titus wants to see me. Start working

on the verification of the economic impact assessments while I'm gone, Major Donner. There were two different sets of figures floating around last week and I don't want to give the wrong one to the media."

"Will do, Colonel."

"I'll be back as soon as I can."

Tucking an errant strand of silvery blond hair into the smooth twist at the back of her head, Julia strode out of her office. Walls in a pale shade of cream stretched endlessly before her, broken by rows of glass-fronted doors and the broad corridors that intersected the rings.

After two tours at Air Force Headquarters, once as an eager, energetic young captain and now as a Deputy Director of Public Affairs, Julia knew her way around these unprepossessing corridors of power. While most officers avoided a second tour at the Air Staff like the plague, hating the long hours and never-ending stress, she thrived on the fast pace and the adrenaline-pumping issues she grappled with daily.

She might even extend this tour at the Pentagon for another two years. General Titus, the Air Force's second-in-command and Julia's gruff mentor, had hinted once or twice that she was heir apparent for the director's position when her boss retired next year.

Brigadier General Julia Endicott, Director of Public Affairs, United States Air Force.

It had a nice sound to it, she admitted with a grin as she turned onto E-ring, the prestigious outer circle that housed the offices of the nation's senior civilian and military executives. Her high heels clicked on the cream-colored marble tiles. Life-sized portraits of past Air Force leaders stared down from paneled walls.

Halting with one hand on the door to the Vice Chief's suite of offices, Julia drew in a deep breath. For all his support of her career over the years, General Titus possessed a temper that matched what remained of his fiery red hair. He didn't suffer fools gladly, and had been known to throw colonels and captains out of his office with equal ruthlessness.

His executive officer rose to his feet at her entrance. "Afternoon, ma'am."

"Afternoon, Dave. I understand the boss wants to see me. Any idea what it's about?"

"No, ma'am. He just said for you to go right in."

Nodding her thanks, she pulled open the heavy oak door to the inner office.

The first thing she noted when she stepped into the huge, blue-carpeted room with a magnificent view of the Potomac was the rare December sunshine streaming in through the tall bank of windows. Shafts of silvery sunlight illuminated the glittering array of memorabilia from three wars arranged on the shelves that took up one whole wall.

Only after she'd stopped before the general and snapped him a crisp salute did Julia notice the stranger in civilian clothes standing quietly a few feet away. Tall and wide-shouldered, he regarded her steadily through steel gray eyes.

Wondering who he was, she waited for General Titus to return her salute and wave her to one of the elaborately carved chairs in front of his desk, as he usually did. Gifts of the Ethiopian government to some illustrious previous occupant of this office, the armchairs were of ebony inlaid with ivory. They were also uncushioned and uncomfortable as hell for anyone who had to sit in them for any length of time. Julia suspected the general kept them in his office for just that reason.

To her surprise, he didn't invite her to sit down. Instead, he jerked his chin toward the silent stranger.

"Colonel Endicott, this is Special Agent Ted Marsh of the Office of Special Investigations."

The curt edge to his voice lifted Julia's brow. Whatever was going down, the general didn't like it. At all.

She wasn't surprised. As the Air Force's investigative arm, the OSI worked all kinds of nasty stuff, from undercover drug busts to old-fashioned, cloak-and-dagger spy rings. Suspecting that the investigator's presence in General Titus's office would mean another long night for her and her staff, she acknowledged him with a small nod.

"Mr. Marsh."

"Colonel Endicott," he returned, his gray eyes holding hers.

The fact that Julia couldn't quite interpret the expression in their silvery depths bothered her.

After two decades of dealing with a sometimes hostile press corps, she'd learned to size people up at a glance. With his hard, lean face and deliberately shuttered eyes, however, Marsh defied easy categorization.

She turned back to the Vice Chief. His grim expression set her nerves tingling. Whatever had happened, it looked to be sensational. She ran through a mental checklist, gearing herself up for damage control with a media pool that would clamor for details the instant the story leaked.

None of her mental checklists could prepare her for what came next, however. His jaw tight, General Titus stood and faced her across the wide expanse of his desk.

"Colonel Endicott, I'm relieving you of all public affairs duties, effectively immediately."

The blunt statement was unexpected, so absurd, she didn't absorb it at first.

"You are now assigned as special assistant to Colonel Richards, head of the Issues Group."

Slowly, as if fighting their way through a protective barrier, his words penetrated Julia's stunned mind. Clutching her notebook in numb fingers, she could only gape at him.

"I don't understand."

"You will remain with the Issues Group pending an Article 32 investigation to determine whether you should be charged with murder."

"What?"

"Murder, Colonel Endicott. Or more specifically, wrongful death, as detailed by Article 131 of the Uniform Code of Military Justice."

Murder! Wrongful death!

Reeling with shock, Julia barely grasped the general's terse explanation.

"The remains of a U.S. airman were recently returned under the new, cooperative agreement with the government of Vietnam."

Julia swallowed, once. Twice. Exerting every ounce of self-discipline she'd inherited from the man known to two generations of combat pilots as Iron Man Endicott, she fought to bring some order to her chaotic emotions.

"With all due respect, sir, what the hell does that have to do with me?"

"The remains have been positively identified as belonging to Captain Gabriel Hunter."

The shock Julia had experienced moments ago didn't compare to the blow that slammed into her now. The leather notebook slid from her suddenly nerveless grasp. Lifting wildly trembling fingers, she pressed them against her lips in a vain attempt to hold back the hoarse cry that ripped from her throat.

"Gabe! Oh, my God, *Gabe?!*"

General Titus leaned his fists on his desktop. "Before you say anything else, Special Agent Marsh will advise you of your rights."

His voice sounded as though it were coming from a deep well. Julia heard the ripples of sound, but they seemed to bounce off the wall of her spiraling disbelief.

They'd found Gabe!

She didn't turn, didn't move, as the special agent stepped forward. Her wide, unseeing eyes stayed fixed on the winter sunlight streaming in through the windows. A distant vision shimmered in her mind, of lush tropical greenery and shell-pocked stucco walls.

"Colonel Endicott, I must advise you that you're the prime suspect in Captain Hunter's death."

His deep voice called her from her private hell. As if her head was too heavy for her neck, Julia turned slowly to face the OSI agent.

"Why?" The question was hardly more than a whisper. She wet her lips and tried again. "Why am I a suspect? Captain Hunter disappeared after an enemy ambush and was listed as MIA over twenty years ago."

"In May 1972," Marsh confirmed.

Julia struggled to draw air into lungs that felt encased in iron. "The Air Force changed his status to KIA ten, no . . . eleven years ago. What possible reason could you have to . . . to connect me with his death?"

Marsh hesitated, glancing at the general as if to confirm how much he should reveal. The Vice Chief stared at Julia for a long moment, then nodded.

"If Captain Hunter was ambushed," Marsh said slowly, "it wasn't by the enemy. His remains were found in a shallow grave just a few yards off the road leading from Saigon to Vung Tao. A single bullet was lodged in his skull, which forensic experts have determined came from a US-issue .38 caliber pistol."

The picture his blunt words evoked all but shattered the last of Julia's control. The thought of Gabe, laughing, daring, devilishly handsome Gabe, in a shallow roadside grave brought the foul taste of bile to her throat.

"The recovery team found a pistol buried under a pile of rubble a few yards away," Marsh told her, his intent gaze never leaving her face. "It's serial number matches that of the weapon you reported missing two weeks after Captain Hunter disappeared."

Aware that she had to respond, to say something, anything, Julia tried to speak around the ache in her throat.

"There's a Report of Survey in my records somewhere that documents the loss. The survey officer concluded that the weapon was probably stolen by someone who had access to my quarters. One of the mama-sans, he thought, although he couldn't prove anything."

The planes of the agent's face seemed to flatten, harden. "The recovery team also found a St. Christopher medal clutched in Captain Hunter's hand. It has your initials engraved on the back, and has been identified as one you wore."

He hesitated, then pulled a laminated card from his coat pocket.

"At this point, I'm required to read you your rights. General Titus will act as witness. Then I must ask you to come with me to a private office so I can take your statement. Colonel Endicott?"

She nodded once, stiffly.

"You have the right to remain silent. Anything you say can and will be used against you in a court of law."

Julia shut out the measured words. Her mind was lost in a dark, swirling world of its own.

Damn you! I thought I was free of you!

She should have known. Oh, God, she should have known she couldn't break his grip on her soul. She'd never been able to fight his hold on her. Not from the moment she'd stepped off the plane in Vietnam that terrible and glorious spring and Gabe Hunter came swooping into her life.